A Lover's Lament

KL Grayson & BT Urruela

D1444551

SPENCER
HILL
PRESS

A Lover's Lament
Copyright © 2015 by K.L. Grayson and BT Urruela

Please visit www.klgrayson.com and www.bturruela.com

First Edition: 2015

A Lover's Lament: a novel / by KL Grayson and BT Urruela—1st ed.
Library of Congress Cataloging-in-Publication Data available upon request

Summary: In a matter of seconds my entire world changed, and it was in that moment that I stopped living and simply began to exist.
In my grief, I sent a letter to the first boy I ever loved. I didn't expect him to write back.
Sergeant Devin Ulysses Clay did what I couldn't: he put the shattered pieces of my heart back together.

A letter from Katie Devora—a letter that I almost didn't open. Her words put a fire back inside of me that I didn't know I'd lost.
The Army saved me from a callous mother and a life on the wrong side of the tracks that was quickly spiraling out of control.
Fighting became my new normal . . . *until her.*

Published in the United States by Spencer Hill Press
This is a Spencer Hill Contemporary Romance, Spencer Hill
Contemporary is an imprint of Spencer Hill Press.
For more information on our titles visit www.spencerhillpress.com

Distributed by Midpoint Trade Books
www.midpointtrade.com

Cover design by: Okay Creations
Cover photographer: RLS Model Images Photography
Interior layout by: Scribe Inc.

ISBN: 978-1-63392-102-3
Printed in the United States of America

We would like to extend our deepest gratitude to all of the service men and women of the United States military and their loved ones. Thank you for your service. Thank you for your sacrifice.

A Lover's Lament Playlist

Prologue | Katie
1996

"Cross That Line"—Joshua Radin

"**K**atie—*Jesus.*" My tongue swirls around Devin's nipple, effectively cutting him off midsentence, and when I nip at it playfully, a low growl rumbles from his chest. I smile against his skin, loving that I have this effect on him. Palms flat against his stomach, I push up to see Devin's green eyes glowing under the dull light of the moon. When I reach for the hem of my shirt, his gaze follows.

"There's something I need . . . something that we . . ." His words trail off, his lips parting as I grip the flimsy material and lift it over my head. My heart is racing with nervousness and anticipation. I've never done this before, and even though I feel safe and treasured with Devin, I'm still a nervous wreck. I may be a virgin, but he most certainly is not.

"What was that?" I let my shirt fall, and Devin's eyes flit between my eyes and chest.

"I, uh . . . I'm . . ." With a quick flick of the wrist, I unclasp my bra. Devin blows out a slow breath and then swallows hard before attempting to finish his thought. "It's just that . . ." My bra joins my shirt in a pile on the floor. "*Fuck,* you're gorgeous," he breathes.

I palm my breasts, rubbing my thumbs over my nipples, and Devin's eyes flare with desire. Strong, warm hands slide up my bare thighs, kissing the bottom of my skirt before sneaking underneath. Slowly, he hooks a finger in my panties and tugs them to the side before slipping it inside of me.

His touch is intoxicating, sucking me in, drowning me in a level of intimacy that I'm not at all used to. Overwhelmed with emotion, I swallow past my heart that is planted firmly in my throat, and my eyes drift shut as the weight of this moment—the moment I'm certain I've spent the last two years waiting for—sinks in.

Devin and I met on the first day of first grade. He stole my Barbie pencil, I cried like a little girl—well, because I was one—and then, forever the peacemaker, my friend Wyatt stole it back. The next day on the playground, Devin pushed me down and walked away laughing. But what he didn't know was that my crying fit the day before was merely nerves on the first day of school. I was a tomboy, ready and willing to play dirty, even if I was wearing a dress. Pushing up from the ground, I ran after him as fast as my little legs would carry me and I plowed right into his back, tossing us both to the ground.

When it was all said and done, Devin had a split lip, my knee was all sorts of ripped up, and at the ripe age of six years old, I'd earned my first trip to the principal's office.

Side by side, Devin and I sat in tiny orange chairs against the wall. "Ya busted my lip." His words caught me off-guard and I looked over at him. He was smiling a big toothless smile, and I couldn't help but grin. It's quite possible that he stole a piece of my heart that day, even if the concept would remain foreign to me for several more years.

At the age of fifteen, I finally admitted to myself that I, Katie Devora, was head over heels in love with Devin Clay. And it wasn't until two and a half years later—three months shy of my eighteenth birthday, and a measly two weeks ago—that I built up enough nerve to tell Devin how I felt. He had me pinned against his truck, mouth slanted over mine, before I finished giving him all of the reasons we should take our friendship to the next level.

A low moan rips through the air, and when I realize it actually came from my mouth, my eyes snap open, slowly regaining focus. My skirt is bunched around my waist and Devin's hand is lodged between my legs while the other holds a tight grip on my hip. As my ragged breathing slows, my body and mind floating back to earth, something akin to worship flashes in his eyes.

"Katie—"

"Don't." I shake my head. My body is vibrating with pleasure, and I need this more than I've ever needed anything. "Please don't stop." *I won't survive if you stop.*

"Fuck, no," Devin breathes. "I couldn't stop if I wanted to." *Thank you, sweet baby Jesus.* It's sad really, but a whimper falls from my mouth when Devin removes his hand from between my thighs. Cupping my face in his hands, he pulls me to him, brushing his lips against mine. "I want this, Katie, more than I've ever wanted anything, but I know you're . . ." His eyes soften, pleading with me to understand what he's saying so he doesn't have to actually say it. "It's just that I need to know you want this . . . with me."

Doesn't he know how much he means to me? Haven't I told him time and time again that the two of us together is so incredibly perfect that even my dreams couldn't conjure up anything better?

Then it hits me. Everything Devin has told me about his relationship with his mom and the way she's treated him, tearing him down little by little. He needs to know that I want him and only him, to be reassured that he's not only worthy but deserving of something this perfect. And if that's what he needs, I'm more than willing to not only tell him how much I love him but show him as well.

Falling forward, my palms land flat on the bed on either side of his head. Slipping from my shoulders, my hair falls down, sheathing us in our own little cocoon. "I can't imagine doing this with anyone but you. You're my dream, Dev. This . . . this is my dream."

"Katie." My name may be just one word falling from his lips, but it's the way he says it, like it's a prayer that he just realized was answered. Devin closes his eyes as though he's fighting his own emotions, and when he opens them, they're glistening with an intense amount of desire, excitement, adoration, and love. But the one thing that's shining through the most is *happiness*.

"Let me show you that I want this just as much—if not more—than you do," I whisper. Popping the button on his jeans, I slowly unzip them. My fingers skim along his waist before dipping into his jeans, where I find him thick and heavy. I wrap my fingers around him and Devin sucks in a ragged breath. I watch his eyes flit between my hand and my face as though they can't decide where to land. "You're more than my best friend—you're it for me, Dev. You're my soul mate. You hold my heart in your hands."

Strong words, I know, but they don't come close to scratching the surface of what I feel for him—of the bond we share.

In the blink of an eye, my hand is ripped from his pants and my body is flipped through the air until I'm flat on my back. *Damn that was hot.*

Propping myself up on my elbows, I blow a chunk of hair out of my face in time to see Devin's pants and boxers fall at his feet. Without breaking eye contact, he crawls his way up the bed. My hips lift instinctively when his hands grip my skirt, allowing him to pull it, along with my panties, down my legs. He tosses them aside without a second glance and his mouth finds mine, hot and fast.

Our tongues duel, battling for control, and right about the time I'm preparing to surrender, he pulls back, scattering kisses across my jaw. "This is happening," he murmurs. "You and me, Katie." My eyes drift shut when his mouth trails down my neck, across my collarbone, and to one breast and then the other.

"You're so beautiful. You're an angel—*my angel*." Looking down, I watch him cup one breast in his hand while his mouth attacks the other. "You have no idea what you do to me, Katie. No idea how you make me feel."

Threading my fingers into his thick black hair, I hold him to me as his lips continue their torturous path down my body. He's moving slow—too slow—and I fight the urge to just shove him where I need him. It's no longer a want . . . I *need* this man. "I think I have an idea." My breath catches on the last syllable when his mouth descends on my clit.

Finally!

My body is on fire, strung as tight as it can go. I've been thinking about this all day, and I'm so worked up I can hardly stand it. Each caress of his tongue is electric, sending thousands of volts of lightning straight through my body. Pressure builds low in my belly and I know I won't last long. "Can't," I pant. "I can't take anymore."

My words only spur him on. Devin's mouth is relentless, the pad of his tongue even more so. I moan, dropping my head back to the bed before deciding that the view of his ceiling isn't near as exciting. Propping myself back up on an elbow, I watch Devin with hooded eyes. His broad shoulders are pressed against my thighs, his head buried, and when he glances up, his emerald eyes devour me at nearly the same intensity his mouth does. His gaze is unyielding, it's yearning, and I beg him to give me a reprieve. "*Please.* Oh, god."

Determination flashes in his eyes right before I squeeze mine shut. My body is at its breaking point, and I'm not sure how much longer I'll be able to last. When the first waves of pleasure crash into me, I tighten my grip on his hair, a deep moan falling from my mouth. He continues to suck and tease, pushing my body further than it's ever gone, and he doesn't stop until he's robbed my body of all of its bones. I'm nothing more than a big pile of Jell-O, sated to the point of immobility.

My heart pounds in my chest, and I fight to open my eyes as Devin removes himself from between my legs. Sitting back on his haunches, he reaches for his jeans and grabs something out of his pocket.

"May I?" he asks, his eyes hopeful.

Cupping his cheek in my hand, I push up until our lips are molded together. I can taste myself on his lips and it's surprisingly erotic. "I've already given myself to you, Devin, you just didn't know it. This . . . this wraps it all up in a nice little bow."

He nips at my lower lip. "I like bows." He smiles, kissing me once . . . twice . . . and a third time before pulling back. With a quick motion, he tears open a wrapper, and without breaking eye contact, he slowly unrolls the condom over his erection, which is bobbing heavily between his legs.

My tongue darts out, sliding across my lips, parting them as Devin's mouth fuses to mine. This kiss is sweet, slow, and incredibly sensual. It's not the kiss of two young lovers; it's the kiss of two soul mates exploring each other for the very first time. We kiss until my lips are numb and my body is thrumming with so much energy that I think I might go insane.

Pulling his mouth from mine, Devin props himself up on his forearms, my head cradled in his hands, his cock nestled between my legs. If he doesn't do this soon, I just might scream. "I love you, Katie."

His words wrap themselves around my heart, which suddenly feels too large for my chest, and I fight the pressure building behind my eyes. "I love you more."

"Impossible." He smiles, brushing a strand of hair from my face. "I'll be gentle, baby, I promise." I nod and Devin slips his hand between our bodies, aligning himself at my entrance. "If it's too much or it hurts, tell me, okay?"

"Okay." Running a hand along his neck, I thread my fingers into the hair at the nape of his neck and tug him toward me while simultaneously shoving my hips upward. His warm, sweet breath fans across my face as he slides into me for the first time. A tiny surge of pain rips through me, but it's quickly replaced with even greater pleasure.

I arch my back, pressing my body into his, our hips rocking in perfect rhythm as I try desperately to remember every single detail. Devin's body is as hard as a rock, his muscles flexing and bending under the weight of my hands. I can feel his heart beating wildly inside of his chest, and I can't help but wonder if he's doing the same thing . . . memorizing this . . . memorizing me.

"Katie," he growls, burying his face in my neck. "I'm not going to last long. This—too much," he pants, thrusting into me one last time before his body goes rigid above mine. His eyes close and a strangled moan rumbles from his chest. He rocks into me several more times, riding out the wave of his orgasm, and my arms lock around his shoulders, holding him to me.

"That was amazing." My fingers trail up and down his back, and I feel him smile against my neck.

"Amazing?" he chuckles. "I was going for earth-shattering . . . life-altering . . . mind-blowing—"

"Trust me," I mumble, pressing a kiss to the side of his head. "It was all of those things too."

"Oh yeah?" He pushes up, his eyes smiling along with his mouth. I love seeing him smile, happy and carefree.

"Yeah. I don't want to move."

"So don't," he says, rolling us over so I'm draped across his chest. "Let's stay here, right like this."

"Forever." Curling my body around his, I take a deep, sated breath, loving the blissful state I seem to have found myself in. Closing my eyes, I listen to the beat of Devin's heart as it plays me the sweetest lullaby.

A loud knock startles me awake and I blink heavily. Lifting my head, I find Devin rubbing his eyes and I realize that we must have dozed off.

"Hi." His voice is husky from sleep and a grin pulls at the corner of my mouth.

"Hi," I whisper. A loud knock sounds again and we both turn our heads toward the door.

"Please tell me you locked your front door."

"Of course." He kisses my nose and rolls off the bed, and I instantly miss the feel of his body against mine. "I locked the bedroom door too, just in case."

"You know," I say, smiling wryly. "We could just cancel the party and stay here." Devin jumps on the bed, bouncing my body, and I giggle when he peppers kisses down my neck.

"I like the way your mind works, but we have about thirty people who won't hesitate to smash through my front door."

"Remind me again why you decided to have a party tonight?"

"Because my mom is gone for the night, Chris's brother bought us a keg of beer, and who else is going to give the preppy kids somewhere to let loose and disobey their families?"

"Fine," I surrender, flopping my arms out to the side. "Let's go get our party on. Just promise me that you won't invite Mary-beth to the next party you have." My lips curl as though I had just smelled something bad and Devin smiles, only this time his smile doesn't reach his eyes. Instead, it fades as though he just realized something.

"What's wrong?" Sitting up, I wrap the sheet around my chest.

Devin slides off the bed, grabs his boxers and jeans off the floor, and tugs them on without saying a word. My stomach churns at the forlorn look on his face, and I scramble from the bed, moving close to him.

"Devin, what's wrong?" My mind races with an endless amount of possibilities as to why he suddenly looks so defeated. Did he not enjoy what we shared? Did I somehow disappoint him?

"Shit," he hisses, stepping away from me. My arms hang limp at my sides as I watch and wait for him to say whatever it is that's on his mind. "I was trying to tell you something before"—he waves his hand absently at the bed—"before . . ."

"Before we made love," I state, stepping in front of him. He must catch the look of anxiety on my face because his eyes soften and he blows out a long breath. Reaching out, he hooks his arm around my shoulders and pulls me against his chest.

"I was trying to tell you something and I didn't get a chance to, and it's big, Katie. I wanted to tell you before we—"

I laugh. "Made love. Come on, Devin, it's not that hard to say."

"It makes me sound like a pussy." I giggle against his chest and he mumbles a curse. "Fine. I wanted to tell you before we *made love,* because it's important."

"Okay." Pulling out of his arms, I give him a curious glance. "So tell me now."

Gripping my shoulders, Devin nudges me back on the bed before wiping his hands on the front of his jeans. "Okay. There's no easy way to say this, so I'm just going to say it."

"Devin, you're scaring me."

"We're moving, Katie. Mom and I are moving."

My brows furrow as my mind works to process what he just said. "You're moving? Like to the country, or across town?"

Devin's face falls and he shakes his head. My chest constricts painfully. "Pennsylvania."

"What?" Jumping from the bed, I shake my head as my throat starts to clog. "What do you mean you're moving to Pennsylvania? Y-you can't move." Clutching my hand above my heart, I rub absently over a dull ache. "She can't just up and move. W-why would she do that? What's in Pennsylvania?"

My chin trembling causes my lips to tilt downward, and I spin away, trying to maintain some sort of composure. Devin's hand snaps out, grabbing my arm. He tugs until my back is pressed against his chest, and then he wraps his arms around me and props his head on my shoulder. "I hate this, Kit Kat." A sob tears from my throat at his use of the nickname he gave me in elementary school. Tears roll down my face and I reach up to wipe them away. "Trust me, the thought of leaving here—of leaving you—rips my heart out, and if there was any way for me to stay, I would."

My mind races with solutions, because he can't leave. He's my best friend . . . He's the person I want to spend the rest of my life with. "What about Chris?" Turning in his arms, I rest my hands against his chest. Chris is Devin's best friend, and Chris's parents love Dev. "I'm sure his parents would let you stay and finish out the year, and—" My words die off in my throat when Devin shakes his head. "Why not?"

"Katie," he whispers, cupping my face in his hands. "I can't let my mom move alone. She needs me."

"You guys don't even get along," I grumble, taking a step back. "She treats you like shit." Devin's eyes widen and I want to apologize for the harshness of my words, but I can't because they're true. Too many times I've sat talking with him over some stupid stunt his mom pulled. I've watched him nearly break down time and time again over the way she's treated him and now *this*. Now she's just going to rip him away from his entire life—from the only life he's ever known?

I take a deep breath, trying to calm myself down, but it doesn't work. Adrenaline, anger, confusion, and sadness . . . They're all running through my veins at warp speed. I can't seem to make sense of any of it, and I need some time to sort through all of this. Everything I thought I knew just changed. My foreseeable future just shifted, tilting my world on its axis, and I need to get a grip on myself before I can get a grip on the situation.

Grabbing my underwear and skirt from the floor, I slip them on.

"Katie?"

Scurrying around the bed, I look for my shirt. I know it's around here somewhere; it couldn't have gone that far. The power of Devin's stare weighs heavily on my back. He's following me around the room, I can feel it. I spot the gauzy material on the floor, along with my bra, and snatch them both up.

Devin steps in front of me as I slip on my bra. "Katie, please talk to me. Don't do this; don't go quiet on me."

"I'm not going quiet." Tugging the shirt over my head, I run my hands down the material, a feeble attempt at pulling myself together. "I just need . . . a minute."

Devin's eyebrows nearly touch his hairline. "You need a minute? No"—he shakes his head and reaches for me, but I dodge him—"what you need is to talk to me. We will work this out. It's only temporary. I'll be eighteen this winter, and as soon as I can, I'll come back. This isn't the end . . . Please don't think that."

"Isn't it?" I ask, whirling around on him. "You're moving to Pennsylvania, Dev. That's like a thousand miles away."

"Eight hundred," he mumbles.

"Great!" I toss my hands up in exasperation. "You've already looked it up, which means you've known for a while."

"No," he states firmly. "She sprung this on me yesterday morning. I tried to tell you earlier, but we were—"

"You know what, never mind." I'm confused. So confused. I just gave myself to Dev and I wouldn't change that for the world, but somehow it seems so insignificant in light of all of this. He's leaving. *Leaving.* My stomach dips and then rolls as I fight back a wave of nausea.

Devin has been a big part of my life for as long as I can remember, and just the thought of him not being here every day—not being able to drive over to his house and see him anytime I want or kiss him anytime I want—makes my chest physically hurt. I've never been shot before, and I hope like hell I never am, but this sharp pain in my stomach must be what it feels like.

Slipping my feet in my sandals, I haul ass toward the door. Devin rushes up behind me, slamming his hand against the solid wood, shutting it before I can slip out. His body is hot against mine, his breathing ragged, and guilt ripples through me. He's the one that's leaving . . . He's the one that has to start over, and here I am acting like this.

"Katie, please hear me when I tell you that this doesn't change anything."

"You're wrong," I say with a sigh. "This changes everything." And by everything, I mean that nothing will be the same. I don't mean it won't work, because I do believe that if we want it badly enough and try hard enough, we can make it work. But it won't be easy. It's something that we'll need to sit down and hash out, but right now I just need to collect my thoughts.

"Please don't do this." His pleading voice is almost my undoing—almost. But I know that I need to step away and calm down before I ruin the very best thing in my life.

"I just need to process this. It's a lot to take in."

"We can make it work, Katie. I promise you, I'll come back."

"I believe you that we can make it work if we both try hard enough."

Devin's body stiffens behind me. "What's that supposed to mean? You make it sound like I wouldn't work at it."

Whirling around, I plant my hands on my hips. "Your mom hasn't had a landline in years, Devin. If I want to see you or talk to you, I have to drive to your house. So explain to me what I'm supposed to do when you're eight hundred miles away."

His shoulders drop, and I can tell that he didn't think of that. "Now, will you please take me home?"

"No."

"What do you mean, *no?*"

"I want to spend every second I can with you, because we're leaving on Sunday."

"What?" I squeal, my eyes nearly popping out of my head. *Great. This just keeps getting worse.* "I—wh—ho—*FUCK!*" This isn't happening. How do I fight this? How in the hell are we supposed to make it work with such little time to even talk about it or prepare? Threading my fingers in my hair, I grip it tightly. "Sunday? You're leaving on Sunday?" My voice rises with each word, along with my blood pressure. "I can't believe this." My pulse is hammering so hard in my ears that it's giving me a headache, and my chin hurts from the uncontrollable trembling.

"Katie!" A loud knock sounds on the bedroom door, and I wonder who in the world managed to get into Devin's house. "Katie, are you okay in there?" My body sags in relief at the sound of Wyatt's voice. Several other voices filter through the air, and I roll my eyes because the last thing I need right now is an audience.

"What the fuck is he doing here?" Devin growls. Stepping around me, he flings the door open. "What?" he barks, the tone of voice causing Wyatt to take a step back.

"He's my friend and I invited him." Wyatt watches the two of us hesitantly, but when I walk straight up to him, he opens his arms without thinking twice. Burying my face in his chest, my emotions get the best of me. They boil low in my belly, slowly working their way up until a strangled cry rips from my throat. Wyatt's arm wraps around my shoulder, but I notice that he leaves the other one hanging loose at his side. Probably a smart idea if he doesn't want it ripped off.

"Enough." A strong hand wraps around my arm and I'm yanked away from Wyatt. "Move," Devin seethes. Wyatt steps out of the way when Devin takes off down the hall, pulling me behind him.

"Let her go."

"Fuck off, cowboy." Devin laughs when Wyatt doesn't come back with more, but I'm not really surprised. These two men, my very first two friends, haven't liked each other since day one. Devin has always been a little jealous and Wyatt a little intimidated, but they've managed to keep the peace for my sake . . . well, mostly.

"Where are you taking me?" I try to pull from his grasp, but he holds on with ease. I finally decide that it'll be easier to just follow behind. We garner several strange looks when Devin drags me through the living room and right out the front door without a word to anyone. Tossing his car door open, he pours me inside then stalks around his car and slides into the driver's seat. It's a short drive to my house, but long enough for my anger to drain and be replaced with a mixture of guilt, sadness, and regret.

If there is one thing I do know, it's that Devin is and always will be my best friend, and I love him more than I will ever love any other man. Gravel crunches under the weight of his car as we pull down my lane, and I shift in my seat to face him.

"I'm sorry." Dropping my head to the seat, I wait for him to look over at me but he doesn't, not even after he throws the car in park.

"I can't believe you."

Closing my eyes, I rub a hand down my face. "I know," I concede. "I shouldn't have told you I needed time . . . That wasn't fair of me. But in my defense, I was overwhelmed. I just wanted a second to process this and put it all in perspective."

"Not that." Finally, he looks over at me, but I don't see any sort of affection, just a distant stare. "You went to Wyatt."

"Huh?"

"I wanted to hold you and talk to you, but you walked away from me. You went straight to Wyatt. My heart was fucking breaking right along with yours and you walked into that prick's arms."

"No," I say, shaking my head. That wasn't it at all . . . was it? "I'm sorry, I wasn't tryi—"

"You should've walked into my arms. You should've let me hold you and comfort you because I'm your fucking boyfriend, Katie. I'm the one that has to say good-bye to the one person that keeps me anchored to this fucking earth. Do you honestly think I *want* to move with her? Do you honestly think I wouldn't choose you in a heartbeat?"

The tight band around my heart pops and I lurch forward, gripping his face in my hands. "You're right. I was wrong . . . *so* wrong." My nose burns with tears, and they quickly build and then fall from my eyes. "Please forgive me," I beg. Guilt churns in my stomach, knotting it up. I can't believe I acted like that. What the hell was I thinking? I can't push him away, and I definitely can't lose him.

Needing to be close to him, I climb over the gearshift and straddle his hips. Pushing my hands through his hair, I pull him toward me until we're nose to nose. "Tell me you know how much I love you and that you know how sorry I am for earlier. Tell me you know that I will find a way to make this work."

Swallowing hard, Devin's eyes penetrate mine. They're glistening under the dull light of the moon shining through the window. "I know you love me, and I know you're sorry. Trust me, I had nearly the same reaction when Mom told me. I didn't handle it well at all." I can see in his eyes that he's being sincere. That's one thing about Devin and me; we've been friends for so long that I can read him like a book. "And I know we'll find a way to make it work, because there isn't another option."

All the breath is robbed from my lungs when he says what my heart feels. There really isn't any other option. Devin and I are meant to be together.

Chapter 1

Katie
January 2006
(Ten Years Later)

"Gone Too Soon"—Simple Plan

"When is she going to wake up?" The strangled voice of a woman rings loudly in my ears, and the thick fog surrounding me slowly dissipates. "I need her to wake up." This time the broken voice is much clearer and I instantly recognize it. *Mom?*

A shiver of fear runs through my body and I fight to move, but something or someone seems to be holding me down. *Why are you crying? Mom!*

"All of her scans came back normal. She'll wake up, Mrs. Devora, I assure you. She's been through a traumatic experience and her body is allowing itself time to heal." I'm not sure who that voice belongs to, but the foreign accent sounds oddly familiar. And what the hell does he mean I've been through a traumatic experience?

"You keep saying that, but she keeps sleeping. I've already lost so much, Dr. Cantrell . . . I can't lose her too." *Wait, what is she talking about? Where am I, and why the hell won't my eyes open?*

Darkness slowly starts to creep in around me, and before I even have a chance to struggle against it, I'm whisked into unconsciousness . . .

My entire body feels heavy and weak. I try to turn my head, but a sharp pain pierces the side of my temple. I whimper but nothing comes out . . . no sound at all. *What the hell is going on? Why can't I move? How long have I been asleep?*

"Go home, Wyatt, get some rest. I'll call you if she wakes up." Mom's voice floats through the air seconds before I feel a warm hand—presumably hers—stroke the side of my head.

"I'm not leaving her. I *won't* leave her." Wyatt's voice sounds unyielding yet strained, and when it cracks, I frantically push against the darkness that seems to have taken control of my body. *Wyatt! Oh, Wyatt.*

I concentrate hard, desperately trying to make a sound or move my fingers, but nothing happens. I growl in frustration—at least I try to.

"Honey, you have to be exhausted. You've been working so hard and spending every spare second here. You need to get a good night's sleep." *No! Don't leave. Please don't leave!*

Somewhere in the midst of my struggles, I hear a chair being slid across the floor and then two warm hands wrap around my right hand, drawing it upward. I'm intimately familiar with those hands and his touch alone seems to calm the panic that had been bubbling inside of me—for now, anyway. "Brenda, I'm not leaving until she leaves with me . . ." Wyatt's voice trails off, along with my mind, as I'm sucked back into the shadows of the unknown.

A soft hum drifts through the air. This whole in and out and not being able to move thing is frustrating the hell out of me, but this time I'm too exhausted to try. The humming continues, and with a touch so gentle that I barely feel it, my fingers are lifted off the bed and entwined with someone else's. The hand is soft and delicate, and I instantly know by the size and lack of calluses that it doesn't belong to Wyatt.

The muffled voice that first woke me up gets clearer and clearer. I try hard not to fight against the wall that's holding me captive, instead hoping that if I stay relaxed, it will lift on its own. I envision myself taking a deep, cleansing breath as my mind follows the voice. "Wake up, sweetheart," she says in between humming her sweet tune. "*Please* wake up."

I'm trying, Mom. I promise you, I'm trying.

Her silky voice starts singing the same song she sang to me when I'd get sick as a child. The words are like a balm for my soul—so sweet and comforting that I allow myself to get lost in them.

"You are my sunshine, my only sunshine—" Her words cut off and everything around me goes eerily still and quiet.

What is she doing? Why did she stop singing?

"Do it again, Katie," Mom says with a hint of a smile in her voice. "Move your fingers for me."

I moved my fingers? Really?

"That's it, Katie." Mom's voice is joyfully high, and I picture her jumping up and down, cheering like she used to do at my softball games. I hear a sequence of loud, solid beeps at the same time I feel my heart pound violently inside my chest. A steady woosh-woosh-woosh pulses behind my ears.

Something is happening. I'm not sure what—and I sure as hell don't have any control over it—but despite the urgent desire to try and move, I stay perfectly calm.

And then I feel it . . . a twitch, followed by another twitch . . . and another.

I hear the door open and then someone starts talking, but I'm too absorbed in the feeling of these little spasms taking place throughout my body to pay too much attention to the conversation. Out of nowhere, my eyelids get yanked open and I cringe when a bright light shines in my face. A garbled moan falls from my mouth, and I can tell by the burning pain ripping through my throat that an actual sound is coming out.

"Katie!" my mom squeals. "She's awake! She's moving!"

My eyelids feel heavy and weak, and each time I try to crack them open, the light in the room blinds me. Someone must notice because the next time I try to open them, the light is turned off, which makes it so much easier. I blink several times, and the blurry figure in front of me slowly comes into focus. "Mo-om," I croak.

"Oh, Katie." She buries her face into the side of my neck. Without thinking, I lift my arm. It's heavy and sore, but I manage to drape it awkwardly over her shoulder as she cries. "I was so scared. I thought I'd lost you too." Her words barely have time to register before my arm slips from her back and my eyelids drift shut, and despite my best effort, I can't get them to open back up. "Katie?"

I thought I'd lost you too.

"It's okay, Mrs. Devora. This is normal. I'm going to go let Dr. Cantrell know that she's starting to wake up."

What does that mean? Who else did she lose?

"Thank you—" Everything around me cuts to black, and my body goes limp as the dark hole sucks me in again.

"Hey, pretty girl." Warm lips touch the side of my head. I have no sense of time, but I hope I wasn't out too long. "I go home for thirty minutes to take a shower and change clothes, and you wake up. What's that all about, huh?" My eyes flutter open and I catch a glimpse of Wyatt's handsome face before they drift shut again.

"She's stubborn as hell." *Bailey!* Wyatt laughs at my sister's accurate description, and the bed dips low next to my hip. "Always stubborn. Even when you're unconscious." Bailey's breath fans the side of my face before she kisses me on the cheek. She whispers *I love you,* kisses me once more, and pulls away.

Every muscle in my body screams when I try to shift in bed. My body feels bruised and battered, and I'm stiff as hell.

"Katie?" I peel my eyes open, and this time two faces are peering down at me. "Don't move, sweetheart." Wyatt is watching me with open adoration. That look, combined with the unshed tears glistening in my sister's eyes, causes my chest to constrict. My gaze bounces around the room, and alarm bells begin ringing in my head when I notice the IV pole sitting off to the side. My eyes follow the tubing, which is attached to an IV in my arm, and a pulse oximeter is clamped firmly around my middle finger.

Everything floating around in my head is still a jumbled mess, and I start to panic because, for the life me, I can't figure out why I'm here.

"Wyatt?" My voice is hoarse and raw, and I desperately need something to drink.

Beautiful blue orbs are watching me, filling with tears, and I feel a few of my own slip down the side of my face. Wyatt reaches out and brushes them off my cheek. "I've missed you so much, Katie."

"What happened? Why am I here?" I ask, trying to make sense of what's going on. *Why did he miss me? How long have I been here?*

Bailey slides Wyatt a sidelong glance that he quickly returns, and it's almost as though they're having some sort of silent conversation. My eyes bounce anxiously between the two as I wait for someone to answer me. Obviously something bad happened or I wouldn't be laid up in a hospital bed feeling like I got hit by a train.

I watch as my sister's head lowers. She swipes a hand across her face and I can see, despite her attempt to hide it, that her chin is trembling. "I ca—" Her voice breaks and she shakes her head. "I can't." Lifting my hand, I reach for Bailey, but she spins away from me and runs out of the room.

Shifting in bed, I make a move to go after her and my entire body screams in protest. Sucking in a sharp breath, my gaze snaps to Wyatt and he runs a shaky hand down the front of his face. "What—" I shake my head, panic and fear settling thick in my bones. "What the hell is going on?"

"Katie—" Wyatt sighs and looks away. His jaw ticks several times, and when his eyes find mine again, they're full of grief. "I think we need to wait for your mom to come back."

My stomach churns as my mind races to try and make sense of what's going on. I come up with absolutely nothing—and that frustrates me even more. "No, Wyatt." With my eyes locked on his face, I reach for his hand. He wraps his fingers around mine and squeezes them lightly. "Tell me," I beg.

But even as I say the words, snippets of memories and broken conversations flash through my mind.

My mom crying.

I've already lost so much.

I can't lose her too.

I thought I'd lost you too.

"Damn it, Wyatt," I growl. His eyes search mine, and I can tell that he's trying to decide what to do. "Please. *Please* tell me." Frustrated, I lift my free hand to my head and wince when something pricks my finger. *What the hell?*

Gently, I run my hand further into my hair and follow what I presume to be stiches, finding that they stop just above my ear. Rubbing my thumb over the pads of my fingers, I hold my hand in front of my face, inspecting it closely. My hand shakes when I see the blood smudged on the tips of my fingers.

Blood on my head.

Sore, stiff body.

What the hell happened to me?

"You had to get fifteen stitches to close the gash above your temple," Wyatt states softly. The distinct sound of tires squealing ricochets through my head, and I squeeze my eyes shut as memories start flooding in. "It took them forever to get it to stop bleeding." I hear what he's saying, but the flashbacks are pouring in too fast for me to stop and ask questions.

Headlights flashing. Honking . . . swerving.

"You also have twelve stitches to a laceration on your left arm."

Metal crunches, glass shatters, tires squeal.

My heart races inside my chest and I grip the fabric of my gown, trying desperately to anchor myself to something.

"Three fractured ribs . . ."

My body flies forward, then it's yanked back again before being tossed violently from side to side.

I wince, clutching my head. *Too much . . . This is all too much.* My breaths are becoming more and more shallow as anxiety trickles through my veins.

"And you have a bruised left hip."

Moaning . . . gurgling . . . My head lolls to the side and I crack my eyes open.

My eyes drift shut. The memory of the metallic taste of blood floods my mouth.

Blood. Lots and lots of blood.

My eyes snap open and I search the room. Someone is missing. Where is Dad? Oh God. No. *No, no, no.* Please, *no.*

My mom comes barreling into the room at the same time realization hits me.

"Da-ad!" I scream. Mom comes to an abrupt halt at the end of my bed and her hand flies to her face, covering her mouth. She blinks once and tears start rolling down her face.

"Katie . . ."

I hear Wyatt say my name, but everything seems to be happening in slow-motion and I can't seem to tear my eyes away from my mom, who's watching me with a look of fear mixed with pain. She takes a hesitant step forward, as if I'm a wild animal and she's trying to decide the best way to approach me. My eyes follow every move she makes, and when she sits next to me on the bed, opposite from Wyatt, she drops her hand from her face so she can brush her fingers along my cheek. Her beautiful eyes are bloodshot and puffy, and the dark circles around them tell me just how much pain she is in. I swallow hard when her bottom lip trembles because I *know*—I can feel it in the pit of my soul—that whatever she's about to tell me is going to rip my life to shreds.

"Katie," she whispers, her eyes searching mine.

"Dad. Where's Dad?"

"Daddy—" Her voice cracks, and once again she plasters a hand over her mouth to stifle a sob. A tight band constricts around my heart. Lifting my hand, I rub absently at the ache in my chest.

"Shhh . . . It's okay." Bailey's soothing voice catches me off-guard.

"Bailey?" I ask frantically, needing to see my sister. She walks to my bed and drapes her arm around mom's shoulder. Tears are dripping down her flushed face and she looks at me for a brief moment, her lips pinched together, before she gives a slight shake of her head.

That one movement is monumental and packs a mean punch of silent words that slam straight into my gut. And that's all it takes to confirm my worst nightmare—the one thing I was most fearful of.

My heart pounds wildly inside my chest, and one of the monitors I'm hooked to makes a shrill sound. A nurse rushes into the room as I fight to keep my emotions in control. She flits nervously around me, checking my pulse and pushing buttons on the machines, and when I struggle to sit up, she helps me. Her eyes are sad, and I instantly know that she's aware of what's going on. "Try to relax," she whispers before exiting the room.

The minute the door shuts behind her, something inside of me shatters.

"No!" I cry. "Ple—ease, no . . ." Slumping forward, I wrap my arms around my stomach. In the blink of an eye, several sets of arms come around me, holding me as violent sobs wrack my body.

"I'm so sorry."

"Oh, Katie."

"We'll get through this."

Words of comfort are whispered, but with the blood rushing through my ears and the pounding in my head, I can't make out who they're coming from . . . or maybe I just don't care. Everything around me becomes muffled except for the two words that keep echoing through my head.

He's gone.

Oh my God, he's gone.

"No!" I cry out, trying to curl myself into a ball, only to feel the grip around my body get tighter. "Nooooo. Oh, God—" I choke on my own words as I fight to suck in air. A mangled cry rips from my lungs when a knife-like pain stabs through the center of my chest, shredding everything in its way as it carves a path straight to my heart and then even deeper as it slices straight through my soul.

Hundreds of memories flash through my head.

Standing on his toes as we dance across the kitchen.

His smile the first time I hit a home run in Little League.

My hand slides into my hair as a memory chokes me.

Waking up in a vehicle, seeing glass and metal twisted around me like a cage I can't escape from.

The memory jars me, and an instant later I see another image.

My daddy tying my hair in pigtails, tugging playfully at each one, telling me I'm his little princess.

I grip my head tighter as the pleasant memory dissipates into something frightening.

My father is covered in blood, his eyes are cracked open—lifeless—and I watch, helplessly, as the color drains from his face.

This can't be happening. He can't be gone . . . he just can't. I didn't get to say good-bye. A deep groan rumbles through my chest at the thought of never getting to see him again, or hug him, or tell him I love him. "Ple—ase," I beg, hiccupping through the sobs.

"I know, baby. I know." This time I recognize my mom's sweet voice, and I fist my hands in her shirt and hold on for dear life.

I have no idea how long we sit here and cry. Minutes . . . maybe hours. But I eventually cry myself to sleep, and when I wake up some time later, the room is dark, lit only by the dull glow of the moon filtering through the window. At some point during the night, everyone must have switched places because Mom and Bailey are both asleep with their heads on the bed at either side of my body. Bailey's arm is stretched across my legs as though she's holding on to me, and I reach out a hand and brush it softly across her forehead. Wyatt is passed out in the recliner next to my bed, his head propped awkwardly on a rolled-up sweatshirt.

Stretching my arms above my head, I let out a big yawn. My heavy lids bob several times as my sleep-induced fog lifts, and within seconds, I'm being slapped in the face with a heavy dose of reality.

My nose burns with impending tears, and I take a deep breath to try and hold myself together—if only for a minute. And really it's only a couple of seconds. Bending forward, I bury my face in my hands and I bawl. My chest physically aches, and if hearts can truly break, then mine has been demolished. The thought of not seeing my dad every day scares the living shit out of me. He was the first man to ever love me, and knowing that he's gone—knowing that he'll never walk me down the aisle or teach my kids how to saddle a horse—is devastating. Squeezing my eyes shut, I try and remember everything about him that I possibly can because suddenly I feel the need to catalog every memory.

Christopher Devora was a bear of man. Six foot two and well over two hundred and fifty pounds. His thick hair was the most beautiful shade of silver, but you never would've known it because he refused to go anywhere without his Stetson. I've been told countless times that my rich chocolate eyes are the exact replicate of his, and I've always taken that as a compliment.

He was so much more than just my dad—and he was an *amazing* dad—he was also my best friend. Sure, I was close with my mom, but growing up I was a daddy's girl through and through. Dresses and makeup? No, thank you! Most days you would find me in a ball cap and cowboy boots, raising hell on the farm. Everything he did, I did, and not once did he make me feel like I couldn't do something just because I was a girl. By the time I was twelve, I was helping him break horses and mend fences, and I could change the oil in every tractor, four-wheeler, and snowmobile in our shed.

"Katie?"

I look up, wiping the tears from my face, and find my mom watching me.

"How long have you been awake?" she asks, stretching her arms above her head. Her eyes are still bloodshot and puffy—from all the crying, no doubt. I can't even imagine the hell she's gone through.

I lean back on the bed. "Not long. Ten or fifteen minutes."

Nodding her head, she offers me a tremulous smile. "You were thinking about him," she observes, already knowing the answer.

"What day is it?" I ask, trying to divert the conversation. My emotions are too raw and I'm not ready to talk about him yet. Or maybe somewhere in the back of my mind I've convinced myself that if we don't talk about it, it isn't true.

"It's Saturday night," she sighs, running a hand over her tired eyes. "God, Katie—" Looking up at the ceiling, she blows out a long, slow breath and then her glossy eyes find mine. "The past forty-eight hours have been hell. After the accident, you didn't wake up and I was scared out of my mind. At first, they didn't know the extent of your injuries, so they were running tests and scans. But all I knew is that you weren't waking up, and I . . . we had lost so much. I just knew I wouldn't survive if I lost you too." The look of sorrow on her face is too much to handle and I instinctively reach for her, pulling her against my chest.

"I can't believe he's gone." She buries her face in the side of my neck and wails. "I can't live without him, Katie, I can't." Her body shakes against mine, her tears running hot down the side of my neck, and I tighten my grip around her small frame, silently promising to help her get through this. He may have been my dad, but he was her husband . . . the love of her life . . . her soul mate. They were supposed to retire and grow old together.

"I'm so sorry, Mama," I cry, desperate for her forgiveness. It should've been me. I should've been the one to die. I was supposed to drive that night, not Daddy. Guilt settles in my gut, shame prickling my skin, and I swallow past the bile rising in my throat. "This is my fault." She pulls back, shaking her head from side to side.

"No, Katie." Her soft hand brushes the wetness from my face, and this time *she* gathers *me* in her arms and pulls me to her chest. "This is not your fault, sweetie. There is nothing you could have done." I open mouth to argue with her, but she doesn't give me the chance. "You guys were hit by a drunk driver."

"What?" I gasp, pulling out of her arms. I vaguely recall being hit by another car, but I had no idea who it was or even how it happened. "Did the other person survive?"

Mom nods her head. "He survived. We don't know much more than that."

Emotion clogs my throat. "He should've died," I choke out over a sob. "Not Daddy. It should've been him." *Or me,* I think to myself, *it should've been me.*

There is no way to explain it, but the thought of this man— this *drunk* man—still living and breathing makes me physically ill. It isn't right, and it sure as hell isn't fair. *He* should be the one taken away from his family—not Dad.

Anger seeps into my body. I try to fight it—try to push it away—but it feels so much better to be mad at him than to feel this gut-wrenching pain. So I let the anger infiltrate my soul, and I let it dull my pain.

Chapter 2 | *Katie*

"Even My Dad Does Sometimes"—Ed Sheeran

"Breakfast is ready."

I jump at the sound of Bailey's soft voice. The shovel slips from my grip, but I manage to catch it before it falls to the ground. "Holy crap," I breathe, my hand clenched above my heart when I turn to face her. "You scared the shit out of me."

"Sorry," she says, yawning. Tucking her hands in her coat pockets, her feet shuffle against the ground, and she yawns again before sitting on one of the straw bales in the corner. My brows furrow and I cock my head to the side. I can't remember the last time I've seen my baby sister up before ten o'clock in the morning, and I sure as hell can't remember the last time I saw her step foot in this dirty barn.

Bailey and I are eight years apart, and when we were growing up, I always used to joke with her that she was an "oops" baby. Of course she wasn't, but I was older so it was my duty to pick on her. Despite our difference in age and my occasional need to make her cry, Bailey and I have always had a great relationship. I've always been the tomboy, never afraid of dirt and hard work, and Bailey has always been the girly girl, in love with designer clothes, manicured nails, and makeup. While I spent hours out in the barn or the field helping Daddy, she sat inside having tea parties and playing with her Barbies. We've always been complete opposites, but best friends nonetheless.

Until recently.

"Bailey?" I ask cautiously, glancing outside to confirm what I already know. Yup. Still dark. "You do realize that the sun won't come up for at least another twenty minutes, don't you?"

She shrugs her shoulders and looks down. "I couldn't sleep."

"Okay," I answer slowly as I turn around to keep shoveling. My hands are tired and achy, but I keep going because if I don't do this—if I don't take care of Mac, Molly, and Toby—then no one will. Bailey and Mom don't understand why I insist on keeping the horses, and I don't understand how they could possibly think of getting rid of them. I know that the horses are expensive and they take a lot of work, but that's why I've taken over the burden. I want to do it. No, I *need* to do it. They're a part of us—a part of *him*—and right now they're the one thing that's keeping me tethered to the past . . . a past that I'm not ready to let go of.

Forty days.

That's how long it's been since we buried my father. January 3, 2006, will go down in history as the single worst day of my life, and I've spent every second since then living in hell— three million four hundred and fifty-six thousand seconds, to be exact. And they've all been filled with a bone-shattering anguish that I wouldn't wish upon my worst enemy.

It took fourteen days for my family to realize that I wasn't grieving properly, but little did they know I wasn't grieving at all. I've merely been existing. And then it took another two weeks for them to convince me to talk to someone.

"I'm worried about you."

And there it is! Of course she's worried about me. That's all I've heard since I walked out of that damn hospital. Frustration bubbles up inside of me, my muscles coil tight, and without thinking, I start firing words back at my sister. "Really, Bailey, you're worried about me?" I scoff. She steps in my line of sight and I catch her glare before continuing. "Don't you have better things to worry about, like the classes that you're failing?" She opens her mouth, but I don't give her the chance to talk. *I'm pissed.* "Or how about your boyfriend? Didn't you tell me you thought he was screwing around on you behind your back?" Bailey's eyes widen as if she can't believe I went there.

And yes, I'm well aware that I'm way out of line, but I can't find it in me to care. Unfortunately, that's what happens when you shut down, and it didn't take long after Daddy's funeral to realize that it's much easier to be angry than it is to be in pain. The downfall is that I've become numb, and not just to my own feelings but to everyone else's as well.

"Fuck you, Katie!" she yells. My heart slams against my ribcage as I wait for her to tear into me some more. Lord knows I deserve it. "Shit," she hisses. Her eyes squeeze shut and she drops her head. "This isn't about me, it's about you." Her voice is softer but still strong, and I'm both proud and jealous that she was able to control her emotions when I wasn't. "I'm worried about you, because you're my sister and I love you."

"Don't worry about me, Bay. I'm fine." That's a fucking lie. I'm far from fine, but I'm dealing with things the only way I know how. I have to get through this in my own way and on my own terms.

"You're not fine." Bailey's eyes are hard and unyielding when they find mine. "You're losing weight and you have dark circles that have become permanent fixtures under your eyes. You work all the time, and when we do see you, it's nothing more than 'hi' and 'bye' on your way out to the barn. You're running yourself ragged and you're going to kill yourself, Katie."

"Right," I say with a snort. Tossing the shovel to the side, I tug the gloves off of my callused hands. "I would hardly con-sider mucking stalls life-threatening." Arguing the other points she made is useless because they're all true.

"It's not just mucking stalls, it's everything. If it's your day off, you're here in the barn from the asscrack of dawn until well past sunset, and if it's your day to work, you're here before and after you put in a twelve-hour shift at the hospital. Seriously, do you even see Wyatt anymore?"

"First, don't worry about my relationship with Wyatt," I warn, my blood boiling at the mention of his name. "It's none of your business. Second, I come here because it's peaceful and it gives me time to think—"

"Dwell," she interrupts. "It gives you time to dwell. I get it, Katie. I get that you're hurting. I'm hurting too, and so is Mom. But what you're doing isn't healthy."

"Healthy? I'm not healthy, I'm in pain! Drexler killed our daddy, Bailey," I yell, running a hand through my hair. "How does that not bother you? He was selfish, and his actions are the reason that Mom will grow old by herself and our future kids will never know their grandpa."

Bailey's shoulders slump. "I get that," she concedes, sadness in her eyes. "I know that Andrew Drexler is to blame, but you need to forgive him so that—"

"What did you say?" I hiss, taking a step back as though she'd slapped me across the face. "Forgive him? You're joking, right?"

"No, I'm not joking, and yes, I think you should forgive him. Look at you," she says, waving a hand in my direction. "You're angry and bitter over something that you can't change. You can yell and scream and cry, and you should do all of those things. Hell, you could even hurt the man that did this, but you know what?" she asks, tossing her hands up at her sides. "It won't bring Daddy back. So you can be angry and keep living this shell of a life that you've been living the past month and a half, or you can grieve with the rest of us and remember all of the good things about Daddy."

The air swirls with tension so thick I could choke on it. We stand for several seconds just staring at each other, and I eventually have to look away or risk breaking down—and I do *not* want to break down. Not now, and certainly not here.

My silence must be too much for Bailey because she says, "I don't want to fight with you, Kit Kat." I flinch at her use of my childhood nickname. "We've just been tip-toeing around you for too long and I couldn't take it anymore. I'll drop it, and I'll leave you alone—for now—but just know that when you do let go of the anger, the pain will still be there. It's not going away . . . not until you deal with it." She spins on her heel and walks toward the door, and when I finally gather the courage to talk, she stops but doesn't turn to face me.

"I'm dealing with it, okay?" I sigh, mostly because I'm tired of arguing, and I hate that my baby sister is schooling me. "I'm going to therapy just like you and Mom wanted. I'm trying to work through it. What else do you want from me?"

Bailey turns around, her face void of any emotion, and she shrugs her shoulders. "I don't want anything from you, Katie. That's the thing, I just want *you*. I want my sister back."

"I'm trying." *Why the hell can't they see that?*

"Well, try harder." She shakes her head before turning away from me and walking out.

"How did that make you feel?" Dr. Perry asks. Folding her hands, she places them neatly in her lap atop a yellow legal pad and looks at me curiously. Apparently, my argument with Bailey this morning softened me, because normally I'm a tough nut to crack—or at least I'd like to think I am. But nope, not today. Today, I sat down on this horrid floral-print couch and spilled my guts before the expert nutcracker even said a word.

"You know I hate it when you ask me that question," I quip, earning a genuine smile from my therapist. A low growl rumbles from my chest and I toss my head back on the couch. It took me three sessions with Dr. Perry to learn that she can read me like a book. I also learned, after a very ugly screaming session— the screaming was totally me—that she has the patience of a saint, and if I truly want to move past the wall I've put up, then

I have to first *open up.* "It made me feel like shit. It made me feel like I'm letting them down."

"Letting whom down?"

Lifting my head, I cock a brow and give her a classic who-do-you-think look. "Mom, Bailey, and Dad." I've known for several weeks that I'm letting them down, but that's the first time I've said it out loud. There's something about saying it aloud that makes it so much more real. "You're waiting for me to tell you *how* I'm letting them down, aren't you?"

Dr. Perry flashes her signature beauty queen smile. "I'm proud of you, Katie. You're finally catching on to this." The corner of my mouth lifts just a fraction before I bite down on the inside of my cheek to keep from smiling. "Wait!" She puts out a hand to stop me from answering. "First, I want to know why you left Wyatt out. Do you feel like you're letting him down too?"

Oh, hell no. I'm not about to dive into that mess right now. "One thing at time, Doc. Take your pick."

Her lips purse but she nods. "Please, keep going."

My body relaxes. There is only so much I can take, and I've just about had my fill. "I don't understand how Mom and Bailey have been able to move on. I don't get how they can go about their days like nothing happened." Anxiety swirls through my body. I take a deep breath and let it out slowly to try and keep myself calm. "They smile, laugh, and carry on just like they did when he was alive."

"Does it bother you that they do those things . . . that they seem happy?"

"No," I answer, nodding my head yes. "Maybe." Leaning forward, I bury my face in my hands and then drag them through my hair. "I don't know," I mumble, shrugging my shoulders. "It makes me feel like they've moved on . . . like they don't care. But I realize that's stupid. Of course they miss him. Of course they care. I just . . . I feel like there's a line drawn in the sand, and they can jump freely from one side to the next while I'm stuck in one spot, completely frozen in place."

"Why would you want to jump?"

"Because I don't like feeling like this," I snap. "I hate it. Anger isn't something I'm used to, but I can't seem to stop feeling it. And I'm completely indifferent to everyone around me. It's like I'm an outsider looking in. I see what I'm doing and how I'm acting, but I can't stop. I *want* to care that I'm hurting them, but I don't. I simply don't care."

My eyes drift over Dr. Perry's shoulder as those words sink in. *Oh my gosh. I don't care.* These are the people I love, the people that love me despite everything I've put them through, and I don't care that I'm hurting them. I wait for the familiar pressure to build behind my eyes or the burn in my nose to signal a breakdown, but nothing comes. *Nothing.* What the hell does that say about me?

"Katie, are you okay?" Dr. Perry tilts her head, trying to catch my gaze, and I look at her and nod. "Can I speak freely for a second?"

This is different. She's never asked that question before. "Sure," I answer, hating how weak my voice sounds.

"You do care, or you wouldn't be here." Her words hit me like a ton of bricks and I look down, suddenly fascinated with the invisible piece of lint on my pants. "If you didn't care, then when they begged and cried for you to get help, you wouldn't have listened. But you're here, and you haven't missed a session. And every time we meet, you open up a little bit more. That tells me you care."

She's right. I know that she's right, but why do I keep acting like a bitch? Why does the thought of being around them and spending time with them make my skin crawl? Why do I insist on keeping myself closed off? Why do I ignore their calls and snap at them when I do see them?

"I don't know. Only you can answer those questions."

My eyes widen and I look up. "I, uh . . . I didn't mean to say that out loud."

"But you did."

"I did," I acknowledge.

"So what's the answer? Why does the thought of spending time with your family make your skin crawl?" My chest tightens and my legs become restless, my knee bouncing at a fast clip. "Why are you keeping yourself closed off from them?" Dr. Perry's calm voice does nothing to soothe me, and this time it doesn't make me want to open up. Nope, this time it pisses me off because she's getting a little too close.

"I don't want to talk about this." Pushing up from the chair, I walk toward the window and stare out at the Great Smoky Mountains. I love it here. The rippling creeks, rolling hills, and—

"Why don't you want to talk about it?"

Son of a bitch, she is good with those stupid-ass, open-ended questions. "If I answer your question, can we change the subject?"

"For now."

My stomach tightens at the knowledge that I should've driven that night. I haven't told anyone else that little piece of information because I'm ashamed. *I'm* the reason my mom lost her husband, and *I'm* the reason Daddy won't be there to walk Bailey down the aisle.

Reaching forward, I grip the base of the window and lean down. My lip trembles and I drop my chin to my chest, then blow out a slow breath. With my eyes squeezed shut, I open my mouth . . . but nothing comes out. I can't. I can't do this.

"It's okay to cry, Katie," she whispers from behind me.

I spin around, my eyes wide, my head shaking frantically from side to side. "Oh, I'm not going to cry." The first tear drips down my face.

Dr. Perry tosses her notepad on the table. Pushing up from her seat, she walks to her desk and grabs a Kleenex, which she pushes into my hand. "I know you're not, but if you decide to, I want you to know it's okay. We all cry. It's nothing to be ashamed of."

"It should've been me," I blurt. Guilt penetrates the solid wall around my heart, and for the first time in several weeks, I feel that horrible pain I've been working so hard at pushing away. My hand rubs absently at the ache in my chest and I suck in a sharp breath. "When I'm around them, I feel guilty . . . because it should've been me. And then I get angry that it wasn't me, and then the anger takes over and all I can think about is Andrew Drexler." Just saying his name makes me want to punch something. I curl my fingers, digging my nails into the palm of my hand. "I hate him," I seethe. "I hate what he represents. I hate that he was so careless. It makes me sick. He's a fucking soldier, Dr. Perry. He's supposed to protect this country, not murder innocent civilians—"

"Katie—"

"No." I shake my head, refusing to let her try and change my mind. "It's true. He murdered my dad. I don't give a shit what he's gone through or how many lives he's saved. It doesn't give him the right to do what he did. It doesn't give him the right to get behind the wheel three sheets to the wind and put everyone else's life in danger."

"Do you think about him often?" Dr. Perry's question throws me off balance. I take a step back.

"Yes, I think about him often," I admit. "I think about him rotting in jail."

"How about your mom and sister?" she asks. "How do they feel about him?"

A maniacal laugh falls from my mouth. "They've forgiven him." My eyebrows furrow and I search Dr. Perry's face for something—anything—that tells me she thinks that sounds as crazy as I think it does. "They've actually forgiven him."

Dr. Perry's knowing eyes watch me. Her stare becomes too intense. Turning away, I walk back to the couch and sit down. Crossing my arms over my chest, I effectively close myself off . . . or put on my armor . . . no difference, I guess.

Dr. Perry follows suit and sits down across from me in her plush chair, but she doesn't look comfortable. She scoots to the edge and props her elbows on her knees. "Katie." Her voice is careful and I lean back, unsure of what she's about to say. "Have you ever wondered what he's been through?" My jaw drops and her words rush out before I have the chance to argue. "Have you wondered what kind of life he's lived, or the things he might have seen at war, or worse yet, what he's had to *do* at war?"

"No!" I answer, a scowl plastered to my face. Shit, I can't even seem to care about my family and how they're feeling—how could I possibly care about how a *murderer* is feeling? "Hell no. Why in the world would I care what he's been through? I don't give a fuck about him. He killed my father." The pain I felt earlier releases its grip around my heart as the anger trickles back in, and I feel like I can breathe again. This is what I'm used to. Anger I can handle. "I don't care what he's seen, or had to do. That's the life he chose. And it doesn't matter what he's been through; it doesn't make what he did right."

"I'm not making excuses for him," Dr. Perry states, reaching for her notepad. She scribbles something down and looks up at me. "I'm trying to find a way to help you move past the anger, and it seems to me that you're holding on to the resentment you feel toward Lieutenant Drexler as a way to keep from moving forward."

"I don't want to move forward," I bite out, grinding my teeth together to keep from screaming.

"Why?"

The truth sits heavy on my chest, but I need to get it off. I suck in a deep breath and let it out roughly. "Because I'll be moving forward without my dad," I lament, gripping my hair in my hands. "Then he'll really be gone." Those last words were whispered to myself, but I know Dr. Perry heard me . . . she hears everything.

"He's already gone, Katie."

Her words float around in my head as if testing themselves out, and when I don't immediately feel the need to punch her, I take it as a good sign.

There's no doubt in my mind that she's right . . . I do need to move forward. Squeezing my eyes shut, I picture the look of disappointment and sadness that I saw on Bailey's face this morning, and a tiny piece of the wall I've erected around my heart falls to the wayside. "Okay," I breathe, opening my eyes. "What do I need to do?"

The look of pride on Dr. Perry's face is unmistakable, and her bright smile beams at me. She stands up, walks over to her desk, and pulls out a piece of paper, which she hands to me before sitting back down. My eyes roam over the sheet, and when it sinks in what she's trying to do, I raise my eyebrows and look up at her.

"Really?" I ask, scrunching my nose. "This seems a little silly. I don't see how reaching out to a soldier is going to make things better. A soldier is my problem, remember?" I ask, dropping the paper next to me. I sit up a little straighter on the couch and cross my legs, knee over knee. "Maybe we should avoid any and all soldiers."

"I can see why you would think that, I really do. But I believe if you get to know one, it might help you look at the situation differently. It might even make it easier to move past your anger so you can move forward with your life."

"Fine. I'll do it," I say, fighting back an eye roll because that would be childish, and it's probably something a twenty-seven-year-old woman shouldn't do. Dr. Perry's answering smile tells me that I've made her happy, and as long as I'm making everyone else happy, then I guess that's what matters.

"Great." Looking down, she scribbles something on her yellow legal pad—I *hate* that damn pad—and then she looks back up at me. "I'll e-mail you a list of participants in the soldier pen pal program so you can get started."

"What am I supposed to say?" I ask, suddenly unsure of my decision.

"Whatever you want to say."

"Fuck you?" I ask without an ounce of sarcasm. Surprisingly, Dr. Perry laughs and a small smile tugs at the corner of my mouth.

"Well, you might not want to use those exact words, but if you think it'll make you feel better, then go for it." I don't know how she does it, talking to people all day every day. It would drive me absolutely insane. Hell, *I* drive me absolutely insane.

Looking at the clock, I notice that my time is almost up. "Well, Doc, it's been fun." I move to stand up, but she reaches out a hand, stopping my movement.

"Wait," she says, looking at me curiously. "You never did tell me why you left Wyatt out earlier. Would you like to talk about it before you leave?"

"No, I would not like to talk about it. We've talked enough for one day. I'm all talked out." *Plus*, I think to myself, *I don't really know why.* I guess that's just one more thing I should add to my list of problems.

"Okay," she says, laughing. "Then I guess we're done for today. I'll send you that list of names, and on Monday you can tell me what you did with it."

"Sounds fantastic." Sarcasm is dripping from my voice, but I don't really give a shit. Right now, I just want to get home, take a shower, and go to bed. Pushing up from the couch, I shake Dr. Perry's hand and make my way out of her office.

"Oh, and Katie"—I stop and glance over my shoulder—"I want you to write the letter, not type it."

"Why on earth would I do that?"

"Because writing it is much more personal." She offers me a small wave and then turns toward her desk. I shake my head as I walk out.

What in the hell did I get myself into? I don't want to write a letter to some stranger, and I sure as hell don't want to write to a soldier. As I head toward the car, my mind races with all the different things I could say to piss him or her off. Then that damn look on Bailey's face pops in my head, and by the time I climb into my car, thoughts of what I should say to try and help me get through this have taken over.

Do I tell them about the accident and who it was that killed my dad? Do I tell them about everything I've been feeling and thinking since I woke up? How much is too much? My mind continues in a thousand different directions, so fast that I can't even keep up with it. Before I know it, I'm pulling into my driveway with absolutely no recollection of driving here.

I put my car in park and stare at my house. It's nothing special, just a small two-bedroom home, but it's mine and I'm damn proud of it. Last summer, Dad worked hard to make the outside look presentable. He repainted the house, added some landscaping, planted a tree in the front yard, and he even hung up a porch swing. Tears fill my eyes when I think about all the things my dad did for me . . . all the things we did together.

Now who will come over when my water heater goes out or my drains get clogged? And who's going to help me install the cabinets that Dad and I spent all winter sanding and staining? Better yet, who will walk me down the aisle on my wedding day and teach my son or daughter to throw a perfect spiral?

I bat angrily at the tears rolling down my face, push myself out of the car, and walk the few steps to my house. Quickly unlocking the door, I nudge it open with a loud creak and slam it behind me. When I flip the light on, the first thing I see is my dad's coat still draped over the back of my couch. He left it here the day of the accident, and I just can't bring myself to move it. If I do, then I'm losing a part of him all over again and I just can't. Once has just about killed me.

Tossing my keys on the table, I grab my laptop and make myself comfy in my recliner. The second I power up my computer, there's an e-mail waiting for me from my lovely psychiatrist.

To: Katie Devora
From: Dr. Carol Perry
Subject: Soldier Pen Pal Program

Katie,

Attached you will find the list that I was telling you about. Pick any one and get started on your path to healing. Good luck. I'll see you on Monday.

Sincerely,

Dr. Perry

I double-click on the attachment and a list of names pops up.

Casey Dean Becker	Jacob Matthew Dicenzo
Patrick Eric Malone	Eric Robert Recendez
Richard Lee Farnsworth	Maxwell Lucas Albert
Jason James Newman	Shane Emil Lopez
Paul Thomas Johnson	Blake Kenneth Haines
Jeremy Michael Wilkinson	Christopher Marcus Holguin
Daniel Robert Gladney	Kevin Aaron Witte
Todd Wilson Blair	Devin Ulysses Clay

I suck in a sharp breath at the sight of *his* name. "Impossible," I murmur, sitting up in the recliner. There is no way that there's more than one Devin Ulysses Clay walking this earth. It's impossible. *Right?*

Scratching my head, I inspect the name, reading it several more times to make sure my eyes aren't playing tricks on me. The hair on the back of my neck stands up and a small shiver runs down my spine. *No way.* What are the chances of this?

I click on his name, but all it tells me is that Devin Ulysses Clay is a twenty-six-year-old sergeant in the US Army.

Well, I'll be damned.

My eyes continue searching for any information I can glean, but it only provides me with a postal address. I grab a pen and paper to write it down. I don't even bother looking at any other names because this is it. Devin is yet another connection to my past—a connection that still doesn't feel resolved.

Closing my eyes, I tip my head back, letting the memory take over, a memory that I can drown my anger in.

I can't believe he's leaving. Tugging my comforter to my chin, I curl up into a ball and cry—really cry—over what all of this means. My mind sifts through memories, one by one, as though it's putting them into tiny little keepsake boxes so I'll be able to pull them out whenever I want.

The day we first met.

Falling out of a tree and sitting side by side in the emergency room as I got a hot pink cast put on my right arm and he got twelve stitches in the side of his face.

Dancing with him for the first time at our Junior Prom.

The look on his face the first time I told him I loved him.

One piece of knowledge keeps trying to fight its way in, so I battle it the only way I know how—with more memories.

Running . . . laughing . . . riding horses . . . swimming in the creek . . . snowball fights . . . skinny-dipping . . .

I'm not sure how long the memories cycled through my head but obviously long enough to put me to sleep. When I wake up to the sound of the rooster crowing, I haul myself out of bed, slip on a pair of jeans, change into a bra and T-shirt, and run through the house. Ignoring calls from both my mom and dad, I scurry out the door in a hurry to complete my morning chores. It takes longer than I'd like, and it's close to noon when I slide into my car and drive to Devin's house.

Last night I apologized, and I know that he accepted my apology because we sat in my driveway for nearly an hour discussing all of the ways we could make things work between us. We talked about letters, payphones, calling cards . . . anything and everything we could think

of to stay connected until he can come back. And even though I know
we're standing on solid ground, that knowledge does nothing to sup-
press this weird tingling I have in the pit of my stomach—a tingling
that tells me something is off.

Speeding through town, I nearly break every traffic law known to
man. I need to see him, to see for myself that we really are okay. I want
to kiss him, hug him, make love to him, and remind him that I will
fight for this . . . for us.

When I pull up in front of Devin's house, I shove the car in park,
pull my key from the ignition, sprint up the front walk, and bang on
the door.

No one answers, so I bang again . . . and again. Running around
back, I head straight for Devin's bedroom window. My feet skid to a
stop when the first thing I notice is that the curtain is no longer hang-
ing in front of it. My stomach rolls, and on shaky legs, I walk toward
his house. Leaning in close, I peer through the cracked glass of the
window.

A sharp pain is carving its way through my chest, and I can't help
but imagine that this is my heart breaking. The pain rips through me,
leaving a trail of shredded flesh in its path, and I clutch my hand over
my chest. Panic grips me, adrenaline pumping through my veins, and I
drop to the ground in a gelatinous pile of arms and legs. Curling myself
into a ball, I bury my face in my arms and sob.

I lost a part of myself that day. Most people would say I was
too young to really know what love is, but I disagree. Admittedly, I'm not sure what part of myself I lost—or how permanent the emptiness is—but I'm sure it must've been significant
if the gaping hole inside my chest is any indication.

"I can't believe this," I whisper to no one but myself. What
are the chances that *his* name would show up on a pen pal list
that my psychiatrist sent me? It's a passing thought, but one
that I can't ignore.

What if his name was meant for me to see? It wouldn't surprise me, considering that Devin was always the one person who

could help me work through my problems, however big or small they were . . . at least until the day he decided to leave me without a word.

Bitterness seeps into my veins, but I fight against it because there is no way in *hell* that I will allow Devin Ulysses Clay to have that kind of control over me, especially after the way he left. And now I have to write him, because if I don't, I'm letting him win—I'm letting the bitterness win—and I'm tired of fucking losing.

No, there is no reason at all that I can't write him a letter. A measly little letter. Who knows? Maybe it will be good for me.

Without giving it much more thought, I open up a Word document to start typing my letter when I remember what Dr. Perry said. "Damn it," I mumble. Shutting down my laptop, I grab the paper I wrote the address on and the pen lying next to it.

Now what? My fingers twirl the pen as I contemplate what to write.

Fuck you! I laugh out loud when I scribble the words on the paper. Then I quickly scratch them out, because as much as I'd like to write that, I'm not *that* big of a bitch.

My phone buzzes on the end table next to me. Looking down, I see Wyatt's name pop up on the screen. I tip my head back and groan. Something has shifted between us over the past several months, and if I'm being completely honest with myself, I've felt different about Wyatt for quite some time. As to what exactly has changed, I'm not so sure, but things are different . . . *I'm* different.

Before the accident, I seriously thought that it was all in my head. I figured I had just gotten too comfortable in our relationship and it was a phase that I would have to work through. After the accident, I began to realize that the love I feel for him is no different than the love I feel for my mom and Bailey. Now the love I felt for Devin . . .

Whoa! Where the hell did that come from? Hell no, Katie, I tell myself. *Not. Going. There.*

My phone continues to buzz so I push the green button to answer the call. "Hello?"

"Hey. Did you make dinner tonight? I just got off work and can head over." His voice sounds hopeful, and something about that just pisses me off. Hell no, I didn't make him dinner. I didn't even make myself dinner.

"No," I snap, dropping my head into my hand. It's been a long-ass day and I'm beyond exhausted, but I don't need to take it out on Wyatt. "I've been busy all day, and I just got done at my appointment with Dr. Perry and now I'm—" I quickly cut myself off. Do I really want to tell Wyatt about the letter I'm going to write? He and Devin were never really on friendly terms, and I'm sure it would only create more waves in our already churning ocean of problems.

"Now you're what?"

"I—uh . . . Now I'm getting ready to make dinner. So if you want, you can give me about an hour and then head over. Is that okay?" Son of a bitch. I don't want him to come over tonight. I don't want anyone to come over tonight. I want to write this stupid-ass letter and then go to bed, dinner be damned.

"Are you okay, babe?" I can hear the concern in his voice and it annoys the hell out of me. I don't say anything though, because I know Wyatt and he won't pursue it. Hell, maybe it's not even concern in his voice, maybe it's agitation. Wyatt doesn't understand what I'm going through and he's done a good job at pushing everything under the rug. As much as I'm annoyed at everyone's obsessive worrying, his lack of concern has put a huge strain on our already strained relationship.

"I'm fine. I'll be fine. See you in an hour."

"If you're sure." And that's his go-to . . . *if you're sure.* He never pushes for more; he's just always happy to take the easy way out. Typical man. "See you soon," he says.

I hang up the phone without saying good-bye. Pushing all thoughts of Wyatt out of my head, I turn to the notepad in my lap and stare at it . . . and then stare at it some more. I tap the pen several times against my mouth. I have absolutely no idea how to even start.

Do I tell him how I feel? Do I speak my mind, and if I do, will it offend him? Do I really care if I offend him? *Nope, can't say that I do. He left me, remember?* Plus, it's not like we'll ever be friends again, especially after the way he tucked tail and ran. It's likely that he won't even respond.

I situate the pen on the top line of the paper and decide to go for broke. I mean, seriously, what do I have to lose?

Not a damn thing.

Chapter 3 | *Devin*

"Warrior"—Evans Blue

The mornings here are when I'm most at ease. The sun scrapes the horizon, teasing the leaves of palm trees with flickers of life. The air is at first cool and light before making way for the broil of midday, and I do my best to enjoy every bit of it. I find that the eastern boundary of our small compound, which is no larger than an elementary school campus, is the best place for catching the sharp early morning rays. I patiently wait here for them to breach the massive walls, our only defense against a harsh reality on the other side.

I slept like shit last night thinking of Jax—or Sergeant David Jackson, as the etched stone now reads.

My thoughts have strayed as of late, reaching deep, dark places they're not meant to go. To him . . . to our first deployment in Afghanistan, which was cake compared to this.

Jax was like a big brother to me there, taking me under his wing. We grew close fighting an enemy that came with tenacity. But at least we knew who we were fighting because they'd bring the fight to our fucking doorstep. It wasn't like this bullshit here, bombs buried around every turn.

Maybe it was my youth . . . when I flipped on the TV and watched the planes barrel into the Twin Towers. It stuck with me, and serving my country was always something I thought about. So after two years of dicking around in community college, I joined the Army pissing vinegar and ready for a fight.

The notification that I'd be shipping right out to meet an infantry unit in middeployment was of no concern to me, and Afghanistan was exactly what I'd hoped it would be. We spent many a long night after a mission was complete talking under the bright desert stars, keeping each other's hopes up with stories of college, girls, and beer. Discussions so vivid, you could almost taste the hops.

But this deployment . . . This is so much different. I didn't sign up for Iraq. I didn't even really agree with it. Hell, I even had *"Fuck Bush"* written in white window paint on the back of my mom's '95 Dodge Stratus in high school. That shit was on there for like two years. Mind you, that was mostly because pissing off Tennessee rednecks gave me a hard-on. I never really belonged there.

As a soldier, I took my doubts about Iraq in stride, but with explosions every other day and the enemy camouflaged so thoroughly within the public, it's made for hard time served. With each passing day, these thoughts have become more frequent, pulling at my attention, taking me to places I know I shouldn't be going but can't seem to help. They burrow into my brain and have their way with me.

I think of what stage of decomposition Jax would be in as visions of blood seeping through the material of his uniform flash through my head.

God, please save me from these thoughts.

It's been three months to the day since Jax was shot. With his head resting in my lap as we waited for the med chopper to arrive, his chest bled out from where the sniper's bullet sat, warm and still. Before taking his last breath, he reached his trembling hand into a pocket and pulled out a letter. His fluttering eyes demanded I take it. I knew all too well what was in that letter, and whether I wanted to or not, I pulled the letter from his hand just before it slumped lifelessly to his side. Every day I ache for him, and with that pain comes the insomnia.

I'm perched on a concrete jersey barrier, sipping black coffee as thick as tar while my squad preps the Humvees for a mission. I let the rumble of the engines soothe me as the sun finally starts to bathe my face in warmth. Throwing my head back, I breathe in slow and deep, the wind whipping my face as I wait for the caffeine to do its job. I take a long sip of coffee, letting it rest in my mouth for a moment before drinking it all down.

This spot, this sunlight, this coffee—it's my release. I often wonder when it will no longer be enough. My eyes are tightly closed, and I feel a single tear roll down my cheek. I quickly wipe it away. *Not here. Not now.*

My thoughts are interrupted by my driver, Private Blake Thomas, shouting from one of our four Humvees idling a hundred feet away. I shift my focus and catch sight of one of my other soldiers, Specialist Jace Elkins, as he thrusts a boot into Thomas's ass each time he attempts to pull the dipstick from the receptacle. I pull a tin of chewing tobacco from my pocket and pack a pungent wad behind my lip. I cup my other hand to my mouth and yell, "Elkins! Don't you have some fucking radio frequencies to be dialing into?" I pocket my tin as Elkins swings around and snaps to attention. Thomas chuckles and resumes his duties undisturbed.

"Hooah, Sergeant, I already did it," Elkins calls back.

"You got ice in the cooler?"

"Roger, Sarge." Elkins is more confident now, borderline cocky, and it's unfortunate for him because his memory's for shit. It's not his fault . . . or maybe it is. He's young, and by his own account he smoked more weed in high school than Cheech and fucking Chong. When I stand before him, he has to tilt his eyes up to meet mine. I get pleasure out of this every time.

"Elkins." I plant a smirk on my face.

"Yeah, Sarge?" I wait a moment and let him sweat.

"Did you fuel up this morning?" I ask, though I know the answer already. His eyes widen immediately, mouth gaping open.

"Fuck!" he shouts as he races to the driver's seat and throws himself in. Thomas caps the oil terminal as Elkins opens the window then sticks his head out of it. "Come the fuck on, T! Lieutenant Dixon is gonna tear into my fucking ass, man."

"I'm coming, man. Fuck, it's not my fault you forgot." Thomas slams the hood, lifts it, then slams it again, and continues leisurely toward the passenger side of the vehicle. He opens the door and carefully climbs in, putting his seatbelt on as slowly as possible. "What about Navas? He's still gotta get the gun up."

"We'll worry about that later, man!" Elkins yells as he tears from the dirt lot. Thomas is wearing a devilish grin you could spot a mile away as the Humvee races to the fuel point.

I give them shit for it, but really, I love their nonsense. I wonder, at times, if it's helped keep Thomas alive even. He hasn't been dealing with the deployment well, but Elkins can always bring a smile to his face. And for the rest of us . . . well, it's a little piece of youth in an otherwise very adult world.

They are the halls of junior high. They are scout meetings and T-ball practice.

They are home.

"Hey, Sarge." Specialist Brooklyn Navas's Mississippi drawl catches my attention, and I turn to see him shuffling his linebacker frame toward me. In one hand, he makes a fifty-pound machine gun look like a child's toy, and in the other, he balances a stack of loaded magazines. "Where the fuck's the Humvee?"

"Fuckin' Elkins forgot fuel again," I say as I grab the stack of mags from his hand.

"Well shit, that's a goddamn shocker. Did he take Tweedle Dick with him?" Navas grunts and spits a rope of tobacco and saliva to the ground as he sets the machine gun down.

"Yeah, they should be back soon." He hands me another stack of mags from his cargo pockets and I line them into my vest while he does the same with his. "Lieutenant DickFuck's probably still sleeping anyway." I think I like calling him that too much. One of these days, he's going to catch me. I'm not so sure I'd mind.

"Oh, you know it. Just got done filling these mags up and he was still snoring the fuck away."

"You wake him up?" I ask, just as our Humvee comes tearing around the corner, screeching to a halt right in front of us. As if on cue, Lieutenant DickFuck exits the officer's quarters, which sits just beside headquarters. DickFuck, or Second Lieutenant Justin Dixon as we're made to call him, is a fancy little twat one year out of West Point. His parents are senators, or some shit like that, and he sucked his way to our unit. Not literally, of course, though it wouldn't surprise me.

A boy amongst men, we were shocked when he arrived because his type doesn't make a good infantryman. But like it or not, here he is. It's obvious he sees this specific assignment as a fast track to senator status. The close relations with locals and the promise of a Combat Infantryman Badge is a future politician's dream, and he knows it. He also knows the line he must meet to stay here, and he dances all over it. He sleeps in up until about the point we need to head out on a mission, and he often skips the more dangerous ones. I wish he'd skip all of them, because it's a fucking nightmare riding with him due to his intolerable arrogance.

He staggers toward us, his eyes sunken and his uniform disheveled, and I slip a glance toward Navas. "Tell me he's not riding with us," I mutter as we load into the vehicle.

"Fuck," Navas grunts.

That would be a yes. *Fuck.*

I watch as Lieutenant Dixon's slender five-foot-six-inch frame rocks harshly back and forth in the passenger seat—*my* seat—as we cruise the rough terrain. He usually rides with Sergeant

Dustin Adams in Bravo Team's Humvee, since the two New Yorkers seem to have hit it off. But apparently their gunner ate some bad goat meat on a mission last night and has essentially created a gas chamber within their vehicle.

So instead, DickFuck is in *my* vehicle messing around with the navigation perched to his left with an almost childlike distraction. He doesn't know how to work it, nor does he ever try to learn, but he likes to play the part.

"Ahhh, you see that shit?" Dixon's head shoots to his right, his eyes peering out the window. His shrill voice breaks the static buzz within our headsets.

"What shit, sir?" Navas asks.

"That chick. She's in jeans, no fucking burka. I'd tear that shit up." The attractive woman walks down the side of the small dirt road. She looks our way and cracks a timid smile, and I see Dixon shudder out of the corner of my eye. He's getting worked up, shuffling in his seat, and I look to Elkins to see if he notices, but his ADD has him off in fuck-fuck land playing with his med-pack.

"I'm shocked she still has her head," I say before catching myself, wishing I could take back my words. I think about the beheading videos that have taken over the media and I feel sick to my stomach. To get my mind off the grisly images, I decide to piss off Dixon. "By the way, how's your wife doing, sir?" I ask, shooting a mischievous smirk toward the back of his head. I know he's trying to think of something clever or witty to say, but he sucks at it, so I soak up the few seconds he takes to think of a rebuttal.

"Pregnant and spending all my deployment money," he snaps. "What about yours, Sergeant Clay?" I know he wishes he could say something insulting, but the gold bar on his chest restrains him.

"No wife here, sir." Not that I haven't thought about it from time to time. How nice it would be to have someone waiting on me . . . someone to go home to . . . someone to miss me.

Dixon twists his head around. "No?" he asks, his beady, life-less eyes scanning me from head to toe. He turns back around quickly. "You're not ugly. What is it then? You can't get a woman? Can't provide for one? How old are you anyway, Sergeant Clay?"

"I'm twenty-seven, sir. And negative, I just don't want one. I don't have time for all that."

"Probably the best choice you could make. My wife, she's great and all, but fuck! We weren't meant to be with one pussy for the rest of our lives. Why else would God have created hook-ers?" He cackles loudly, making me flinch at the sound it makes over the headset.

"Roger that, sir!" Elkins says, chucking the med-pack to the side. Apparently, he's become bored with it.

"Oh, shut the fuck up, Elkins, you wannabe playaaa," Navas chimes in, kicking a heel back toward Elkins but not even com-ing close.

"Shiiiit, I bet I've fucked more bitches than you have, old man," Elkins shouts up through the turret hatch, as if the head-set on his head was useless.

Navas laughs and tilts his body toward Elkins. He shifts a hand down to his crotch and pretends to jerk off. "Are you fuckin' kidding me? That's some dumbass shit you're saying, boy. I was a Marine for twelve years, travelin' around by ship to ports all over the world. You do the fuckin' math!" Navas shouts, pretending to come all over Elkin's face before angling back forward.

I look up through the turret hatch and see Navas smiling down at me. I know him well, and because of that, I know he's lying his ass off. He's not the fuck-around type. He was mar-ried to his high school sweetheart for fifteen years and they had two beautiful children together, a son and a daughter. She died of breast cancer a year ago, just before he joined the Army and came to our unit. He fought with our leadership for a month straight to even get on this deployment. They wanted him to stay back, for his kids' sake, but he'd have none of it. He said he needed to be with his guys. I respected him for his decision, but I worry about him and his kids nonstop out here. It keeps me awake most nights.

"You ever been to Thailand, Navas?" I ask, slipping bits of jerky into my mouth while consciously shoving the thoughts deep down. Deep enough to never see the light of day. Until they inevitably do.

"Yeah, a shitload a times. Why?" Navas questions.

"You ever fuck a lady boy?" I ask, smiling.

"What the fuck? A lady boy? Fuck no!" Navas laughs and fakes throwing up into his mic. *Do they not hear how loud that shit is? Pull the mic away from your faces, assholes!*

"You know, I've heard surgery is so good over there that you can't even tell a procedure has been done," I say, causing the radio to sit silent for a moment. Then Elkins and Thomas burst out laughing, and Dixon goes back to playing with the navigation.

Navas clears his throat and turns his attention back to Elkins. "Elkins, you're twenty years old. You got a lot more living and a hell of a lot more fuckin' to do before you get to my level."

"Well . . . Thomas is a fuckin' virgin!" Elkins huffs and prods a finger into Thomas's ear, causing him to jerk his head away.

"I'm not a virgin, you fucking asshole." Thomas keeps his attention on the road, his rich olive-colored eyes watching intently as he guides the Humvee off the dirt path and onto a paved four-lane highway. This particular road is essential for travel and is one we use nearly every day.

"One girl and a hand job is pretty much a virgin, dude," Elkins chides.

"I told you that in confidence, fuck stick. Fuck you! With all the Arkansas trailer trash you've been with, your dick is about ready to fall off anyway. I'll take my one bitch and a hand job any fucking day, bro," Thomas snaps, shooting a glare toward Elkins through the rearview.

"Fuck you, dude!" Elkins yells, playfully kicking the back of Thomas's seat, causing the Humvee to swerve. I backhand him hard on the arm.

"Hey dumbass, don't fuck with the driver—" I swallow my next words as an explosion erupts in the distance, so strong it violently rattles our Humvee. Navas instinctually dives from the turret hatch down into the vehicle.

"Well, fuck," he says, climbing back onto the turret strap almost as quickly as he came down.

"What the fuck! Where the fuck was that from?" Thomas asks, slowing the vehicle down a bit.

"Keep driving, Thomas." I reach for my headset and click the button that communicates between each Humvee. I call up the last one in our convoy. "Gator three Alpha, this is Gator four Bravo, are you guys okay?"

The radio fizzles a second before Sergeant Adams' voice breaks through. "Roger. We're all good. Nothing hit any of us."

"Roger that. Sounds like it came from our six o'clock. Making a U-turn. Over," I say, directing Thomas to make the turn. He clutches the steering wheel so hard his skin turns white as he traverses the unpaved median, the easiest place to plant a roadside bomb. I hold my breath. I don't know why, but I always do.

"FUCK! You guys see that?" As Navas says this, I see what he's talking about. An enormous plume of thick black smoke breaches the clouds about a mile down the road, just off the highway. It owns the sky. This is a bad one.

"What the fuck, man? Must have been a car bomb. No way we would've felt it from *that* far away otherwise." I take it all in for a second, wondering what exactly we are about to encounter and praying that there are no casualties on our side. Or women. Or children. *Fuck, why does anyone have to die?*

I tap Lieutenant Dixon on the shoulder. "Sir, do you want me to call this in to headquarters? See if we can get some support?"

"Oh, yeah, yeah, I was just about to have you do that," Dixon says through a tight jaw. His sweat now runs freely down the back of his neck. I can hear the fear behind his words and it makes me hate him that much more.

I call in the blast and ask for another squad to meet us on-site just as we pull up to the carnage. No US casualties that I can see. No women or children either. I'm thankful for that at least.

The target was an Iraqi police checkpoint. I see a shredded engine block at the bottom of a hole that's three feet deep and five feet wide. The pit is charred black and contains mangled pieces of what was once a Geo Metro. More parts lie upwards of a hundred yards away, and three police trucks are lying damaged around the pit. The distinct smell of cooked flesh and burnt fuel begins to creep into the vehicle, thick and nauseating, as we come to a stop. I scan the area through the windshield and see some police scattered around the hole with missing arms or legs—or in some cases, both. They writhe on the ground, moaning in agony. They paw at raw stumps or tightly grip limbs hanging by threads of skin.

Others are just fragments of human beings left adorning the sides of neighboring homes to bake in the afternoon sun. The police who remain untouched are coated black with ash and wandering aimlessly, some howling into the sky.

Erratic rounds start to come in around us, some kicking up dirt and rocks while others pierce homes and damaged police trucks.

"Where the fuck is that coming from?" I ask, peering as best I can through the window.

"Elkins, grab me the binos," Navas barks down through the hatch. Elkins frantically digs through the trunk compartment using a slot in the back. He locates the binoculars and passes them off quickly. Navas waits for the fire to stall, then takes a long look through the binos as I anxiously wait for word. He slowly lowers himself into the vehicle and sets the binoculars beside him. "Son of a bitch!" The words erupt from his mouth. "Motherfuckers!" He tears the headset from his head and throws it to the Humvee floor. "It's the other fucking checkpoint. The fuckin' IPs are firing on us from the other fuckin' checkpoint, man. God fuckin' damn it!"

I look to Dixon whose hands fidget with his headset, his gaze fixated on the navigation and bottom lip clutched nervously between his teeth.

"Sir, we've gotta do something. There are either dumbass motherfuckers at that checkpoint, or we've got enemy dressed like IPs," Navas says to Lieutenant Dixon.

No response.

"Sir, we've gotta do something! We're just sitting ducks here." I try my hardest to subdue the anger in my voice, but I fail to do so and Dixon picks up on it.

He whips his head around and locks his nervous eyes onto mine. "What exactly do you expect us to do, Sergeant Clay? Let me think for a goddamn second!" He turns back around and gnaws at his thumbnail. I look out my window and spot one of the policemen who isn't wounded but dazed and cowering behind a truck. He has a radio clipped to his belt.

I wait no more.

"What the fuck are you—?" Effectively cutting of Lieutenant Dixon's next words, I quickly swing open my door, hurling myself to the ground and slamming the door shut behind me, effectively cutting off Lieutenant Dixon's next words. I wait for the gunfire to slow, clutching my helmet to the ground with both hands. Once it finally does, I get up, duck my chin to my chest, and barrel toward the policeman's location. A few poorly aimed shots crash in around me and my stomach turns with each strike and puff of dirt. It's as if they're shooting at us blindly.

Several excruciating seconds later, I reach the truck and kneel before the frightened policeman. He doesn't look at me but mutters prayers under his breath and rocks back and forth. His face is pale and eyes are wide. His mouth gapes as he fights for oxygen. I grab him by his shoulders and shake him until he looks at me.

"Do you speak English?" I shout slowly. He shakes his head from side to side, his eyes still unfocused.

"FUCK!" I release him and snatch the radio from his belt, clipping it to my own. I leave him there on his knees and run to Sergeant Adams's truck, which is positioned strategically behind ours. I hear a few more rounds fire behind me and I say a quick prayer of my own: *Lord, get me through this day.*

I meet Adams behind his door, sweat running freely down my face and temples throbbing. He stands with his rifle, scanning the road adjacent to us, and lowers it upon my arrival.

"The fucking gunfire's coming from the other checkpoint a half mile down the road," I say between heavy breaths.

"Not a fucking surprise. Dumb bastards."

"I need the 'terp. I've got one of the IP radios. We need to call these fuckers ASAP . . . see what the fuck is going on."

I pass the radio off to Adams and he chucks it to Mike, our interpreter, then orders him to make the call. Before Adams can get another word in, I take off in the direction of my own vehicle, my heart attempting to punch a hole through my ribcage.

Looks like it's gonna be another long day in hell.

Chapter 4 | *Devin*

"Weight of the World"—Young Guns

Come to find out the shots were fired by a bunch of frightened IPs in response to the explosion. This led the checkpoint down the road to assume the other one was being overrun. Sure, why not fire blindly toward another checkpoint based solely on assumption? *Dumb fuckers.*

After helping the IPs load the dead and wounded onto new trucks that arrived, we eventually made our way back to base. The whole mess took the lives of fourteen Iraqi Police and one dedicated suicide bomber. It stole six hours of our day. As we quietly cruised the road back to base, I couldn't help but wonder which of those made me more upset. I'm a little ashamed of that.

After reaching base and debriefing from our mission—and getting my ass chewed out by Dixon for taking matters into my own hands—my squad and I took up our usual spots on lawn chairs around a fire pit in the center of the three tents our company stays in. It's not so much a fire pit as it is a giant ashtray, since protocol dictates that we can't have fires at night.

A smattering of blue chemical lights cast a glow around us. The moon dominates the night sky, shining flawlessly with the absence of pollution. We have canteens full of oversweetened Kool-Aid and a carton of cigarettes between us. We won't smoke them all, but after missions we wish we could forget, we certainly give it a valiant effort. The Army owns almost every hour of every day we spend in this place, but this time . . . This is ours.

About two canteens deep, my squad's conversation turns to "sickest anal stories," but I tune them out. I'm lost in the moment. I'm lost in that shining freckled orb in the sky. I'm wondering who else could be looking at it too . . . at that very moment. With my legs outstretched and hands behind my head, I nearly forget I'm even in a combat zone. I lose myself in thought as the conversation flickers around me. I shut my eyes and drift far, far away.

I'm reading Cormac McCarthy on a Hawaiian beach. The story is about a man and a boy on a journey in a desolate wasteland. The ocean is as blue as I've ever seen it, and so clear I can spot dolphins playfully jousting in the distance. A beautiful girl sits beside me. A romance novel is cradled in one of her hands, while the other rests against my chiseled abs. I love her touch. Her frequent glances and heartbreaking smile make my body numb. She tells me she loves me. Twirling a strand of her hair between two fingers, she bites the edge of her lip, then she tells me I'm her everything. This is perfection. This is my oasis. This is—

"Time to go, brother. Going to be an early morning." A swift kick from Navas is the sobering thud that jolts my eyes open, and immediately my heart sinks back into its resting place. I groan and rise to meet him. He's right. Five a.m. will be here in no time.

After a quick field shower, which pretty much consists of baby wipes and bottled water, I make my way to my bunk. In the tent where we sleep, our cots are lined up one beside the other with equipment strewn about. Posters of half-naked women are duct-taped against the tent's walls, and a stale, dingy aroma sits heavy in the air. It's not much, but it's our home for now.

When I reach my cot, there's a letter positioned on my pillow. I turn to Navas, who has entered behind me, and ask, "We get mail?"

"Yeah, man. The radio dispatcher just dropped them off. Who the fuck is writing you anyway?"

"I'm assuming just some random person from that pen pal shit," I say, thinking back to the program I reluctantly signed up for a few months back. I'm not even sure why I did, since I haven't bothered to read any of the letters that have come to me, but it's hard seeing these guys get letters and packages from home. And don't get me wrong, I'm happy for them, but I'm envious too, and I fucking *hate* envy. It's such an ugly shade on anybody. So I do my best to hide it.

I pick up the envelope, and just as I'm about to toss it with the others, I notice the name and address. My heart lodges at the base of my throat.

Katie Devora
1224 N. Main St.
Rock River, TN, 62442

"Holy fucking shit!" I exclaim, drawing Navas's attention.

"What's up, man?" he asks, but I ignore him.

Katie has been on my mind a lot over the years, and even more so after spending some time in this hellhole. But I never thought I'd hear from her again . . . not after the way I left her. And how did she even find me? A dull ache stabs at my chest, and I blow out a slow, labored breath.

I feel an immediate urge to open the letter, a force too powerful to deny. *Katie fucking Devora!* Slipping a thumb into the nook of the envelope, I slide it open quickly and pull the letter out. Almost immediately, I'm hit with the smell of perfume . . . *Katie's perfume.* The smell is faint, not like she sprayed it on but as if it were simply passed from hand to paper.

For better or worse, my nose has become quite sensitive to the smell of women in just these first few months of deployment.

We often stop at the main operating base located on the Green Zone to drop off detainees, and many of the female soldiers stationed there wear some sort of scent. We animals could smell them from a mile away.

But Katie's perfume brings an onslaught of memories that make my legs go weak and causes me to stumble back. I take a seat on my cot to compose myself. I don't unfold the letter right away, instead choosing to let the soft floral essence float around my nasal cavity for a bit. I close my eyes and breathe it in slowly, letting the fragrance remind me of my biggest regret. My only regret, actually, and one I've never quite gotten over.

From the second I saw her, I knew I was a goner . . . and that was in the first fucking grade. Two pigtails swung freely from either side of her head, and when she turned around and locked her large brown eyes onto mine, I just knew I had to steal her pencil. I wanted her chasing me, because if she chased me, it meant she liked me. The second she dove onto my back and brought me tumbling to the ground, I knew I'd met my match.

And boy, did I ever. In the years that followed, it became crystal clear that Katie would be the woman I was going to marry—a woman who would take my bullshit and throw it right back at me, a woman with a stubborn will and the kindest of hearts. And I knew, the first and only time we made love, that I was a complete goner. From that moment on, Katie Devora owned me.

Squeezing my eyes shut, I allow myself to remember that moment . . . the feel of her mile-long legs as they wrapped around me, pulling me into her and digging her heels into my back if I tried to move away. I see her perfect tear-dropped tits waiting for my eager mouth.

My dick throbs in my uniform bottoms, and I look down at it as if it's grown a face. *What the fuck is wrong with me?* Ignoring the feeling, I unfold the letter and begin to read.

Dear Devin,

I'm not sure the best way to start this letter, but considering our past, I feel the only way is with complete honesty. So . . . here goes.

I'm not writing you because I want to; I'm writing you because I need to . . . well, at least that's what my therapist says. She wanted me to connect with a soldier, so she sent me a potential pen pal list. And although I vaguely remember someone telling me in passing that you had joined the military, I think I'd blocked it out. So you can probably imagine my surprise when I saw your name. Seriously, what were the chances?

I've been having a hard time lately, and connecting with a soldier is supposed to help me heal. At first I thought seeing your name was some sort of sign, a tiny ray of hope from the man upstairs. Because if anyone knew how much you helped me before, it would be Him. But now that I'm actually sitting down and writing this, it's doing nothing but bringing back all of the insecurities and anger that I was left with nearly a decade ago.

You left me. Without a single word. I'm pissed at you for that, and honestly, I'm not sure I'll ever be anything but mad at you. You made a decision to leave me with no way to reach you or find you. You left me at home to drown in my own heartache, and that's what I did. I didn't even get the chance to say good-bye . . . just like with my dad.

You probably haven't heard, but my dad was killed in a car accident. I was with him, and his death has completely destroyed me. In fact, according to my therapist, I'm not grieving the loss of him very well. She seems to think that writing you—or any soldier, for that matter—might help me let go of some of my hurt and anger. But I can see now that reaching out to you probably wasn't the best idea.

Anyway, I think Dr. Perry has a screw loose and has absolutely no idea what she's talking about. However, I am desperate to find closure and move on, because the woman I've become is not the woman I want to be. You would probably still recognize me if you saw me, but the carefree, happy girl you once knew . . . she's gone . . . buried right alongside her dad in a cold, dark grave.

Despite what you're probably thinking right about now, I'm not a completely angry, closed-off bitch. Writing you just seems to have pulled that out of me. Honestly though, I don't care what you think, and I can't bring myself to give a shit about anything, really.

I'm getting off track, and that's the exact opposite of what this letter is supposed to do, so I'm going to do what's best for me right now. I'm going to tell you what happened, but for my own sanity I'm going to pretend that Devin Ulysses Clay is a complete stranger . . . shouldn't be too hard, I guess, considering I haven't heard a word from you in years. So here goes nothing.

Six weeks ago, my dad and I were on our way to dinner when a car in the opposite lane crossed the center divide and slammed into us head-on. I woke up two days later in the hospital to find out that my father had died on impact, and the man responsible for his death was a soldier home on leave.

Sergeant Clay, my dad was my best friend—my biggest supporter—and now he's gone. And instead of grieving his loss and remembering all of the great things about him, I'm consumed with anger and resentment toward the young man who so carelessly stole my father's life. He was a soldier, for Christ's sake. Aren't soldiers supposed to be strong, upstanding men? Aren't they supposed to be trained in the art of discipline and control? Or has the military gone to shit and now they're producing nothing but careless, uncontrollable monsters who think it's okay to get behind the wheel drunk?

Who does that anyway, drive drunk? It makes me angry, and I hate this anger that has somehow taken over every aspect of my life. But I can't seem to move past it. It controls me in ways that I can't even explain. It's an entity, in and of itself, growing inside of me to epic proportions. It's the last thing I think about when I go to bed at night and the first thing I think about in the morning, and on most days it occupies every minute in between.

Bailey tells me that the first step is forgiveness, but please tell me how in the hell I'm supposed to forgive a "mistake" that destroyed my entire world? How do I move on from this? How do I erase this deep-rooted hatred that has spread from a smolder to a full-blown inferno inside my soul? Honestly, I'm not sure I can erase it, or move on, and that terrifies the ever-loving shit out of me.

My dad was a good man . . . a kind man. He was a hard worker and the best damn father a girl could ever ask for. He was my hero, and nothing and no one can bring him back. But it sure will be satisfying knowing that Lieutenant Drexler will rot in prison for what he took away from me and my family.

Can you even relate to what I'm going through and what I'm feeling? Of course you can't. Because what I'm feeling is a gaping hole of emptiness in the spot where my heart should be.

I haven't told anyone about these feelings, except my therapist. Sure, my mom and sister know I'm having a hard time, but they're oblivious to the things that cycle over and over in my head. They don't know that there have been days I've thought about what it would be like to leave this earth, and I hope they never do because I don't want to disappoint them more than I already have.

So, do I feel better after writing this letter? I'm not so sure. If anything, at least it will appease Dr. Perry, and it's given me the opportunity to tell you that you're a fucking dick and I hate you for what you did. Most of all, I hate that I don't know why you left. What changed to make you pick up and leave the way you did?

You know what? Don't answer that. I don't care.

Have a good life, Sergeant Clay.

Sincerely,
Katie Devora

My breathing is ragged and my heart is racing at a pace that seems inhuman. My fingers grip the letter tightly as if the longer and tighter I hold it, the kinder the words will become. Her letter absolutely gutted me, but I shouldn't be surprised. Maybe leaving her without a word was a dick move, but she had no idea what I saw . . . the way she looked at Wyatt, the way she turned to him with her problems. I would never be able to compete with the likes of him. I could feel it in my bones, even before talking to her dad, that Wyatt would be her knight in shining armor. Sure, at the time I didn't want to believe it, but I could *feel* it.

Katie may have loved me then—fuck, I know she did—but I had every reason to believe that my love for her wouldn't be enough.

Without permission, my mind drifts to the last night I saw Katie. The night I promised her we'd find a way to make it work. The night I ultimately walked away, shredding both her heart and mine in the process.

"Goodnight."

"Goodnight." She giggles when I cup the back of her neck and bring her mouth to mine. Reluctantly, I let go, and with a smirk, she walks away, only looking back once to give me a little wave. My eyes stay fixed on her until I know she's safe inside the house.

Katie lives out in the country, and it's much darker out here than in town. So dark, in fact, that a light tap against my passenger-side window causes me to instantly go into panic mode. Spinning around, I pin myself against the driver-side door. Mr. Devora's enormous frame comes into view, but even after I realize it's Katie's dad and not some masked murderer, it still takes several moments to collect myself.

He throws a hand up in apology and then motions for me to get out of my car. My eyes dart to the door Katie just walked in and then back to Mr. Devora before I finally do as I'm asked and climb out. He walks around the car and puts a hand on my shoulder; I feel like if he applied any pressure at all it would rip my arm right off. The strength he's acquired from working on a farm has never been more apparent than now as my teenage arm disappears under the grip of his hand. He flashes a bright white smile beneath a thick brown mustache that even Tom Selleck would be proud of.

"Sorry, buddy, did I scare you?" His voice comes off much softer than you'd expect from such an intimidating figure. He always has a way of instantly making me feel comfortable, though a quick change in facial expressions and I'd be back to cowering like I'm fourteen again.

Mr. Devora and I have always had a pretty good relationship. He knows how I feel about Katie, and for years I've helped them both around the farm. He also knows about my home life and has often made a point to act as father figure toward me. I've always appreciated him for that.

"No, it's okay, I just didn't see you. It's dark out here in the country." I try my best to not sound like a child, but I can't help but think I do anyway. I guess that's just a repercussion of knowing him since I was a toothless little boy. He'll always be Katie's scary dad to me.

"I just wanted to talk with you real quick. Do you have a few minutes?" My mind runs through all the things he could want to talk to me about, and I come to the same conclusion each time—he knows I just had sex with his daughter!

Chills rack my body when I remember just how many guns this man owns, and for a split second I consider jumping in my car and taking off because I'm sure that this will be the end of me. I'm going to die at the hands of Katie's dad, and he's gonna bury me in some secluded spot on his property, never to be heard from again. Well, fuck, it was a fun ride, I guess.

"Yeah." My voice squeaks and I swallow hard, hoping he didn't hear it. "That'd be fine, Mr. Devora. What's going on?"

"Head over to the fire pit, and I'll go grab a couple of Buds." I clear my throat and can only manage to nod my head as I make my way to the side of the house where the fire pit sits, four chairs surrounding it, with only a few embers still smoldering. He makes his way inside and I grab a seat, my entire life running through my head. I wonder how long it'll take my mom to notice I'm gone . . . and how long it'll take her to sell all of my shit.

The back door slams shut and the soft glow of the fire casts a massive shadow as Mr. Devora approaches. In my head, I'm saying as many Hail Marys as I can, but I'm messing up half the words. I'm thinking right about now that this is going to get me a first-class flight to hell. Leave it to me to try and find religion just seconds before my life ceases to be.

I see his hand lift amongst the shadows and I squeeze my eyes shut, waiting for the bullet to pierce my skin and leave me bleeding to death in the dirt. "Well, you gonna take it, or you gonna make me drink 'em both?"

His voice with its slight drawl forces my eyes open, and I see he's holding a Bud Light out for me to take. I immediately relax and accept it from him. Popping the top off, I toss it back, hoping the alcohol will calm my nerves. I down about half the bottle before noticing him look-ing at me as if to say, "You better slow it down, boy." I've always loved that Katie's dad would give me beers from time to time, and I have his old-school cowboy ways to thank for that. But he's never been a fan of my tendency to drink them entirely too fast. Little does he know, it's my fear of him that makes me guzzle them in the first place.

Mr. Devora pulls out a chair, plops down next to me, and takes a swig of beer. "You've known my princess for a long time now, and you guys have gotten pretty close," he says, matter of fact.

"Yes sir, we have." I'm instantly taken back to just a few hours earlier when I was buried deep inside his princess, and as wonder-ful as it was, I'm coming to terms with the fact that I may have been *jeopardizing my mortality by doing so. This man could crush me with his bare hands, and I'm just waiting for it to happen. Well, at least I'll have had one last beer before I go.*

I take another long swig and place the bottle between my thighs. "Is that what you needed to talk to me about, sir?"

"Well, kind of. I also wanted to talk to you about your future. Where you're headed. Your plans after school." *He waits for a moment as if trying to find the right words and an acceptable way to present them to me.* "I know all about your home life, Devin, and what I haven't learned from Katie, I hear from Brenda. She and your mom used to be very good friends. Do you remember that?"

I nod my head. "Yes, I remember. Not a whole lot, but I remember our families hanging out when I was little . . . before everything happened." *I drop my eyes to the ground and start fumbling with the pocket of my jeans. It's not a part of my life I'm particularly proud of.*

"That's right. Your father and I used to be pretty good friends too. After he took off, I looked after your mom the best I could. Brenda and I both did. We would stop over all the time with meals and stuff for you. Do you remember that?"

"Yes, I do." *Come on, how could I forget Brenda's pot roast?*

"You were a good kid. Incredibly resilient considering everything you went through." *The fact that he used past tense to describe me as 'a good kid' further convinces me that tonight will end differently than I had originally planned.* "After a few months of that, when things got really bad, your mom got very angry with us. She told us to never come back. We've always wanted to continue helping, but we also wanted to respect her wishes." *I nod, unsure of what to say. I'm not certain where he's going with this at all, unless he's just allowing me to reflect on my life before he takes it. But what I do know is that I don't need him to remind me of the choices my mom has made.*

I think back to that night, seven years ago, when Mom, all messed up on Percocet and cocaine, completely lost it on the Devoras. She destroyed half of the breakables in our house as they stood shocked in the doorway with freshly made lasagna in one hand and a new bookbag for me in the other. She screamed about them taking pity on her . . . saying that they were trying to prove they were better parents than she was. They reluctantly left me there with her as she continued destroying the rest of the house and subsequently went on a two-week bender. When she came out of it, she ordered me never to see the Devoras again. Seeing as I am head over heels in love with their daughter and always have been, that was never an option. I got pretty good at sneaking around, and my mom was usually too fucked up to know what was happening anyway.

"So, do you know what I'm trying to say?" Mr. Devora's words tear into my thoughts, and I realize I've missed the last part of what he said.

"I'm sorry, sir, I don't really." My words are barely audible and I avoid making eye contact with him.

"What I'm saying is, I understand your situation isn't ideal. Shit, to be perfectly honest, it sucks. You weren't dealt the best hand in life, but I just want to make sure you never let that dictate your future. It's easy to fall into a familiar cycle." I cock my head and do my best to interpret his last words. In my understanding, he just said "Don't be a fuck-up like your mom." I try my absolute hardest to keep my face from showing how offended I really am, especially coming from him. "There are a lot of good schools in the area and a lot of good programs. Have you thought much about what you'd like to do next?" he asks.

I want to lie and say yes, but I don't even know what I'd pretend to be interested in, not to mention the fact that I won't even be here.

"No, I haven't really figured it out just yet." I feel foolish saying it, and I can feel his judgmental eyes lumping me in with all the other Tennessee trailer park trash, so I quickly scan my brain for something else—anything that would prove my worth to him. But inevitably, there's nothing to say but the truth. "I'll actually be moving to Pennsylvania in the next few days with my mom. So, I'll have to figure something out up there."

Mr. Devora's mouth drops open and he cocks his head to the side as though he's trying to decide if he heard me right. And then it happens.

His brows furrow and his eyes harden, and I get the distinct feeling that this is it. I just pissed off the daddy bear.

Fuck. *Diverting my eyes, I search for some way to get out of this conversation . . . hide under a rock, maybe? Peace Corps? Antarctic exploration? Anything to get me as far away from this man as possible.*

"So you're leaving?"

I nod, and when he stays silent, I take a chance and look up.

"It's your mom, isn't it?" *His words throw me off because I was expecting him to be pissed at me. But judging by the tone of his voice, he's pissed* for *me.*

"My grandmother, actually. She isn't doing well. They're talking about putting her in hospice and Mom wants to be closer to her."

"Wow." *He blows out a slow breath and runs a hand through his hair.* "I'm sorry about your grandma, and I'm sorry to hear that you're leaving."

"Yeah," *I grunt.* "I'm not really happy about it."

"I bet." *We both go silent, and it's not a comfortable sort of silence. It's more of an awkward silence where I can tell that he wants to say something, and I know that it'll be something I don't want to hear.* "So, what does this mean for you and Katie?"

There it is. "I'm not really sure, sir. I care about your daughter—a lot—and I'm not . . . I don't . . ." *I clear my throat, frustrated because my words don't seem to want to come out.* "I really want us to stay together. I—"

"Listen," *he interrupts.* "How is this going to work? How are the two of you going to make it when you'll be living so far away?" *He holds up a hand when I open my mouth to speak, and that just pisses me off.* "I know you're going to tell me that you'll come back, and I believe that you will. But what will you do when you come back? Where will you live? Will you go to college, and if so, how will you pay for it? Where will you work?" *With each word out of his mouth, my heart beats faster because I don't have those answers. His eyes lock on something over my shoulder for a couple of seconds before landing on me.* "I want to see you succeed, Devin, I really do. But I love my daughter with all of my heart, and I want the best for her."

All those years of knowing him, all the talks we've had and the bonding that's been done flies right out of the window with his last statement. In not so many words, he just told me that he doesn't believe in me and I'm not good enough. I wish he'd just come right out and say it.

I finish off the beer and timidly pass him the empty bottle. Standing, I avert my eyes and hope to hell he will let me go so I can go lick my wounds.

"I just want what's best for her," he repeats, this time his voice unyielding, as though to drive home his point. I nod blankly and make my way back to my car. "Devin . . ."

He stops me in my tracks and I turn to face him. "No, it's okay, I totally understand what you mean." Turning around on my heel, I head toward my car, yank open the door, and climb in, hoping to wash my hands of this entire conversation.

"Do you?" he asks skeptically as he approaches the car. Cranking the engine, I close my door and roll down the window. Each of his hands are cupped against the window frame and he's leaning in toward me. "Devin, I think very highly of you, you know that. This—"

"No, really, I completely understand. You want your daughter to be with someone a little less like me, and a little more like Wyatt, right? Someone that comes from a thoroughbred family, someone that is destined to get into an Ivy League school and make more money in one week than I'll make in a year." My chest tightens because I know that I'm right. That's exactly what Christopher Devora wants, and I can't fucking blame him. Hell, that's what I want for Katie.

Shifting the car into drive, I'm hoping that he'll get the hint and remove himself from my car. Reality just slapped me in the fucking face—with a little help from Katie's dad—and as much as I hate it, I know what I have to do.

His eyebrows furrow and he glares at me for a second before pushing away from my car. "Devin, that's not—"

Before he even has a chance to finish, I shove my foot on the gas and speed away from the only real home I've ever known. Mr. Devora's large frame slowly fades away in my rearview mirror, and when he's no longer visible, it hits me that I'll probably never see this place again . . . or the girl I love.

Never could I have provided Katie with the type of life she deserved, and that night it became clear that I would only be holding her back. She deserved someone who could give her the world . . . someone like Wyatt.

Fucking Wyatt.

I hadn't even thought of that name in about a decade, and now here it is again digging itself underneath my skin. I wonder for a moment if they ended up getting together. Since the day I left her, I just always assumed that's how it would turn out—that Wyatt would be there to pick up the pieces, and she would welcome him with open arms.

Wyatt is the one Katie's dad wanted her to be with all along . . . the one that fit the perfect husband mold for his dear daughter. He may have thought highly of me, or so he said, but I could see it beneath the surface. Wyatt had the great home life, the family money, and the excellent grades. I was just the kid from the other side of the tracks with the messed-up mother.

Katie has no idea that it was her dad's last words to me that ultimately gave me the courage to walk away from her, to leave her without notice. And she would never dream that those words are also the reason why I'm where I am today.

As awful as it sounds, I contemplate throwing her letter with the others and joining the rest of my platoon in their slumber, not even bothering to respond. But I'm torn. I want to write her back and explain what happened. I also want her forgiveness—badly. But haven't I put her through enough already? Wouldn't telling her the truth be counterproductive?

I could leave *us* out of it entirely, because despite what she may think, Katie Devora has always been—and will always be—my best friend, and there's not a second that's gone by I haven't thought of her and wondered how she was doing. I want to be there for her, especially since I can read the desperation in her sentences, the pain in her words. I feel that pain, too. I *know* that pain. It sits heavy in my bones. Could I offer her some sort of comfort?

Maybe we are all monsters, created by war like some lab experiment gone wrong. Maybe I should tell her the man that took her father's life deserves to be hanged, along with every drunk driver. Maybe I should tell her that I want nothing more than to kill him with my bare hands for hurting her, because even after all these years, she still means the world to me.

Maybe I should just be honest.

I remove a pad and pen from my duffel, and then I sit and stare at the paper, scanning my brain for the right words to say. I manage to write *Dear Katie* before uncertainty takes hold again.

Closing my eyes, I picture the two of us on that last perfect night. Feeling her lips on mine, my skin against hers, and knowing that everything was going to be okay. And then the reality of it all settling in . . . Wyatt with his straight A's and bloated trust fund, her father and his unattainable expectations, my inadequacies. Shaking my head, I push the memory away.

Grabbing the flashlight from my pillow, I shine it at the pad, and before I know it, the pen begins to move. I don't process every word I write; I only write from the heart. Letting the words flow out of me freely, I scrawl with feverish intent, letting truth dictate the message. For the first time in years, I let my heart take the lead.

Chapter 5 | *Katie*

"Sad"—Maroon 5

"Hold up." Maggie drops her fork on the plate and leans forward, resting her elbows on the table. "You actually went through with it? You wrote him a letter?" I nod my head at the same time I shovel a bite of pizza into my mouth. "And you told him what happened and how you were feeling . . . and you didn't hold anything back?" Nodding again, I reach for a napkin and she slides one toward me. "Wow," she says, a look of disbelief on her beautiful face.

"*Wow?*" I ask, a little annoyed that she finds it surprising. "Why *wow?*"

"Why not *wow?*" Maggie relaxes back in her chair, giving me her patented you-won't-win-this-argument look, and I roll my eyes. "You've just been so . . ." she trails off, biting on her lip as though she's looking for the right word.

"Closed off?" I offer.

Her eyebrows push into her hairline and she laughs. "'Closed off' is one way to put it, but I was going to say bitchy. But we can go with 'closed off' if it makes you feel better." I open my mouth to argue and she cocks a brow, daring me to deny it. I snap my mouth shut. "What'd you expect me to say, that you've been a ray of fucking sunshine? Because we both know that sure as hell isn't the truth."

Magdalena Garcia—a.k.a. Maggie—has been my best friend since the first day of college when she stopped me from accidentally walking into the men's bathroom. She has been and always will be the most upfront, in your face, tell-it-like-it-is person I've ever met, so her boldness shouldn't be a surprise, but her words sting nonetheless. They shouldn't—I know they shouldn't—but they do. I've been a bitch of epic proportions to everyone, including her, and I'm lucky she's put up with me for this long. I don't really have anyone to blame but myself either, but I'm still not in the mood, not after my recent fight with Bailey.

"Don't," she says, waving her fork in my direction. "Don't you dare look at me like I just kicked your fucking puppy."

"I love you, Maggie, but I deal with this shit from everyone else in my life, and I'm not about to sit here and put up with it from you." Pushing from the table, I drop my plate in the sink. I walk toward the living room, but she snags my arm in her tiny hand and whips me around.

"I've kept my mouth shut for three months." I stare at her blankly, hoping that if she says her piece, I can get the hell out of here. Wait, we're at my house. I need to get *her* the hell out of here. "That's twelve weeks, Katie. Do you know how hard that was for me?"

I fight back a smile because it's nearly impossible for Maggie to keep her mouth shut for longer than a minute, so the fact that she went twelve weeks is a complete miracle. "I let you fester and bitch and *close yourself off* because it's what you felt you needed to do. And maybe this wasn't the best time to say anything, but I saw something different in you tonight and . . ." She shrugs her shoulders and looks down.

"And what?" I ask, dropping into the seat I'd just vacated.

"When you were telling me about the soldier pen pal program—and about Devin—I saw a little part of you that I haven't seen since before the accident."

"Really?" *She really saw that?*

"Yes, really," she says, laughing. "You smiled. Sure, you smiled at the thought of writing 'fuck you' to a man that's defending our country, but you still smiled . . . and I've missed that smile."

I knew that I was hurting everyone—hell, it was my intention. But seeing the forlorn look on Maggie's face makes me realize, for the first time, just how far I had taken it. "Sorry, Mags," I say, reaching my arm across the table. I wriggle my fingers, urging her to take my hand.

"I'm not sure I'm ready to kiss and make up," she says, amusement shining in her large hazel eyes as she cocks her eyebrows suggestively. "I think you'll need to do a little more than just apologize." I sigh and pull my arm back. Her hand flies across the table and snags mine. "Okay, fine," she says with a dramatic eye roll. "I forgive you. Now tell me more about this letter. I want to know exactly what you said to Devin. I hope to hell you laid into him."

She's like a dog with a bone, and I should've known that she'd read way too much into it. "There isn't anything else to tell." I shrug, dislodging my hand from hers so I can steal a pepperoni off her half-eaten pizza slice. "I said my piece, opened up to him about my dad, and then I pulled up my e-mail and picked a different soldier that I'll write to next time."

"Except you won't," she mumbles dismissively. "Anyway, did you cry when you wrote it?" She takes a swig of her soda and waits for me to answer. I've missed this, sitting here shooting the shit with my best friend. And even though I don't particularly want to talk about *this* subject, I also don't want to lie to her.

"I did." I nod, fighting the urge to look away. Her hand freezes midair and she blinks at me several times before slowly lifting the pizza to her mouth.

"Why are you staring at me like that?"

"Sorry." She swallows and then takes another drink of her soda. "You just threw me for a loop there. I thought maybe when you told me you opened up to him in your letter, it was just a fluke that you actually answered me, but then you just did it again."

"I did." Apparently, that's my universal answer tonight, and surprisingly, it feels good. At first, I wasn't sure if writing the letter was therapeutic or not. And honestly, I'm still not sure, because when I crawled into bed that night, I was nothing short of pissed off. But this seems like progress so I'll take it.

Devin hasn't written me back, and initially I was sort of bothered by it. I thought for sure that he would at least reply to tell me that he was sorry, or maybe that I was a bitch and didn't deserve the release I was so desperately looking for. It's possible that his lack of response bothers me more than his harsh words would have, and maybe that's because everything surrounding our falling-out is nothing but a big mystery to me.

Maggie pushes her plate to the side, the corner of her mouth tipping up in a classic shit-eating grin. "I wonder how far I can push my luck."

"Try me."

"Have you heard—?"

The front door slams shut, and we both turn in time to see Wyatt kick off his boots. "Fucking Wyatt," Maggie growls under her breath. "He totally just cock-blocked me."

She crosses her arms over her chest and huffs. I giggle, watching Maggie act like a petulant child.

"What?" she asks.

"You don't have a cock, Mags, and we aren't having sex."

"But that's what it would feel like," she answers with a completely straight face. "You were loose and ready to go, and I was totally going in for the kill, and BAM!" She smacks her hands together and shakes her head slowly from side to side. "Wyatt walks in and ruins it all."

I toss my head back and laugh, noticing instantly how foreign it sounds even to my own ears. But even though it's foreign, it feels *good*.

I'm finally able to catch my breath when Wyatt steps into the kitchen. He eyes me skeptically and then gives Maggie a pointed look. "Magdalena."

"Cock blo—"

I slap a hand across her mouth, and we both lose ourselves in another fit of laughter. Wyatt watches us curiously and I half expect him to demand to know what's so funny, so I'm caught completely off-guard when he simply smiles—and not just at me, but at Maggie as well.

Maggie and Wyatt have never really gotten along, but they've tolerated each other for my sake. I've always chalked up their dislike for one another to nothing more than a clash of personalities. Maggie is as loud and rambunctious as they come, and Wyatt is, well . . . not. Wyatt is more of a straight-laced kind of guy, quick to walk away, and always—as taught by his mother—reserved.

With slow, measured steps, he walks over and slides into the chair next to me. "You're smiling . . . and laughing." I nod, dropping my hand from Maggie's face. Wyatt leans forward, placing a gentle kiss on my lips, and then pulls back, watching me with open adoration. I wait for that familiar tug inside my chest, the one that I used to get when he would kiss me, the one that I haven't felt in months. My eyes roam his face, desperately searching for something—anything.

Nothing.

All the feelings of uncertainty and guilt that I've been pushing away for the past several weeks rush to the forefront, and my stomach drops. *How did this happen? How did we get here?* I've already lost so much; I can't lose him too.

Something in my expression must change because Wyatt's face falls and he eyes me with a hint of confusion. *Did he notice it too? Could he tell that my heart didn't flutter and my breath didn't catch in my throat like it should have?* I'm completely frozen in place because I feel, without an ounce of uncertainty, that this isn't a phase. This isn't something I have to work through. This is just how I feel.

A dull ache resonates in my belly at the thought of hurting Wyatt. Unable to hold his gaze, my eyes drift over his shoulder. Maggie is watching me intently, and if I didn't know better, I'd think that she just read my mind. She knows me, and she's been around the two of us more times than I could ever try and count. She sees it too.

Clearing her throat, Maggie breaks eye contact and looks at Wyatt. "It's because of me, Wy-Wy." Wyatt's jaw clenches at the nickname she gave him years ago. She's using their general dislike for each other to break the tension, and even though I don't think it'll work, I'm thankful that she's trying. "I'm the one that made her smile."

"I'm sure you did, Magdalena," Wyatt states flatly. His eyes plead with mine, begging me to explain what's going on. Everything inside of me is screaming to make this right, to pull him into my arms and reassure him that we are okay. But I can't, because we are *not* okay. He runs a finger down the side of my cheek and offers me a hesitant smile. "Is everything alright?"

I've waited months for him to push me for answers, and he chooses now? "I'm fine." I pause, giving myself the opportunity to lay it all on the line, but like always, I chicken out. How do you tell your boyfriend of seven years—who is now your fiancé—that you're not in love with him anymore? "I'm fine," I repeat, even though he hadn't questioned me after I said it the first time. My voice is even and controlled, and the lack of emotion should speak volumes. Wyatt's eyes flit between mine and he opens his mouth, but the loud shrill of his radio cuts him off.

"Shit," he hisses, rushing into the living room. Wyatt grabs his radio off the coffee table, where he must have set it when he walked in, and slips his boots on. Then he comes back into the kitchen and grabs a bottle of water from the refrigerator while he waits for the dispatcher to give details surrounding the call.

Wyatt is a third-generation volunteer firefighter, and over the past several years, I've learned to stay calm until I know what the emergency is. The town we live in is quite small, with only about seventy-five hundred residents. Therefore, the fire department responds to anything from a fully engulfed structure fire to minor medical emergencies.

A loud voice crackles through the radio. "Attention Rock River Fire Department and Rock River EMS. Report of a two-vehicle ten-fifty on Highway 25 near the intersection of Placard Road. Report of airbag deployment with multiple occupants. Unknown injuries. No further information at this time."

"I gotta go, baby." Wyatt dips down so we're eye to eye. He cups my cheek in his hand and kisses me twice before pulling back. "I don't know what's going on with you tonight, but when I get back, we're gonna talk about it."

He spins around and hauls ass through the house. "Be safe!" I yell, my words dying off when the front door slams shut.

"What the fuck was that?"

"A ten-fifty is a car accident," I answer dryly, dragging my gaze back to Maggie.

"Nope, not that," she says, her lips pressed into a firm line. "The other thing."

"What *other thing?*" I ask, pretending I have absolutely no idea what she's talking about.

"Alright." Sliding her chair back, she gets up, walks to the cupboard, and grabs two wine glasses. "If that's how you wanna play this." I follow her movements as she strolls to the refrigerator and picks out a bottle of wine, then pulls the stopper from the top. Gripping the two glasses in one hand with the bottle clenched in the other, she falls into her seat at the table. "I've got all night, Katie." There's a smirk on her face when she fills both glasses with my favorite red wine and pushes one toward me.

"There's only enough there for another two glasses."

Her smile grows and she tips her goblet in my direction. "Well then, it's a good thing I have two more bottles in my car . . . and a change of clothes."

"Great." I groan and tip my head back, draining half of my glass. It's a damn good thing I don't have to work tomorrow, because it sure would suck spending twelve hours in the hospital taking care of other people while nursing a hangover.

Placing the goblet on the table, I move it around slowly, waiting for her to say something. Maggie's eyes sparkle with amusement, and I watch as she takes several small sips of her wine. Minutes tick by, and eventually she reaches for the newspaper on the counter and flips through the pages. She sure as hell isn't making this easy on me, that's for sure.

"You're a pain in my ass."

Maggie levels me with unyielding eyes. "*Igualmente,* my friend."

"I hate it when you do that. You know I can't understand Spanish."

Maggie snorts with laughter as I finish off the Stella Rosa. Lifting up the bottle of wine, she refills my glass and then offers me a cocky smile. "*Si dejaras de ser una perra, yo no lo haria.*"

When she starts speaking Spanish, I typically just ignore her, because if I play into it, she won't stop. She simply loves to torment me. So instead, my mind races, trying to figure out the best way to put into words what I'm feeling. When I draw a complete blank, I decide to just go for it.

Drawing in a deep breath, I push down the anxiety that is keeping me from opening up. "I'm not in love with Wyatt anymore."

Maggie's smile falters, and her shoulders rise and fall when she sighs. "I know."

The casual way that rolls off her tongue irks me. "Really?" My tone is much sharper than I intend, and Maggie frowns at me. "How the hell did you know when I just figured it out myself?"

"Did you, though, just figure it out? Really?" Her eyes narrow and she crosses her arms over her chest. "Because I've seen it for at least the past year."

"No," I say firmly, unwilling to believe I could have been blind for that long. "The past several months, yes, but—"

"Seriously, Katie?" she snaps, pausing momentarily to look at me like I've grown a second head. My eyebrows are practically in my hairline as I wait for her to continue. "Fine. How often do you and Wyatt go out?"

"That's not fair, Mags. You know damn well that I've pushed him away since Daddy died." Just the mention of my dad's death causes a thick band to constrict around my heart and my eyes instantly well up with tears.

I watch as regret replaces determination on Maggie's face. "I'm sorry—"

"Don't be." Waving her off, I take another sip of my wine. "We should be able to mention it without me going into freak-out mode. Keep going . . ." I urge, wanting to move past this as quickly as possible.

"Okay, how often did you and Wyatt hang out before the accident?"

She already knows the answer to that because she's always with us, but I know she's trying to make a point so I play along. "A couple of times a week."

She nods, accepting my answer. "And who was initiating those get-togethers?"

I open my mouth to reply and then quickly snap it shut. *Son of a bitch.* "Wyatt," I whisper. My mind works furiously to recall a time when I initiated anything with him, and I come up completely empty.

"And how often have you sent me a last-minute text to come over and hang out with the two of you?"

No. There's no way that I've been avoiding alone time with Wyatt. *Right?* We've spent plenty of time together, just the two of us. "Okay, yes, I would invite you over, but Wyatt always stayed the night after you left and we sure as hell weren't knitting scarves in bed."

"But don't you see? He's your *fiancé*, Katie. Not only do you guys not live together, but you don't even spend every night together. Sean is just my boyfriend and we spend every single night together—*alone*. And I don't doubt that you and Wyatt have been intimate, but I do question how much passion there is between you."

Her words pierce through the armor that I've spent the last several months shielding myself behind. My leg bounces rapidly under the table. Nervous energy builds up inside me to the point that I feel like if I don't move or do something, I'll explode. A tiny part of me wants to blow up at Maggie, to tell her to fuck off and mind her own business, but I can't. It's been my defense mechanism for far too long, and it's time I act like an adult.

"Fuck." Burying my face in my hands, I groan. "What the hell is wrong with me?" Nausea rolls through my stomach at the thought that I've led Wyatt on, and I take a deep breath to try and keep from throwing up. She's right. She's completely right. "How did I not see this sooner?"

"Okay, first, nothing is wrong with you, sweetie." Maggie's soft hand lands on my arm and I look up, meeting her gaze. "Second, I don't think you saw it because you didn't want to see it. There is no doubt in my mind that you love Wyatt; you're just not *in love* with him."

Pressure builds behind my eyes and I shake my head adamantly. "I'm not. I want to be . . . God, do I want to be in love with him. The thought of hurting him makes me physically ill. But why? That's what I don't get. He's perfect for me, Maggie. He's an amazing guy. How did I just fall out of love with someone like that?"

Thoughts. Hit. Brick. Wall. *Holy shit.* Is that what happened with Devin? Did he just fall out of love with me? Did he sleep with me and then decide that what he was feeling was nothing more than friendship? That it was easier to cut and run rather than deal with the fallout of an emotional woman?

"I'm not sure." Maggie watches me for several seconds, and then she stands up, grabs both of our wine glasses, and nods toward the living room. "Let's go in there and talk." Numbly, I follow her into the living room and curl up in the corner of my couch while she makes herself comfortable in the recliner. "Permission to speak freely."

"I think I'll need more wine for this." I reach my hand out and she looks down, realizing that she's still holding my glass. With a cheeky smile, she pushes it into my hand and then drains the rest of her wine. "Permission granted."

"Is it possible that you've never *truly* been in love with him?" My brows furrow and she reaches a hand out. "Hear me out. You guys have been together for, what, five years?"

"Seven," I say, a wave of nostalgia washing through me. Wyatt and I had been friends since kindergarten, so when he'd built up enough courage to ask me out our sophomore year in college, I didn't think twice about saying yes. Because even though I'd never thought of Wyatt as more than a friend, what did I have to lose? And well, we've been together ever since. It was easy and comfortable, and not once did I regret the decision. We liked the same things, we had a ton of fun together and I just generally enjoyed being with him. The first time he kissed me, I had all of the universal "first kiss" symptoms. Butterflies took flight in my stomach, my palms were sweaty, and the itch to kiss him again was strong. It took another year, but we eventually slept together, and even though the first time was beyond awkward, it eventually got better.

Wyatt was the first person I'd slept with since that ill-fated night with Devin. In the beginning, I compared the two, which always led to a tremendous amount of guilt. One day, I just decided that I couldn't continue to compare Wyatt to Devin. Devin was gone and he wasn't ever coming back. I knew that I had to cherish what I had, because even though our connection didn't feel as strong as the one Devin and I had, I was still aware that it was a connection most people would die for.

Eventually, I began to crave Wyatt. There were times when he was all I could think about, and his presence would soothe me in ways that nothing or no one else could. So no, what Maggie is saying is not possible. "I was in love with him." The words fall easily from my mouth because they're true. I did love him; I just didn't love him enough. I didn't love him the way a woman should love a man, the way a woman should love her soul mate.

"I can't argue with that look on your face."

"How do I . . . what am I . . . *shit*." Tipping my head back, I stare at the ceiling. My hand slides into my hair. Wrapping a thick chunk around my finger, I twirl it as I sift through my own thoughts. "I don't want to hurt him." It sounds stupid when I say those words aloud, because that's all I've been doing. I've already hurt him enough, and now—

"You need to let him go. You *have* to let him go."

"I know." A thick lump forms in my throat and I swallow past it. Rubbing my hands nervously over my legs, I look up. "I know I do."

"It's going to hurt him, there's no way around that. But it's better to get it over with now." I nod my head because I know that she's right. It doesn't make it any easier though.

A tear slides down my face, and Maggie gets up and walks over to me. Wrapping her arm around my shoulders, she sits down and pulls me against her side. "He's going to be angry, but you owe it to yourself—and to Wyatt—to do this now. I want you to be happy, Katie. You've been through so much and you deserve to be happy."

"So does Wyatt." I sniff, tucking my face into the crook of her neck. Maggie's hand runs a soothing path up and down my back, and without fighting it or even thinking too much about it, I accept the comfort she's offering.

"Yes," she says, chuckling. "Even Wy-Wy." A half sob, half cry falls from my mouth and I swipe away my tears.

"I love you, Mags. You're the best."

Maggie's grip on me tightens and she presses her lips to my head. "If you knew what I called you in Spanish earlier, you might not think so."

Chapter 6 | *Katie*

"Slow Dancing in a Burning Room"—John Mayer

"Katie?"

My eyes snap open and I find Wyatt propped up on his elbows, watching me. The sheet is bunched around his hips and the muscles of his abdomen twitch under the weight of my stare. My eyes rake over his half-naked body and I will myself to feel something. At some point during the night, I finally gave up trying to fall asleep and I moved to a chair across the room.

"Sorry if I woke you up," he says, rubbing a hand across his tired eyes. "Is everything okay?"

Oh my gosh, I can't do this. I can't hurt him. My arms and legs feel weak, and my heart is beating so hard that it could possibly fly right out of my chest. *Shit.* I suck in a sharp breath. "No," I blurt.

Wyatt's brows furrow and I know he's waiting for more, but that one word is all I can seem to get out. Guilt crawls up my throat, threatening to make itself known—the same guilt that could potentially keep me from doing what needs to be done.

Wyatt flings the covers off and moves to get out of bed. Urgently, I hold up a trembling hand. "Please," I beg, shaking my head. Wyatt's eyes widen and his lips part, and the look of panic on his face nearly brings me to my knees. *"Please."*

I love Wyatt. I'll always love Wyatt. But he deserves so much better. He deserves a woman that will love him, heart and soul. A woman that will open herself up and give him everything that life has to offer. I'm not that woman. Not for Wyatt—probably not for anyone.

And it's the thought that Wyatt deserves better that pushes the words from my mouth. "I can't . . ." My voice cracks, and I look up at the ceiling and squeeze my eyes shut, a feeble attempt to gain some sort of control. "I can't do this anymore."

"What?" With two long strides, he's kneeling in front of me. "You can't do what?"

I blow out a slow breath, reminding myself that I'm doing the right thing, even if it's one of the hardest things I've ever done . . . well, second hardest thing. The first was burying my father. Okay . . . third hardest thing. The second was getting over my first love.

"Katie?" His pleading voice is thick and raw. "Look at me." He cups my face in his warm hands, forcing me to look at him. "You can't do what?" His blue eyes are swirling with insecurity and concern.

Just say it. Set him free, Katie. "Us."

Wyatt sighs, his shoulders drop and he nods at me with a look of understanding. *Uh, what? Did he not hear what I just said?* "You've been under a lot of stress, and I know I haven't been making it eas—"

"No," I interrupt.

"Hear me out, okay?" He slides his hand in mine and gives it a gentle squeeze. "I know I haven't been what you've needed me to be since the funeral, and I hate myself for it." I shake my head vigorously, but he keeps talking. "I didn't know how to handle it. I didn't know how to handle *you*. And then when you shut down, when you closed yourself off, I-I froze. It scared the hell out of me, and instead of pushing you to talk about things and comforting you, I abandoned you." A pained look overtakes his face.

"You didn't abandon me," I quickly argue. Okay, yes, he did give me space, essentially acting as though nothing happened and everything was fine when it most certainly wasn't fine, but there is no way in hell I'll let him take the blame for this. "This is com—" Wyatt pushes a finger against my lips, effectively shutting me up.

"I did. I gave you space because I thought it was what you needed, and every single time you told me you were fine, I just accepted it and moved on, knowing that you weren't. I should've insisted that you open up and talk to me, and I wish I could go back and do it over again, but I can't. What I will do is promise you that I'll never act like that again. I'll promise to be there for you, no matter what." Anguish rolls off of him, slamming into me, and my chest physically aches. *Fuck.* "I let you down and I'm sorry. I'm so sorry."

His words cut through me like a knife, and I'm not sure how much more of this I can take. "Stop," I beg. "Please stop. We both could've handled the whole situation differently, but this has nothing to do with that. This—" *Shit.* Pressure builds behind my eyes, and I blink several times to try and keep the tears at bay. *This is so fucking hard.*

My hand fists in my lap and I fight the urge to look away, but that would be the cowardly thing to do and he deserves so much more than that. I take a deep breath and blow it out. "My feelings have changed, Wyatt."

His brows dip low and he drops my hand. "What do you mean?"

"I can't marry you."

A vein pops out in Wyatt's neck, and in one swift move he stands up and takes a step back. "Are you serious? I-I don't understand."

Pushing from the chair, I take a step toward him. I've never seen him look so helpless and lost, and I want nothing more than to wrap him in my arms and tell him that everything will be okay. But I can't. "I don't want to hurt you, Wyatt."

"You don't want to hurt me." His gravelly voice drips with disbelief. "What the fuck does that even mean, Katie?"

Spinning on his heel, Wyatt turns and paces the length of my room with his hands planted firmly on his hips. When he makes his second pass, he stops in front of me. His blue eyes are full of unshed tears, and the sight nearly breaks my heart in two. "Despite what we just talked about, what did I do? Tell me what I did. Was I not attentive enough?" He steps forward and nudges me back. "Did I say the wrong things, or take you to the wrong places?" His voice goes from raw to hard and unyielding. "Tell me what I did!" he shouts.

"Nothing," I blurt, pushing him back a step. "You didn't do anything, don't you get that? This isn't about *you,* Wyatt, it's about me. I'm not in love with you anymore, and you deserve better than that." I look down. A sense of calm washes over me and my shoulders sag in relief. "I deserve better than that." My voice is softer and more reserved, because I can feel it in my heart that I'm doing the right thing. He may hate me now, but someday . . . Someday when he's had time to think, time to move on, he'll understand.

"I don't believe you."

"I'm sorry, Wyatt." Our eyes meet and I rest my hand over my chest. "I didn't see this coming. It crept up on me, and I think that if you look at it—*really* look at it—that you'll—"

"Fuck!" His loud voice thunders through the room, and I flinch. In all the years we've known each other, I've never heard him yell like that, and I hate that I'm the cause. "I don't want to look at it, Katie! I love *you.*"

He shoves a finger into my chest and I stumble back. Catching myself on the dresser, I stand tall, determined not to back down. Regret flashes across Wyatt's face. Cautiously, he reaches for me, but I step back.

"It's okay," I whisper. I know that he wasn't trying to push me, but I don't want him touching me. I'm too open, too raw, and frankly, I'm not sure what it will do to me.

"I just want you." His words are laced with conviction, his eyes shining with passion, and I don't doubt for one second that he means it. "I want the life we've talked about, the life we've planned. I want the white picket fence and the tire swing in the front yard." Slowly, he steps toward me. My feet stay planted as I listen to him beg me for all the things my younger self promised him years ago. "I want those three kids. Two boys and a girl, remember?"

I nod feebly and he takes another step in my direction.

"Don't you see that in your future?" Ever so gently, Wyatt cups my face in his hands. "Because I do. I see all of that . . . *with you.*"

It sounds amazing—all of it. And I hope that one day I'm lucky enough to experience everything that he's talking about. But as the words fall from his mouth—as I picture it all in my head—I don't see it with him, and that brings on a whole new wave of guilt. "Wyatt." His name is but a whisper, packed full of more emotion than an entire fucking romance novel, and I can tell by the stunned look on his face that he understood the meaning loud and clear.

Wyatt's eyes widen and he steps back. The passion in his eyes fades, quickly replaced with frustration and pain. "Damn it, Katie!" Spinning around, he moves across the room. A low growl rumbles from his chest as he slides his fingers through his thick blond hair, tugging at the strands.

This is not at all how I saw this going. Honestly, I'm not sure what I expected, but I thought that maybe I could get him to see that this is for the best. I know now that never would've happened because tonight I broke his heart, and I know all too well how that feels. How could I ever expect him to understand—let alone someday forgive me—when I'm walking away after promising him forever? I'm still not sure I could ever forgive the man who broke my heart, so why should I expect anything different from Wyatt?

Unconsciously, my thumb rolls my engagement ring around my finger. I look down, watching as the diamond catches the light, scattering specks of color around the room. For the first time since we got engaged over a year ago, the white gold princess-cut ring feels foreign on my finger. The weight of the diamond, like the weight of my guilt, sits heavily, and I slip it off while at the same time letting go of the lie that I've been living this past year. It's cathartic in a way that I can't even explain. In a sense, I feel lighter. However momentary it may be, the monsters inside of me have calmed, and for once I feel like I can actually breathe.

A low grunt catches my attention. Looking up, I find that Wyatt has put on his jeans, and I watch him tug his T-shirt over his head. He drops to the bed, his elbows on his knees and palms covering his face, rubbing it roughly several times. *Please don't break,* I think to myself. *You deserve so much more than the broken girl that I've become.*

Slowly, I move toward him. His face tilts up, his glassy eyes finding mine, and it's impossible to miss the tearstains on his cheeks. Instantly, my nose burns—the kind of burn that comes right before I turn into a blubbery mess of tears and snot. We watch each other for several seconds, and when I'm confident that I have some control over my emotions, I push the ring into the palm of his hand.

Wyatt looks down at where I have my hand wrapped around his, and then his eyes dart back up to mine. "You are an amazing person, Wyatt. You are kind and generous"—I swallow hard past the lump in my throat—"and smart and funny, and I am lucky to have had you in my life. One of these days, you are going to make someone very, *very* happy. And I don't deserve your friendship, but I'm selfish enough to ask for it, because the thought of not having you in my life is terrifying." Wyatt's jaw clenches, a fresh batch of tears collecting in his eyes, and I suck in a shuddery breath. "You may not believe it right now, but I never meant to hurt you. You were my very first friend and your happiness means the world to me, which is why I need to do this." Wyatt's lips pinch into a thin line and I know that he has something to say, but I need to get this out or I may never get the chance again. "My only regret is that I didn't do it sooner"—he flinches, and I rush to explain—"because I knew months ago that my feelings had changed. But I was greedy. I was scared to lose you . . . scared to lose your strength and your friendship. I see now how unfair that was to you, and for that I'm *so* sorry."

Wyatt's chin trembles, the movement so slight that I almost miss it. Then in the blink of an eye, his face transforms, almost as though he's slipped on a mask. He wrenches his hand out from under mine and stands to his full height, shoulders back and chin up. "I don't want the damn ring." He shoves it at my chest, and I scramble to catch it before it falls to the floor. "And I don't want your friendship, Katie. I don't want your apologies, I don't want your fucking excuses, and I sure as hell don't want *you*." Brushing past me, he rushes toward the door. Gripping the knob, he flings the door open and then comes to a dead stop.

"You know what?" Twirling around, he stalks toward me. His cerulean eyes are nearly all black, and they're burning with hatred—and quite possibly disgust. I stand frozen as he rips the ring from my hand. "I do want it. I want to destroy it," he seethes, "the same way that you've destroyed me. And then I'm going to throw it away, along with every fucking memory of you."

Speaking isn't an option. I have no defense, no argument, and I certainly have no right to beg for absolution. My lungs ache as I fight to suck in air. *I broke him. I actually broke him.*

"Don't give yourself that much credit." *Holy shit! I've got to stop doing that.* "It's going to take a lot more than *you* to break me."

"Wyatt—"

"No!" he growls, his eyes bouncing around my face. I feel like he's looking for the girl he fell in love with, but he's not going to find her. She died months ago.

With a heavy sigh, Wyatt turns and walks out of my room without a backward glance. Seconds later, I hear the front door slam shut.

He's gone. My hand reaches for my chest, ready to rub the ache I felt the last time I lost a man that I loved. But the pain isn't there like it was before, so I drop my hand to my side.

I stand motionless in my room, waiting for regret to smash into me. I clench and unclench my hands, expecting them to feel numb and tingly, but they don't. There are no tears bursting to break free, and my heart isn't threatening to bounce from my chest. The only thing I feel is a sense of calm that I didn't know I possessed.

Okay, I obviously haven't given it enough time. *It's coming, I know it's coming . . .*

Feeling surprisingly at peace, I walk into the kitchen, passing right by Wyatt's running shoes sitting by the back door. I'll have to worry about those later because this is just the calm before the storm. Any minute now, I'm going to go into full panic mode.

Grabbing a bottle of water from the refrigerator, I twist off the cap and chug half of it. My gaze drifts toward the clock and my jaw nearly drops. It's only four o'clock in the morning . . . no wonder I'm fucking exhausted. Well, that was about the shittiest possible way to start the day. On the plus side, my day can't get much worse. *I hope.*

Hooking my foot around the leg of a chair, I tug it out from under the table and plop onto it. With an exaggerated sigh, I close my eyes and tip my head back, letting a sense of nothing-ness wash over me. My body is relaxed, not an ounce of tension to be found. My pulse, calm and steady, creates a gentle thud in my chest, and my breaths are slow and easy. I want to feel bad, or guilty, or *something*, but I can't because I know I did the right thing. I just wish that it didn't take breaking Wyatt's heart to feel this sense of relief.

With languid movements, I sit up, chug the rest of my water, and look aimlessly around the kitchen. Normally, I wouldn't head over to Mom's to take care of the horses for another hour or so, but I'm wide awake and a sunrise run with Mac is just what I need.

Pushing myself up, I toss the empty water bottle in the trash and then I turn to grab the wine glasses left out from last night. My eyes catch on the stack of mail sitting at the edge of the table and I sift through the envelopes, sliding each one to the side just enough so I can see the next. Phone bill, utility bill, car payment . . .

Everything inside of me stills. My heart literally stops beating before kicking into overdrive, and I slowly drag the tattered envelope out from the middle of the stack.

Tilting my head to the side, I examine the messy penmanship of Sergeant Devin Ulysses Clay. My finger runs a deliberate path along the worn edges and a slow smile builds, tugging at the corners of my mouth. The urge to rip it open is strong and I bite down on my bottom lip, trying to determine whether or not I should read it. A tiny shiver runs through me, and I decide that, for once in my life, I'm going to do something without overthinking it.

So what if I pissed him off? So what if the hope blossoming in my chest completely contradicts the bitterness I still feel toward him? Scooping up the envelope, I toss it in my messenger bag, along with my notepad and pen. I run to my room, quickly changing into a pair of jeans and a sweatshirt, and then I slip on my coat, grab my keys and bag, and dart out the door.

Chapter 7 | *Katie*

"Be Still"—The Fray

A thin fog blankets the rugged landscape, which is lit only by the dull glimmer of the moon. My hair whips around my head, the cool air stinging my cheeks, and for the first time in a long while, I feel the urge to smile.

Mac breezes past a cluster of familiar trees, and on instinct, I duck my head for three beats to avoid the branches I know are hanging low enough to knock me in the face. Slowing down would be the smart thing to do, but Mac loves to run just as much as I do. Plus, I've been riding this path my entire life, and I'm certain we could take it backward and blind without so much as a stumble.

The soft glow of the sun peeks out over the horizon and I push Mac faster. I've been making this ten-minute trek to the edge of my parents' property nearly every morning since being cleared by the doctor, because it's the only place I seem to find solace. As a child, my dad would bring me out here to watch the sun rise; as a teenager, Devin and I claimed it as "our spot"; and as an adult, I come here to drown in the memories of the two of them.

Mac slows to a trot when we hit the clearing, and I know we've made it in time. I tug on the reins and we come to a stop at our usual spot next to an old oak tree that sits several feet from the edge of the creek. Orange and red hues kiss the earth, and it's in this brief moment, when everything is neither dark nor light, that my anger and sadness seem to fall away. Everything around me is quiet, and I tilt my head up to the sky, close my eyes, and breathe in the crisp morning air. The fresh rays of sunlight should hold promises of a new day, but for me they've been a reminder of what I've lost—*until today.* Something inside of me has changed. I can't pinpoint it exactly, but there's a tiny sliver of hope that wasn't there before.

My face warms as the minutes tick by, and only when I'm certain that the sun has risen do I open my eyes. Twisting, I slide off Mac, walk to the oak tree and plop down. That damn letter has been burning a hole in my bag since I ran out of the house, so I waste no time pulling it out. Unable to wait a second longer, I slide my finger under the lip of the envelope, rip it open, and pull the letter out. Tiny smudges of dirt are scattered around the edges of the stark white paper, and I immediately picture Devin sitting down after a long day of work, trying to decide how to reply to his best friend-turned-lover-turned . . . nothing. My stomach churns at the thought of what he could have written, and for a split second, I wonder if I'm better off not reading it at all.

Will his words give me peace? Did he decide to come clean about what happened, or did he simply write to finally tell me good-bye? I don't want to care, but that last thought doesn't sit well with me.

Screw it, I tell myself. *It doesn't matter what he wrote. His words won't change a thing.* Because when it comes right down to it, he still left, my dad is still gone, and no words or mis-placed apologies are going to fix either of those things. And with that last little pep talk—depressing as it may be—my trembling hands unfold the letter.

Dear Katie,

Wow, well my skin is still buzzing! When I saw your name on the envelope, I just about had a stroke. In fact, I think I reread those two words about a hundred times just to make sure it was really you. The address isn't the same—I'll take that as a good sign, although your old address will be etched in my memory for life.

So you found me through the pen pal program, huh? And through a therapist, no less. The world truly does work in mysterious ways. I've thought about you often over the years and always hoped you were doing well. And as mad as you may be at me, hearing from you is one of the best things to happen to me in a long time, which I guess is pretty stupid to say considering how things ended. But you have to believe me, Katie, I never wanted things to be that way. You know I loved you. Those moments we spent together are the best memories I have. You don't even know how many tough times those memories have gotten me through. We were inseparable, you and I . . . partners in crime. I don't want you to think I take that lightly.

I had my reasons for leaving, reasons that are probably best left unsaid. I wouldn't expect you to even begin to understand what was running through my head at the time. You know what I was going through back then, and at the time, we were just two people in two very different places. But I digress . . . That is not what I wanted this letter to focus on at all.

I'm so incredibly sorry to hear about your father, and I can't imagine the pain you must be going through. I know how close you two were, and just reading your words makes me ache so much for you, Katie. I'm just so very sorry.

How is your mom handling everything? And Bailey?

You know my pops walked out on us when I was just a kid and how devastated I was when he disappeared. I'm not trying to compare my situation to yours, not by a long shot. I only mean to say that after going through what I did with all of that, struggling with it like I did but still knowing he was alive and well at least, I can't even begin to understand how you feel right now. I want you to know that, no matter what happened in the past, I will always be here for you. If you ever need to talk, or vent, or just rip into someone, I'm here. I even have e-mail. You could totally bitch me out on there anytime you want!

God, so the man who hit you was a soldier? I wish I could say I'm surprised, but there is an abundance of substance abuse in the military. There are a lot of people numbing themselves, and I can't say that I blame them. When we lose people day in and day out, watch our friends die, and take lives that we don't want to take, how else are we supposed to cope? I've lost so many friends over here that I'm beginning to lose count. Just three months ago, my best friend was one of them. Jax bled out in my arms. He was a polite Mormon boy from Utah without a hateful bone in his body.

So to answer your question, are we all monsters? No, we're not. We are fathers, brothers, husbands, and sons. We are dreamers, lovers, and God-fearing men. Are some of us monsters? Yeah, we are. Some of these soldiers kill with a thirst, and others can gun a man down and not even think twice about it. Unfortunately, there are some who wear the uniform that do not live within the code of ethics our uniforms represent. But the majority of us are just like you . . . people dealing with something so traumatic, so heartbreaking, and so horrific that the heart never quite learns to mend. Many of us, including myself at times, have learned to patch together the broken pieces of our hearts using whatever means necessary— and yes, that sometimes results in harm inflicted upon ourselves and others.

I wish I could tell you that I've never driven drunk, but that would be a lie. I didn't change much after leaving Tennessee. And as ashamed as I am to admit it, I got worse once I moved to Pennsylvania—and worse yet after my grandmother passed away. Mom lost her shit completely when Grandma didn't leave a penny to her name, and it all went downhill from there. I started smoking all the time and drinking. I fell in with the wrong crowd. I just wanted anything other than to be there with her in that fucking trailer.

It was my twentieth birthday, and I was on my way back from a bar with my buddy. I was drunk and nearly unconscious in the passenger seat when my friend, who was also plastered, ran into a telephone pole going fifty in a thirty-five. The doctors said the only reason I avoided major injury was because I was passed out and wearing a seatbelt. My buddy wasn't so lucky. He broke his C-2 vertebrae and has been a quadriplegic ever since. His entire life changed that night, Katie.

Even though I walked away from the wreck, my life changed that night too. I've had tremendous guilt since then and often think about the harm we could've caused others. To think we could've done something like what happened to your dad—to your family—it rocked me to my core. It still does. I joined the Army soon after that. I didn't want to be that person anymore. I didn't want to be defined by those actions, and although I knew you were long gone—that I had effectively pushed you from my life—I still wanted to be worthy of you.

The man who took your father's life could have easily been me a few years back. What's worse is that I hadn't even experienced combat yet. We spend our days here immersed in death—women, children, and loved ones killed on a daily basis—and when we go back home, we aren't the same as we were when we arrived. We become numb, our emotions sedated. Death becomes merely a noun, something we neither process nor heal from.

I make no excuse for the man who killed your father. Maybe he is a monster, one of those who kill with pleasure. Maybe he's a young, dumb grunt who has no regard for the sanctity of human life. Or maybe he's one of many who drink away the pain they can't begin to understand. No matter the circumstance, a life was taken—the life of a wonderful man— and for that I am so incredibly sorry. I can only imagine that

that soldier is sitting in a cell at this moment wishing he could take your father's place.

I'm thinking right about now that I've probably done more harm than good. I hope I haven't heightened the ugliness you see in all of us, me especially, because that wasn't my intention. I only hoped to explain the potential side effects of playing Russian roulette with roadside bombs and bullets for an entire year. And then another year and another and another . . .

Don't treat your grief as we do. Don't let it simmer until, before you know what's happened, it's boiling over the edge. Don't let this one man and his actions change who you are and who you were meant to be. Don't let him own your existence.

I know it must be hard, Katie. I'm no expert; I just know I haven't been doing it the right way. Hell, I don't even know what the right way *is*. But I do know that by hanging on to all this stuff and burying it deep down inside, it'll all catch up to me one day. I can feel the cracks forming already, and I know the foundation will eventually come tumbling down.

I hope to hear back from you. I really enjoyed your letter, although it's possible that it might be the first letter in pen pal program history where a soldier was called a "fucking dick."

But seriously, thank you for writing. And thank you for not letting the past dictate the future.

Sincerely,
Devin
devinuclay@yahoo.com

The letter falls from my hands, the papers floating aimlessly until they come to rest noiselessly on the ground. My mind is racing at warp speed as I work to process his words, but I can't. There's too much, too many emotions, too many things he said that I wasn't prepared to hear or read, and now I can't seem to focus on anything at all except this overwhelming, indescribable emotion that's creeping its way through me.

My brows furrow when I think back to the letter that I wrote him and the callous things I said with abandon. And yet here he is, this soldier—this man who should feel like a stranger but doesn't—fighting for our country, living in his own version of hell every single day, trying to give *me* peace. He clearly has his own cuts that run just as deep, if not deeper, than mine, but he's offering me comfort in the only way he can—with his words.

I don't regret expressing my feelings in the letter I wrote, but after reading his response, I feel like I don't deserve his compassion. I want it though. God help me, I want it.

I squeeze my eyes shut as his words drift around in my head.

So to answer your question; are we all monsters? No, we're not. We are fathers, brothers, husbands, and sons. We are dreamers, lovers, and God-fearing men.

But the majority of us are just like you . . . people dealing with something so traumatic, so heartbreaking, and so horrific that the heart never quite learns to mend.

Lieutenant Drexler's face pops in my head. I've only seen it once, pictured on the news, but it's been branded in my memory and now I can't help but wonder. Does he have a precious little girl or boy running around who will now grow up without him? Will his kids mourn the loss of their father the way I have mine? Does he have a wife who is scared and lost and lonely? Is his mother crying herself to sleep every night because the son who safely returned from the battlefield will never really return home now?

Not once have I allowed these possibilities to enter my mind. I haven't wanted to consider anything about the man who killed my father, and I'm still not sure I want to. But Devin's words have opened a gate, and it doesn't matter how hard I push, the damn thing won't shut.

I can only imagine that that soldier is sitting in a cell at this moment wishing he could take your father's place.

We spend our days here immersed in death—women, children, and loved ones killed on a daily basis—and when we go back home, we aren't the same as we were when we arrived.

Is Lt. Drexler's pain as raw as mine?

Does he think about us as often as I think about him?

Pressure builds behind my eyes, making them burn, and a few tears manage to slip past the confines of my lashes and drip down the side of my face.

If I gave him the opportunity to explain or apologize, would he take it?

Is that something I'm strong enough to do?

A wave of heat washes over me, and without warning, a strangled cry flies from my mouth.

Don't treat your grief as we do.

Don't let this one man and his actions change who you are and who you were meant to be.

Don't let him own your existence.

Clutching at my stomach, my shoulders curl inward, heaving as my body expels three months' worth of grief, pain, anger, and guilt. "Oh, God," I moan, slipping my hands in my hair, wrapping them around the windblown strands. Slow and steady, my body rocks back and forth as my mind replays all the times I've taken my emotions out on my family. I've ignored them, shut them out, and refused their comfort and love. I've said hateful things in fits of anger and sorrow . . . things that I can't ever take back. I tug roughly on my hair, needing to feel some sort of physical pain in exchange for all the pain that I've caused. My breath hitches when I suck in a deep breath and another round of sobs wrack my body.

Lifting my head out of my hands, I tilt my tear-streaked face up to the sky. Raw, nervous energy courses through me and I push to my feet, needing to move somewhere—anywhere. Walking toward Mac, I grab onto his reins and lead him toward the creek. "What is wrong with me?" I mumble, my eyes searching the clouds for some hidden answer. "I don't want to do this anymore." My chin trembles and I swipe away the tears running down my face, but they keep coming and I eventually give up.

Minutes tick by, or maybe hours, but the sobs finally subside. I'm exhausted—beyond exhausted—and already regretting the decision to pick up an extra shift at work tonight. Every muscle in my body aches, and I feel as though I could crawl in bed and sleep for hours on end. I take a deep, cleansing breath and blow it out slowly, letting everything from Devin's letter sink in.

I have absolutely no idea why his letter hit me the way that it has. His words are merely a different version of the same thing everyone else has been trying to tell me, but they *feel* different. Or maybe it's just because it's Devin. There's a reason he was my best friend for so long. He was the first person I gave my heart and body to, and maybe that's the reason I haven't been able to shake this unmistakable connection to him—even after ten years.

There's also a reason his name was on that pen pal list. I've been treading water in a choppy sea of guilt and anger, and he just inadvertently threw me a lifeline. If it were anyone else, I'm not sure it would've made the same impact. So, without thinking twice, I make the decision to grab on to that lifeline he tossed me, and I'm going to hold on to it with every ounce of strength I have left.

Something nudges my shoulder, pulling me from my thoughts, and I turn around and come face-to-face with Mac. Using his nose, he frisks my shirt for treats and I laugh, patting him gently on the neck. "Sorry, big guy. There's nothing in there for you." He lets out a soft huff before dropping his head to graze on the grass. My eyes drift to my bag that is propped up against the tree, and I notice that Devin's letter is exactly where I dropped it. "There's one more thing I need to do before we go, Mac." I give him one last quick rubdown on the head and then make my way to the tree.

Sitting down cross-legged, I grab the letter and read over it once more. This time, however, my heart feels lighter and I can't help but grin as different parts of the letter begin to stand out.

You know I loved you.

Those moments we spent together are the best memories I have.

Devin's words slice through me, leaving me feeling more open and vulnerable than I've felt in a very long time. *He has the power to hurt me again.* How is it possible to feel such a strong connection with someone I haven't even talked to in a decade? I mean, seriously, he treated me like shit, and yet after a very simple apology, I'm dying to reconnect, dying to tell him everything. That should scare the hell out of me, but it doesn't.

I have no idea who this man is anymore. Sure, I know the boy he used to be, but I have no idea what type of person he's turned into. What happened after he left Tennessee? What was his life like in Pennsylvania? Did he meet someone else and fall in love? Did he go to college, and if not, why?

Sure he touched on some of those questions in his letter, but the woman in me—the woman who clearly still harbors some sort of feelings toward her first love—wants details. And lots of them.

A slow smile spreads across my face, and when I take a deep breath, I have an unexpected release of tension. There is no doubt in my mind that a higher power is at work here, and I smirk at the thought that I could very well have my dad to thank for this. Shaking my head, I close my eyes. It would be easy to hold on to my resentment and anger toward Devin, but when I look back on our friendship and all the things we've been through, I'm grateful to be given a second chance.

I'm not sure why, and maybe it's foolish of me, but I have a feeling deep in my bones that I can trust him. A tiny voice pops in my head telling me I shouldn't be feeling this way after everything that happened with Wyatt this morning—especially considering both of our pasts with Devin—but I push it aside.

The need to write Devin back grows with each passing second, so I grab my notepad and pen from my bag, intent on doing just that. He needs to know that I may have lost so much of who I used to be, but one thing hasn't changed—my ability to forgive. Now, I may not be able to forgive Andrew Drexler, but Devin is a completely different story. I want him to know that the words I wrote, although true at the time, were written out of anger and confusion, but that his words have touched me. The process may be slow, but I will make things right with my family and with Devin.

So as my pen hits the paper, I open up the deepest part of me and let it all out, hoping against hope that I hear back from him again.

Chapter 8 | *Devin*

"Lover, You Should've Come Over"—Jeff Buckley

I wake before the sun has checked in for the day and scan the tent, noting my men still sleeping heavily. My morning ritual, at least on the days I have time to do it, requires a bit of privacy, and I make certain I have it before I begin. Most of these clowns will just jerk it in their cots in the middle of the night with the rest of us passed out around them. There's always been something odd about that to me. On a regular basis, I've woken up to the sounds of heavy breathing and skin slapping skin, and it pisses me the fuck off. If I'm not dog-tired, they'll get a boot heaved in their direction, aimed straight for the dick and with the express purpose of putting them out of business for a while.

No, jackin' the beanstalk in public isn't for me. Unfortunately, that leaves only one other place to do it—the Drop Zone. Porta-shitters, as we like to call them, sit for weeks without being emptied and capture every bit of the sun's heat. It's like a fucking hothouse in there, and one breath in that motherfucker while beating off and your dick is in full retreat.

So there's a trick to doing this just right; you have to prep him first. You get him up and going, and then you quickly finish in the shitter. For most of these guys, the bikini-clad chicks above their cots or the porno mags stashed in their bags are a necessity for a proper jerk-off, but I'm an imaginative guy. I close my eyes and my mind becomes like a time machine of fuck. Marilyn Monroe in *Some Like it Hot* . . . bam! . . . cum everywhere. Farrah Fawcett in her iconic red swimsuit bent over the counter . . . set the time machine and go.

This time my mind goes for none other than Jackie O. She's spread-eagle, with my tongue lightly flicking her throbbing clit while she's begging for my dick. And, of course, I'm making her call me Mr. President. I laugh at the last thought but notice it's at least gotten the job started. Since my dick is half-mast and ticking its way to full form, I slink my way to the tent's entrance.

Stepping out, I'm met by the sun creeping softly over the tops of the barriers, and I hurry toward the porta-shitters, positioned just past the Humvees in front of the eastern wall. This two-hundred-yard walk is the most important part of the process. You have to walk with speed but not urgency, in hopes that you don't attract attention from the few others also awake—all while the imagined porn still plays in your head.

I manage to make it into the shitter undetected and quickly go to work on my shaft while my left hand pinches my nose like a vise and my eyes squeeze tightly shut. Only this time it isn't someone famous that I picture. It's Katie.

Even as early as it is, the Drop Zone is like a sauna, and beads of sweat collect on my forehead. I try desperately to hold in my breath as the seconds tick down. Just as my lungs begin to demand air and my body stiffens, I toss my head back with a stifled groan. My body recovers from its high much quicker in this setting, but at least the job is done. *Two weeks of combat stress gone, just like that.*

I take in a deep breath of the noxious air and regret it instantly. Opening my eyes, I turn to exit but notice that I've unloaded all over the toilet seat. *Fuck!* Most of these assholes would just leave it, but I think of how pissed I'd be walking in on a jizz-covered seat so I wad up some toilet paper and wipe away the evidence.

When I'm done, I toss the wad into the pit and thrust myself through the door, relieved to feel the fresh air again.

Just as I step out, I see Navas exiting the crapper beside me. At first I say nothing, caught off-guard by his sudden appearance and feeling awkward having just shot off a load a foot beside him. He has a curious smirk on his face as he eyeballs the sweat now dripping down my forehead. His gaze drops and he catches sight of my hands fumbling with my belt; his smirk turns into a full-blown grin. *He totally knows.*

"H-h-hey," I stammer. "What are you doing up, man?" I add, composing myself a little.

"What's up, buddy?" The way he says it and the grin planted on his face lets me know he's got me figured out. "Little bit sweaty, huh? Were you battlin' a shit or beatin' your dick?"

"Monster shit, bro. You know how that goes. A week of built-up MREs and the turds are like grappling hooks. What are you doing up this early?" I repeat, hoping to change the subject as we slowly make our way back to the tent.

"Chatting with the niños. . . . you know my mom. She'll only let me talk to them once a week. Says it's just too hard on them otherwise, and with the ten-hour time difference, this is the best time to do it."

"And at least you're not having to fight anyone over the phone," I say as we reach the tent. I motion toward the smoke pit. "You want a cig?"

"No, man, I'm good, but I'll chill with you." We both take a seat as I spark up the cancer stick. Fuck this place for getting me hooked on these things. I hate them, but they're just the buzz I need before and after these long-ass days.

Navas peers into the distance, appearing to be deep in thought, and continues. "Why the fuck they gotta have one phone and one computer for an entire combat outpost is beyond me. Even at this hour, I still had to wait for DickFuck to get done talking to his wife. Motherfucker spent like two hours in there, and at one point I could hear his ass getting off, asking her to twist his nipples and shit."

I think to my own release in the shitter moments earlier and chuckle to myself. Put a man in combat—or prison, or a fucking office with a view, it doesn't matter—and he will eventually find his dick in his hand.

I look harder at Navas, who still seems lost in thought. "How are the kids?" I ask.

"You know, they miss me. It's weird because it's like, what do I talk to them about? They ask me what Daddy's doing over here and I can never find the right words to say . . . nothing that a four- and six-year-old would understand anyway. So I tell them we're over here helping people." He stops and runs a hand through his hair. "I've never felt like more of a liar," he says, exhaling loudly, and I can see the pain in his eyes. "And then my mom gets on with her usual rant. She thinks I chose war over my kids, and she uses every chance she gets to remind me of it."

"That's fucked up. Seems like there's not much good that can come of that." I'm not sure what else to say. I haven't spoken to my mother in years. Though she was physically there growing up, she left right along with my father all those years back.

"Yeah, that's just who she is. Mexican women, man, what can you do?" He looks over to me as I light another cigarette. "You know that shit's gonna kill ya, right?"

"Not before this place does." I laugh, but immediately feel uneasy as I often see myself not making it out of here alive. Call it a premonition or what have you, but it feels so fucking real. I can even sense Jax standing just beside me, his hand resting on my shoulder as if waiting for me to join him. *I'm coming, buddy. I'm coming.*

I fight the thought away, and it takes everything I have to do so. Navas notices and pats me on the shoulder. "You alright, brother? Where'd you just go, man?" *Fuck!* I need a distraction . . .

I point to Navas's cargo pocket where I know a cigar rests, impatiently waiting to be smoked after mission. "You think those things won't kill you?" I send him a big, plastic smile, so mastered you'd think I was Beaver-fucking-Cleaver.

"Fuck it, man. If it's not one thing, it's another." He knows me well enough to read through the bullshit, but he also knows, as his squad leader, I'm not going to be the one crying like a little bitch. That's all Lieutenant Dixon, and I'd really like to keep it that way. "The way it's going, if I do make it back, I'll be walking dead," he says, smiling.

"What do you mean?" I look at him curiously but carefully, so as not to seem judgmental.

"I don't know. It's weird," he says, "but do you think we'll ever learn to feel again? After all this, I mean." I know exactly what he's talking about, but I wait for him to continue. Navas isn't always so generous with his emotions, and I make certain I take advantage of the times that he is. It's obvious he's hurting, and it seems to get worse with each phone call home.

"It's like all this death and destruction, losing buddies, and the kids growing up without me, I've lost my sense of feeling. I don't hurt. I don't ache for home. I just exist. I don't feel like I have control anymore. *But I need this.*" He emphasizes those last words, and I know it's because he's afraid of coming off too soft in front of me.

"I need this too, man. But as much as I wish I could, I can't empathize with you. I don't have anything back home. I don't have anyone that needs me. You . . . You have your babies, man. Kids that need their father." I stop and look Navas in the eyes. He's stooped over in his seat as if the weight of the world is resting squarely on his shoulders, but he perks up when I pause as if asking me to continue. I hesitate for a moment but then I do. "I feel for you, man. I feel for your family. For me, this all kind of seems normal now. I get anxious when I'm stateside. Too much time to think . . . and wonder. I think when that day comes and we finally hang up our boots, we'll look in the mirror and not recognize who's staring back. And I have a feeling we're going to miss this. *We will miss the hell out of it.*"

"I couldn't agree with you more." He nods, looking relieved that someone understands. "I think that's a big reason I'm back here. Besides being with you guys, I just didn't feel right back home. Like I was there for my kids, but I wasn't really there, ya know? Growing up, this was all I ever wanted to do. Now, I just don't know. It's like it's changed me. *Fuck . . .* it's too early for this shit, huh?" He shoots a forced smirk my way, but the sadness in his eyes is too prominent.

"Never too early, my friend. I'm here anytime you need to shoot the shit. The kids, man, they'll adapt. Eventually, they'll be old enough to understand the meaning behind all of this. As for us, I can only hope that when the last shots are fired, we are able to cope with what we've seen and done and come back stronger. The Army way, right?" I let out a sarcastic laugh as I rise to my feet, flicking the cigarette butt into the fire pit. Navas doesn't move, just continues to stare into nothing.

I rest a hand on his shoulder. "We have another five months to figure it all out. Don't let it get to you too much. Let's get through this shit and get these guys home safe, huh?"

Navas rises to his feet and faces me, and for a brief moment he embraces me before letting go and making his way toward the tent. There is no love like that of your brothers-in-arms.

"Let's get some fuckin' chow," he says, slipping through the tent's entrance. I follow him in and scan the cots. Some of the guys are fork-deep in their MREs, while others are still getting their asses out of bed. I dig through a box of MREs at the front of the tent.

Chicken. Chicken. Chicken. I'm so fucking sick of chicken. "Damn it, you fuckers, this is a brand new box. Who the fuck took my tortellini?" As I say this, I see Elkins plop the pasta into his mouth with a wide smile.

"I hope you choke on it, Elkins. You know I've got infinite dibs on the tortellini." I smile at him then grab two of the chicken MREs. I toss one to Navas and tear open the other. We take a seat on our cots, one beside the other, and dig in.

"Sarge, you know those officer fucks clear out the good ones before they give us the box, right?" Elkins's words come out slightly distorted as he's still working on a mouthful of *my* tortellini.

"Enunciate, Elkins, I can't understand you with that dick in your mouth." I lock my eyes onto Elkins with eyebrows furrowed as I fork a piece of dry chicken breast into my mouth.

Navas pulls my attention from Elkins by tossing a bag of peanut butter M&Ms at my back. In the world of MREs, peanut butter M&Ms are like gold. They are coveted and often bartered. I quickly forget about how awful the chicken tastes.

"That reminds me, when Dixon got done in the comm center, he told me to tell you there's a meeting at 0700. Some kinda mission briefing or something," Navas says.

I eyeball my watch. *0650. Damn it.* I shovel the remaining chicken into my mouth, retrieve my notepad and pen, and begin to head out, saluting Navas with the bag of M&Ms before departing.

The room is packed tight. The other squad leaders and I stand at the back against the wall. Lieutenant Dixon and the three other platoon leaders take up seating at two tables that separate us from the front of the room. On the front wall, there's a large map of Baghdad with our area of operations marked boldly in red. Our company commander, Captain Kendricks, stands before us. He's a Mr. Clean clone and is nearly as large as the map itself. Our brigade commander, Colonel Birch, is beside him, which tells me this is serious. He's based out of the Green Zone and only comes here for the most important briefings. He's an extremely short man and looks like a midget standing next to Captain Kendricks, but he's stocky with a spark-plug personality. He's old-school Army and therefore barks his words rather than speaks them.

He starts off with his usual introduction, the whole "I'm proud of you" and "keep up the good work" bullshit, but my mind takes off after that. I think about Katie and the letter I sent. *I know the military mail system sucks, but damn, does it have to take this long?* I've even checked my e-mail twice a day every day for a week straight, hoping to hear from her—but no such luck. I subtly wrote my e-mail address in below my name on my last letter hoping she'd see it, but I'm guessing that she didn't, or she just didn't want to write back. With each day that passes, I'm a little more convinced of it.

I guess her therapy in regard to me is already complete. She took out her anger and told me how she feels. What more can I expect after what I've done to her? And I do want her to feel better, but I just hope she has more to get out. I'll take cuss words and insults from her over silence any day.

I can't shake the feeling of seeing her name and reading her words again. It takes me back to middle school, and unbelievably, her handwriting is just the same. So beautiful and flawless you'd think it was fake. We'd pass notes back and forth, my chicken scratch and her artwork, and we'd do it all day long. By the time we caught the bus home, we had filled up five sheets, front and back. I still have every last one, since I always insisted on keeping them. She fought me every time, but I always won. The nights out here when I'm hurting so badly I'd rather die than bear the pain, I read those notes and can feel her there beside me, giggling as I throw paper airplanes at Wyatt's head.

A tear rolls down my cheek, catching me off-guard, and I quickly wipe it with my hand before anyone can see. Almost immediately, I receive a quick jab in the ribs from Sergeant Adams, who is standing beside me. "Wake the fuck up, dude. Kendricks is looking over here," Adams whispers, which for a New Yorker comes out more like a yell. Dixon looks back at us, face red, and he jerks his head toward the front of the room. I roll my eyes at Adams and direct my attention to the front.

"We have orders to make a major offensive push," Colonel Birch says with his laser pointer hovering over the map. He circles it around a specific area. "Intelligence we've gathered is telling us that this area of Saidiyah has several large weapons caches and roadside bomb manufacturing facilities. For the next two weeks—at least—infantry units out of Forward Operating Base Falcon will be conducting massive door-to-door raids throughout this entire neighborhood. We will be going around the clock, twenty-four hours a day with two units from First Armored Division and 101st Airborne, who are leading up the raid and defense efforts. They need us to serve as their quick reaction force. If shit goes down, we're there to assist." He clears his throat and drops the laser pointer on the table.

"We only have your platoon to execute this specific mission since the rest of the company needs to continue with the mission at hand, so we need you guys to suck it up for the next few weeks. It's going to be some long hours, but this is pretty damn important, so keep your heads on straight. I'm going to leave you with Captain Kendricks here, and he can let you know how the rotations will go. Stay strong, gentlemen, we're halfway through."

He nods to Captain Kendricks and heads out of the room as fast as his short legs can take him. I can't help but smirk.

Captain Kendricks waits for the colonel to exit before addressing us. "As Colonel Birch stated, this is a major task for such a small contingent, so hours will be long. Staff Sergeant Richards and Staff Sergeant Baker, being that you're both higher ranking and more experienced, we will have you cover the night shift . . . Eight p.m. to eight a.m. It's more likely that if shit is gonna go down, it's going down at night."

Richards and Baker nod toward Captain Kendricks and he continues, shifting his focus to us. "Clay and Adams, that means you guys are on first shift. We need you to grab your guys, divvy them up between three trucks, and be on your way. Coordinates, unit call signs, and all that shit will be provided to you by your platoon leaders."

"Hooah, sir," Adams and I say in unison as Captain Kendricks turns his attention back to the platoon leaders.

"PLs do not need to take part in these missions, but I will leave it to your discretion. Those that don't will be here in HQ with me. I need you all to stay behind for a second so we can go over the details. The rest of you can head out. Are there any questions? No? Good! Let's get to work."

The four of us pile out of the room as the captain continues his discussion with the platoon leaders. "Hey, Clay, you pussies enjoy your twelve hours twiddling your dicks in the sun. Baker and I will worry about doing some real infantry shit." I look back and see Richards with a shit-eating grin on his face. His thick red pornstache straddles his upper lip like a saddle. Baker juts his chin out and smirks at me.

I turn back around without saying a thing, but Adams whips his head back toward them. "Oh, fuck you, Richards, we don't speak ginger. Baker, can you please translate for the hellspawn?" Adams chuckles and looks to see if I am too, which of course I am. A good ginger joke goes a long way with me. But I'm also partly laughing at Adams's constant need for affirmation. *I like the guy, but fucking sh—*

"Shit, you think the New York garbage that comes out of your mouth is any better? You guys stink of envy," Baker snaps at Adams as they reach the door.

I try not to give a shit about what they're saying, but they're right. Here in beautiful Baghdad, they only really like to come out and play at night. The days are left to roadside bombs and excessive sweating. I'm about to say something, but I cut myself off because it's just not worth it. My focus is Katie and the possibility of an e-mail sitting in my inbox. How fucking amazing would it be to hear from her. Just then, a voice catches my attention.

"Yo, Clay!" Sergeant Tavares, our radio operator, calls from the communications room. The buzz of radio chatter plays like an orchestra behind him. "Come here for a second."

I turn and approach him as the others exit the building. I notice a letter in his hand and my heart leaps into my throat. I try to restrain my excitement, but a heavy buzz sits just under the skin. *Maybe it's not even mine.*

He hands it to me. "This came in with the mail shipment last night, and I forgot to drop it off to you." I snatch it from his hand and narrow my gaze before flipping it over.

Katie Devora.

A smile cracks my face. "Thanks, dude."

I don't even look at him. Keeping my eyes locked onto the letter, I turn and quickly make my way toward the exit. Before I can get the door open, the shrill voice of Lieutenant Dixon calls out from the conference room. "Clay, come here real quick. We need to go over this shit."

I slowly turn and fight the desire to strangle him right then and there. He holds up a notepad with a page full of writing and jams a finger into it. My shoulders drop a bit, as I know what's about to come, and I have to force my eyes not to roll as I walk toward him, reluctantly slipping the letter into my cargo pocket.

My temples beat like drums as I clench my teeth tightly together, withholding all words because the only ones I want to use have four letters. We're cruising down the road with Thomas at the wheel, Navas in the turret hatch, me in the passenger seat, and our interpreter, Mike, seated behind me.

Twenty-five fucking minutes Dixon blabbered on. He has a unique way of making what should take five minutes last a lifetime, and I was too busy getting the squad together afterward to read Katie's letter. If we were the first vehicle in the convoy and not the third, it's likely we'd end up in the Euphrates River because no way my mind is focused enough to navigate. I can only think of Katie and the letter that's currently burning a hole through my pocket.

A buzz over the radio headset draws my attention. "Hey, Sergeant, it looks like Adams's trucks are falling back. Do you want me to have the lead vehicle slow down?" Navas asks.

"No, they're okay. They know where we're going. They'll be covering for the 101st at the southern end of the target area anyway. We've got the northern end, so they'll be cutting out of here shortly."

I turn my attention to the navigation. It's loaded with little icons representing all of the coalition vehicles. The raid and defense forces have already positioned themselves around the neighborhood, and we are just a few miles away.

I watch as Sergeant Adams's convoy pulls off the highway. "Yup, there they go. A mile or so up the road and we're there." I shift my gaze to Thomas, who has a distant stare, his body sagging in the driver's seat.

"Thomas, you awake, guy?" He snaps to attention like a teenager caught sleeping in class and quickly nods his head. "Sure doesn't seem like it. You get okay sleep last night?"

I know he didn't. I woke up several times throughout the night, as I often do, and I found him reading with a flashlight or just lying there, staring at the tent's interior. Since the grisly scene at the checkpoint, he just hasn't been the same. I haven't been able to get him to talk either, which isn't normal for him. He'll usually at least open up to *me*.

"Slept like a baby, Sarge," he lies.

"Alright, I'll take your word for it." I point toward a group of palms just outside our target neighborhood. "Park under those trees over there. Face that clearing."

Thomas does as ordered while our other two Humvees station themselves a hundred yards on either side of us in their own defensive positions. The sun is shining brightly overhead, but the outstretched leaves of the palms will keep our vehicle well shaded. A crisp morning breeze funnels down through the turret hatch and teases my face.

Curious bystanders of all ages stand in the middle of the dirt roads that connect the neighborhood, watching infantry squads work. The neighborhood bustles with activity as the troops search homes for weapons, artillery rounds, roadside bombs, and insurgents ready for a fight. We can't see much of it from our positions since half walls close off most of the neighborhood, with only a few roads leaving room for visibility. But we can hear American forces calling out orders loudly and an orchestra of Arabic chatter.

I radio Sergeant Adams to ensure his squad has taken up their own positions and then check in with the raid contingent's leadership. Thomas has his head resting against the steering wheel, already fast asleep, and Navas's hand is burrowing deep inside a bag of pork rinds.

Ensuring first that Navas can't see me, I slip the envelope from my cargo pocket and quickly open it.

The first thing I notice—almost immediately—is her e-mail at the very bottom of the letter. My cheeks hurt from the smile that owns my face. *Looks like I'll be spending a hell of a lot more time at the comm center.*

Dear Devin,

To say that I was shocked to see a letter from you is an understatement. After the way you left things, I certainly didn't expect you to respond, and I wasn't at all prepared for your words. My head is telling me that I'm an idiot for continuing communication; it tells me that I should be angry and that you don't deserve a second of my time. My heart, however . . . My heart remembers our friendship, and because of that, I want to believe that in that particular moment in time you really did think you were doing the right thing. Because I know you—at least I did—and the boy that I grew up with, the boy that I fell in love with, wouldn't have ripped my heart out unless there wasn't any other choice . . . at least that's what I keep telling myself. But I can't help but wonder if you realize now that you made a horrible decision . . . because I do think you made a horrible decision.

Oh my God, if she only knew that my heart has ached for her since the day I left. I'd give the world to change what I did. Horrible decision? Try the biggest regret of my fucking life. I won't tell her about her dad's talk with me though. I can never tell her that he's the reason I disappeared without a trace.

And I'm not just saying that because I was the one left. I'm saying that because I know how much you meant to me—how much I loved you—and I know that I would've walked to the ends of the earth to make sure that we made it. But you didn't give me that choice. You didn't believe enough in my love for you, and as much as I want to forgive you, I can't. Honestly, I'm not sure I'll be able to forgive you until I know what happened, but it sounds like you'll take that to the grave.

So, you're probably asking yourself why in the hell I'm taking the time to write you if I'm still upset with you and can't forgive you. It's because even though the scorned woman in me is still upset, the little girl that pushed you down on the playground would still very much like to get to know the friend that she lost.

Fuck, I'd give anything to be back in Tennessee making memories again. I want this girl. I've always wanted this girl. How the fuck am I gonna deal?

It's also because the part of me that's broken, the part I'm desperate to fix, was more than touched by your words. In fact, I'm incredibly grateful that you pushed the past aside and decided to respond to my letter, despite the fact that the tone of it was less than cordial and no one would've blamed you for simply wadding it up and tossing it away.

But I do want to thank you for sharing the story about you and your friend driving drunk. As much as I hate to hear about how much his life changed that night, I'm so very glad that you both survived. And the guilt that you're holding onto from that night . . . let it go. Please let it go. The fact of the matter is that, yes, you could've caused harm to others, but you didn't. You didn't rip apart a family, or take someone's life, and although I understand where your guilt comes from, I'm begging you to move past it. You've learned from your mistake and you used that to make yourself a better person. You should be proud of that. I know I am.

My focus drifts from the letter to the lump that's formed in my throat. I swallow hard before continuing to read.

And I'm so sorry about your best friend. I can't imagine how hard it was to lose him. I know it's not exactly the same, but I feel like I can somewhat relate to that. I don't think I told you in my first letter—actually, I know I didn't because I haven't told anyone—but I have this memory of waking up and seeing my dad for a couple of seconds right after the accident. If I close my eyes, I can remember everything so perfectly . . .

He was covered in blood—it was literally running in streams down his face. I kept watching his chest, trying to see if he was still breathing, but I couldn't focus because I was fading in and out. I don't remember much else, but it haunts me. I don't sleep well because when I close my eyes at night that is what I see. Why do I see that though? I have so many memories of him, and yet that's the one that always pops up. How do you do it? How do you close your eyes and not see your friend? Or maybe you do . . . Maybe the memory of him bleeding out in your arms is what keeps you up at night. It probably sounds sadistic, but as much as I hope that you're not haunted by those memories, I find it somewhat comforting to know that maybe I'm not in this alone.

The letter falls to my lap and my eyes close tightly. I think of Katie, fighting for consciousness in the passenger seat, watching her father die before her eyes, and I can't help but feel more connected to her in that moment, having been through the same with Jax. I ache for her, too. I imagine her lying in bed some nights, the pillow collecting tears beneath that beautiful masterpiece of a face. In my mind, she's clutching a silver frame, her father's picture staring back at her. *I have to take her pain away.*

I don't know how you do it; how you cope with everything that you've had to witness or do. Unless you're like me and you aren't really coping with it at all. My guess is that you're living one day—one second—at a time, just getting by. That's what I've been doing. But I want to change that. I want to stop just existing. I want to live again, and your letter did that for me. So if you don't mind, I'm going to very gently throw your words back at you.

Don't treat your grief as I do. Don't let it simmer until it's boiling over the edge. Live your life, not just for yourself, but also for your friends who have lost their lives. Take them with you wherever you go and do all the things that they'll never get to do.

I've read your letter several times now, and each time I get to the part where you think you've done more harm than good and I have to smile because you have absolutely no idea how much good you've actually done. I made a huge change in my life today, one that left me with a flicker of hope, and then I read your letter and that flicker exploded. I can't explain it—I wish I could—but in the words of my father, "Some things aren't meant to be explained, they just are."

So, I'm not going to think about it too much. I'm just going to be grateful that things happened the way they did, and I'm going to work toward making changes. I know it won't be easy, but I want to forgive Lt. Drexler because I know that's the only

way I'll move past all of this. Or maybe not forgive him . . .
Maybe that wasn't the right word. How about make peace?
That sounds better, don't you think? I want to make peace
within myself toward Andrew Drexler. I think I'll work on
myself first though. It seems appropriate that I get comfortable
in my own skin again before I try making amends with
anyone else.

Anyway, I'm sure you're tired of hearing me babble on and
on. I'll bet when you wrote that you hoped you'd hear back
from me, you probably weren't expecting all of this, were you?

I really do hope that you're doing well. And from the tiny
snippet of your letter, it seems like you had a rough go of it in
Pennsylvania, but I'd like to hear more about that . . . about
your time there. How is your mom? I hope she's managed to
clean herself up, but I have a feeling you're rolling your eyes
right about now.

I'm so sorry to hear about your grandmother. I know how
much she meant to you and how much you enjoyed spending
your vacations there as a child. I bet it was nice getting to see
her more after you moved though, wasn't it?

Well, I could probably go on and on with any number of
the questions running through my head, but right about now
I'm thinking that baby steps are in order. I noticed your e-mail
address on the last letter you sent and I contemplated e-mailing
this letter to you, but I didn't want to do that. Seems silly, I
know, but e-mailing you rather than writing felt like I was
making a first move toward something—what that something
is, I have no idea. I just know that I'm not ready to make any
first moves, not when it comes to you. I will, however, put the
ball in your court.

I hope to hear back from you.

Sincerely,
Katie
katie.devora@yahoo.com

I'm taken aback for a moment when I realize that she just might be okay with the idea of opening her life back up to me. All I want is the chance to know her again, to learn about the new Katie, and the road she took to get here. I want her to learn about me too, and how different I've become. How much better I've become. *Or have I?*

I read it over three more times, and the smile that I'm sure is plastered on my face could light my way through the desert night. I haven't felt this in a while, and it feels really damn good.

Six hours have passed since we took up our position and a whole lot of nothing has happened. Radio chatter from the hundreds of units involved in the mission acts as ice picks buried in my eardrums. I've read the letter basically a hundred more times, and I still can't wipe the big, goofy smile off my face.

I know that woman like the back of my hand, and when I'm reading her words, I can hear her saying them just as she would have back then, hand gestures and all. She'd put her hand on her hip and give me the cutest little I'm-trying-really-really-hard-to-look-pissed-off faces. I'd place my hand on her hip, just where the pelvis frames her ridiculously sexy stomach, and I'd slip my other hand to the small of her back, lightly running my fingers back and forth, effectively rendering her body useless. Or that's how it used to be at least.

"Fuck! I'm so fuckin' bored!" Navas whines. "Why have you been so quiet today, man? Both of you fuckers." I quickly fold up the letter and place it beside me, readjusting the bulge that's developed.

"Well, Thomas is still passed the fuck out." Thomas's head is now lodged between the steering wheel and the door. "He's going to be hurting tomorrow . . . Me, I'm just in my own little universe, man. This shit is mind numbing."

"Yeah, man, it's gonna be the death of me. Two more weeks of this and you're gonna have to pull the barrel outta my mouth," Navas says with a laugh.

"I know, I almost wish something would happen just to break up the boredom." I immediately feel unclean. The words ring in my ears as the thought of a Humvee blown to smithereens owns my thoughts. "I mean, within reason."

"I know what you mean, man. I wouldn't mind putting a couple rounds into some unlucky insurgent," Navas says. "Fuck, is that sick or what? I think I need a vacation."

"You and me both, brother." I check my watch and it's as if the second hand has stalled, moving ever so slowly around the watch face. "Six more fucking hours." I throw my head back against the headrest, tilting my eyes toward the window.

The noise from the neighborhood has died down, which tells me the squads have moved on to the next block of homes. Iraqi civilians have now gathered in packs, conversing in the street with agitated looks on their faces. Some peer out toward us before turning back to the others and pointing.

I let out a loud sigh, my palms squeezed tightly to my sides. *I need to get the fuck out of this Humvee.* Just then I feel movement and turn around to see Navas out of the turret and crouched just behind me, smiling. His perfectly white teeth glow against his tan skin, and as always, it gets me to smile too. "What?" I ask.

"What's eating you, pumpkin?" His smile grows impossibly wider, and he slaps the back of his fingers against my arm. "Spill it, man."

"It's nothing." I pretend to play with the navigation. "Really, I'm just tired."

"Dude, I'm the only one awake. Talk to me." I try my best to stealthily slide an elbow over the envelope lying beside me, but I'm too late.

"Oh shit, man! Katie?" he asks, the smile returning to his face. I slip the letter into the envelope and shove it in the side door compartment. I can feel Navas's smile burning a hole through the back of my head, but I refuse to turn around.

"What'd she have to say? Was she cool?" He pokes a saliva-soaked finger into my ear and I pull my head away quickly, scrunching my nose and throwing a wild punch that he easily outmaneuvers.

"Cocksucker, you know I fucking hate wet willies."

"I know, that's why I do it!" He chuckles, causing Thomas and Mike to both stir in their sleep. "So . . . Was she cool?"

I take a moment to think, tugging at the frayed edges of my sleeve. "Well, let's just say we won't be doing *The Amazing Race* together anytime soon."

We both laugh, and just as I'm about to continue, a gunshot fires in the distance, echoing toward our position. Another one pops off and then another, and clusters of civilians run feverishly back toward their houses.

More shots ring out and Mike is awake and nervously looking around, but Thomas somehow remains sleeping.

"Thomas, wake the *fuck* up!" I nudge him in his side, but he doesn't move. "*Thomas, wake your fucking ass up now!*" I hiss, and he finally wakes, startled and confused.

"There's some shit going down. I need you to pull it together." Thomas nods his head in affirmation, though he still isn't fully there. I direct my attention back to Navas.

"You see anything up there?" While I wait for him to respond, I peer out the windshield opposite the neighborhood toward the field stretching a mile into the horizon. Palm groves and large boulders are scattered across it, making it hard to spot enemy movement.

"I don't see anything. Nothing through the binos. Nothing in the field or adjacent neighborhood, but there's a lot of cover that way," Navas yells down through the hatch. "You think it's a sniper?"

"That's what it sounded like to me. Who the fuck are they shooting at though?" Two more rounds pop off. I notice movement in the neighborhood, but I can't make out what's going on.

As I'm about to have Thomas drive toward the houses, a mob of civilians—at least ten to fifteen—exits the neighborhood and makes its way to our position. They're frantically pointing toward the field and then back at the street. A woman slips between the mob carrying something in her arms. It looks like a little sack of potatoes covered in a light blue shawl. A deep red quickly overwhelms the blue. *Fuck.*

The group nearly reaches our position when another shot rings out. It hits nothing, but most of the men and women go scrambling for cover. The woman with the bloody shawl doesn't even flinch but continues shuffling forward. She weeps relentlessly.

"Mike, let's go!" I say as I exit the Humvee, and he quickly follows suit. The woman meets us behind the cover of my open door and maneuvers one hand around to pull back the shawl. My stomach tightens and I feel vomit working its way to the surface. I also feel an insuppressible rage as I stare into the lifeless, doll-like eyes of a young girl, no more than five years old.

Blood pours from an entry wound in her chest. My heart lurches beneath my rib cage, and I instantly want to kill every last one of these desecrators of innocence. I want to make them suffer. I want them to wish that their Allah would rip the life from their bodies because the pain is just too unbearable.

"Navas, call the fucking medics! Get them over here now!" I yell, my voice breaking.

I grab a blanket from the trunk and lay it on the ground behind our Humvee. Mike is trying to talk to the woman, but his words are interrupted by her screams. I meet them back by the door and gently take the girl from the woman's arms and into my own.

One more round tears through the leg of a civilian clinging to the outer wall, blocked partially by a palm. He wails in pain.

Mike ducks and pulls the woman in closer to us. We move in unison back behind the Humvee for better cover.

"It's her daughter," Mike says. "She says the gunfire came from the field. That there's a man shot in the street, too." He points to the neighborhood as I set the girl on top of the blanket and check her pulse. *Nothing.* I grab a pressure dressing from my med-pack and hold it tightly against the wound as our other Humvees pull up behind us, parking side by side. I lift the girl using the blanket and lay her back down between the vehicles. Our platoon medic, Specialist Benedict, races from the back seat of one of the Humvees and meets me by the girl's side. The other doors begin to open.

"Stay the fuck in the vehicle! We're taking fire! Let your gunners hold up a defensive position while Benedict works." Mike guides the woman to Benedict and they both kneel down beside us. The woman is hysterical now, rocking back and forth. Her screams cause the hairs on the back of my neck to rise. "Benedict, I need you to see what you can do here. I'm going to take our Humvee to that field to find these motherfuckers."

"Roger that, Sarge!" He quickly goes to work, though for just the briefest of moments, his eyes say exactly what I already know—this girl is gone.

I motion for each gunner to point their weapons in opposite directions, and then I head toward my own vehicle. Mike starts to do the same, but I put a hand up to stop him. "Stay with them! Talk her down," I say, climbing into the vehicle and pointing in the direction of the field. "Thomas, *go!* As fast as you fucking can!"

He pulls out slowly at first, mindful of the three kneeling behind us, but once the coast is clear, he puts the pedal to the floor. The engine roars as the Humvee picks up speed, tearing toward the field. We get about a mile down the road when we see a man leap from behind a large boulder, throwing his sniper rifle down and taking off in the opposite direction. As we come up beside the boulder, two more men throw down sniper rifles and ammunition, pick up AK-47s, and take off.

The first man is about a hundred yards away when Navas rips off a string of shots from his machine gun. They tear through the man's back, putting a hole straight through his stomach. He grips at the open wound with both hands as he falls to his knees, finally settling face-first in the sand. Navas then directs his machine gun toward the second man and he fires. The rounds don't hit the man but tear into the ground just behind him. The insurgent throws his AK-47 to the ground and then himself, putting his hands behind his head. The third man sees this but continues running. He turns and fires rounds at Navas, forcing him down into the safety of the vehicle. More rounds come in, one after the other, preventing Navas from resuming his post and firing back.

"Navas, stay down, I've got this one." I open my door and exit, and with the Humvee between the fleeing insurgent and myself, I rest the barrel of my rifle on the hood. I position the red crosshairs on his head as he turns to fire again, and then I gently squeeze the trigger. The round erupts from my barrel and rips a hole through his head, taking off a piece of his skull. Blood spurts from the wound as he crumples to the ground.

I race to the other insurgent, who remains facedown on the ground, and I quickly zip-tie his hands together. Navas scrambles back in the turret to pull security while I snatch the insurgent up by his arms and drag him back to the Humvee. I throw him into the back seat carelessly, then I walk to the boulder they used for cover and find a small cache of weapons including sniper rifles, AK-47s, a rocket-propelled grenade launcher, and several cases of ammunition. One by one, I place them in the back compartment of the Humvee.

When I'm all done, I return to the vehicle. The insurgent is angrily speaking Arabic to Thomas, who just as angrily ignores him.

"Shut the fuck up!" I scream at him, though he doesn't understand what I'm saying. He looks defiantly at me then spits in my direction, missing me by an inch, and continues rattling off shit I don't know or care to know.

"I said *shut the fuck up,* motherfucker!" I repeat with fire burning in my eyes. I want to kill him . . . I want to rip the soul from his body, but we need him. We need a live body for the detention facility. He continues talking, but this time I say nothing. I leave the driver's side of the vehicle and swing open the back door, charging in and punching him squarely in the face. He topples over, and I grab him by his arm and yank him back to a seated position. He wipes his bloody nose on his shirt and continues eyeballing me. I punch him again, and then again, until he finally averts his eyes to the Humvee floor.

The anger swells in me like a storm as I think of that little girl, her mother now in utter despair. I take one more hard shot at him and feel his jaw crack beneath my knuckles. He wails loudly and I notice Thomas flinching.

The insurgent's will is completely broken. He's now obedient, his face bloodied and swollen. I pull him toward me, close enough that our nostrils nearly touch, and I jerk his chin so that his eyes meet mine. In this moment, I've nearly lost all control. I am standing on the edge of a cliff and the wind is picking up.

"I will fucking destroy you. Do you understand me?" I raise my fist again and he cowers back into the seat.

"Navas, come down here real quick," I say. He removes himself from the turret strap and joins me outside the vehicle. He looks at me, wide-eyed and nervous, as if he knows what's to come. I pull in close to his ear. "This isn't good, man."

"I know," he whispers.

"Fucking rules of engagement. If the higher-ups see you shot that fucker in the back with no weapon, we're fucked." My mind races to come up with a plan as I do my best to stifle my concern.

"What do you think we should do?" His voice cracks, and the look in his eyes lets me know immediately that his children are on his mind—and the fact that he could get five to seven years of hard time at Fort Leavenworth. Tears well in his eyes.

I think for a moment, peering off toward the other Humvees, which are merely specks in the distance. I then look out the other direction to a large palm grove, the biggest of the lot, located just a few hundred feet away and dense with foliage.

"We are far enough that they can't see us. You radio in and tell them we found two insurgents with a sniper rifle and small arsenal. We exchanged fire, killed one of them, and the other one surrendered after a scuffle. Have them call it up to headquarters and get a disposal team down here." I take a second to look into Navas's eyes to ensure he understands. "I'm going to take care of the other body."

Chapter 9 | *Katie*

"Fight Song"—Rachel Platten

"So, you girls got any big plans this weekend?"

"Nope." Shoving the last of the leftovers in the refrigerator, I shut the door and then pause. I can't remember the last time I've had actual plans aside from hanging out with Wyatt. "When do I ever have plans?" Pulling out a chair at the table, I plop down and take a drink of my water.

Maggie turns her inquisitive gaze to Bailey, who is currently shoveling a bite of brownie into her mouth. Covering her mouth with the back of her hand, she looks at us sheepishly. "No plans," she mumbles.

Swallowing her bite, her gaze locks on mine. She looks a little nervous, almost hesitant, and I offer her a small smile, my eyes as open and inviting as I can get them. Because I'm truly glad she accepted my invitation to come here tonight. Her eyes flash with an unknown emotion and a tentative smile tugs at the corner of her mouth.

Bailey had been avoiding me, and rightfully so, and I ended up having to play hardball to get her to sit down and talk to me. I knew I had been wrong so I wasn't above a little bit of groveling, even though the thought of apologizing nearly killed me. It's difficult to swallow your own pride, but I knew it had to be done. So I showed up at Mom's early one morning, like most other mornings, only this time I had already taken care of the horses and I was waiting inside when Bailey crawled out of bed.

Her steps had faltered when she walked into the kitchen to find me sitting at the table with Mama, eating a bowl of cereal. I could see it in her eyes, the urge to flee, and I knew that it was now or never, so I did the only thing I could think of doing. Flinging myself from the chair, I rushed to my sister, wrapped her in my arms, and apologized for being such a bitch. But more than that, I begged her to forgive me and promised that I was going to make things right. I knew that we weren't going to just snap back into place, and I knew I was going to have to work at earning her trust and friendship back, but it was a start. We talked for two hours that morning before I finally had to leave for work, but by the time I left, I really think she had a better understanding of what I had been going through after Dad died—and vice versa.

"You know what you guys need?" My mouth waters when Maggie snaps off a bite of her licorice, my eyes following the delicious red rope as she waves it in the air.

"A piece of that," I answer, trying to snatch the yummy goodness from her hand. Bailey laughs heartily and Maggie bats me away playfully before pulling an extra piece out of the bag and handing it to me.

"You're an addict."

"I am." I nod in agreement then bite off a chunk of my cherry-flavored kryptonite.

"You girls need a night out on the town."

Bailey and I both answer at the same time, only her answer is an enthusiastic "*Yes!*" and mine is a very firm "*No!*" They both turn to look at me.

"Why not? It would be fun." Bailey nods in agreement to what Maggie says, but I just shake my head.

"I've been so tired lately, I can barely make it through work these days." The evil twins give me a pointed look. "I know, I know. I've already started cutting back my hours. No more extra shifts."

"I'm glad," Bailey says softly. "You really had me worried there for a while."

"I told you I've been working on things and I meant it." She watches me inquisitively and then nods before popping another bite of brownie in her mouth. It was much easier convincing Mom that I was trying to turn things around than Bailey, and I make a mental note to try and do a few extra things to strengthen her belief in me.

"So—" My phone vibrates, skidding across the table, and Maggie stops talking, picks it up, and flips it open.

"Hey!" Reaching across the table, I yank it from her hand. The sight of his name on my screen causes me to clench my teeth in frustration, and I let out a loud huff as I type out a quick response.

"Who is it?" Bailey asks, looking at me curiously. When I lock eyes with Maggie, I know instantly that she saw who it was from.

"Wyatt." Flipping my phone shut, I toss it on the table and bite off another chunk of my licorice.

"How is Wyatt?" Bailey asks. *Oh shit.* She doesn't know that we broke up. I give Maggie a help-me-here look and she widens her eyes in a what-do-you-want-me-to-do look. Bailey's gaze slowly travels between the two of us. "I'm missing something here. What am I missing?"

I already know that this won't go over well. Bailey has always been a big fan of Wyatt. "We, uh . . ."

"They broke up."

"What?" Bailey gasps at Maggie's declaration. "What do you mean *you broke up?*" she asks, her head whipping in my direction. "What happened? He left you, didn't he?" Shaking her head in disbelief, Bailey pushes away from the table.

"She left him," Maggie states nonchalantly, shrugging when I glare at her.

"You broke up with him? Why on earth would you do that? You guys have been together forever."

"I don't love him." It really is that simple.

"You—you don't love him?" Bailey's head rears back as though I just slapped her. "How can you *not* love him? You don't just fall out of love with someone, Katie."

"Okaaaay," Maggie drawls. "I think it's time for me to go." Excusing herself from the table, she shrugs on her coat, grabs her purse, and then bends down, whispering a quick "good luck" in my ear before walking out. All the while, Bailey continues to stare at me in shock.

"What do you want me to say? I've felt this way for a while, and I refuse to apologize for doing what I need to do to be happy."

"But I thought you were working on things. How is this working on things?" Disappointment flashes across Bailey's face. "I can't believe this."

"You don't have to believe it." As much as I want Bailey's support on this, I know I'm not going to get it. She scoffs, crossing her arms over her chest, and frustration bubbles up inside of me. "It doesn't concern you, Bailey. You don't have to understand it; you don't even have to like it."

My skin prickles with annoyance as Bailey leaves her spot at the table and follows Maggie's lead of shrugging on her coat and grabbing her purse. I'm not going to beg her to stay. As much as I don't want her to leave right now, and as much as I do want to fix things between us, I refuse to let her opinion on this matter sway me at all. I know I did the right thing. "Bailey—"

With a heavy sigh, she twists around to look at me. "I don't understand this, Katie. I don't understand *you*. Wyatt is a good man, and he doesn't deserve this."

"He is a good man, but I did what's best for me, Bay. That's what I need you to understand."

"Whatever."

Her dismissal pisses me off, and I shove up from the chair and follow her toward the door. She reaches for the handle, and in a last ditch effort to keep her from leaving, I grab her arm. "Quit being so stubborn and let's talk about this."

"Pot meet kettle," she mumbles before opening up the door, slipping through it and shutting it softly behind her. I walk numbly to the couch, dropping down with a big sigh then burying my face in my hands. What the fuck just happened?

The loud buzz of my phone vibrating from the other room grabs my attention, so I walk in and pick it up to find yet another text from Wyatt. About a week after our breakup, the texts came rollin' in. It started with *"I'm sorry for the way I acted"* and slowly progressed to *"Please don't do this, we can make this work"* and *"I love you so much."* Despite my numerous replies that nothing has changed and I still feel the same way, he just won't give up.

Forgoing a reply—because it wouldn't do any good—I decide to call it a night. I make quick work of getting ready for bed while this evening's events play out in my head. Crawling into bed, I grab my laptop off the nightstand and power it up, deciding to quickly check my e-mail before catching up on some much needed sleep.

I recline against my pillows, watching as my Dell slowly brings itself to life. Opening up the browser, I log into my e-mail. The hourglass flips over and back several times on the blank screen, and I stretch my arms over my head with a big yawn. When my e-mail finally loads, my entire body goes still—except for my heart . . . I'm pretty sure it's trying to launch itself out of my chest.

A grin plays at my mouth, and I lean forward to make sure my tired eyes aren't playing tricks on me. I'm staring at an e-mail from Devin. *Oh my God, I'm staring at an e-mail from Devin!* Excitement bubbles up inside of me, and I wipe my sweaty palms on my comforter before taking a deep breath and opening the message.

To: Katie Devora
From: Sergeant Devin U. Clay
Subject: Thank God for e-mail

Katie,

I am so happy that I can e-mail you now. It makes things much easier knowing I don't have to wait three weeks for a response. So, thank you for that! I spent the better part of a twelve-hour mission today reading your letter and deciding how to respond. I'm still not sure the best way to start, so I'm going to go with my heart.

It kills me—fucking kills me—to know that I hurt you the way I did. But I want you to know something . . . I want your forgiveness. I need it, Katie, and I'll work my ass off for it. And you will forgive me. It might take time and a whole lot of groveling on my part, but it will happen. One of these days when the time is right, when I think that you're ready—when we're ready—I'll share with you all of the reasons behind me leaving. But now is not the time. For now, I simply want to prove to you that you can trust me, that I'm here for you, and that I'll never hurt you like that again.

Thank you for putting your anger away and responding, especially in your time of grief. You won't ever fully understand what that means to me. God, Katie, I can't stop thinking about you, your dad, your whole damn family. I hate that I wasn't there for you when you needed me most, because you know I would've been there in a heartbeat. But I'm here for you now. I'm sure you've already gone through several different stages and emotions, but I want you to know you can come to me.

Speaking of emotions, I truly believe that the feelings you're having in reaction to your father's death are normal. All the amazing times Jax and I had together—going through Basic, graduating together, making Sergeant, drunken nights in small German towns—they aren't what I see when I close my eyes. I only see him lying there in my arms completely lifeless, eyes closed, body limp. I think some of it has to do with not getting to say good-bye, and a lot of it has to do with wishing it was us who died and not them. I'd give anything to switch places with Jax, as I'm sure you would with your father. They call it "survivor's guilt," and they say it's a bitch to get over.

Of course, that's assuming it's something you can actually "get over." I don't see it ever going away. I'm devastated that I lost him, but truthfully, I still feel him around me all the time. I think he's watching over me, or maybe I'm just fooling myself.

You asked me how I do it . . . The answer is easy. I don't. I see him when I close my eyes. He's in my dreams, my nightmares . . . He's always there. I can't help but think that maybe we just need time, you and me. Maybe, in time, our memories won't haunt us quite as badly. Maybe, in time, we'll be able to process it easier. Or maybe that's just wishful thinking.

You are right, though. (I bet you enjoy hearing that, don't you?) I can't let this stop me from doing my job—from getting these men home safe. It's a burden I accepted when taking on this rank, and it's one I take very seriously. But being in this position means much of what I feel must be restrained. I can't let them know I'm hurting and that I'm weak. Sometimes the pressure of it all feels like it's going to suffocate me. And other times, I feel like I'm right where I belong.

I love these guys, and the bonds I've formed with them are like nothing I've ever felt. You know I was kind of a loner growing up. I had a few friends here and there, but I didn't really feel like I could relate to any of them. And then to come over here, to fight and bleed next to these guys, to do something so much bigger than us . . . it means everything. No matter how this place changes me down the road, I will always be grateful for these friendships. These men are my brothers.

It means even more when you're seeing a real difference. When you know in your heart that you're doing something good, something that changes the life of another human being for the better. That's how it was in Afghanistan, but here . . . not so much.

Like today, for example. Something happened during a mission—something that's left my head spinning. I don't even know how to make sense of it all. The absolute disregard for life by these animals perplexes me. To kill a child, to steal her from her parents without regard is something I will never understand. They call us murderers. They call for our heads even, and yet they kill each other with reckless abandon. I like to think I joined the Army and was deployed to this hellhole to do some sort of good—to make a difference in the world—but it doesn't feel like we're making much headway.

I don't mean to pummel you with the depressing details of this place, because I know you're dealing with your own grief. It's just nice to have someone to talk to about it all, especially someone who's not over here questioning the same things I am.

Trust me, I won't be complaining in a few months when my ass is boarding a plane back to the States, I can promise you that! I miss beer so damn much—oh, and pizza . . . can't forget the pizza. Is that little pizza joint still in town, the one we used to eat at every Friday night after football games? God, I miss that place. I remember when Mom worked there for a couple of months and she would bring home leftover pizza from their buffet—okay, seriously, I can't talk about food or it'll drive me insane.

Anyway, speaking of my mother . . . Unfortunately—or fortunately, depending on how you look at it—she's out of the picture. We spent the better part of my first two years in the Army faking the funk. I'd fly to Pennsylvania for a week or two of leave and stay at her house. She'd make dinner and play "mom." Then she'd try to convince me she was sober, and she did look a little better, but I'm not a fucking idiot. I caught her a few times doing a line or key bump. In the weeks I spent with her, I'd meet twenty different versions of Josephine, each more psychotic than the last. She'd be nice only when she needed something from me—usually money—and I just grew tired of it.

For a year or so, I felt this built-up resentment in the pit of my stomach and it was dragging me down. Ugh, you can't judge me for this next part, okay? I spent about two hours one random night writing out how I felt . . . all of it. I mean, this thing ended up being like five pages long. I spent thirty minutes on the phone telling her what I'd written, pretty much chewing her ass out. She got pissed off and turned it around on me, blaming me for my dad leaving because she said he never wanted kids in the first place. We argued off and on, and then her last words to me were, "So what? It's in the past." I said "fuck you," hung up the phone, and never called again. It's been three years now since we last spoke, and I can't say that I've missed her.

As crazy as I'm sure all that sounds, I felt better after I did it, like a weight had been lifted. I wasn't burdened anymore, because I'd laid it all out on the table and washed my hands clean of it. This is actually my first time thinking about her in a while, so thanks for that (and yes, I'm being a smartass).

I did have a great two years with my grandma though. I worked odd jobs and took some classes at a community college nearby. With what free time I had, I read her books. Her favorite author was Nicholas Sparks. We'd often get to that dreaded last page of the book, and as the final words poured from my lips, she'd flip those eyes open wide, let out a long, satisfied sigh, and then start in on a story about grandpa and her falling in love. She said they fell in love with each other over and over and over again. She missed him terribly in the years she spent without him, and it seemed the closer she got to the end, the more excited she was to see him again. It may sound dumb, but it was just a really beautiful thing to be a part of.

Sorry, I think I may be the one babbling today. And enough about me anyway. Tell me about you. It's been a decade, so what have I missed? What does Miss (or Mrs.?) Katie Devora do? You know I'm a soldier out here playing in the world's largest sandbox. What are you doing with your life? Can I take three guesses? Teacher, nurse, or social worker. I know how big that heart of yours is, and you always said that you wanted to do something to help others.

Well, it's been a really long day and my eyeballs hate me right now so I'm going to hop off of here. But I want you to know that it's been nice to talk to someone, particularly you. I'm glad we have a faster means of communication, because I don't want to wait weeks in between hearing from you again—not after the last decade we've spent apart.

PS. How is your mom and Bailey?

Sincerely,

Devin

My body is a jumbled mix of emotions as I lean back against my headboard and take in everything he wrote. My heart aches for Devin and what he's witnessed and endured both at war and at home. I don't know how he does it, how he copes from day to day, but I could tell by his mad rush of words that he needed to get what happened today—or maybe it was yesterday—off his chest. He also mentioned that it was nice to have someone to talk to, and my stomach flutters at the thought that *I'm* that person. A sense of peace, belonging, and friendship washes over me, and I squeeze my eyes shut because the feeling is so familiar that it physically hurts.

And for the first time, it hits me—I *miss* him. I miss our friendship, the connection that we shared. I miss being able to talk to him without being judged, and I miss the way he used to support me without swaying any of my thoughts or actions.

I miss Devin.

Somewhere in the back of my head, there's a tiny vision of me crying in the middle of his driveway after I found out that he'd left, but I push it away and focus on his words.

How in the world can his words affect me this way? It took about a year after he left to face the facts that he wasn't coming back, and another year to convince myself that whatever feelings he had for me weren't real. About a year after that, I finally realized that I'd never be the same. So for him to be able to easily infiltrate my life this way after a decade of *nothing* . . . Well, it's scary really. Because if he hurt me once, he could do it again.

That thought alone makes my stomach churn, but I take a deep, cleansing breath, pushing past the nausea. Because right now I want nothing more than to take all of this for what it is and go with it. I don't want to live in fear. What I want is to move forward.

Just as I'm about to reply to his e-mail, my phone vibrates again.

Wyatt: Please call me

"Come on, Wy," I mumble, to no one but myself. "Please don't do this." I sit for several minutes, trying to decide what to do, and when I blow out a breath and look to the side, my eye catches on a picture wedged into the side of my mirror. My first thought is *how in the hell is that picture still up there?* Then, as my eyes linger on the photo of Wyatt and me, arm in arm, the day after we got engaged, I instantly think of Devin.

Why did he ask if I was a Miss or Mrs.? Is he curious because he thinks that this . . . whatever *this* is . . . is more than what it is? Or maybe he realizes he made a colossal fucking mistake and wants me back. If that's the case, then no way, mister. You snooze, you lose, and Lord knows I'm not going down that path again. Right? *Right!* But what if . . .

Maybe he's engaged. Or, worse yet, married. Holy shit, what if he has a family?

My chest tightens at the thought of building an emotional connection with him if he belongs to someone else, and for a split second I hesitate to respond. Emphasis on *split second,* which is over when I hit 'reply,' all thoughts of Wyatt completely gone.

To: Sergeant Devin U. Clay
From: Katie Devora
Subject: Are you married?

Devin,

I hope I'm not coming off too forward, but I feel like we moved past that a while ago . . . say, in the first grade ;). So, here goes nothing. Are you married? You don't have a girlfriend, wife, or family at home, do you? I'm going to be blatantly honest, and if I'm way off the mark, then, well . . . we'll just pretend I never wrote this e-mail.

Your words have struck a chord with me. They hit me where it hurts, in the best way, and maybe it's just nostalgia, but I feel a connection when I read your letters/emails. But I'm not going to lie, the thought of restarting our friendship—which I assume that's what this is since we both continue to reply to each other—with someone that is already emotionally invested in another person doesn't sit well with me. And considering our past, it wouldn't be fair to your wife or girlfriend either.

But it's not just that, even though that's *huge*. Whatever this is, it scares the shit out of me. Not just because of the way things ended between us, but because you have the power to hurt me. And frankly, I won't survive being hurt again.

My fingers tap nervously against the keys, my teeth chewing at my bottom lip as I reread what I wrote. *Shit.* I sound like an idiot. Who the hell writes that to someone they barely know anymore? It's none of my business if he's in a relationship. Right? And should I tell him about Wyatt? Does he have a right to know about that, even though it's over?

Damn it! Twisting a chunk of hair around my finger, I twirl it several times, deciding whether or not this connection we're building is worth it. Only when I start to get an actual headache does it hit me that I don't have a choice in the matter. The connection has already been established, whether I like it or not.

So screw it . . . It's not like I have much more to lose.

Alrighty, now that I've gotten the awkward part out of the way, on to something else. HOLY SHIT. It kills me to know that these are the types of things you're seeing and dealing with on a day-to-day basis over there, and my heart aches for the innocent children that seem to be getting caught in the crossfire. I know you probably feel helpless in those situations, and I'm not going to pretend I know anything about it, but I'm sure you're doing everything you can. You have to remember you're only one person in an army of soldiers fighting against evil. There are going to be days when you conquer and others when you capitulate. But don't lose sight of why you chose to do this. I have no doubt that you will make an impact, big or small, and people's lives will be better for it.

I want you to know how proud I am that you took this path in life. You always were so incredibly strong, so I shouldn't be surprised that you decided to go off to war and fight for our country. Thank you for that, by the way.

And don't ever feel like you're pummeling me with too much. Do you remember all the shit I hit you with in that first letter? And let's not forget all the stories I made you listen to growing up. Plus, I enjoy hearing about your life in the military, and we all need a place to vent. I'm glad that I can be that outlet for you. So as much as I appreciate the offer that I can come to you—and I do believe you when you say that—I want you to know that I'm here for you as well.

Okay, now that the mushy stuff is out of the way, let me answer your question. I'm a nurse. I work at a local hospital, alongside my best friend, Maggie. We both work in labor and delivery, which I love. It's so exciting to watch new life being brought into this world. These little, innocent people are so perfect, and seeing them open their eyes for the first time and take their first tiny breath warms my heart. And trust me, my heart needs all the warming it can get these days.

I realize now that I've been working too much though, using it as an escape. I've been picking up as many shifts as the hospital will allow in an attempt to ignore the pain. And it helped—it really did—but I was hiding behind it. I was working myself into exhaustion, so that at the end of the day I couldn't do much more than pass out.

I've also been taking care of the horses. You remember Mac, right? Well, I still have him! Mom wants to get rid of the horses because she says they're too expensive and too much work, but for me, they're a way to keep my dad's memory alive and I'm not ready to let go of them yet.

But one of these days, I'll get there. After my last letter to you, I vowed to try and do better. I think you'll be proud to know that I haven't been picking up as many shifts, and I hired a young high school boy to help out on the farm. I've definitely got more time on my hands, but I guess that isn't always a bad thing. I think the fact that I can get through most days—emphasis on most—without spending every second stewing over the accident is a move in the right direction . . . don't you?

I've already started making amends with my mom and sister, who are doing great, by the way, thank you for asking. Mom was much, much more forgiving than Bailey, but you remember how stubborn she can be. I know it'll take time with her though. Some of the things I said to her and the way I acted are inexcusable, but I'm confident that she'll forgive me in time . . .

And, who knows, maybe in time you'll be able to patch things up with Josephine. I hate hearing how things went down between the two of you, although I can't say that I'm surprised—not after the way she started acting after your dad left. But it isn't your fault, so don't think that. She is the mother; she should have handled things differently, both when you were growing up and as an adult. I don't blame you for not staying in contact with her. No child should have to work that hard to have a relationship with their parent. But I digress—this is Josephine we're talking about. I'd like to think that it will only make you stronger when the day arrives that you become a father. (Don't freak out by that prospect LOL)

Okay, enough with all the heavy stuff . . . Tell me something about you that I don't already know, something that's happened in your life since we've been apart.

I'll talk to you soon . . . e-mail IS GREAT!!

Sincerely,

Katie

With a smile on my face, I hit send, then shut my computer down, place it on my nightstand, and curl into bed. My eyes drift closed as my mind pulls forward visions of Devin as a young man. Just before I doze off, I start to wonder what he looks like as an adult. Are his green eyes as piercing as they once were? Does the dimple in his left cheek still stand out every time he smiles?

If I saw him now, would my body have the same reaction to him that it once did?

Chapter 10 | *Devin*

"Existentialism on Prom Night"—Straylight Run

Another day has passed and I still can't get Katie out of my head. Visions of her dance in my head the moment my body hits the cot. She claims my dreams and then consumes every bit of my mind every second I'm awake. And not only has she infiltrated my brain, she's reclaimed the empty spot in the center of my chest too.

If I had a hard time sleeping before Katie came back into my life, then I'm a complete insomniac now. As of late, I've been finding myself at the communications center on nights like these—nights even a thousand sheep couldn't cure. Katie's e-mails have provided a link to my past life, to memories of childhood mischief and young love. *Fuck, I miss those days . . . so much simpler.*

As my fingers settle against the keyboard, I think about the improbability of it all. Never in a million years did I want to join a fucking pen pal program, and I have absolutely no explanation for why I did. And for Katie to find me amongst the thousands of other names . . . I'm just one lucky son of a bitch.

But I can't help wonder whether luck played a hand in this at all, or if it was something more . . . something bigger than all of us. I never once believed in a God—not with the upbringing I endured. But when you see the delicacy of life and how quickly it can be snatched right up, you start to yearn for a higher power. You begin to feel His presence and see it in ways you can't begin to understand: a dud mortar round landing undetonated just before you, a sniper's bullet that pierces your body armor and travels its way around your back but leaves you unscathed, a piece of shrapnel lodged in the side of your helmet that could have been in your brain. A second chance at love . . .

Not many people find what Katie and I once had, and even fewer get another shot at it. I know she isn't thinking in terms of rekindling what we had before, but if she thinks that "restarting our friendship" is enough for me, she couldn't be more wrong. Of course I want to be friends again, but I want it all. I want her back. *Baby steps,* I remind myself.

To: Katie Devora
From: Sergeant Devin U. Clay
Subject: Nice subject line!

Katie,

Talk about coming right out of the gate . . . Then again, I wouldn't expect anything less from you. So to answer your question—no, I'm not married. There is no wife, girlfriend, or family at home, so you can rest easy tonight. And I'm not gonna lie, I really like knowing that you're becoming emotionally invested, because I'm already there. Your letters have the same effect on me, and this connection . . . It's not just nostalgia. It's real, and in case I haven't already made it clear, I feel it too.

You mentioned that this—the prospect of us—scares the shit out of you because I have the power to hurt you. Don't let it scare you, Katie. I know that's easy for me to say since I'm the one who walked away, but I didn't just rip your heart out that night—mine was shredded as well. And knowing that I hurt you is something that I'll have to live with every day for the rest of my life. So trust me when I say that I won't hurt you—not now, not ever. Never again will I walk away from this or from you. My word means shit right now, as it should, but I'll prove it to you. Just give me the chance.

Now, since you managed to completely avoid my not-so-subtle way of asking you what I don't really want to know but I need to . . . Are you seeing anyone? Married? Boyfriend? Little ones? This works both ways, you know ;).

Okay, enough with the . . . what did you call it, *awkward* stuff? Haha-haha yesssss! A nurse! How good am I, huh? I can't even imagine what kind of challenges that sort of profession presents, but it sounds like you have an amazing job. Every day you get to see the instant bond between child and parent, and that must be pretty incredible.

I am so damn proud of you, Katie. And I think it's okay that you used work as an escape for a while because that's who you are. You've always been one to bury yourself in some form of work when you get stressed out or pissed off. Hell, I can still remember you getting in fights with your mom or Bailey, and what's the first thing you'd do? Stomp your tight little ass—yes, I was always looking, and no, I'm not sorry—straight out to the barn and start mucking stalls. You'd crank up that song I hated . . . What the hell was it? Oh yeah! That "Tearin' Up My Heart" song by the Backstreet Boys, right? I knew as soon as that song came on that it was my cue to leave. And from the sounds of it, you haven't changed all that much. But I have to ask . . . Do you still listen to that song? No, really, I want to know!

Now, if my memory serves me correctly, you'd always walk away from the barn refreshed and ready to face your mom or Bailey head-on . . . hopefully that hasn't changed. And speaking of your mom, I'm so glad you're not listening to her about getting rid of the horses, especially knowing how special they were to your dad. You should never be sorry for wanting to hold on to that. But I do think it was a good idea to get some help on the farm, and it sounds like you could use a little time to yourself.

Maybe you should think about a vacation . . . say, to Maui, when I come home on leave? I mean, I'm cool with the Bahamas too. (That wasn't subtle at all, was it?) So you just mull it over, and we'll come back to it later. How about that?

My fingers pause as I decide which part of her letter to address next. I don't want to talk about the fucking military right now any more than I have to. Living it day in and day out is enough. And I sure as hell don't want to talk about my mom. What I really want to talk about is Katie. With a smile on my face, I decide to answer her last question.

So you want to know something about me that you don't already know . . . hmmm . . . You realize that's going to be hard, right? Okay, got one! Before my first deployment, I bought an acoustic guitar to bring with me because Jax played. He was crazy good and I begged him to teach me. He finally relented and we used to practice together every chance we got. Well, you spend a year playing with a guitarist as amazing as Jax, and you get pretty damn good yourself. Grace—that's the name I gave my Fender—is with me on this deployment as well.

So what about you? Tell me something I don't know. And while we're at it—getting to know each other again and all—how about you tell me your biggest fear in life. I don't recall that we ever talked about that.

Okay, it's late as hell here and I have an early mission tomorrow. I hope you have a great day and I can't wait to hear back from you.

Always,
Dev

Tired as all fuck, I shut down the computer, push away from the table, and make my way toward the porta-shitters to take one final piss before passing out. As I get closer, I hear muffled cries coming from inside one of them. I tiptoe until I'm just outside the door, where I hear a loud snort accompanied by more

stifled weeping. I lightly tap on the door and the crying immediately stops.

"I'll be out in a minute." I recognize Thomas's voice as it
bounces against the plastic walls.

"Thomas, it's Clay. You alright, man?"

"Yeah. I, uh . . . I just need a minute."

"I got ya." I take a leak in the shitter next to his and then
walk around the corner to wait for him to exit. When the door
squeaks open, I see Thomas slink out, his eyes fixed on the
ground. "Hey," I call out without moving, "come have a smoke
with me."

He doesn't face me and continues in the opposite direction.
"I'm good, Sarge," he says, waving me off.

Taking a step toward him, I reach out with a cigarette and
lighter. "That wasn't a request, Thomas. *Get your fucking ass
over here.*"

Thomas stops and slowly faces me. Without making eye contact, he takes the cigarette and lighter from my hand. He flicks
the Zippo twice before it sparks to life, and then he lights the
cancer stick and tosses my lighter back to me.

"You need to talk to me because I know this shit is eating
away at you." I take a drag. Thomas doesn't look at me or touch
his own cigarette, but I don't miss the quiver in his chin or the
tick in his jaw. He's fighting to hold something back, and I need
to get him to open up.

"I'm good, Sarge," he says through gritted teeth. I can tell
by the way he's shifting on his feet that he wants nothing more
than to get the hell away from me.

"Was it the car bomb? The girl?" Nostrils flared, he sucks in
a sharp breath. I'm pushing him, I know it, but this is what he
needs. "Was it the body? All of it?" I ask.

"I said I'm good, Sarge!" His eyes snap to mine, hard and
unyielding, completely inconsistent with the tears that are pushing against the confines of his lashes. He's like a child trying

desperately to be a man, and I want to take him in my arms just like I would a child. But that's not what we do here . . .

"Thomas, we will stand here all fucking night if that's what it takes to get you to talk. I'll have you know I was in a three-day firefight with no sleep while you were still a fucking senior in high school, so you don't wanna have that contest with me. Now, tell me what's on your mind."

He rubs at the tears with his palms, but whatever is going through his head must be too much—too powerful. I watch as his chest heaves several times. When he finally looks up, his glassy eyes find the sky, and for a moment I see peace. *Only for a moment.* And then he looks to me and shakes his head.

"It's not the body. I could give two fucks about that moth-erfucker. I back the team in this shit one hundred percent, just like we agreed before we got here."

"So, what is it?" I ask, already knowing the answer. Like most of us here, it's not any *one* thing, just a big pile of bullshit.

"The girl. The IPs. Fucking everything, man. I thought I wanted this, I really did. But if we lose one more fucking guy—" Thomas cuts himself off, tears welling in his eyes once again. I can tell he wants to let it all out, but he can't in front of me. *He won't.* It's the infantry way . . . and sometimes I hate it. "I don't know how I'm gonna hang." His voice quivers with each word as if he wishes for anything but for them to escape. He drops his head, embarrassed.

"You're gonna fucking hang, Thomas. You know why?" I don't give him time to respond. "Because of the other one hun-dred and fifty hard dick motherfuckers in those tents." I jab a finger in the direction where they're all sleeping. "You will keep fighting, because they would keep fighting for you. You think I don't feel what you feel? I do, man. Every. Fucking. Day." Stepping forward, I wrap my hand around the nape of his neck and pull his face closer to mine. "I need you to fight for *me.* I need you to fight for *them.* I need you to make sure these guys get home. This is what we signed up for, and I'll be God-fucking-damned if I'm gonna let you quit on me now. You're a fucking warrior, you hear me?" His eyes have strayed from mine, back to the ground, so I tighten my grip on his neck. "Look at me!"

When he does, my heart clenches at the tears now falling freely down his cheeks.

"Can you find a way to get through this? We have your back, brother. We just need you to have ours. Now, do you?"

"Roger, Sarge," he says, his voice barely audible.

"I can't hear you, Thomas. Do you have our backs until we get out of here? That's all I'm asking."

Thomas looks me in the eyes, wipes away his tears and straightens his back. "I will always have your back, Sergeant."

"Good. Now get some fucking sleep. I know you need it." I pull him in close and throw one arm around his shoulders before letting him go and pushing him toward the tents. He stumbles a bit but catches himself, and I see a grin pull at the corner of his mouth.

Lighting another cigarette, I watch him walk inside his tent, and when I'm certain he's gone and no one else is around, my shoulders slump forward, my head hanging low, and I give in to my own pain. The tears come quickly, running down my face before being absorbed by my uniform. *There's rust forming on my armor.*

Chapter 11 | Katie

"Breathe Again"—Sara Bareilles

"Hi, Katie." Sean bends down and kisses me sweetly on the cheek. "I haven't seen you in a while. You're looking good."

"Hey!" Maggie protests, slapping his arm playfully. "What am I, chopped liver?"

"Damn it, woman," he laughs, rubbing at his arm. "No slapping. What did I tell you about that?"

"That it's for the bedroom," Maggie croons, pushing from the chair, stepping directly into Sean's arms. He scoops her up and tosses her over his shoulder. Maggie squeals, reaching to me for help, but I bat her hand away, laughing along at their playful antics. "Where are you taking me?" she says as Sean turns to walk down the hall.

"Where else? To the bedroom."

"We have company," she screeches, wriggling around, trying to break free.

"Damn." Lowering Maggie to the floor, he keeps a firm hand on her waist until she has her footing and then backs her against the wall. An image of Devin gripping my hip as he slams into me pops in my head, and I blink my eyes several times. *Where the hell did that come from?*

"I thought I was going to get away with it." Sean's voice is low and gravelly, his lips grazing Maggie's when he talks.

I sit, stunned silent by the amount of sexual energy coursing through the room. Looking away is probably the polite thing to do, but for some reason I can't. The chemistry between these two is fucking hot. It's palpable. It's exactly what I want. My eyes follow Sean's hands as they slide up her body. He cups her neck, pulling her mouth to his, but instead of kissing her sweetly like I expect him to do, he devours her, plunging his tongue into her mouth. They're instantly dueling for power.

"You taste so fucking good, Katie." Devin's eyes, shining with lust, are pinning me to the bed, holding me hostage.

The memory slams into me so fast that I don't see it coming, but I'm quickly drawn back to the present when the faint sound of moaning catches my attention.

My jaw drops at the sight of Maggie and Sean. Their hands are everywhere, exploring places that they certainly shouldn't be exploring in the presence of another human being. I glance away, my eyes bouncing around the room, but maybe I'm a voyeur at heart because curiosity gets the best of me, and I can't help but look at them.

Maggie tangles her fingers in Sean's hair, holding him to her, and when a faint whimper falls from her mouth, warmth settles low in my belly. Heaven help me, this is like watching live porn, and coupled with my random flashbacks of losing my virginity to Devin . . . well, let's just say I'm certainly worked up.

Sean pulls back. Maggie's eyes flutter open. "I have to meet a client for dinner," he says, linking their hands together, "but I wanted to stop in and tell you I love you. That was your be-waiting-for-me-when-I-get-back kiss."

"That was one hell of a kiss," I mumble. Both Maggie and Sean's heads snap toward me. "Well"—I shrug unapologetically—"it was. I could seriously go for a stiff drink and cigarette after watching that."

Maggie's eyes widen with amusement. "You don't smoke."

"Exactly."

Sean grins and kisses Maggie one last time before heading out the door.

"He's my lobster," she says with a sigh, dropping next to me on the couch. Maggie is a *Friends* addict, and one of her favorite episodes is the one where Phoebe tries to convince Rachel that Ross is her "lobster" because lobsters mate for life. So, being a *Friends* addict myself, I know right off the bat what she's talking about.

"Can I have a bite of your lobster?"

Maggie snorts and smiles over at me. "Sorry, sister. We need to find you your own."

"I don't think I have a lobster," I say, feeling a twinge of discomfort in my chest. In a few years I'll be thirty, and although I know I'm not in the best place right now to start up a relationship, it's still something I long for.

"You have a lobster," she affirms. "He's just still out there swimming around, trying not to get eaten." Pulling her knee up on the couch, Maggie angles her body toward mine. "Okay, I'm seriously starving so we have to stop talking about food. What do you want to do tonight?"

"What are my choices?" I ask, mimicking her position on the couch.

"Do you want to watch a movie?"

"Nah, I watched a movie this morning." I worked the past three nights, which means I have the next couple of days off. This morning was spent watching *The Breakfast Club,* and when I went to start it over, I decided once was enough. So I invited myself to Maggie's where I've spent the better part of the afternoon.

"We could get dolled up and go have a few drinks."

I look down at my yoga pants, T-shirt, and tube socks. The thought of replacing them with skintight jeans and heels makes me want to cringe. "Pass. Next option."

Maggie looks around, making a clicking noise with her tongue. "I got it!" Jumping from the couch, she darts down the hall, and a couple seconds later she runs back with her laptop in tow. "Power that baby up," she says, handing me her computer before she walks into the kitchen.

By the time I turn the computer on, Maggie comes strolling back in with a pint of vanilla ice cream, a bottle of chocolate syrup, and two spoons.

"Sorry." She shrugs, sitting on the couch next to me. "I only have vanilla, but we can totally coat it in chocolate."

"Don't ever apologize for feeding me ice cream or chocolate." Handing the laptop to Maggie, I grab the ice cream and peel open the lid, then pour the syrup all over it. Grabbing the spoons, I hand one to her, snuggle against the couch and we both dive in.

"What's the laptop for?" I ask, shoveling the first bite of creamy deliciousness in my mouth.

A slow grin spreads across Maggie's face. "We are going to find you a lobster."

"Oh no. Nonono." Shaking my head, I make a move for the computer, but she pulls it out of my reach.

"Oh yes. Yesyesyes."

"Maggie—"

"Oh, come on. Loosen up. This could be fun," she quips.

"I don't even know what *this* is." I scowl, dipping my spoon in the container for another bite.

"Marry me dot com."

"Absolutely not," I mumble around the ice cream in my mouth. "I will not do a dating site."

"Why not?" she whines, giving me her best puppy-dog eyes.

"Well, first, because I just don't want to. Second, it's too soon. Wyatt and I just broke up."

"Semantics," she says, waving her hand through the air dismissively. "You were over Wyatt long before you cut the cord.

Moving on will be a good thing. How about Mark from the surgical floor?"

"He has a boyfriend."

"Oh," Maggie says with a pout. "How about—?"

"How about you drop it?" I say, licking my spoon.

Maggie gives me the stare-down, and I return it with a cheeky grin. "Fine. Your loss," she says, shrugging.

I watch quietly, eating away at the ice cream as Maggie pulls up the Internet and logs into her MySpace account. My eyes bounce around the screen, watching her click through several people's profiles. Eventually, I get bored and grab the remote. I don't know how she has time for all that. I certainly don't. Well, I didn't until now . . .

Turning on the TV, I find the news and drop the remote, listening as the anchor talks about yet another shooting in the city. "What is this world coming to?" I whisper.

"Katie?"

"What?"

"You need to update your MySpace page."

"I know," I answer, my eyes glued to the TV.

"No, seriously." I glance over at Maggie and she points to her computer. "Your profile picture is from like two years ago, and there are a massive amount of pictures of you and Wyatt. Oh, look! According to your profile, the two of you are engaged."

"Who cares?" I shrug, turning my attention back to the TV. "It's not like I'm ever on MySpace anyway, and I don't interact with anyone on there. I should probably just delete it."

"You will not delete it," she protests, poking me in the side. Laughing, I bat her hand away. "Awww, there's Bailey . . . when she was sweet," she mumbles. "Speaking of Bailey, how did things go the other night?"

"Not good. She's mad at me. *Again*."

"She has nothing to be mad about. It isn't her decision. And she's your sister; she should want you to be happy."

Stabbing my spoon in the ice cream, I set the tub on the coffee table. "Can we talk about something else?" I ask. When I look up at Maggie, I see her eyes soften and she offers me a sympathetic smile.

"Sure," she says, looking down at her computer.

A loud boom startles me, and I turn my attention back to the flat screen that is nestled against the wall. Flashes of bright orange light illuminate the screen. The horrific scene fades and a petite blonde comes into view, her high-pitched voice resonating through the speakers.

Four people were injured and two killed early Saturday morning when a roadside bomb struck a US military convoy.

Devin. Oh my gosh, Devin!

My heart nearly explodes from my chest as I struggle to comprehend what she's saying.

The attack occurred thirty kilometers south of Baghdad. This comes just two days after a string of bombings across Iraq have killed thirty-nine people, three of whom were American soldiers.

I place a trembling hand over my mouth as thoughts of Devin race through my head. *Is that where he's at? Is he okay? Are his men okay?* My adrenaline spikes, pumping nervous energy through my veins, and I scoot forward on the couch. Dropping my hand from my mouth, I prop my elbows on my knees and listen carefully, each word causing my stomach to twist in knots.

A military spokesperson tells us that the four injured on Saturday were, in fact, American soldiers, and all are expected to make a full recovery. The two fatalities were not Americans but Iraqi civilians.

Several emotions hit me all at once with a force so powerful I feel it in my bones.

Fear.

Anxiety.

Relief.

He's alive.

The breath whooshes from my lungs and I drop my chin, tangling my fingers in my hair. *He could've been killed. His troops could've been killed.* It's possible that he was one of the four men injured, but knowing that all the soldiers will make a full recovery and no US military deaths occurred helps to calm me down.

But my fingers twitch, the urge to write him and reach out to him stronger than it's ever been. More than anything, I want to know he's okay and that his men are okay, which terrifies the hell out of me because it means I've let him in. Somehow, in this short amount of time, I've allowed my feelings to come out of hiding and I've begun to care about him. *You never stopped caring about him*, I think to myself.

Squeezing my eyes shut, I push back the onslaught of emotions. How did this happen? Not only have I let myself get close enough to the one person who could hurt me again, but on top of that, he's a soldier—someone who could easily be ripped away from me at any moment.

"Katie?"

The soft voice reaches through the fog, pulling me out, and I rub my eyes, determined not to cry. When I finally peek up, Maggie is watching me carefully.

"Are you okay?"

"Yeah." Straightening my back, I run a shaky hand over my face. "I'm good."

"Really?" she asks, her eyebrows raised. "Because whatever that was"—she waves her hand in my direction—"it wasn't okay."

"Stop it. I'm fine. I just . . . that reporter . . ." Unable to get my words out, I finally give up and flop back on the couch. A couple of seconds pass and Maggie stays quiet, so I close my eyes, take a deep breath, and say, "That news story scared the shit out of me. I've never paid much attention to the news. I've never had a reason to . . . until now."

"Because of Devin?" she asks. I nod my head, listening to her fingers tap the keyboard of her laptop. "Remind me what his last name is? Devin what?"

"Clay. Devin Clay." I pause, afraid to open my eyes because I'm sure I sound like a complete nutcase, and I don't want to see it reflected in her eyes. "I know it's silly. We haven't talked in a decade, Maggie, but it's like we never stopped." My hand fists my shirt, right above my heart. "I can't explain it, but I *feel* it . . . Reconnecting with him was meant to happen."

"Does he have really short dark hair?"

"No idea," I quip, tossing my hand up in exasperation. I let it slump down covering my face. "I only know what he used to look like, and he hated short hair. It was always shaggy, but yes, it was dark." Memories of threading my fingers through the curls at the nape of his neck flash through my head. "His hair was fucking sexy. It was rugged in a bad boy sort of way. I can't picture him with short hair. I bet if he has short hair, then he's probably not near as good-looking," I rationalize, hating that I desperately want to know what he looks like. I want to know if his dark lashes still make his green eyes pop, and if the dimple in his left cheek still stands out the way it used to. "Yup"—my body relaxes—"I bet he hasn't aged well. If I saw him, I probably wouldn't feel a thing."

I know that's a fucking lie, because it wasn't Devin's looks that I fell in love with. It was his heart and his mind and so many other things that I'm not going to list because I am *not* interested in a relationship, damn it!

"Maybe you'd feel a *little* bit more than nothing," she says suggestively. Flinging my arm off my face, my eyes fly open and I stare at Maggie. She glances down, smirking at me and then at her computer. "Because he sure as hell doesn't look like a man that hasn't aged well. Mmm-mmm-mmm. Nope, that soldier is sex on a stick."

"Maggie," I breathe, my eyes painfully wide. "You can't look him up."

She shrugs. "Too late, already did. Wanna see?" she asks, showing me her laptop.

"No!" Popping up, I quickly shut her laptop. Maggie's mouth drops open. "Good Lord, Mags, he's going to think I'm stalking him or something. You can't just do that," I say frantically. "You can't just look someone up like that."

"Why the hell not?"

"I . . . I don't know. You just can't. It feels wrong."

"Oh, trust me," she says. "It's *so* not wrong."

"Okay. Well, maybe I don't want to know what he looks like anymore because that's not what it's about for me. I'm not interested in anything more than what we are right now, which is two old friends who have managed to—"

"Or maybe," she says, pushing my hands off of her computer, "you need to stop worrying, stop thinking, and just look. Maybe"—she opens her computer, which is still open to MySpace, and I cross my hands over the screen, shielding it from view—"the connection you feel toward Devin is strong, not because he's an *old friend,* but because he's your lobster." She waggles her eyebrows, a grin tipping the corner of her mouth.

"Oh good God, Maggie." Pinching the bridge of my nose, I take a deep breath, fighting the urge to strangle my best friend. She can't do this. She can't plant these crazy notions in my head. "He is *not* my lobster."

"Really? Your eyes light up when you talk about him," she says. "He's been able to pull things out of you with letters— fucking *letters,* Katie—that no one else could pull out of you. And just now when you were watching that news story, you nearly hyperventilated. Hell, I nearly hyperventilated just watching you." She drops a gentle hand to my arm. "You two have a connection. I know you feel it because you've told me. And you're right. It doesn't matter what he looks like because that connection is there, and it's real. But what if that connection has the potential to grow? What if that connection could blossom into so much more than friendship? What if you guys could not only get back what you lost but gain so much more?"

Damn it. How does she always know the precise thing to say to get me to change my mind? Doesn't she know I'm not ready for this? *I mean, I'm not ready for this . . . right?*

No, I know what I want and what I don't want, and anything other than being friends with the only man to ever break my heart is something I definitely do not want. And if that's the case, then seeing his picture won't change anything.

But what if it does?

Shit.

Slowly, I drop my hands. Devin's picture fills the screen, and every last image of the teenager-turned-man I had conjured up in my head falls to the wayside because the *real* him is so much more than I'd imagined. My heart races as my eyes roam over his profile picture, which was obviously taken at the beach.

His entire body is ripped, chiseled to perfection—much more so than the last time I saw him half naked. I can't help but think that this is the type of body I read about in books. Board shorts sit low on hips. A thick, corded arm is slung over the shoulder of another man, equally as gorgeous in a rugged sort of way. As expected, Devin's green eyes pop under thick dark lashes and pair perfectly with his straight nose and full lips, which are split into a breathtaking smile. He's always had strong features, but they're different now . . . more defined. And if that jawline isn't enough to make any girl swoon, the single dimple in his left cheek—the one that I've always loved—would more than do the trick.

"Please tell me we can look at more pictures." Maggie's warm breath fans the side of my face, bringing me back to reality. I don't even want to know how crazy the two of us would look to an outsider as we sit here drooling over a picture on a screen.

"Absolutely," I say, nodding my head.

Maggie fist pumps the air. "Yes!" Clicking on the arrow, she slowly scrolls through pictures. There are several of Devin by himself, a few of him with some friends drinking beer, and one of him with a girl. She's a tall blonde with sparkling blue eyes. Her body is tucked in close to his, her left arm wrapped around his lower back. Devin's arm is hooked around her neck in a kid-sister sort of way, but it does nothing to ease the tension in my stomach.

My mind drifts to my last e-mail and the very important question that I asked him. *Is this his girlfriend, or maybe his wife?*

Suddenly, I want nothing more than to rush home and check my e-mail. I know Maggie would let me use her computer, but my letters to and from Devin are just that . . . they're mine.

Biting the inside of my cheek, I continue to take in the various photos when a thought pops into my head. "Maggie?"

"I know, I know." She blows out a slow breath, her eyes glued to the screen. "You're one lucky bitch."

"What if I'm not ready for this?" Her head snaps toward me. "What if I'm making a huge mistake?" I ask. Her eyes bounce around my face, uncertainty swirling in the depths of her whiskey-colored eyes.

"But what if you're not," she breathes, her eyes imploring me to really consider what she's saying. "What if this is a second chance? You've told me how much Devin meant to you and how crushed you were when he left. But what if it just wasn't your time? What if the two of you needed to separate so that you could come back together, stronger and more solid?"

"What if I let him in and he leaves again?"

A slow smirk plays at the corner of Maggie's mouth. "Then I'd rip his fucking balls off." I offer her a tremulous smile and she sobers up. "But I don't think it'd come to that. You want to know why?"

I nod.

"I think that Devin is probably a fairly smart fella, which is why he's been writing you. Now, I don't know exactly what the letters say, but you did tell me that he's apologized more than once. I'd bet just about anything that he realizes he made a big-ass mistake—a mistake that he won't make again."

I want to believe her—I really do—but there are too many "what-ifs." Starting with, "What if I'm making a big-ass mistake by thinking he won't hurt me again?"

"Katie." Maggie sighs, scooting forward on the cushion. "Life is one big chance. You can either choose to sit on the sidelines and always take the safe route, or you can jump into the game. I think you need to jump into the game. Fate has fucked with you enough, and this time I think it's working in your favor . . . either that, or your old man is pulling some pretty big strings from upstairs."

My mind drifts back to the silent plea I made to my dad the day of his funeral.

"You promised you'd never leave me," I cry, making no attempt to wipe away my tears. My throat tightens, making it hard to talk, but I need to get this out. Lowering myself, I kneel next to Daddy's casket, which is perched just inside the ground. His name, Christopher James Devora, is etched into the nameplate. My chest hurts—physically hurts—and I rub at it, trying to ease the pain.

"I'm not sure I can do this without you." My words break on a sob and I bury my face in my hands. "Show me the way," I beg, my shoulders heaving. "Put me on the right path, and I promise I'll follow it . . . I promise. But you have to give me a sign, Daddy," I plead, finally gathering the strength to look up. Gently, I place my hand against the side of his casket, my fingers drifting over his name. "I need to know you're with me."

Devin's name was on that pen pal list for a reason—I know it was. Would I have formed a bond or friendship with any of the other soldiers, or did fate and something entirely too big for me to understand bring Devin back to me?

Unspoken words linger heavy in the air, their meaning so powerful and intense that I'm too scared to speak them.

"Maggie, I need to go."

Chapter 12 | *Katie*

"How to Save a Life"—The Fray

I can't stop smiling. Even if I could stop, I don't know that I'd want to. I left Maggie's in a hurry to get home, hopeful that I'd have a message from Devin waiting in my inbox. Plus, I was shaken over what I'd seen on the news and admittedly rattled by the realization that maybe—just maybe—he and I were supposed to come back into each other's lives. And who knows, maybe we're meant to be nothing more than friends, but I needed to get home and process it . . . process everything. I didn't get much time to take it all in though because the second I pulled up my Yahoo account and saw his name, I had to read what he wrote—and I wasn't disappointed.

His words put a big, goofy grin on my face. Oh, and the fact that he isn't married and I didn't inadvertently become an emotional mistress. That makes me smile too. *A lot.*

After hitting reply, I sit and watch the cursor blink steadily on the screen. I want nothing more than to lay it all on the line. I want to tell him that news of the roadside bomb scared the shit out of me, and that in that moment, I was desperate to hear from him and talk to him—that I would've given anything to be able to pick up the phone and call him, just to make sure he was okay. I want him to know I was worried, to know that I care.

But as my fingers continue to press against the keyboard, unmoving, my mind goes completely blank. Laughing at myself—because this Devin, and I know how to talk to Devin—I decide to do what comes easy . . .

To: Sergeant Devin U. Clay
From: Katie Devora
Subject: Tearin' Up My Heart

Devin,

The Backstreet Boys, really, Dev? Did I not make you listen to that whole damn album every day that summer? It was NSYNC, not Backstreet Boys. Come on, don't you remember my crush on Justin Timberlake? Honestly, this is just unforgiveable!

Nice knowing you, soldier . . .

Sincerely,
Katie

With a smile on my face, I hit send.
Oh shit, I hit send!
Clicking on his e-mail, I hit 'reply' and try again, hoping like hell he doesn't see that e-mail and think I was serious. *Way to go, Katie.*

To: Sergeant Devin U. Clay
From: Katie Devora
Subject: How to save a life

Devin,

Okay . . . I forgive you. Not just for mistaking NSYNC—the best boy band of the '90s—for the Backstreet Boys, but because you're a man and well, that was probably unfair of me to assume you could keep all those songs straight. My bad ;)

And no, I don't jam out to "Tearin' Up My Heart" when I'm pissed off anymore. I gave you a little clue, in the form of the subject line, as to what my go-to song is these days. I feel like the whole song is somehow about me, only I'm the one being saved.

Now, to answer your other question, the one I looked right over. No, I'm not married and I'm not seeing anyone. I will be honest with you though. I did just recently get out of a long-term relationship.

Pursing my lips in contemplation, I remove my hands from my laptop and thread them through my hair. Do I tell Devin that it was Wyatt I was engaged to? A part of me wants to leave that little bit of information out, but somehow it feels wrong—and I've had enough wrong in my life to last a lifetime.

I was engaged to Wyatt. The details don't really matter and maybe someday we'll talk about it, but I recently broke things off and it didn't go well. It probably makes me sound like a horrible person, but I wasn't happy, and with everything that happened with my dad . . . well, life is just too short and I couldn't drag him along any longer. I couldn't do it to myself either. So I called off our engagement, and in case you're wondering, which is incredibly presumptuous of me, I'm doing really well with it. That's how I know I did the right thing.

Anyway, I don't want to bore you with all of that. So you want to know something you don't already know about me? There's not much to tell, but I'll give it a shot.

Do you remember me telling you I work with my best friend, Maggie? We met in college and became fast friends. It sounds pathetic, but I don't have much of a life outside of work and Maggie. And everyone loves Maggie—except Wyatt. They never did get along, but she's gorgeous and funny, and she's one of those people that lives by her own set of rules. She does what she wants when she wants to do it, and she doesn't give a shit what anyone else says. She is the best girlfriend I could ask for, and I know that you would absolutely love her. I can totally picture the two of you shootin' the shit over a couple of beers next to the fire pit, and trust me when I tell you that she can dish it out just as good as she can take it. I hope that one day you get to meet her.

And you want to know my biggest fear, huh? That's a tough one. Okay, before my father was killed, my biggest fear was death. I'm sure that answer sounds cliché, but it's true. I can remember lying awake at night, and I'd start thinking about death and the fact that once we're gone, we're never coming back. No more sunsets on my favorite hill, or riding Mac in the rain. Never again would I feel the burn in my legs after running, or the ache in my chest after laughing too hard. It's scary, thinking of all the things you'd never get to experience again. Some nights, when I would think about it too much, I'd have to get out of bed and go do something to quiet my brain.

Anyway, after Daddy's death, I'd say my biggest fear is no longer death itself but losing a person I care about. And not just anyone, but someone that owns a piece of my heart . . . someone I'm invested in. Losing my dad nearly destroyed me, and I'm not sure I'd survive something like that again.

I told you mine, now you tell me yours. It's only fair ;)

Always,
Katie

My mouse hovers over the 'send' button, and I suck my bottom lip between my teeth as I contemplate whether or not to mention the roadside bomb I heard about on the news. Is that something that I can just bring up? Because I really want to know . . .

PS. I saw on the news that there were a few bombings, and I'm sure that's an everyday thing for you, but I'll be honest . . . It sort of freaked me out. I've never known someone at war, so when I heard about it, well, it scared me, and I thought of you. And I guess . . . I just want to know that you're okay, and that your men are okay, and I want you to know I'm thinking about you and praying for you. Also, I'm not sure the whole phone situation over there, but I'm always available on my cell . . . You know, if you ever want to call me . . . (533)-224-9892

Chapter 13 | Devin

"The Fear in Love"—Don't Look Down

Fuck these mornings. The ones where I wake up after a restless night of sleep about ten minutes before mission. The ones that limit personal hygiene and add unnecessary stress to an already long day. The ones where I barely have time to take a piss, let alone check my fucking e-mail in the comm center.

I rush to get into uniform, brush my teeth quickly, and meet my guys near the trucks. They laugh their asses off as I approach, my uniform half on and sweat already running down my cheeks. I pierce a hole through them with my eyes as I finish strapping on my gear and tightening my helmet.

"You motherfuckers can't wake a guy up?" I yell, slamming a fist into the hood of the Humvee. I make my way to the passenger seat and look over at headquarters just before climbing in. It's like I have X-ray vision. I see straight through the walls into the communications center and to the computer that sits there, taunting me with an unread e-mail from Katie. I huff and sink my ass into the seat, slipping my headset on and slamming the door shut.

"Hey, what can I say, Sarge? You had one thumb in your mouth and the other one up your ass. It was just too cute to fuck with." Navas cackles and nudges my elbow with his boot. "I swear we were coming to get you in five minutes."

"Five more minutes and I would've had to go out on mission without pants." The Humvee pulls out of the spot and toward the gates as the other two vehicles follow behind. "Thomas, you're the driver. It's your job to wake up the boss."

Thomas waves to the two men guarding the front gate as we pass through it before glancing over at me with a smile. He's looking a lot better since our talk.

"It wasn't my fault, Sarge. Navas said to leave you there. That you needed your beauty sleep." He laughs and steers the Humvee onto the main road. While I'm okay with the extra sleep, I was hoping to at least be up in time to check my e-mail before heading out on mission. Now, that's all I'm going to be able to think about right now. Fuck, that's all I'm going to be able to think about all day, for that matter. It's going to make for a long twelve hours.

The air conditioning pumps out lukewarm air, which does little to alleviate this early afternoon sun. The heavy armor on the Humvees and the heat of the engine make the vehicle like an oven during this time of day. I try my best to stay comfortable, setting each hand against the A/C vents, soaking up every bit I can get. Thomas is passed out—as usual—resting his helmeted head against the steering wheel. I wonder how he can even manage sleeping with how steamy it is right now. Then again, even though there are times I can't sleep if my life depends on it, there are other times I can pass out in five seconds using my helmet as a pillow. There's no rhyme or reason to it, really; it's just the way of a soldier. You learn to adapt . . . eventually.

But this heat is a different story. I'll never get used to this.

Navas is talking about some episode of *The Office* where Dwight sets the office on fire as a safety test for his coworkers, but I'm not really listening. He goes on these tangents about episodes of *The Office* as if they actually happened in his life—like he was telling me an old story of his or something. It's funny as shit, but I couldn't care less right now.

My head is stuck on Katie and how much clearer my mind has been since we've started talking again. I can't shake the feeling that this is something that was supposed to happen . . . that our paths have crossed once again for a reason. But why now? Why when I'm deployed thousands of miles away without the option of seeing her—or the assurance that I ever will again? For all I know, I'll be one of a hundred flag-draped coffins lining the back of a C-130.

That terrible thought is broken up by a loud "hey" that roars into the headset. It's so loud it jolts Thomas from his sleep for a moment before he nuzzles back into the door panel.

"Are you listening to me, asshole?" Navas grunts.

"Yeah, yeah, man, *The Office* and Dwight, and all that."

"You're a dick! You're supposed to be my best friend, man. That means entertaining me on boring-ass missions," Navas says, his voice purposely whiny, which makes me laugh because it seems so unnatural coming from a man his size.

"If I didn't know any better, I'd say that turret strap has cut off the circulation to your balls. You might want to think about standing for a while, bro. Maybe getting some blood back into those little guys." I laugh, and so does he, but he stifles it quickly.

"Don't make me pull these bad boys out." He tilts toward me and spreads his legs, gripping his crotch in his hand. "I wouldn't want to give you a complex." I reach a hand out before he can move away and slap the back of my fingers against his balls—*hard*. His knees jerk together, and he nearly falls out of the turret strap on top of our interpreter. Mike, being all of a hundred and twenty pounds, cowers against the side of the door, but Navas catches himself and then clutches his balls, howling in pain.

"You . . . are such . . . a fuck," he pants in between gasps.

"Well, don't put that shit in my face. I don't want to catch anything." I laugh loudly as he fidgets in the turret.

"Just wait, you fuck, I'm not playing around. I'm getting you back tenfold."

"Don't make me pull rank, specialist," I joke, tilting my head back and shooting him a smile up the turret. "You owe me some fucking push-ups when we get back, bitch!"

He smiles back, shooting me a middle finger salute. "Yeah, good luck enforcing that while you're sittin' in the comm center!"

I relax into my seat and check my watch. Of all our missions, this has been by far the most boring, but I'm careful not to mention it . . . or even think about it. Not anymore. Not after the girl.

"Since you don't wanna listen to me, fucker, you get to talk," Navas says. "So what's up with Katie?" As soon as he asks it, her face teases my thoughts. I don't want to talk to him about this. Hell, I don't even know what's going on myself. I take a moment to respond, but I guess it's too long for Navas's liking. "Hello . . . You either listen or talk, one or the other, but we aren't just going to sit here in silence. I won't allow it."

"Okay, then you talk," I say.

"No, no, no," Navas says, "you lost that privilege. Now you get to tell me what's going on with Miss Katie Devora. Or is it *Mrs.* Katie Devora?" He smirks at me, but just the thought of her being married to Wyatt makes me shudder. *There would at least be wedding pictures up already, right?*

"Come on, man. Nothing's going on. What could even happen anyway? I'm a million miles away and a decade too late." I think back to her engagement photo with Wyatt, and I feel my fingernails dig into my palms. Yup, I totally stalked her MySpace page and there he was, front and center. I always hated that kid, but knowing he's going to fucking marry *my Katie* makes me want to go crazy.

"Don't give me that bullshit. I know you, man. You haven't used the comm center this entire deployment, and all of a sudden you're there, what, three times a day over the past week? That's sayin' something." He stops, but before I can get a word in edgewise, he continues. "I've noticed a change in you, I'm not gonna lie. You're not so fucking mopey these days. I know I can be depressing sometimes, but you were starting to get like *Sophie's Choice* level of depressing on me. I can't be havin' any of that."

I laugh and finally decide to let the words spill. *What do I have to lose?*

"I don't know. It's just been nice having someone to talk to that doesn't have a hand in any of this and can take my mind away from everything. Somebody I have a past with. I just wish I still had a chance . . ." I trail off, realizing I may not really want to share the next part with Navas, but he finishes it for me anyway.

"You looked her up, didn't you?" he asks, knowing full well I did, having figured out how to read me long ago.

"It's your fucking fault, man!" I say, convinced I never would have if it weren't for him. Oh, how much easier this mission would be if I hadn't.

"She's a fuckin' knockout, isn't she?" He stretches his head down the turret hatch and looks at me inquisitively. He has a ridiculous smirk on his face. "Isn't she?"

"Shit, she was a knockout when we were kids. Now it's just unfair for every other woman on the planet."

"Sounds like a good thing to me."

"Well, I'm not with her, now am I?"

"Is she seeing somebody?" he asks, and I have to fight my desire to elbow his face to shut him up.

"You know I hate talking about this shit, right?"

My words go unnoticed as Navas keeps talking. "In the year that I've known you, you've talked about this girl relentlessly. For a while there, I knew more about her than I did about you. You may think you're Mr. Independent, trying to act all tough and shit, but you're just like me, a tough candy shell with a gooey caramel center." Annoyed, I tilt my head back to look at him again. Catching his playful smile, I refrain from throwing my elbow into his face. "We're lovers . . . It's just how God made us."

"Yeah, well, I'm also a killer, so keep it up, dick!"

"Okay, okay, come on, I'm just playing. Don't be ashamed of who you are, man. Ladies don't want some emotionless hard-ass. They want a man who can love them better than anyone else," he says, likely hoping it's enough to get me talking. It works.

"She was the one that got away, man. And I don't think anything or anyone will ever change that. She's it for me . . ." My voice trails off for a moment, and Navas takes it as his cue to chime in.

"So, she's seeing someone, huh?"

"Yeah, man, she is. And of all people, she's engaged to my childhood nemesis. The guy wanted her so bad when we were growing up, but she only had eyes for me. I should've known he'd swoop in the moment I left."

"Why did you two end anyway? You never did tell me that part of it."

"Conversation over, motherfucker."

I'm not about to tell him about my biggest mistake, because then I'd have to tell him that, for the first time in my military career, I want to tear this uniform off, burn up my enlistment papers, and hop on a plane back home. For the first time in my life, my world seems so much bigger, my options limitless, my chances of happiness now visible.

And I know what he'd say. He'd tell me to go and get my girl. But I also know after seeing her picture with Wyatt that it would be nearly impossible.

Slouching down in my seat, I close my eyes. I still want to read that e-mail that I hope to hell is waiting for me because maybe then the fact that she's getting married will be hammered into my head. Maybe then I'll be able to accept it and take this for what it is . . . a fucking friendship. And as much as it'll kill me, I'd rather be friends than nothing at all.

Chapter 14 | *Katie*

"Fall"—Ed Sheeran

"I think I'm ready." My eyes widen at my own admission and Dr. Perry raises an eyebrow, clearly unsure as to what I'm talking about. "Drexler," I clarify, "I think I'm ready to deal with Andrew Drexler."

"What do you mean by *deal* with him?"

Dropping my head back, I look up at the ceiling fan, watching the blades go around and around. *Who the hell has a ceiling fan in their office?* "Katie?"

"I'm thinkin'," I mumble. What exactly *do* I want? I'm not really sure. I just know that I've come so far and I'm starting to feel happy again. I've found the place I thought I'd lost forever, but one thing is still there in the back of my mind. "He sent me a letter awhile back. I need to read it, or maybe meet with him. I don't really know." Sitting up, I lock eyes with Dr. Perry. "I just know that I want to move past it once and for all, and he's the one thing left standing in my way."

"Standing in your way of what?"

"Life. Happiness. Forgiveness. You name it."

"Who do you want to forgive?" Her probing eyes see way too much, and even though I want nothing more than to look away, I don't. "Him, or yourself?"

I shrug. "Both, maybe. It's hard to explain. It's just . . ." My words trail off as I think of the best way to put it. "I want to move on. I've moved past so much of my anger and resentment, but I want to move past *all* of it. I want to . . ." I sigh, rubbing a hand over my face when my throat grows tight. "I want to be able to think of my dad without thinking about *Drexler*. I want peace."

The smile on Dr. Perry's face widens and something inside of me relaxes. "I'm proud of you, Katie, and I think it's a great idea."

"You do?"

"Absolutely. I think you're ready. But maybe just start by reading his letter, and then if you still feel unsettled, you can contemplate speaking with him."

"Sounds like a good idea." I smile and rub my hands along the front of my thighs, then push up from the couch.

"Goodnight, Katie. I'll see you next week."

With a small wave, I turn toward the door when Dr. Perry calls out to me. "Oh, by the way, how are things going with your pen pal?"

"They're going great." *Better than great*, I think to myself as I leave Dr. Perry's office, much lighter than ever before. And I know there is really only one person to thank for that—the same person who has somehow managed to hijack my head, considering I find myself thinking about him nearly 24/7.

"Goodnight, Kelly!" I wave at Dr. Perry's secretary on my way out, tugging my phone from my pocket the second I slide into my car. Three missed calls pop up on my phone, and I roll my eyes at the sight of Wyatt's name. He's really backed off lately; in fact, I haven't heard from him in several days. So why is he calling me again all of a sudden?

Just then, my phone vibrates in my hand, lighting up with Wyatt's phone number. Curious as to why he's rapid-fire calling me, I flip open my phone.

"Hello."

"Katie, hey . . . I, uh . . . I didn't expect you to answer."

"I was with Dr. Perry. I'm just heading home. What's up?" Transferring my phone to speaker, I start my car and pull out of the parking lot. I hear the faint sound of a woman giggling in the background. "Is everything okay?"

"Uh . . ." Wyatt grunts and then more giggling ensues. I cringe, wondering what in the hell is going on, and I'm seconds away from asking him just that when he says the last thing I expect to hear. "No, everything isn't okay. I was calling because I have Bailey, and she's"—Wyatt grunts—"*shit*, are you okay?" There's another grunt followed by some rustling sounds, and now I'm wondering if Bailey really is okay and why in the hell Wyatt is with her.

"Wyatt? What do you mean you *have Bailey?*"

"She's wasted," he says, sighing. "She refuses to let me take her to your mom's, and no way in hell am I bringing her to my place."

"Bring her to me." I can't help but laugh. Bailey is a funny drunk, although I can't help but wonder why she's drunk at six o'clock in the evening. "I'll be home in two minutes."

"Thank God," he says with an exaggerated groan. "We're sitting in your driveway."

"Almost there." I disconnect the call as I turn onto my street. Sure enough, Wyatt's truck is parked in the driveway and he's standing outside, leaning against his sleek black Chevy. Pulling in, I throw my car in park and start laughing hysterically at the sight of Bailey's face squished against the glass of the passenger-side window.

Wyatt walks around the truck and opens the passenger door, sticking a hand out just in time to stop Bailey from toppling to the ground. Scooping her up, he tosses her over his shoulder and I shake my head, laughing.

"It's not funny."

"Oh, but it is." Unlocking my front door, I hold it open for Wyatt and he walks in and places Bailey on the couch. I reach down to tug Bailey's heels off, causing her to stir and roll onto her side. Her eyelids bob heavily several times and she swallows hard.

"Are you going to be sick?" I ask, pointing to the trashcan and motioning for Wyatt to bring it to me.

"He cheated on me." Her words are slurred as she clumsily reaches up to wipe away some tears that have gathered in her eyes. My heart clenches, and I kneel down on the floor next to the couch to run a soothing hand along her forehead. No wonder she's hammered this early in the evening.

"I'm sorry, sweetie." Wyatt hands me the trashcan and I place it on the floor, just in case she feels the need to hurl later—which she most likely will. "He doesn't deserve you, Bay. You're too good for him."

"But I wanted him." Her eyes drift shut and when she sighs, the smell of her breath nearly knocks me on my ass. Okay, so her drug of choice tonight was tequila. Nice. That should be a lovely smell in the morning when I'm cleaning up whatever mess she makes.

"I know you wanted him, babe." Brushing the hair out of her face, I lean down and kiss her forehead, glad that she's too drunk to remember that she's mad at me. "But sometimes what we want isn't always what's best for us."

A faint snore falls from Bailey's mouth, and I pull an afghan off the back of the couch and tuck it in around her. Standing up from the floor, I come face-to-face with Wyatt. "Thanks for bringing her by."

"You don't have to thank me." Lifting the hat from his head, Wyatt runs his fingers through his hair before readjusting the Stetson. I always loved it when Wyatt wore his cowboy hat. It made me think of my daddy. "She said she didn't know who else to call." Wyatt props a hip against the wall and cocks his head to the side. "Why didn't she just call you?"

Great. Not exactly the conversation I want to have. Turning toward the kitchen, I wave for Wyatt to follow me so we don't disturb Bailey. "Well," I say, grabbing a bottle of water from the fridge, "we aren't exactly on speaking terms."

"Why's that?" His southern drawl has always grown thicker when he's concerned, and it's more than prominent now.

"She got mad when she found out that you and I broke up." Looking down, I fidget with the cap to my bottle, unsure as to why I suddenly find it hard to look Wyatt in the eye. I sure as hell was able to look him in the eye when I broke his heart.

"We didn't break up."

My head snaps up. "Uh, yeah we did."

"No." Wyatt takes a step toward me. My entire body freezes. "You broke up with me. To say that we broke up is a complete lie, because if I remember correctly, I didn't really have a choice in the matter."

"No, I guess you didn't." Glancing down, I take a deep breath. "I'm sorry, Wyatt." For the first time since it happened, guilt over breaking up with him slices through me. Not because I regret ending things with him—because I don't—but because I feel bad for hurting him. And I'm not going to lie, having him here in my house again is familiar and comforting, and I'm finding it mildly unsettling.

I jump at the feel of Wyatt's warm hand on my face, but I don't look up. This is all so confusing. I can't bring myself to meet his gaze, but when he hooks his thumb under my chin, tilting my head up, I don't have much of a choice. His eyes are intense, swimming with emotion, and I get a sinking feeling in the pit of my stomach.

Please don't do this.

"I don't want you to apologize, Katie." He swallows hard. "What I want is for you to give me another chance."

"Wyatt," I say, groaning. Furrowing my brows, I shake my head. "Please—"

"Just hear me out," he says, holding up a hand. "I get it. I get why you broke things off. You've gone through so much lately, and I—I wasn't there for you like I should've been. And I can't tell you how sorry I am for that, but I can show you. Let me show you."

"Wyatt." I stare at him for a few seconds, hating that he's putting me in this position. "I haven't changed my mind."

"Let me change your mind," he pleads. "We were great together, Katie, and yes, somewhere along the way we drifted apart. But I know that we can find our way back to each other. I just need you to give me a chance."

"I don't—"

"Dinner," he blurts. "Just have dinner with me. Let's talk. That's all I ask."

"I don't know, Wyatt." My stomach rolls with uncertainty, but turning him down on the phone was much easier than telling him "no" in person.

"Think about it." Slowly, he backs away from me with a hopeful smile on his face. "Just think about it."

"Okay," I concede. "I'll think about it."

He doesn't say another word. Turning around, he walks out of the house, shutting the door quietly behind him.

Completely defeated, I drop into a seat at the kitchen table. Telling Wyatt that I'd think about having dinner with him was a huge mistake, because I know deep down that no matter how familiar it felt to be around him again, I made the right choice. And no dinner is going to change that.

My phone vibrates in my pocket and I groan. "Come on, Wy." Scooping my phone out of my pocket, I'm prepared to see Wyatt's number—yet again—but the number is completely foreign to me. *Who the hell is this?* It's probably some damn telemarketer, and usually I'd just send them to voicemail, but for some unknown reason I decide to answer.

"Hello."

"Katie?"

I'd know that voice anywhere. A tiny wave of electricity buzzes through my body, sending a shiver down my spine. *No way.* The sinking feeling in my stomach from before is now a swarm of butterflies that decide to take flight all at once. I push up from the table, knocking the chair over in the process. "Devin?" My voice comes out way too breathy, but I don't have time to care because I'm too busy being shocked, and excited, and hopeful . . .

"Hi." His rich, gravelly voice floats through the line, soaks into my skin and wraps itself around my heart. I've wanted to talk to him—to hear his voice saying the words that he's written—but I didn't realize I needed it until now.

I can't believe he called.

He's on the line, no doubt waiting for me to talk, but I'm utterly speechless. The only thing I can think of is that now that I've heard his voice again, reading his words won't be enough. I'll crave this . . . this connection. It'll be my new weakness, my new drug of choice.

"Is this a bad time?" I can practically see him frowning through the line.

"No!" I take a deep breath to try and calm my nerves. "No, it's perfect. You just caught me off-guard. I didn't expect to hear from you, and now here you are on the phone and it's so different, you know?" I cringe, loathing the way I'm rambling but completely unable to stop it. "Hearing your voice, it's just . . . it's . . . it's too much . . . it's been so long . . ."

Devin chuckles and goose bumps scatter up my arms. He's laughing at me, and I don't even care because the sound of his laugh is like a heating blanket, warming me from the outside in.

"Katie?"

"Yeah?"

"You were engaged to Wyatt." Okay, I wasn't exactly expecting him to say *that*. He obviously got my e-mail.

"Were. Past tense."

"I've never been so fucking relieved to read something in my life."

"Yeah?"

"You have no idea," he says. "And Katie?"

"Yeah?"

"E-mail or phone?" he asks.

"Is this a trick question?" A slow grin spreads across my face.

"You're supposed to just answer," he says, laughing. "You aren't supposed to answer a question with another question. Now answer the question, Katie." His commanding tone causes shivers to run down my spine. I forgot how *alpha* he could be.

"Phone." I didn't have to think twice. Our words may have reconnected us, but hearing his voice only confirms the one thing I've suspected all along: what we had never went away.

"Good answer."

My cheeks are hurting—seriously, they're cramping up—and if I don't stop smiling soon, I'm afraid I'll have this goofy-as-hell grin for the rest of my life. But it feels good . . . really good. "What would you have done if I said e-mail?"

"I would've hung up and e-mailed you." He chuckles. "You've never been one to ramble, so is it because you're nervous . . . or is it just me?"

My racing heart kicks up a few extra notches because it's totally him. I'm tempted to tell him that I do ramble and he just doesn't remember correctly, because telling Devin that it's him is the equivalent of slicing my chest open and laying my heart on the line—and quite frankly, my heart has been through enough lately. But as tempting as it is, I know that I have to tell him the truth. We've come too far and built too much in such a short amount of time, and whatever this is, I don't want to jeopardize it . . . or lose it.

"It's you." Leaning forward, I prop my hands on the counter. *Holy shit, that was terrifying.*

Devin blows out a slow breath but doesn't respond. *Oh shit.* My stomach tightens as I try to come up with a way to dig myself out of this. "I'm sorry, I shouldn't have—"

"I like your answer."

"You do?" That knot in my stomach unravels, taking with it the urge to throw up.

"More than I probably should," he says with a sigh. The line crackles, going completely silent for a few beats, and I'm worried that the call was somehow dropped when I hear him clear his voice. "I have a confession to make."

"Okay . . ." My nerves are running at high speed, so I grab a pot from beneath the sink. Maybe if I keep myself busy, I'll be more relaxed.

"Shit," he says, laughing. "I really don't want you to think I'm some sort of stalker . . ."

"Spit it out, Sergeant," I quip.

"I stalked your MySpace page," he breathes, quickly rushing to explain. "My friend Navas, that fucker, had me convinced that I needed to see you again, to see what you've been up to. Don't get me wrong, I wanted to know what you looked like after all these years, but . . . are you laughing at me?"

"S-sorry." I gasp to catch my breath. "I'm laughing because—" My abs constrict, tears of happiness—and quite possibly relief—running down my face. I suck in a breath. "I totally stalked you too."

"You did?" He sounds surprised, which makes me laugh harder.

"Yes, I had to. Maggie made me!" Filling the pot up with water, I place it on the stove, setting the temperature to high.

"She *made* you?" he teases. "How did she make you?"

"She's evil, Devin. She's a little devil, and she's enamored with you and your chiseled abs."

"I think Maggie and I are going to be great friends."

"I'll tell her you said that." Wiping the wetness from my face, I pull the angel hair pasta from the cupboard.

"And you . . . were you enamored with my chiseled abs?" I smile, picturing Devin with a shit-eating grin on his face.

"Nah. Your abs could use some work, if you ask me," I joke.

Devin's laugh is deep and throaty, and it does things to me that a laugh should never be able to do to someone. It's quickly becoming my favorite sound. "I'll have to remember to do an extra set of sit-ups tomorrow."

"Your smile."

"Huh?"

"It was your smile that got to me." Without permission, my mouth continues to spew exactly what's running through my head. "I miss seeing the way it lights up your face. And that dimple in your left cheek . . . I shouldn't be surprised that it's just as sexy now as it was then."

He sucks in a sharp breath at my confession. Then the line goes quiet, and I can't help think that I'm crazy for opening my mouth and saying those things. *What the hell was I thinking?*

"How are you, Katie?" Devin's voice is infused with so much emotion. I take a deep breath, thankful that we're finally getting the chance to talk while simultaneously trying not to dwell on the fact that he didn't mention what he thought about me. I know I don't look the same. *What if he doesn't find me attractive anymore?*

"Good," I answer honestly. I drop the pasta into the near boiling pot of water. "I'm good. I had a session with Dr. Perry tonight, and I told her that I think I'm ready to read Andrew Drexler's letter."

"Wow," he breathes. "That's a huge step. But you're strong, and if anyone can do it, I know you can. I'm so proud of you."

Hearing him tell me that he's proud of me gives me an enormous amount of confidence, but it also makes me nervous. "I don't know if I can forgive him."

Closing my eyes, I conjure up a vision of my dad. He's smiling, his round cheeks red from laughter, and I wonder what he would want me to do. "He'd want me to forgive him," I murmur, quickly repeating those words as they sink in. "Daddy would want me to forgive him."

"One step at a time, that's all you can do. Read the letter first, listen to what he has to say and then go from there. You don't have to forgive him right away—or at all, for that matter—but at least you're taking that step. Just remember you're taking that step for you, and no one else."

"Wait a minute . . . is this Dr. Perry?" I quip. "No really, what did you do with her?"

"Ha ha."

The faint sound of water sizzling catches my attention, so I open my eyes and whip around. "Shit." Quickly, I turn the temperature of the stovetop down and blow across the top of the steaming water until it stops boiling over.

"Are you okay? Did you hurt yourself?"

"No, I'm fine. Just a little cooking mishap. And in case you're wondering, no, I'm not a better cook now than I was before you left."

"Duly noted." Devin yawns through the line and I look at my watch. *Six forty-five.* I wonder what time it is where he's at. "What are you cooking?"

"Do you really want me to tell you?" I ask. "Is it going to make you dream of food?"

"Tell me, woman. Let me live vicariously through you."

"Okay," I drawl. "Wait for it . . . wait for it . . . spaghetti!"

"Mmmm." Devin moans, deep and long. The vibration in his voice slams into me like a tidal wave. Desire pools low in my belly, and a vision of the two of us naked and writhing in bed flashes through my head.

"That sounds so good," he says.

"It—" My voice squeaks and I clear my throat, thankful when the words come out right the second time around. "It is. It's become my specialty."

"Oh yeah? What's your secret?"

"Well, if I told ya, I'd have to kill ya."

"Wow, now I'm *dying* to know."

"Fine, fine, twist my arm, why don't you? It's chicken."

"What?" He chuckles. "Chicken?"

"Yeah. I put chicken in the spaghetti rather than beef. It's amazing! I'll make it for you some time."

"I'm gonna hold you to that."

I hope you do, soldier. "It'll be great. We can have a spaghetti picnic under the stars. If you're good, I'll even pack Cool Ranch chips and Mountain Dew."

"You remembered," he mumbles as though lost in thought. I nod my head, but by the time I remember I'm on the phone and he can't actually see me, he starts talking again. "And on this picnic, will you serenade me with Backstreet Boys too?"

We both fall into a fit of laughter as we argue the age-old question of who is better—or worse, as Devin likes to say—Backstreet Boys or NSYNC. Then I go on to tell him about Bailey, why she's upset with me, and how she ended up here tonight—leaving out the fact that Wyatt brought her. He doesn't need to know *everything*.

Devin tells me some funny stories about his friend Navas, and I can tell by the way he talks about him that Navas is a good person. I'm glad that Devin has someone like that in his life—someone he can trust and talk to that's there with him, day in and day out. If I'm being honest, I'm a little jealous that I've been replaced, and then I wonder if that's how Devin feels when I go on and on about Maggie.

Devin is yawning nearly every other word, and when I glance at the clock in my kitchen, I notice that we've been on the phone for nearly an hour. "You sound exhausted. What time is it there?"

"Ummm . . ." The phone buzzes and crackles a few more times. "Almost two fifteen."

"In the morning? Oh my gosh, Devin, why didn't you tell me I was keeping you up?"

"Because I wanted to talk you, Katie." My shoulders relax, but I still feel bad. He probably has to get up at the asscrack of dawn. "And trust me, I don't sleep much anyway."

"We're going to discuss that the next time we talk," I say, causing him to chortle. "But I'm letting you go because you need to get some sleep."

"Okay."

"Okay."

Neither of us says a word or makes the first move to hang up. I'm instantly transported into the "you hang up, no, you hang up" antics we used to play as children, before his mom disconnected their phone. "I'll try and call you again soon," he says.

"You better."

"Katie?"

"Yeah?" Walking into the living room, I curl up in the recliner and lean my head back, closing my eyes.

"This was—"

"Great," I interrupt. "It was great." He mumbles in agreement, and suddenly I feel the need to ask him about *us*. I need to know if he feels this connection or if it's just in my head, because I can feel myself starting to fall again. And wouldn't it be a bitch if there was no one there to catch me?

"Devin?"

"Yeah?"

"This friendship . . . it's, um . . . I mean, I feel like . . ." I bite my lip, frustrated that I can't seem to put into words everything that I'm thinking and feeling. Taking a deep breath, I reach down deep, grasping whatever courage I can find. "Since your first letter to me, I've felt . . . I just . . ."

"I feel it, Katie."

Everything around me blurs as tears fill my eyes. "You do? Because I feel it, and it's powerful and overwhelming and I thought I had moved past it, and then all of a sudden, there it was again, and . . ."

Devin sighs, a rush of air sounding through the phone. "God, Katie. I don't know how to explain it, but you're not alone. I feel the same way, only I knew that I never moved past it. Believe me, I tried because I thought it was best, but it's always been there for me. Why do you think I was so quick to reply to your letter when I tossed all the other letters away?" My heart constricts. I had no idea he'd tossed other letters away . . . He didn't tell me that. "And yes, it's powerful and overwhelming, but in a good way. Christ, what we had . . . I'd never felt anything like it before, and now, there just aren't words for it."

I sniff, wiping my face with my arm. "I can't tell you how relieved I am to hear you say that. I didn't know . . . I thought maybe it was just me. That maybe I was making it so much more than it was—"

"It's everything." His voice grows thick with emotion. "Whatever this is between us . . . It's big, Katie. Bigger than you, bigger than me . . . and ten years hasn't changed that."

"So, what now?"

"I don't know." If it's at all possible, his voice seems lighter, as though a weight has been lifted off his shoulders. "But I think that I'm going to like figuring it out."

My lips lift at the corners, a grin splitting my face. "Yeah?"

"Definitely."

"Well, okay then. So call me when you can?"

"Soon. I promise."

My heart soars as I let go of all the insecurities I was having about Devin. I know that when I lay my head down tonight, he'll consume my dreams. "Goodnight."

"Katie?"

"Still here. You'll totally have to hang up first."

His boisterous laugh fills the room—and my heart. "I'll hang up first, not because I want to but because I'm fuckin' exhausted and I have to be up in like three hours. But I need to tell you something."

"What's that?" Pushing my foot on the floor, I rock back in the chair, completely content and happy. For the first time in a long time, I feel genuinely happy.

"It was your eyes." Adrenaline pumps through my veins. Warmth radiates throughout my body and the smile that's been plastered to my face since hearing his voice again . . . Yup, it just got a little bit bigger. Devin clears his throat. "You've always been gorgeous, Katie, and I knew that no amount of time would change that. But from the first time I laid eyes on you in the first grade, it's always been your eyes. And when I get to see you again—and I *will* get to see you again—I'll tell you exactly why they've always captivated me."

"Or now . . . You could tell me now."

"Some things need to be said in person." I can hear him smiling through the phone. "Katie?"

"Yes?"

"I'm so sorry for hurting you." His voice cracks on the last word, and that crack resonates all the way to my soul. "I'll never be able to—"

"I forgive you." Once again, the words rush from my mouth before I have any time to think about them. But I'm okay with it, because right now I feel so incredibly light as my heart flops over inside my chest.

Devin breathes heavily into the phone for several seconds. "Goodnight, Katie." I get the feeling he'd stay on all night if he could.

"Goodnight, Devin," I say with hesitation. The click and buzz of the dead line sends my heart plummeting into my stomach because I have no idea when I'll get to talk to him again.

Visions of that news story I saw the other day flash through my head.

If I'll ever get to talk to him again.

Chapter 15 | Devin

"The Proof of Your Love"—For King and Country

I'm buzzing. My whole fucking body is buzzing and her voice still rings in my ears as I return the phone to its cradle. I can hardly fight the smile that's streaked wide across my face, so much so that my cheeks are aching. How can someone thousands of miles away make me feel this . . . this . . . euphoric? And how in the hell I'm supposed to concentrate on anything else now is beyond me.

Stepping out of headquarters, I head toward our tents, wondering what she's doing at this very moment. It makes me sound like a fucking pussy considering I just got off the phone with her, but what can I say, the girl makes me stupid. She makes me think and feel things that I haven't let myself think or feel in a long-ass time—things like marriage, kids, love, and a future away from here. A future where I can go to bed with her gorgeous body wrapped around mine and wake up every morning to her beautiful face. Those are the things I'm thinking of, the things I'm dreaming of, and the things I'm determined to make happen, because what I feel for Katie surpasses normal human reasoning. I have to make it back to her. I have to feel her in my arms and make her mine. There isn't any other option.

"Well, I'll be damned," a voice calls out just as I'm about to enter the tent. I look over my shoulder, and under the moonlight

I see Navas seated by the fire pit with a half-smoked cigar clenched between his fingers. I stop in my tracks, then spin around and walk toward him. Hooking my foot around the leg of a chair, I pull it toward his and take a seat.

"What?" I ask, feeling the smile still tugging at the corners of my lips. I fight the damn thing the best I can, but it's a losing battle.

"That shit-eating grin you got. It about blinded me when you walked past." He laughs and slaps a hand against his thigh.

"I don't know what you're talking about," I say, pulling a cigarette from the pack and lighting it.

"The fuck you don't," Navas says with a chuckle. "You pretty much live at the comm center now! You really are into this girl, huh?"

"You already know I am, fucker."

"Why don't you want to talk about it?" he asks, looking me intently in the eye as if trying to read me.

"I don't know, man. I guess I figured you'd think it was all crazy. Fuck, sometimes I even think it's fucking crazy." I take a long drag of my cigarette and think about the words that just came out of my mouth. It's something I've thought a lot about.

"What's crazy about it?" he asks.

"I don't know. I haven't talked to the girl in ten fucking years." *And you have no idea what I did to her,* I think to myself, knowing full well that not talking to her for ten years doesn't mean shit.

"Have you talked on the phone, or webcammed, or has it just been letters and e-mails?" His eyes quiz me even harder now as he puffs at his cigar. He looks like a mob boss interrogating a potential snitch. I can't say I like these reversed roles very much.

"First phone call was just now," I say, letting the fresh memory of the conversation tug at my attention. God, her voice is perfect. So soft and delicate . . . the kind a guy would be lucky to have whispering "good morning" from the pillow beside him. *I wonder if her heart raced like mine did during our call?*

"No, shit?! That's cool, man. How'd it go?"

"It was . . ." I trail off, my thoughts still on the call, my mind filled with images of her wrapped tightly in my arms. "Perfect."

"You going to call her again tomorrow . . . or, fuck, I guess it'd be tonight?" he asks, rising to his feet and throwing the cigar butt in the pit. Taking one last drag of my cigarette, I flick it to the ground and then follow him to the tents.

"Yeah, I think I just might do that."

My day went by as slow as hell, mostly because I was counting the minutes until I could get back to the comm center. *Good God, I sound like a fucking girl.* I look around, half expecting someone to walk up and shoot a bullet through my man card.

When I'm certain I'm alone, I pick up the phone and dial her number. Each ring raises my level of anxiety, and I shift around nervously in the seat. *I hope she picks up.* Another ring and I'm wishing I had actually scheduled a call with her.

"Hello?" Her sweet voice sends a jolt of electricity through my system, leaving me breathless and at a complete loss for words. "Hello?" she says again, bringing me to my senses.

"Hey, sorry, it's Devin . . . hi!" *Fuck, I just sounded like a little kid.*

"Devin." She releases my name in a husky breath, and the sound makes my dick go instantly hard. Closing my eyes, I picture us sitting together on the couch, her legs straddling my hips, my hands roaming ever so slowly up her arched back—

"I was hoping you would call. Honestly, I wasn't sure if you would or not, but I was hoping . . ."

"You were?"

"Mmm-hmm," she purrs. The sound is too fucking erotic, and I have to reach down and rearrange my junk.

"This whole time difference thing makes it a little difficult. I wasn't sure when would be the best time to call you."

"You can call me anytime." Her voice may be soft but her words speak volumes, and something inside of me clicks—something that I've been worrying about. *This is real.* "No matter when it is, I'll do my best to answer . . . promise." The sweetness in her promise makes me ache to have her near me, and I have to change the subject before I do something stupid like beg her to marry me. Because that would totally be stupid. *Right?*

"How was your day?"

"Uneventful," she says with a sigh. "I had today off, so I went for a run this morning and did some shopping this afternoon."

"Run?" I laugh, remembering how much she used to despise running in PE. "The Katie I know isn't a runner."

"*Knew* . . . the Katie you *knew* wasn't a runner. A lot has changed over the last decade."

The smile falls from my face for several reasons. First, because she's right. A lot *has* changed. And second, because it does nothing but drive home the knowledge that I don't *really* know her anymore, and maybe more has changed than I think.

"Okay, I totally lied." Her husky laugh travels south, and my cock goes from rock solid to throbbing against the confines of my zipper. "I'm *so* not a runner. But I tried! I really did try. I got up at the break of dawn, laced up my ASICS, and ran around the block."

"You ran around the block?"

"It's a big block."

"You're so full of shit," I joke, feeling the smile slide back onto my face. "I bet you didn't even run the whole way."

"I hate you."

"Because I'm right. You totally walked, didn't you?"

"I jogged," she corrects. "There's a big difference. And enough about me." She huffs, but the amusement is clear in her voice. "How was your day?"

"Boring . . . But a boring day is a good day over here." I pause and think about how lucky we've been as of late. Not much has happened since the incident with the girl, and the missions have run smoothly thus far. In my experience, that means something is bound to happen. There's always a calm before the storm.

"What's it like over there? And what do you do . . . Wait, am I allowed to ask that?"

"Yeah, you can ask that." I laugh, secretly loving that she wants to know more about me. "It's nothing too special. We're on something called a combat outpost, so it's pretty small . . . just bare essentials. A few buildings, one of which I'm in now, and some tents we stay in. A couple of porta-potties but no shower."

"No shower? Yikes!" She laughs but catches herself, as if she feels bad for jesting me.

"No, you have no idea. Our tents have a smell that could be collected and used as a biological weapon. It's beyond bad." She laughs loudly through the phone and it makes me want to continue, if only to hear that sweet sound again. "I do my absolute best with baby wipes and water bottles, but some of these guys over here have a misunderstanding of what good hygiene is. I swear this guy Elkins hasn't changed his uniform in months. You could stand it upright without him in it."

"Oh God," she slips out between laughs.

"As far as day-to-day life though, it has its ups and downs. There are incredibly slow, dull moments, and there are times when I feel like I'm in an action movie . . . and some days I wish it *were* a movie." *At least then I could pick up after the credits start rolling and go home, safe and sound.*

Katie clears her throat. "It's crazy it's only been a little less than twenty-four hours since we last spoke. It felt like a whole lot longer." *There's the girl I grew up with,* I think to myself, *never afraid to say exactly what she's thinking.*

"You seriously have no fucking idea." My head falls back between my shoulders, and I run a hand along the back of my neck. "Right now, a lot of our job is just sitting around in a

Humvee doing nothing, so time drags on at a snail's pace. After the day I had, I feel like it's been weeks since we've talked."

I pause for a moment and a crackling static takes over the line. "Am I going to make a fool of myself if I say you were the only thing on my mind the entire twelve-hour mission?" I laugh, but it's the nervous kind that comes out all wrong.

"Really?" she asks, her voice laced with disbelief.

"I haven't stopped thinking about you since I got your first letter."

"Devin . . ." The rough sound of my name falling from her lips is almost my undoing. What I wouldn't give to hear her say my name like that, naked and writhing beneath me. "I like it. I like that you think about me . . . that you couldn't stop thinking about me." She pauses. My heart is pounding against my ribcage as I wait for her to continue—and she will continue. I can feel it. Her honesty and openness amazes me . . . Everything about my girl amazes me.

My girl. Fuck, that sounds good.

"I'm happy to hear that you think of me because you, Sergeant Clay, have taken up *way* too many of my thoughts as well. So it makes me happy to hear that the feeling is mutual. I'm glad I'm not alone in this." My chest tightens. This girl couldn't get more perfect. How in the hell I got so lucky, I'll never know.

"More than mutual." The words jump from my mouth before I can stop them. Damn, it probably makes me sound like a fucking pussy, but it feels good telling her that. I shake my head, even though she can't see me. "I looked forward to your letters and e-mails, Katie, but now that we've talked . . . I can't tell you how nice it is to be able to call you after the long-ass day I had. You know I'm gonna crave your voice now, don't you?" I hear a quick intake of air, and I can't hold back the smile tugging at my lips. My eyes drift to the clock and I cringe—I forgot about the time difference. "I hope it's alright that I'm calling at this time."

"Of course," she says. "Like I said, call me anytime. If I'm not around to answer or have something else going on, I'll just e-mail you and you can give me a call back. Deal?" *God, how could I not agree to everything this woman says?*

"You've got yourself a deal." And because nothing in my life is ever easy, I hear a long whistle followed by an explosion off in the distance. The sounds put my body on high alert. I straighten up in my seat, stiff as a board, and listen for any more sounds.

"Devin?" I hear her, but I don't respond right away. I listen as another long whistle sounds and another blast hits—closer this time. "Devin, what is that?" The panic in her voice reclaims my attention.

"Hey, it was nothing," I lie, shifting the phone to my other ear. I cock my head and listen for more.

"Are you sure? It didn't sound like nothing." *Damn it.* This is the part I didn't want her to be exposed to—the part I wanted to pretend didn't exist. I want to end the call before the mortar rounds strike closer and the sound of the explosions cannot be mistaken, but I can't bear to let her go. The commotion on the other side of the door in headquarters has picked up now, and I know shit is about to go down. *Just a little bit longer. I need to talk to her just a little bit longer.*

"Nothing out of the ordinary, I promise." The last word is cut in half by a whistle that punishes the eardrums and is followed by an explosion that rocks the walls of the building as if they were made of paper. The phone clicks and buzzes, but I hear Katie faintly calling for me on the other end.

I can hear chaos outside and I know this is bad. They've successfully targeted their mortar rounds and there are sure to be more to come. "Katie?" I call frantically into the receiver, needing to know I didn't lose her, desperate to hear her voice one last time.

"Devin? Devin, I'm scared. I can't los—" Her trembling voice is muted by the static buzz, but I know exactly what she was saying because it's the same thing I was thinking.

And maybe that's what motivates me to continue. Maybe that's what pulls the next words from my throat.

My words are rushed, and I don't even know if she can hear me, but she needs to know . . . I *want* her to know. "I want you back. I want us, Katie, and I'll—"

The line goes dead—my words cut off—and I'm thrown from my chair as another explosion rocks the earth beneath my feet.

Chapter 16 | Katie

"From Where You Are"—Lifehouse

"Devin?" All the blood drains from my face, my heart racing so fast it's literally seconds away from exploding. "Devin!" The shrill sound of a woman screaming penetrates through the blood pounding in my ears, and I look around before realizing that woman is me.

"No. *Nononono.*" Snapping the phone shut, I rub my fingers over my temples, trying to drown out what I heard. Devin's words were broken and barely audible when they completely cut off. Images of him lying on the ground, hurt or worse, start playing through my mind, and I look around, frantically trying to decide what to do. I *need* to do something. I can't just sit here and do nothing.

My body freezes at the realization that there isn't a damn thing I can do. Devin is half a world away, and I have no other way to contact him. "Oh, God." My limbs go numb. Fear courses through my body, robbing it of normal function and control. On unsteady legs I push from the couch, and with jerky movements I walk across the living room into the kitchen, my phone gripped so tight in my hand that my knuckles are painfully white.

I can't do anything. Just like with Daddy, I'm helpless.

Sucking in a shuddery breath, I send out a quick text—a cry for help—and then I toss my phone on the counter and brace myself for impact. With my hands planted firmly against the sink, I bow my head, allowing myself to be absorbed into the all-consuming and far-too-familiar sense of dread. Call it what you want . . . panic, fear, terror. It's all the same. And right now, like the blood in my veins, it's flowing through my body.

Chills race up my arms, leaving a trail of goose bumps in their wake, and the sob that's been building inside my chest finally rips free, causing me to collapse to the floor. My vision blurs, tears sliding thick and fast down my cheeks. Images of my dad in the car, blood running from his face, flash in my head . . . only it's not my dad's face I see, it's Devin's. Pulling my knees to my chest, I bury my head and cry.

Time passes, each vision tearing off another chunk of my heart. Maybe I've been here for minutes, maybe hours; I honestly have no idea. But when I hear my mom's soft voice, my head snaps up.

"Katie." She rushes toward me, dropping to her knees. Pulling me against her chest, her familiar arms curl around my body, wrapping me in the warmth and love that I knew only she could provide. "Katie, sweetheart, what's wrong? You're scaring me, honey."

"Devin." Pulling back, I wipe the tears from my face but they're quickly replaced. "We were talking and there was th-this loud noise, and he said that everything was o-okay but it wasn't." My words break as my chest heaves. "It wasn't okay"—my head shakes frantically—"because I h-heard it again, this l-loud whistle . . . and then there was a b-boom . . . and then he was gone. Just like th-that, he was gone, and I don't know w-what to do. I can't l-lose him, Mama. *I can't.*" The thought of losing him—again—is nearly unbearable. A tight band constricts around my chest, robbing air from my lungs, and threatening to squeeze the life out of my heart.

Bile rushes up my throat. Scrambling from the floor, I run to the trashcan. A burning sensation rips through my stomach as I expel all of its contents.

Mom sweeps my hair out of my face, securing it in a band. Seconds later, a cool, wet cloth is pressed against the back of my neck. With each surge of my stomach, I bawl, breaking down bit by bit until there's nothing left. Only then do I allow myself to drift toward the dark tunnel of the place I was before . . . the empty hole I buried myself in after Daddy's death.

How could I put myself through this again? How could I care for a man that could so easily be torn away from me? I knew Devin was a soldier and I knew the risks that went along with that, yet I still allowed myself to fall for him . . . care for him . . . love him. Another rush of bile crawls up my throat, but this time I'm able to swallow past it.

"Come on." Wrapping one arm around my back, my mom guides me gently to my room, tucks me in bed, and then climbs in next to me. I snuggle against her side, and she kisses the top of my head and then whispers, "Devin, huh?"

My eyes snap up. Mama is watching me, but instead of looking upset or confused, she looks curious. I told her that Wyatt and I broke things off, but I never did tell her about Devin . . . not even that we're talking again after all this time. I decide she needs an update.

So I tell her about the pen pal program, and we talk about Devin and what he's been through, and how he's managed to break through my walls and steal a piece of my heart. She smiles when I relive the moment I read his first letter to me and how his words were a punch to my solar plexus, then she laughs when I tell her about the way he made fun of me trying to run. My eyes drift shut as I describe hearing his voice for the first time in so long, and the way it literally made my heart flop around in my chest. When I open my eyes, I see that she has tears building in hers.

"So what do we do now?" *She said we.* Air rushes from my lungs. Tilting her head to get a better look at my face, she smiles. "How do we find out if Devin is okay?"

"I, uh . . ." Scanning through every letter, e-mail and conversation in my head, I try to think of anything to help me out, but I come up empty. "I have no idea. I don't even know where to start. There is a number on my phone, one that pops up when he calls, but I don't know if I'm allowed to call it— or even if I should. Not after what I heard on the phone." I don't know the fucking rules or procedures or anything, and it's driving me insane. Rubbing a hand over my face, I thread my fingers into my hair, gripping it at the roots. *What do I do?*

"I wish I had some answers for you, sweetie, but I don't." Mama sighs, readjusting herself on my pillows. "Devin always was a smart young man, and I'm sure he could tell how scared you were on the phone." I nod, remembering his words and the way he was trying to comfort and reassure me when all hell was obviously breaking loose around him. "I'm sure that, whenever he can, he'll find a way to reach out to you."

"I know." Biting my lip, I suck it into my mouth. "But that doesn't help me now. I'm scared for him. I want to know that he's okay."

"I know, honey."

"He's more than my friend," I whisper, tucking my head under her chin. "I know it sounds silly, but I feel like I'm right back where I was when I was eighteen. It's like nothing has changed. My feelings haven't wavered, and if anything, they've only grown stronger. He feels it too," I add, just in case she's wondering if the feeling is mutual. Under thick lashes, I peek up at my mom to find her smiling. "It's sort of scary because it's not like I forgot that he left me, Mama. And I do believe him when he says he'll never leave me again. But what if this time he doesn't have a choice?"

Sayings these things out loud, telling someone else all of the feelings that I have for Devin, is freeing in a way I never expected. It's almost as if, after he left all those years ago, I balled up everything inside, tucked it all away, and never talked about it again. "Do I sound crazy?"

"Not crazy," she whispers.

"I never felt for Wyatt what I feel for Devin, and it's terrifying because I haven't even seen him in ten years."

"Love doesn't have an expiration date, Katie. There is no cookie cutter for it, and there sure as hell aren't instructions. It just *is*. Who says you can't fall in love with someone who's already broken your heart? Who says you can't move on and then fall in love all over again from thousands of miles away via letters and e-mails? That's the great thing about love . . . it finds you. And when it's true love, it doesn't go away, and you just know. You don't have to wonder or guess, because it just . . . *is*."

"That's exactly how I feel." A sense of peace blankets me, a smile tugging at the corner of my mouth. "How did you get so smart?"

Mama laughs. "It's a mother thing. You'll understand one of these days."

"I love you. You know that, right? I know I was a pain after Daddy . . . after Daddy died, and I know I said some things and did some things—"

"You've already apologized. No more." Kissing my head, she slides from the bed and I sit up, wishing she would stay. There is just something about being wrapped in your mother's arms. For a few moments, I was a kid again, and her words and soothing touch had the ability to make everything better. "We all grieve in our own way, on our own schedule. I knew you'd get through it, you just needed time."

"Where are you going?"

"Home. I need to take care of the horses."

"No." Flinging my legs over the edge of the bed, I stand up. "I'll do it. I told you I'd take care of them."

Mama cups my face in her hands. "Not today." Her words may be simple, but they're firm, leaving no room for discussion. "You need to be here. I know you're worried, but try to stay positive and strong until you hear something."

That's easier said than done. "Okay, Mama. Thank you."

Following her through the house, I give her one last kiss before watching her walk out the front door. She shuts it gently behind her and I'm left standing in my living room. Everything is quiet and I feel lost, so I do the only thing I can do . . . I communicate with Devin the one way I know how in this moment.

To: Sergeant Devin U. Clay
From: Katie Devora
Subject:

Devin,

I left the subject line empty because I simply didn't know what to put. I'm scared. No, scared probably isn't a strong enough word. I'm terrified. I have no idea what happened today . . . Sure, I can take a few guesses, but what I know for certain is that you were torn away from me, your words cut off, and in a split second, you were gone. And right now I just really need to know that you're okay. Actually, you have to be okay because there are still so many plans we need to make and things that I need to tell you.

My mom came over after our phone call. I needed someone to be with me because I felt like I was falling apart. I told her all about how we became reacquainted, and I half expected her to go all Mama Bear because of the way things ended between us. But she didn't. She stepped up to the plate and took care of me, just like I needed her to do.

Okay, so I'm going to go about my day, cleaning the house and doing laundry, but don't think for a second that you aren't consuming every single spot in my head. Because you are, and that won't change until I hear back from you—and I will hear back from you. Please call me as soon as you can.

Love,
Katie

It's been twenty-four hours since I heard Devin's voice. Twenty-four hours of waiting, worrying, and pacing . . . and I have been doing a *lot* of pacing. And where there is pacing, there is thinking, and right now, I'm thinking about all of the things I may never get to say to Devin.

To: Sergeant Devin U. Clay
From: Katie Devora
Subject: I want you

Devin,

I had a dream last night that we were on the phone. You were laughing at something I said and there was a loud bang. It was a weird dream, because even though you were on the phone, I could see you. I watched you get thrown across the room and you were lying there, writhing in pain, and there wasn't a damn thing I could do. I was screaming, desperately beating at the invisible wall keeping me from getting to you, but it wasn't doing any good. I was frantic to get to you, but I couldn't.

That was it . . . I woke up in a cold sweat and then realized it wasn't a dream. I realized that it was real, only in reality, I don't know if you're okay. I don't know if you're lying somewhere, hurt . . . or dead. I've decided that I don't like the unknown . . . It leaves too much room for my mind to wander, and my mind doesn't usually wander in the right direction.

I have to work today. I'm not sure if working will be a good thing or a bad thing. You're still consuming every inch of space in my head . . .

and my heart. I forgot to tell you that the last time we spoke, but it's true.

Love,
Katie

Clasping my hands together, my gaze flits around the room, avoiding the computer sitting right in front of me. My stomach rumbles, but I don't dare put anything in it, not with the amount of throwing up that I've been doing.

Thoughts of Devin fill every second of every day. Yesterday after work, I broke down and began searching the Internet for any information that I could find. I had no idea what to search for, so I started combing through headlines on the Internet, hoping to see something—anything—that might give me some sort of peace . . . some sort of comfort in the hell I've been living. I found nothing.

Gritting my teeth, I try to fight the tremble in my chin, but it's a lost cause. My throat burns, constricting with emotion, as tears fall from my face. Wiping the tears away is pointless—I gave up on that a long time ago.

To: Sergeant Devin U. Clay
From: Katie Devora
Subject: I want us

It's been forty-nine hours, twenty-two minutes, and fourteen seconds since I've heard from you. I've checked my e-mail hundreds of times, hoping to see a reply, and each time I come up empty, a little piece of me breaks away. My phone has become a permanent fixture in my hand because I keep waiting for you to call.

I miss you. How did that happen in such a short amount of time? I miss seeing your name in my inbox . . . I miss reading your words, and with each passing second, I'm convinced that I may never see them again. I need to see them, Devin. You've always been a part of me, but this is still new and I'm not done exploring. I'm certainly not ready to let go.

I'm still holding on to hope.

Love,
Katie

"Hi, honey."

"Hi, Mom." It's the third time she's called today. I canceled my appointment with Dr. Perry, and I haven't shown up to take care of Mac, Molly, and Toby all week. I would never leave her to do it, so I've hired out extra help on top of the kid I've already got going there. She's worried . . . She should be. I can feel myself slipping, giving up hope with each passing second. I can see myself going down the road I've recently traveled . . . the one where I shut down because being numb is so much easier than feeling the pain.

"I'm making lasagna for dinner. Would you like to come over?"

"Nah. Thank you, though," I answer. "I made a pizza a little while ago." Closing my eyes, I cringe. Lying to her is not the grown-up thing to do, but I hate to make her worry, and right now, I just need to be alone.

"How about breakfast in the morning? I can make your favorite."

"I have to work."

"Don't do this, Katie," she pleads.

"Don't do what?" I hiss. "What am I supposed to do? Should I just pretend that he didn't exist, pretend that something horrible didn't happen—"

"I know it looks bad—"

"Looks bad?" I scoff, pressing my thumbs into my temples because, damn it, I do *not* want to cry right now. "It doesn't look bad, Mom, it *is* bad. I've done everything I can do, and I keep coming up empty-handed. I've contacted every military facility I can find, but nobody knows anything, or they just don't want to tell me. So either something terrible has happened, or . . ." My words, along with my thoughts, trail off.

"Katie, I don't want you to be alone right now."

"I have to go, Mom." Ending the call, I power my phone down, lock my door, grab my laptop, and crawl into bed.

To: Sergeant Devin U. Clay
From: Katie Devora
Subject: What do you say?

Devin,

My mind is fucking with me something fierce. I've considered the fact that maybe I've been duped . . . Maybe you're not responding to my e-mails or calling because this was all some sort of joke or game and I've been played. But then I read the letters you've sent me and I know that couldn't be it. Then I get mad at myself for even thinking it, because you promised you wouldn't hurt me again. And I do believe you.

Last night I cried myself to sleep because this pain that has settled in the center of my chest is becoming too much to bear, and each day it hurts just a little bit more. I had another dream about you, only this time you weren't hurt and it had nothing to do with our last phone call. In fact, you were here with me. We were in bed. My head was resting over your heart. Your left arm was wrapped around my shoulder, your finger drawing circles over my bare arm. It was per- fect. We were happy and didn't have a care in the world. And then I woke up and realized that I may never get to feel your skin against mine again, and that thought alone nearly brought me to my knees.

I want that, Devin. I want to see you. I want to feel your lips brush mine, to feel our fingers link the way they used to. But at the same time, I want to start over because we're two different people than we were back then. I want the firsts all over again with the man that you've become. I want the first date, the first awkward kiss—because there always is one (remember ours?)—the first non-awkward kiss, the first everything. I want to snuggle up next to you and fall asleep to the beat of your heart. I want to be woken up in the middle of the night by your touch . . . the list goes on and on, but basically, I want it all.

More than that, right now, I just want to hear from you. If I can't feel you, I want to hear your voice.

Love,
Katie

Chapter 17 | *Devin*

"Fighting My Way Back"—After Midnight Project

F ive fucking days I've been stuck inside this building with the entire company up my fucking ass. We stand all day, one beside the other, in the hallways, one hundred soldiers deep, with nothing to do but let our thoughts run wild and nothing more than what we were able to carry in both arms.

A lucky enemy mortar round hit our ammunition point, which led to secondary explosions best saved for the Fourth of July—and for way fucking further away than two hundred feet. Our own artillery shells and tracer rounds burst under the heat of the flames, arching aimlessly in a blaze across the sky.

Disregarding our own safety, we watched the show outside for a little while as the shells erupted into beautiful reds, oranges, and yellows. Eventually, we were called inside by leadership, who, by the way, have been staying in their own buildings and in their own rooms. So while we're left here like homeless people under an overpass, the pricks have been sleeping comfortably in their cots.

Not that there's been much sleep to be had. From behind these walls, it's sounded like the entire compound was in the middle of Armageddon. Two days ago the explosions stopped, and since then, explosive ordnance disposal teams from the Green Zone have picked through spent rounds, carefully loading those that failed to detonate onto trucks to be taken to the middle of nowhere and manually blown up. God knows what shape the compound is in right now.

As for headquarters, there wasn't any significant damage and no one was injured, thankfully. Some asshole in Third Platoon claimed he was hit with shrapnel, but it ended up only being some shards of glass from a broken window. What he really meant to say was that he's being a bitch and wants to go home.

Our radio communications are still up, but that's been our only connection to the outside world. Which means . . .

No phone.

No Internet.

No Katie.

I'm lying beside Navas in the middle of the hallway with the rest of the platoon sprawled out around us, and it feels like these walls are beginning to close in around me. I haven't really spoken to anyone in a while. I'm sick of talking and sick of pretending we aren't stuck inside this hellhole.

A blanket is tucked under each armpit and my head sits snugly against a pillow as I stare at the same *Sports Illustrated* I've read a thousand times before. All I can think about is Katie and what's running through her mind during all of this. I know she heard that last explosion, because I could hear her talking right before it hit. Her last words float around my head . . . *Devin, I'm scared.*

No one has cared about me—not since her—and I've never had anyone anxiously waiting for my return. But she does, and hopefully she is. In the meantime, it breaks my fucking heart that she might think I'm dead, just another person to leave her behind.

God, if I could only call—if I could just hear her voice— everything would be okay. The magazine falls from my hands. My temples throb with each flicker of the fluorescent light, and

I pin my eyes on the communications center just a few steps away. Knowing I can't get in there annoys the hell out of me.

Elkins chuckling strikes my ears like nails against a chalkboard, and I want to fucking scream. I want to grab the nearest officer and shake the living shit out of him. *Let me fucking out of here! Fix the fucking phone!*

The screeching sound of the main door opening makes me pop straight up and draws most of the eyes in the building. Captain Hendricks enters the main hallway and stops, scanning us as we all keep our eyes locked on him. We wait anxiously for him to speak, but he scurries quickly past us and into the operations center, joining the other officers. I drop back down and shut my eyes, but just as my lids are about to meet, I hear footsteps exiting the operations center. I look up to see Lieutenant Dixon making his way toward the front door, but he stops just before he gets there.

"Alright, we just got word from EOD that nearly all the ordnances are cleaned up and taken care of. We will still have engineers and communications teams here for the next few days to get everything back in working order, but you'll be able to go back to your tents tonight at 2100 hours." He finishes and turns to exit, and I quickly rise to my feet.

"Sir?" He stops in his tracks and turns to me. "What about the comm center? When will it be back up?"

"Did you not hear me, Sergeant Clay?" he snarls. "Communications teams will be getting everything back to working order in the next few days. You think you're the only one that wants to use the phone?" I envision myself strangling him, my thick hands squeezing his neck as he flails helplessly.

"Well, I didn't know if maybe they gave you a time frame . . . *Sir.*"

"Should be up tomorrow," he mumbles before strapping his helmet on and exiting the building.

"*Motherfucker,*" I hiss under my breath, dropping back to the ground.

I listen as the last truck rumbles out of the front gate and down the road. My cot feels like a California king and our tent like a suite at the Ritz right about now. I'm curled up in the dark, using my flashlight to light my way out of this place. I scan every line of every letter and email Katie has written me as I listen to the faint sounds of men working outside the tent, the very men I'm relying so desperately on to bring me closer to her—communication-wise at least. I pray they get the lines up before we set out on our mission tomorrow. I'm looking at three hours of sleep at the rate I'm going, but I don't care. I can't sleep because my mind is just too frantic, and I know it won't calm down until I talk to Katie. All I want to do is let her know that I'm okay . . . that I'm still here and I'm not going anywhere.

The alarm on my watch blasts for what has to be five minutes before I realize it's not a dream. Navas and a few of the others are half awake and grumbling for me to *shut it the fuck off,* and I finally shake the sleep away enough to mute the annoying sound.

0500.

The glaring numbers burn holes through my pupils. I glance over to my left and see the pile of letters beside me. It immediately reminds me what I'm doing up so early and kicks me into gear. I'll check every hour if I have to, but I *will* reach her before mission.

I labor out of bed and throw on my gear before making my way to the entrance of the tent. Peeking out, I see that the crews have finished working for the night. Equipment and maintenance vehicles are still scattered around the base, but there's not a noise to be heard or movement to be seen. I step out of the tent and walk toward headquarters, all the while counting the charred remnants where each mortar exploded. The walls of the Hesco barriers are painted black with soot and dotted with fresh holes, and a guard tower is still midrepair. Two small buildings used for storage are now in shambles, but the rest of the base seems to be intact. A quick chill shoots down my spine as I realize just how lucky we were.

We could've been killed. *I* could've been killed.

Just before entering headquarters, I look up to the sky and imagine God looking down at me. I mouth a "thank you" to Him, and in my head I say a short prayer: *Please let it be fixed, Lord. Please.*

Stepping inside, I first look through the open operations center door. For a second, I think I should just ask the radio operator if communications are back up, but I can't. If he tells me no, I don't know what I'll do.

Instead, I enter the communications center, take a seat and power up the computer, crossing my fingers tightly as I do so. The little bar dances back and forth across the computer screen, over and over and over again. My stomach tightens and my foot bobs at a pace any crack addict would appreciate. The seconds feel like hours as the word "loading" works its way under my skin.

And then it happens . . . the chime . . . the system booting up. *It's fixed!* Every tense muscle in my body relaxes. I settle into the seat and let out a long sigh of relief. Then, without hesitation, I quickly pull up my e-mail.

There are four messages from Katie, and I read each of them—more than once. With each one, my heart both breaks and then mends, and when my mind finally puts together the messages she left me in the form of subject lines, my heart expands to epic proportions.

She wants me.

She wants us.

I say, hell yes.

Tears blur my eyes, but I blink them away. I have to let her know that I'm okay. I check my watch.

0600.

Struggling to do the math in my head, I finally realize that it's only ten where she's at, so I rip the phone from the cradle, dialing her number as fast as my fingers will move.

Chapter 18 | *Katie*

"We Can Try"—Between the Trees

Dipping my hands into the hot, soapy water, I reach for a glass and then perform the same monotonous routine that I've been performing on this load of dishes for the past twenty minutes.

Scrub. Rinse. Repeat.

My eyes have been locked on a little girl playing in her yard across the street, but my mind isn't processing what my hands are doing or what my eyes are seeing. I've had a one-track mind for the past several days, and it's been on Devin.

I've carried my phone around in my hand like it's attached to my body, and every time it rings, my heart stutters to a stop. But it's never him, and with each day that's passed, what little hope I had left has slowly started to fade.

A soft knock sounds at the door, but instead of moving to answer it, I just yell at whoever is there to come in. Probably not the smartest idea, but right now I don't really care. My mind drifts back to thoughts of Devin when I hear the front door open and then shut, followed by the soft shuffle of someone walking toward me. Hopefully it's not a serial killer. I take that back—

"Hey, Kit Kat." At the gentle sound of Bailey's voice, I close my eyes, take a deep breath and pray to whoever is willing to listen that she takes pity on me, because I'm not up for much of a fight right now.

Pulling my hands from the sink, I dry them off with a towel and then turn around and prop myself up against the counter. Bailey is standing in the doorway, her shoulders hunched forward, her hands wringing together. I can't help but wonder what in the hell she's so nervous about.

My silence must be unnerving because she takes a step forward and says, "Thank you for taking care of me the other night."

Scrunching my nose, I think back to what she's talking about, and then I remember her drunken evening. "You were gone when I got up."

"Yeah"—she clears her throat—"sorry about that. I should've waited for you to get up, but I was embarrassed and still a little frustrated with you . . . well, more with myself . . . Anyway, I just needed to get out."

"How did you get home? You didn't have your car."

"My car was only a mile down the road at the bar, so I just walked." Bailey's eyes dart to the kitchen table and then back to me. "Mind if I sit?"

"Oh, um, no . . . go ahead, sit." I stay standing. Right here, I feel absolutely nothing, but if I move . . . well, if I move, that might change. And I really don't want that to change.

Bailey pulls out a chair, sits down and props her elbows up on the table. The room is eerily quiet, and judging by the way she's shifting in her seat, it's making her uncomfortable.

"Mama told me about Devin," she blurts. I can't say that I'm surprised.

"What do you want me to say, Bailey?"

"Nothing." Her eyes soften and she shakes her head. "I just . . . I wanted you to know that I'm here for you if you need me. I know things have been a little rough between us, but you're still my sister, and I want you to know that if you need a shoulder to cry on, or someone to sit down and eat a pint of cookie dough ice cream with, I'm your girl."

Her words wrap themselves around my heart, and suddenly, the urge to close myself off isn't as strong. But I don't give in because giving in means feeling, and right now I'm specifically trying *not* to feel.

"Thank you, Bailey."

She huffs and cocks her head to the side. Those three little words must not have been what she was expecting. "I'm sorry, Katie. There, I said it. I'm sorry for pushing you and for getting mad about the whole Wyatt thing. You were right, it wasn't my business. I just—"

My phone rings, cutting her off, and both of our eyes dart to the tiny silver contraption as it jumps across the table with each vibration. My heart stutters to a complete stop, and much like every other time my phone rings, adrenaline pumps through my veins. Closing my eyes, I attempt to calm myself down, but it doesn't work. *It never fucking works.*

"Here." My eyes pop open in time to see Bailey reach for my cell. She looks at the screen and then up at me. "Unknown number. Want me to hit 'ignore'?"

"NO!" Lunging forward, I snatch the phone from her hand, flip it open and push it against my ear. "Hello?"

"Katie." His voice cracks through the line; it's the sweetest fucking sound I've ever heard. Tears spring to my eyes and my trembling hand flies to my mouth. All of the tension instantly drains from my body as I slump against the cabinets and slide to the floor in a blubbering mess.

Bailey pushes from the table, runs across the room, and drops to her knees beside me, enveloping me in her arms. The faint sound of Devin's voice filters through the phone, but I can't hear him over the cries coming from my mouth.

"Devin," I gasp in between sobs. "Oh, God. I didn't . . ." A strangled moan rips through my lungs, my body rocking forward as my mind finally allows me to believe that this is real.

He's alive.

"Please don't cry, Katie. I'm okay." Devin's voice is soft and gentle, and I can tell by the hitch in his voice that he's feeling just as emotional as I am. My lungs fight to suck in air, and when I'm finally able to catch my breath, my eyes look heavenward and I mouth a silent "thank you" to whomever has been listening to my prayers. Looking down, I find Bailey watching me questioningly, and I give her a tremulous smile and nod. She slowly releases her hold and kisses me on the cheek before walking out of the room, presumably to give me privacy.

"I can't help it." I hiccup as I fight past the burning in my chest to just speak. "The explosion . . . and then the line went dead . . . You never called or e-mailed, and I had no way to get ahold of you, and . . ." With each word, the tears are returning at full force, emotion clogging my throat. "I thought you were gone. I didn't think I'd ever hear from you again, and—"

"And now you're hearing from me," he breathes. "Because I'm okay. Shit, Katie, I can't stand to hear you cry."

"I'm just glad you're okay." My voice is thick—strangled. "You have no idea what went through my head, Devin. I just got you back, and then the thought of losing you, it . . ." The words fell from my mouth before I even had a chance to process what I was saying, but now that they're out there, I don't regret saying them. Because it's true. He's back in my heart—hell, he never fucking left.

"I don't want to lose you," I whisper, batting away my tears. Devin's breathing sounds labored and heavy as though the weight of the world was just lifted from his shoulders.

"You're not going to lose me, Katie," he vows. "Getting ahold of you, getting back to you, it's all I thought about. *You* were all I thought about." We both go quiet but the faint sounds of sniffling and heavy breathing still pass through the line. I'm not sure who's doing what, but I honestly don't care.

"I got your e-mails."

I suck in a breath and hold it. *Did he put together my hidden message?*

"Did you mean it?" For the first time since reconnecting with Devin, he sounds unsure, and I hate that sound in his voice. It's something I don't ever want to hear again, not when it comes to us.

"Yes." I nod, even though no one is around to see it.

"I need to hear you say it, Katie."

"I want us." I infuse as much conviction as I can into those three little words, and Devin must catch on to it, because a huge sigh filters through the phone. "I want you," I continue, needing him to know how much this means to me—how much *he* means to me. "I've never stopped wanting you, Dev."

"God, Katie"—a string of incoherent words fall from his mouth before he clears his throat—"I can't tell you how bad I've wanted to hear you say that. And I feel the same way. You own my fucking heart, Katie. You always have and that's never going to change."

Tears are dripping down my face, but I'm unable to keep myself from chuckling. Not because what he said is funny but out of pure happiness. This euphoria is something I haven't felt in a long-ass time, and it's leaving me with a feeling of giddiness. "Now what?"

"Now we wait four more months until I get to come home. It's gonna be the longest four months of my entire fucking life," he says with a laugh.

"And then what?" I ask, needing to hear him say what my heart desperately wants to hear. "When you go on leave, then what?"

"Then I'm coming home . . . to you. And we're going to make up for every fucking second of the last ten years."

I nod, brushing at the never-ending stream of tears. Best thing I've heard in . . . ten years. I'm aware that when he goes on leave it doesn't mean that his tour is over, but one step at a time. We'll deal with that later.

Taking a deep breath, I hold it in and then blow it out slowly. This is really happening. "I like the sound of that. A lot."

"Katie?"

"Hmmm?"

"I don't have a lot of time to talk because we're getting ready to leave on mission, but I want you to know that if I could've called after the explosion, I would have. You know that, right?"

Shit. There for a second, I completely forgot about the explosion. "I don't even know what happened that day. Why didn't you call? Why couldn't you at least e-mail me to let me know that you were okay?"

Devin groans, and I picture him dropping his head back and running a hand through his hair like he did when we were kids. "Trust me, I would have, but those damn mortar rounds took out our communications center and it took days to get it up and running again."

I didn't even think of that. "That's not at all what was running through my head," I say, a shiver racing down my spine.

"I don't want to know what was running through your head."

"Hell no, you don't." My head falls back against the cabinet as relief sinks in, seeping its way through my body.

"I'm sorry, Katie."

I'm not sure what he's apologizing for, but the way his words come out makes it sound like everything. "You're forgiven." A smile spreads across my face because, in my heart, I know that he really is forgiven . . . for everything. Before, I wasn't sure if I'd ever be able to forgive Devin for the way he walked away from me, but that seems so insignificant right now compared to everything else that has happened. "No more apologies, okay? From now on, you and me, we keep moving forward."

"I like the sound of that," he says with a hint of playfulness in his voice. Heat radiates through my chest, and I reach for the spot that's been aching the past several days, only to find it gone.

The phone line gets scratchy and I hear several other voices before Devin speaks again. "Katie, I hate to do this, but I've gotta go. We're getting ready to leave, but I promise that I'll call you as soon as I can."

"You promise? No matter what time, you promise you'll call?"

"I promise," he says, laughing.

"Good. Because if I don't hear from you soon, you're in serious trouble."

"I find that incredibly intriguing, Miss Devora. What would be my form of punishment?" he says suggestively.

"Hah!" I bark out, a huge grin splitting my face. "Of course you would turn that into something dirty."

"You didn't answer my question. What's my form of—?"

"Goodbye, Devin." I sigh, feeling like the weight of the world has been lifted from my shoulders.

"Bye, Katie."

Chapter 19 | Devin

"If It Means a Lot to You"—A Day to Remember

I'm shedding my equipment beside my cot, just after mission, when Tavares bursts through the entrance of our tent, his frantic movements catching our attention. His eyes lock on mine and when I see the look of pity on his face, my blood runs cold. I know he's here for me . . . *but why?*

In three long strides, he's standing before me. His mouth opens and closes several times as though he has something to say, but he just doesn't know how to get it out.

"What's up, man?" I ask, dropping my body armor to the ground and unbuttoning my uniform top.

He remains silent and looks over to Navas, who is holding a Hot Rod magazine but has his eyes locked on Tavares, waiting for him to speak as well.

"Dude, Tavares, what the fuck is up?"

"We need you over at HQ . . ." His eyes flit around my face and his voice trails off. I can tell he wants to say more, but can't.

Now I'm annoyed.

"Who is *we*, Tavares?" I ask, trying to keep my voice as calm as possible.

"Captain Kendricks," he says before turning on his heel.

"No," I snap. He looks over his shoulder, and the determination must be written all over my face because he spins around to face me. "Tell me what's up."

"I'm not really sure. Kendricks didn't mention anything." I don't believe him, but I won't try and press him for more. I've known Tavares long enough to understand he says what he wants to and nothing more. If there is one thing in this life I've mastered, it's the ability to read people.

I follow Tavares to headquarters and the short walk is awkwardly quiet. He leads me inside to Captain Kendricks's small office. Tapping on the door, he's met with a deep grunt from the other side. Then he opens the door, motions for me step into the office and closes the door behind me. I take a seat, having absolutely no idea what's going on, but my mind runs through a hundred different scenarios. Not one of them is good.

Kendricks continues to shuffle through papers without acknowledging my presence. He finds what he's looking for and finally looks up. He has the same look of pity Tavares had, only his seemed forced, most likely out of habit. His conversations with the men below him are business, and only business.

"Well, Clay, I have some bad news." He pauses, crossing his arms over his chest. I'm immediately grateful that he tells it like it is; I respect a man that can do that. "We got a Red Cross message tonight, and . . . well"—he clears his throat but keeps his eyes on mine—"your mother died two days ago." He stops, presumably to let me process what he's just said. My mind is numb as I fight to comprehend his words. "There's not a lot of information there," he says, handing me a stack of papers, "but there's a number to call, and of course, we will have to get you on a plane out of here as soon as possible." I grab the paper from his hand and notice that mine is trembling. My hand never fucking trembles.

My mother is . . . dead. Gone. A rush of breath pushes through my lips and I close my eyes, only instead of thinking of Josephine, my thoughts travel to Katie.

Will I get to see her? Will she come to Pennsylvania to see me?

I should feel bad that this is where my thoughts are going, but I don't. Not after the hell my mother put me through.

"A plane, sir?" I know what he's saying, but in this moment, my mind isn't here.

"Yes, we gotta get you out for the funeral. It says in the message—I mean, you can read it yourself—but the funeral is in three days. We will have to get you on a chopper and to the Green Zone in the morning, and our operations men have set up a flight for you out of the country tomorrow evening. You'll be home by Friday," he says, handing me another piece of paper. I glance at it and see my itinerary. He stops for a moment, and for the first time during this meeting, he has a genuine look of pity on his face. "I'm sorry for your loss, Sergeant Clay."

"Thank you, sir," I mumble, my eyes drifting to his marble-topped desk as I mentally make plans to call Katie. *I have to call her. I have to see her.*

"Clay?" Captain Kendricks's deep voice catches my attention, and I look up. He wants to say something else but stops himself and simply nods.

"Do you know when the chopper will be here, sir?" I ask to fill the awkward silence that's taken up the room.

"0600 the bird will be here, so get your stuff together tonight and be prepared at 0530."

Nodding, I stand, the Red Cross message clenched in my hand. Without a word, I walk to the door before realizing how rude I must've come off. I spin back around.

"Sorry, sir. I'll be at the helipad at 0530."

He nods, accepting my explanation. "I'm sorry again, Sergeant Clay."

The walk back to the tent is almost like a dream. My senses have dulled and my mind struggles to understand. I wait for the urge to cry or feel an overwhelming sense of loss, but it never comes. I'm only numb.

The line rings several times and I wonder what they're going to tell me, if anything. My desire to call Katie is growing by the second, but I have to find out what happened to my mom first. As foul as that woman could be, she was still my mother, and I hope at the very least she died peacefully, though at her age I know that's impossible.

The line clicks and a woman's voice comes through.

"Red Cross Emergency Communications Services. This is Sharon. How can I help you?"

"Yes, ma'am, my name is Sergeant Devin Clay. I'm a US Army soldier deployed to Iraq, and I just received a Red Cross message about my mother's death."

"Oh, I'm so sorry to hear that, Sergeant Clay, and I must say, thank you so much for the sacrifices you and your family are making." Her words are saccharine sweet, but I have a feeling she does these sorts of calls entirely too often and her words are merely a script that runs through her head. I hear her typing away on the keyboard.

"Thank you very much, ma'am. Do you have any information for me?" I ask as she continues to type.

"Just . . . one . . . second . . . Yep, here we go. Josephine Clay, myocardial infarction, died April 18, 2006. The funeral is on April 23rd." She types again before continuing, "Now, Sergeant Clay, did your Command give you all of the funeral and travel information?"

"Yes, ma'am. Is there anything else I should know?"

"That should be it. Please give us a call if you have any problems with your travel arrangements. We are here to serve you, and again, if you don't have any further questions, thank you so much for what you're doing over there." Her words barely register because my mind is on one thing and one thing only.

It's been ten long years, and I'm ready to get my girl.

"No, I think I'm okay. Thank you, ma'am." I quickly hang up the phone and snatch it back up again, dialing Katie's number as fast as I can. With each ring, my heart pulses rapidly through my veins, a warm buzz sitting just under my skin. The excitement over seeing her is almost too much to comprehend, the thought of my mother no longer being on this earth, at least for the moment, being pushed beneath the surface.

"Devin?" Katie's voice crackles over the line and I can't help but smile. And then, without warning, an image of my mother and father holding each of my hands and swinging me in the air flashes in my head, bringing reality crashing down on me. Katie says my name again, but before I can answer, another memory comes barreling in. This time we're walking through Cedar Point, looking for rides suitable for an eight-year-old. I've got a snowcone in one hand and a stuffed bear in the other.

My legs go weak and I yank out a chair before dropping onto it.

"Devin? Are you there?"

My chest tightens and nose burns, and when I open my mouth to talk, my voice is choked with tears. "Katie."

Chapter 20 | *Katie*

"Carry On"—fun

"Wyatt—"

"Come on, Katie," he says, cutting me off, "I've been your best friend for years. And I was your fiancé, for cryin' out loud!" *Doesn't he realize that this isn't going to change anything?*

Looking at my watch, I notice the time. "Wyatt," I say, sighing, "can we talk about this later? I'm going to be late for my appointment." Pushing the driver's side door open, I step out of my car, shut the door behind me and click the lock before heading toward Dr. Perry's office.

"Just say yes," he says before giving a muffled apology for raising his voice. "Hell, you've already said yes, you just haven't followed through yet. It's dinner. One dinner. Give this to me, please."

"Fine," I relent, mostly because I'm getting tired of hearing him beg, and I'm hoping that I'll be able to prove to him—once and for all—that we are *over*.

"Really?" I almost laugh at the shock in his voice. "Okay then. How about Friday night?"

"Friday night is fine." Pulling on the door to the building, a gust of wind catches it and I grunt, trying to get it open.

"What time should I pick you up?"

Blowing a chunk of hair out of my face, I shrug out of my jacket and drape it over my arm. "You aren't picking me up. This isn't a date. I'll meet you at Bobby's at six."

"Bobby's?"

"Yes, Bobby's." I knew he wouldn't like that. Bobby's is a bustling café that is usually packed full of college students. It's not a good place at all for someone who wants to have a nice, intimate dinner—which is exactly what Wyatt wants. "Now I have to go. I'll see you then." I hang up before he finishes saying good-bye.

Walking up to the building, I pull open the door and step into Dr. Perry's waiting room.

"Good morning, Katie."

"Morning." I smile, signing in at the front desk before taking a seat against the wall.

"You can actually head on back. Dr. Perry is ready for you."

"Thank you." I drop the magazine I had just picked up and weave my way to Dr. Perry's office. She's already sitting in her plush chair, waiting for me with a giant smile on her face.

"Long time, no see, Miss Devora."

"Yes, well, it's been a long week," I say, hanging my jacket on her coat rack before walking over to that beautiful floral-print couch that I love so damn much. *Not.*

"Tell me about it."

I can't stifle the laugh as I drop onto the worn cushion. "How did I know you were going to say that?" Dr. Perry laughs too, and without a second thought, I tell her absolutely everything that's happened. We talk about Devin, and how I not only forgave him but let him back into my heart. We talk about Bailey and Wyatt and Mama, and when I'm finally done telling her everything about everything, she leans back in her chair and simply stares at me with a huge grin plastered to her face.

"What? What's that look for?"

"I'm speechless." She laughs again. "I don't really even know where to go with all that."

"Well, you could start with Devin. Do you think I'm stupid for letting him back in?"

"Do *you* think you're stupid for letting him back in?"

"Nice deflection."

"Thank you." She nods, her eyes sparkling with amusement.

"I think it feels right. I think it's the most right I've felt since before my dad died . . . Hell, it's probably the most right I've felt since before Devin left ten years ago. It's like as soon as I opened my heart up to the possibility of letting him back in, all the remaining resentment and sadness over what happened with him just went away. Suddenly, the gaping hole in my heart wasn't so empty anymore, and I like that feeling." My shoulders relax as though I needed to get those words out.

"Sometimes in life, we have to go with our heart instead of our head," Dr. Perry says, offering me a gentle smile "We have to trust that our heart will lead us on the right path, even if it's not the path we originally expected to be on." I nod, waiting for her to continue, waiting for her to give me the confirmation that I've already given myself. She smirks and shakes her head. "You're not stupid, you're human, and you're in love."

I suck in a sharp breath.

In love?

Am I in love?

Don't get me wrong, my feelings are still strong . . . but in love?

"Don't think too hard about that." Dr. Perry scribbles something on her notepad before dropping it on the table between us. "It's just an observation and not something you should be scared of. You're an incredibly intelligent woman, Katie. You just managed to get off track, but I'm not really worried about you."

"You're not?" *Really? Because I'm sort of worried about me.*

"No." Dr. Perry shakes her head and pushes a chunk of hair behind her ear. "You've got an amazing support system. I've watched you grow stronger every single time you've come in, and you're starting to make tough choices without getting overwhelmed. Plus, when you walked in here earlier, you looked lighter than I've ever seen you look. You looked happy."

"I am happy."

"Good."

"Can we talk about Wyatt now?"

Dr. Perry tosses her head back and laughs. "Absolutely! Let's talk about Wyatt."

"Am I leading him on by going to dinner with him?"

"No," she states firmly. "You know what you want, and that's Devin. What you're giving Wyatt is closure, and I think it's something that he deserves."

Well, I didn't think of it that way. "Closure, huh?"

"You didn't get closure when Devin left you. He just took off, and you were stuck behind to pick up your own pieces." I cringe when her words bring up an onslaught of memories—bad ones—but I get where she's coming from. "It seems Wyatt still needs closure, and maybe one last dinner will help drill home the fact that you haven't changed your mind."

"Alright." I nod. "How about Bailey?"

"Who's asking the questions here?"

"You are," I say, grinning.

"More than likely, Bailey feels guilty for the way she's been pushing you on top of everything you've gone through. Cut her some slack. She's your sister."

"So next time I see her, I just hug her and tell her I love her?" Because that's really what I want to do.

"I bet she would love that."

"I bet you're right."

"Now it's my turn." Dr. Perry folds her hands in her lap, and the smile slowly falls. "Let's talk about Andrew Drexler."

The first thing I notice is that when she says his name, I don't instantly panic. My body doesn't freeze up and my blood doesn't start to boil. "What about him?"

"Have you read his letter yet?"

It's sitting on my dresser at home. "Nope."

"Is there a reason why you haven't?"

I'm scared. "I haven't had time." My words come out more like a question and less like the statement I was going for.

Dr. Perry notices. "Haven't had time or haven't made time?"

"I've just come really far . . . at least I feel like I have."

"You have," she confirms.

"And I don't want him to set me back. I don't want to go back to that place."

Dr. Perry cocks her head to the side, her eyebrows furrowing. "You won't." Her words are laced with so much conviction that I almost believe her.

"How do you know?"

"Trust yourself, Katie. You're ready for this, and I think it's the closure that *you* need."

She's right.

I've felt so good these past couple of days, but something is still off—something that feels unresolved. Maybe it's this. "Okay," I say, pushing up from the couch. "But I better go do it now before I talk myself out of it."

"By all means"—Dr. Perry stands and motions toward the door—"go get your closure."

I slip on my coat, grab my purse, and pull open the door, and then I turn back to Dr. Perry. "Thank you."

"You're welcome, Katie." The look of pride on her face is unmistakable, and it gives me that extra push I need. "I'll see you next week."

No good-bye is needed. I simply give her a smile and step out of her office, determined to get home so I can read that letter.

My arms hang loosely at my sides before I shake them out as though I'm preparing to go for a run. Everything inside of me is screaming to do this, to get this over with, but the blood pumping in my ears is making it difficult to concentrate.

Closing my eyes, I count to ten while taking several slow, deep breaths. When I open my eyes, they instantly land on a photo of Devin and me that I found in a shoebox tucked away in my closet. We were probably about ten years old. His arm is draped around my shoulders, mine wrapped around his back. We both have mud caked to our faces and he's holding up a catfish. I'm not sure what it is, but there's something about that picture—that memory—that gives me courage.

Pulling open the top drawer of my dresser, I pull out the letter that my mom gave me several days ago. The envelope is stark white but worn around the edges, a telltale sign that it's been passed around and most likely opened numerous times.

Slipping my finger under the flap, I open the envelope and pull out the letter. My hands shake as I unfold it, and when I see handwriting scribbled across the paper, my heart nearly pounds out of my chest.

With the letter gripped in one hand, I situate myself on the bed, propping up on the pillows.

"Come on, Katie," I whisper, giving myself one last pep talk. "You've got this."

Dear Brenda,

I'm sorry doesn't seem like enough, but I'll say it anyway. I'll repeat those words over and over again for as long as you need. I don't expect your forgiveness, and it's not something I'll ever ask for, because I don't deserve it. I hurt you in a way that no human being should ever hurt another human being, and for that I'm truly sorry.

There's no excuse for my actions that night. I made a stupid decision and I got behind the wheel drunk. My lawyer tried to play it off that I'm scarred from my time served overseas, but I insisted that he stop. I didn't allow him to play the same card that so many other soldiers use as an excuse. What I've witnessed and gone through while at war holds no bearing over my actions that night.

But I do want to tell you what happened because you deserve to hear. My buddy Tom and I went out for dinner. I hadn't seen him since high school graduation and we were enjoying our time catching up. One beer led to another and then another, and before I knew it, I'd had close to seven beers. At the time, I thought I was good. Hell, I used to drink way more than that in college. But what I didn't take into consideration was that I hadn't had a lick of alcohol in over two years. Again, not an excuse, but I really want you to know what happened and why.

Anyway, I left the restaurant that evening knowing I shouldn't drive, but I didn't have anyone else to call. Tom had had more to drink than I did, so I decided to drive home. The house I was renting was only a mile down the road, so no big deal, right?

A half a mile from home I crossed the center line, and in the blink of an eye, I took someone's life—someone who, from what I've been told, was a loving husband, devoted father, and one hell of a farmer. But I know I didn't just take one life that night, I took four. I recognize that, in losing your husband, I managed to destroy not only your life but also the lives of your two daughters.

I hate that I survived. I would give anything to trade places with your husband, and I want you to know that I think about him—and about you and your daughters—every second of every day. I've prayed for your happiness and for comfort for your girls, and I hope that someday you're able to find peace despite the disaster that I caused.

Sincerely,
Andrew Drexler

I read the letter three more times before dropping it at my side. My pulse is steady and calm, not rapid and uneven like I anticipated it would be. Tears are running down my face because I believe that Andrew Drexler is truly sorry for destroying our lives. I do think that he would move heaven and earth to trade places with my dad, and that belief releases a rope of tension that I didn't realize was wrapped around my heart.

Something inside of me opens up, and as I swipe away the tears running down my face, I notice that I'm smiling. I'm actually smiling. I'm not sure what I was expecting from Andrew Drexler's letter, but it sure as hell wasn't this.

But I'll take it, because Dr. Perry was right. I needed this closure. I needed the opportunity to listen to his apology and make my decision whether or not to accept it. I'm damn glad I read his letter, and now I know why my mom and sister have accepted things so much easier than I have.

They opened their heart way before I did and they forgave him. They accepted Andrew's apology for what it was, they grieved the loss of their loved one and did what Daddy would want them to do.

Suddenly, the need to write Andrew Drexler back slams into me like a freight train, and I jump up, grab my notebook and a pen off my dresser, and drop back down on the bed. Opening up the notebook, I situate it on my knee. I'm ready to give my heart the closure that it needs, and as I transfer the words from my head to my heart and onto paper, I realize that it wasn't really closure that I needed, just love. Because the love of my family and my love for my dad ultimately led me to be able to forgive.

Dear Andrew,

I forgive you.

Thank you for serving our country. Thank you for your letter of apology. I hope that you're able to find the same peace that I have.

Sincerely,
Katie Devora

Chapter 21 | *Katie*

"Break Your Plans"—The Fray

"Devin?" A dull buzz is crackling through the line, and that coupled with the noise coming from my living room makes it hard to hear. Pushing up from the couch, I hold my hand over the receiver. "I'll be right back," I whisper to the room full of cackling women.

Mom and Bailey both smile and nod, but leave it to Maggie to open her big ol' mouth. "Who's on the phone?" she asks as she refills everyone's wine glasses.

"Devin—"

"Oooh, Devin," she croons before I even finish. Rolling my eyes, I walk out of the room as she yells, "No phone sex. It's not polite while you have company over." I hear my mom and Bailey crack up just as I shut my bedroom door.

"Devin?" At first I think I lost him—a dropped call or something—but then I swear I hear him breathing through the phone. "Devin? Are you there?"

"Katie."

"Hey! I thought I lost ya." Yanking the covers back on my bed, I climb in and prop myself up against the headboard.

"Um . . ." Devin clears his throat. "My day . . . it, uhh . . . shit."

His voice is too gentle, his thoughts too scattered, and the hairs on the back of my neck instantly stand up. "What's wrong? Are you okay? Are your men okay?" I ask, pushing myself upright as though it'll help me hear him better. My body tenses as I wait for his answer.

"No," he breathes. I hear rustling as though he's moving around or running a hand over his face. "I mean, yes. I'm okay, and my men are okay."

"Oh, good," I say, feeling my tightly coiled muscles relax.

"But I do have something to tell you."

"Looks like we'll be on the phone a while then," I say, settling back against the bed, "because I've had one hell of a day, and boy, do I have some stuff to tell you. But you first."

"My mom died." His words come out flat and completely lifeless, and it takes a couple of seconds for my mind to process what he said.

"What?" I gasp, flinging myself out of bed. "Oh my God, Devin." Tears spring to my eyes and I shake my head. "I'm so sorry." My heart aches, not because Josephine is gone—as bitchy as that might sound—but it aches for Devin. She may have been a shitty mother, and I had hopes that Devin would be able to find peace where she is concerned, but she's still his mom and now that's no longer an option.

He doesn't respond, although I'm not really sure what I expect him to say. I know the numbness that he's probably feeling right about now. Hell, I've been there—and not that long ago. "What can I do? I want to help. Please tell me what I can do."

Devin sucks in a breath and I swear I hear him sniff. That sound absolutely breaks my heart. Closing my eyes, an image of a ten-year-old Devin pops into my head. We were sitting by the creek and he was crying because of something his mom said, and I can picture him now, a grown man grieving the loss of the woman who's caused so much pain in his life. She doesn't deserve his tears.

"I'm going home," he says, his voice thick with emotion. "I get a four-day leave."

He's coming home? Oh my gosh, he's coming home! "You're coming home." It's not a question, just something I repeat to convince myself that what I heard is true. Excitement bubbles up inside of me, and despite what he just told me about his mother, I can't stop the smile from erupting on my face.

"I'll be home early Friday."

"Okay," I breathe. My mind instantly starts making a list of what I have to do to be able to go see him.

I'll actually get to see him.

I'll get to touch him, and hold him, and kiss him.

I'll get to tell him—

"I was hoping you could come . . . you know, out to Pennsylvania . . . to see me." There is insecurity in his words that softens my heart. I obviously haven't done a good enough job of convincing him that I really do want *us,* and everything that goes along with that.

"I'll be there. I don't want you to go through that alone." And he would have to go through it alone. Devin has no one. His father has been absent for longer than I can remember, and he's an only child.

"You will?" he asks, his voice full of disbelief. "You're going to fly out there?"

"Yes," I say. "Of course, I'll have to rearrange a few things. I'm supposed to work on Saturday and Sund—"

"You don't have to take off, Katie."

"Stop it," I scoff, walking out of my bedroom and into the kitchen. I pull my work schedule out of the drawer to see who's off that might want to pick up some extra shifts. "I want to take off; it's just short notice so I'll have to find my own coverage."

My mind drifts to all the other things I'll have to do like book a flight and find a hotel—because I don't want to be presumptuous and assume that Devin wants me to stay the night with him. And honestly, I don't even know where Devin will be staying.

"I'm getting a hotel," he says, catching my attention.

"Huh?"

"You said you don't know where I'll be staying." Shit. Saying stuff out loud is becoming a habit for me. "I'll be staying at a hotel, and if you come, you'll stay with me."

The way he says that, as though I don't really have a choice, causes my mind to conjure up all of the things I'll get to do to—I mean *with,* do *with*—Devin over the next four days.

"Okay," I say, cringing when my words come out way too raspy.

"Other than take off work, what else do you have to do?" he asks. "You've got someone to help with the farm, right?"

"Yes. I'm not worried about the farm, and other than that, I'll just have to cancel dinner plans with Wyatt and—"

"Dinner plans with Wyatt?" he interrupts in a tone I haven't heard in about a decade.

Dropping my work schedule on the table, I stand up straight. Did I hear him right? Is he mad? He can't be mad; I haven't even had a chance to tell him why I was having dinner with Wyatt.

"Yessss," I drawl out. "Wyatt asked me to dinner Friday night, and with everything that's happened, I felt the least I could do is meet with him." Plus, it'll be nice to tell Wyatt about Devin myself before he ends up hearing about it through the grapevine. It sounds asinine, I'm sure, considering that I still haven't seen Devin. But if he really is coming home on leave in four months, and we really do decide to give this a whirl—which we are, otherwise I'm kicking him in the damn balls—then everyone will find out anyway.

The last thing I want is for Wyatt to think I broke things off with him to be with Devin, because that's far from the truth. Plus, I was hoping Wyatt would be able to get some closure, once and for all.

"So you said yes?"

"Of course I did." My brows furrow, and I bring my hand to my hip. "He was my best friend for years, Dev. He picked up the pieces that you left behind, and—" Devin flinches and I close my eyes. "I didn't mean it like that. I wasn't trying to make you feel bad . . . and I'm sorry, but it's true. You have to understand that he's been there for me through everything, and I broke his heart. He needs closure and I owe that to him."

"Fine." My blood runs cold at the sound of Devin's voice. "I understand. Do whatever you've got to do."

"Don't be like that," I plead. "The dinner means nothing, and I'm going to cancel it, just like I'm going to find a way to get off work. I promise you, I will try my absolute hardest to make sure I'm there with you the entire time you're home, okay?"

"Okay."

What? That's it?

"Devin, I—"

"Look," he says curtly, "I've gotta go pack. I'll e-mail you my itinerary. You just let me know if you're able to rearrange your busy schedule."

"Excu—" I pull the phone back and stare at it.

Did he just hang up on me?

"Katie?" I look up at the sound of my mom's soft voice and find her standing in the doorway of the kitchen. "Is everything okay?"

"Josephine passed away."

"Oh no," she croons, stepping further into the room. "What happened?"

"I . . ." It hits me all at once that I didn't even bother to ask him how his mom died, and I instantly forget that I'm mad at him. "I don't know."

"How's Devin holding up?"

"Not good, from the sounds of it," I answer, looking down at my phone and then up at her. "He's shutting down." I should know. I was the queen of shutting down for several months. "I can hear it in his voice."

"Well, then it's a good thing he has you, isn't it?" she says, pulling me into her arms. "Because you know a little something about that, and maybe you'll be able to help when you get to him."

"How did you know I was going to him?" I ask, pulling away from her just a fraction.

"Because you love him."

"He's your lobster," Maggie sings, sashaying into the room with Bailey following close behind.

Mom laughs and gives her a sidelong glance. "You and that damn lobster."

"Hey," she says, holding up her hands, "blame Phoebe." She walks up to the table and grabs my work schedule. "What's this for?"

Mom fills her and Bailey in on what little I told her, and then Maggie turns to me. "I'm off those days; I'll pick them up for you."

"Really? Maggie, you just made my freakin' year." Stepping out of Mom's arms, I walk straight over to Maggie and pull her in for a hug.

"That's what friends are for. Plus, Sean is out of town, so the extra work will keep me out of trouble."

"I love you, Mags. You know that, right?"

"Of course you do," she says and laughs, wrapping her arms around my shoulders. "What's not to love? I'm amazing."

"And conceited," Bailey mumbles, earning herself a slap on the arm from Mom.

"I'll owe you big time," I say at the same time Maggie pulls away from me.

"Nope." Gripping my shoulders, she spins me around and leads me to my bedroom. "You owe me nothing." Pulling my suitcase from the closet, she tosses it on the bed and opens it up. "You're my best friend, Kit Kat, and I want you to be happy. Now get packed and then I'll help you book a flight."

"Thank you."

"You can thank me when you see the lingerie I've got waiting for you at home. I'll get it for you later, but you're taking it with you."

"First, I'm not taking lingerie with me." Because how fucking embarrassing would that be if I took lingerie and then we didn't even . . . bowchickawowwow. "Second, why in the world do you have lingerie for me? You just found out about this trip."

"It was something I picked up for your bachelorette party, but since you went all *Runaway Bride* on me, I figure I'll give it to you now."

"I didn't go all *Runaway Bride*," I argue, giving her my best pouty face.

"Semantics." She waves her hand through the air, and I can't help but laugh at her crazy ass. "There was going to be a wedding, now there's not. We don't really need to hash it out any more, especially since you've got more important things to do."

Spinning on her heel, Maggie walks out of the room and I'm left staring at my empty suitcase, wondering what in the hell I'm going to pack. My gaze drifts to the picture of Devin and me that's tucked in the frame of my mirror. I walk over to my dresser, pick up the photo and run my thumb across it.

"Ten years," I whisper to myself. Closing my eyes, I send a silent prayer up to the big man . . . God, or my dad . . . right about now, I'll take either one.

Please don't let him break my heart again.

Chapter 22 | *Devin*

"I'd Hate to Be You When People Find Out What This Song Is About"—Mayday Parade

"Katie? Hello?"

All I hear is static before the phone line clicks and switches back to a dial tone. I slam the receiver into its holster and run my hands through my hair, trying my best to calm down. *Of all the times for this shit to cut out.*

I take a deep breath in and reach for the phone again before stopping myself. I wonder for a moment if I even want to call her back. I don't know if I'm pissed, jealous, or maybe both, but right now all I want to do is spend time with my men—who also happen to be my friends. And when I want to escape these thoughts of Katie and my mother, they're the best antidote available.

I rise to my feet and head toward the exit, all the while doing my best to pretend she wasn't planning on seeing Wyatt and fighting to shake thoughts of them together . . . holding each other, kissing each other, fuck—

No. *Hell* no. I'm not fucking going there.

The chopper came just as expected at 0600. The quick ride to the Green Zone was a blur as the rhythmic whip of the blades forced my tired eyes shut. Navas spent several hours the night before pulling everything out of me, though I fought tooth and nail against it. And as I now sit at the military air terminal waiting on the C-130 to arrive, my eyes burn while scanning the enormous room full of hundreds of other military personnel funneling in and out. I try and catch sight of one I may know, as unlikely as it is, because in this moment of total isolation even in this crowded room, all I want is familiarity.

What I really want is Katie, but all I can think of right now is that she needs space . . . that as much as I want to talk to her, as much as I want to see her, she does have unsettled business and I can't get in the way of that—no matter how much I may need her. She tells me that she's over Wyatt, that what they had is in the past, but how can it be when it just ended? I want to believe her, but a tiny voice in the back of my head is holding me back, keeping me from believing that I ever had a chance. So I spend the next thirty minutes running our phone conversation through my head, and when my plane finally arrives, I breathe a sigh of relief.

The C-130 flight to Germany went by in a flash, and as I shuffle onto my second-to-last flight of the day, a nine-hour trip across the Atlantic, I'm actually grateful for the ridiculously early chopper—and even Navas for his hours of concerned interrogation—because my sleep on the C-130 flight was better than any I've gotten in a very long time. I think, more than anything, it's the knowledge that—at least for now—I'm out of harm's way.

In usual cruel fashion, thoughts of my guys come into focus. Seeing the snug, pleather Lufthansa seats in rows before me, I can't help but feel guilty that I'm not back there with them. If something happens to one of my men while I'm gone, I don't know what the fuck I'll do.

I pour myself into my seat and slip the window shade open.

Light comes in waves through the little oval window, first blinding me, then exposing the busy airport tarmac and gorgeous city of Frankfurt. I'm taken aback by just how differ-ent this place is compared to where I've just come from—how oblivious these people are to what others are going through at this very moment.

I'm startled as an older woman slides in beside me, and I can't help but stare. She looks like my mother, only with dirty blond hair instead of dark, which stretches the length of her back. And just like Josephine, her skin is weathered and tan. It's as if my mom is sitting right next to me.

Since she appears noticeably disturbed by my gawking, I pull my eyes away from her and force them to look out the window. I don't want to think about my mom, but the woman beside me brings the memories in waves. The worst ones dominate any positive thoughts I could ever have of her. I hate her for the years I lost with her. I hate her for not letting me say good-bye. I *hate* her for choosing the drugs over me.

The house is unusually dark, and with the shades drawn, it's hard for me to see much of anything. I slip my backpack off and set it on the couch, making note of the geometry homework that I know is inside and still needs to be finished. A house this dark when I get home from school usually means Mom is out for the night, but her car is in the driveway and I can hear rustling sounds and muffled conversation coming from her room in the back of the house.

I flip the light on and I'm stopped dead in my tracks, eyes wide, as I take in my surroundings. The glass coffee table is shattered to pieces, her favorite sculpture—a stone representation of St. Francis, the patron saint of animals—sits just inside the metal frame of the table with bits of glass sprayed out around it in every direction. The bookshelf is toppled over with books scattered all across the hardwood floor.

If I hadn't seen this a time or two before, I'd be three blocks away by now and yelling for the neighbors to call the cops . . . but this is no home invasion. It hasn't happened in a long time, but my mom has been known to destroy shit when she either couldn't get any blow or prescription pills, or when she's had entirely too much. As I creep down the hall, I'm debating which of those scenarios I'd rather deal with.

Just feet from her bedroom door, her rail-thin body bolts from the room, but she stops immediately when she sees me. Her hair is matted and drenched in sweat. Her eyes are wide with dark circles settled beneath them, and the size of her pupils tells me she's clearly high as a kite.

I can't move. In this moment, I am terribly afraid and my brain tells me to run as fast as I possibly can, but my legs won't cooperate. When she first stepped into the hall, she looked confused and full of despair, but now, as she inches toward me, the evil in her eyes sends chills down my back. Her jaw is clenched and she grinds her teeth so hard I can hear it. She lifts a thin finger and jabs it in my direction.

"You!" Her voice is ragged, her breathing heavy, and the veins in her neck are thick and pulsing. At this point, she likely doesn't even know who I am, though the way she scowls at me right now makes everything seem uncomfortably personal.

"You little fuck . . ." she growls, taking two more steps toward me, so close I can smell the bourbon on her breath. I back up a few steps, knowing full well when she mixes alcohol with pills or coke, she becomes someone else entirely. Not a human, but an animal, desperate for prey, that wants nothing more than to cause harm. She wants someone else to hurt as much as she does. And unfortunately, that someone is probably going to be me.

"Mom, wha-what's wrong?" I stammer, reaching for the knob to my bedroom door as I back up. My hand comes in contact with the cool metal and I cling to it, ready to yank myself inside if need be.

"What's wrong?" She stops moving and stands up straight. The angry, evil look on her face looks almost comical, like she's remembering a joke she heard a few hours earlier. "What's wrong?" She laughs as though that same joke was the funniest thing she'd ever heard. "What's wrong is you . . . What's wrong is that I had a perfect marriage until you. What's wrong is I fucking hate you," she hisses, and though I've heard these words before, this is the first time I actually believe them. "You're a fucking tumor."

I fight it with all my might, but a tear makes its way down my cheek. I didn't want to cry, not in front of her, but since the first one has fallen, it's as if the floodgates have opened. This is my mother, the woman who is supposed to love me.

The tears fall faster than I can dry them. I dab my shirt against my eyes, hoping that when I pull it away, she will be back in her room. But instead, she's even closer. My back is flush against the door and she brings her finger to my face, causing me to flinch and draw back. I smack my head against the wall, but that doesn't stop her. Instead, she slides her pointer from my chin to my eye, collecting some of the tears, and then she pulls her hand back to examine it. She looks down at me and then back at her finger with disgust before wiping it on my shirt as if she could catch something from it.

"Fuck your tears. Do you know how many tears I've cried over you stealing my life from me? How many tears I've cried because I didn't listen to your father and get rid of you like he told me to do?" The last part cuts through me like a knife, my heart exposed to the cold, hard world and forever changed because of it.

But I'm not sad anymore, though the tears still pour. No, now I hate her. In fact, right now, I could kill her. I want to erase her from my memory and pretend my mother died a long, long time ago.

Just as I'm about to lose it, she turns and charges back to her room, slamming the door so hard I can hear every picture in her room tumble to the floor. Pushing my door open, I quickly slip inside, shut it behind me, and burrow into bed. I bury my face in my hands, and for longer than I'd like to admit, I cry.

The tears begin to dry and I pull a picture from my nightstand, the only one I have of my mother and father together—the only one I have of my father at all. I'm eight years old and seated in both of their laps, all of us with Mickey Mouse ears on. It's my favorite picture, probably because it's the last time I remember us being happy. I managed to swipe it from my mother before she burned every picture with my father in it, everything he ever bought or touched or looked at . . . My childhood literally went up in flames.

I stare at the picture for an eternity, and for the millionth time, I coat it with a fresh layer of tears. Once I've cried my last tear, I make my way to the kitchen and pick up the phone, because right now there's only one person I want to see—the only one that can take this pain away. And she's the only family I'll ever need.

"Katie?" A voice tugs at my consciousness, pulling my eyes open, and for a second, I have no idea where I am or who could be talking to me. I rub my palms into my eyes and try to wipe away the fogginess.

"Sorry, I didn't mean to wake you. Your eyes were open just a few moments ago and you seemed alert." *Really? Alert?* My coherence finally returns and I recognize the woman, who sort of looks like my mother, looking very motherly at me. *My mother. I'm on a flight. My mother died. I'm heading home.*

"How long have we been flying?" I ask.

"A little over six hours. Do you not remember speaking with me a few times along the way?" she asks, sounding concerned.

I scan my brain but come up empty. Then, as if making sure my limbs are still intact, I scan each sleeve of my uniform and both pant legs, and then I look around the plane, taking everything in. "I'm sorry, I don't. I . . ." She puts a hand up to stop me.

"Don't worry about it. I can only imagine what little sleep you all get over there. Thank you for what you do, by the way. I have a lot of family that served and continue to serve. I was actually over in Germany visiting my son and his wife. He's in the Army and they had their first baby, so I got to see him. Now I'm making my way back to Memphis via JFK." She pauses briefly, putting a hand to her mouth to capture a yawn, then continues. "Of course, we've discussed all that, so sorry if I'm repeating myself."

I shake my head. She's not repeating anything, to my knowledge. I'm a little embarrassed and shocked that I had conversations with this woman and don't even recall them.

"Wait, so what about Katie?" *Did I talk to her about Katie?* "You sure do talk about her in your sleep . . . a lot." She giggles a little and then catches herself.

"Really? What was I saying?"

"Well, you weren't making a whole lot of sense. It seems you are desperate to get to her though, and judging by the way you were calling out to her, I'd say that you love her very much. I guess that's why I asked. I'm hoping for a good love story to pass the time. Oh, how I love a good love story!" She smiles at me, squeezing her hands to her chest. I'd rather just settle my head and arms on top of the tray table and go back to sleep, but she's too damn sweet. I can't be an ass to her.

"An old flame, I guess you could say." It's the only thing that comes to mind. I search for more, but there's nothing. Nothing my clouded brain can come up with, and nothing I want to share with this complete stranger.

"And are you on your way to see this *old flame?*" She puts a hand on my shoulder. "Gosh, I'm so sorry! Look at me being all nosy and obnoxious!" She shakes her head from side to side, scolding herself under her breath.

"No, you're fine, ma'am. I know how these long flights can be. I'm sorry I've been a rude neighbor." I force a smile. "To tell you the truth, I'm not really sure if I'll see her or not. I hope to, but it's been a long time and a lot has happened." *Yeah, Wyatt has happened.*

"Oh dear, you don't know if you'll see her? Tell me she knows you're on your way home."

"She does." I'd love nothing more than for this conversation to end, and if this were one of my guys, I would've told him to shut the hell up already. But I try my best to remember where I am and who I'm talking to. "I sent her my itinerary. The rest is up to her."

She almost speaks but catches herself, then looks to be deep in thought before she continues. "Take it from a mother, though I'm sure you have your own to give you advice"—*if she only knew*—"but stop being such a guy!" She laughs and pats my shoulder softly. *If this conversation goes on any longer . . .*

"If you love this girl, which it sounds like you do, you need to make sure it happens. You need to do everything in your power to see her, to show her that you love her." She waits a moment, settling back into her seat, and bowing her head. "Gosh, I'm sorry. Terry—that's my boy—he tells me all the time I talk way too much to strangers. I just can't help it."

"You're fine, ma'am. I appreciate it. I really do." I check my watch and let out a groan as I realize only twenty minutes have passed. "I'm sorry, I hate to cut the conversation short, but I'm exhausted. I might try and get some more sleep." I fake a yawn, though I don't really need to . . . I could sleep for days. But even if I couldn't, I don't want to talk about Katie. And I certainly don't want to think about the possibility of not seeing her.

"Of course! Please do, sweetie. You deserve to get some rest."

"See you in New York, though I'm sure we'll be having more sleep conversations before we get there, for which I apologize ahead of time." I force a laugh and one last smile, then nuzzle my head into my arms, folded over the tray table. As I drift off to sleep, there's only one person on my mind . . . *Katie.*

"Can I come over?" I ask, my voice trembling over the phone.

"Of course. Is everything okay? Are you okay?" It's amazing how, almost instantly, Katie's voice can soothe the worst of pains. I desperately want her in my arms.

"I'll tell you about it when I get there. I just gotta get out of here."

"Come over, please. I'll wait for you outside."

"Okay, I'll see you soon." I hang up the phone and head out the door. If my mom had given me two more damn months before she had her meltdown, I'd be sixteen and able to drive to Katie's house. Instead, I curse her under my breath as I grab my bike from the side of the house and quickly pedal away.

The ride goes quickly, and before I know it, I'm pulling onto the gravel road that leads to Katie's property. The porch light is on, casting a dull glow over her body, and just seeing her brings me relief. Skidding to a stop, I jump off the bike, drop it to the ground, and Katie instantly propels herself at me. She envelops me in her arms, holding me tighter than she ever has before. The warmth of her touch and the soft reassurances she's whispering against the side of my neck make my heart throb inside my chest. I squeeze her back, nuzzling my nose into her shoulder and letting a few tears pass from my eyes to her skin. My heart is home.

"Come inside," she whispers, taking my hand and pulling me toward the door. In this moment, I am at her complete mercy. She has my heart, and she always will.

"Devin, I don't even know what to say." She runs her hand softly down my cheek and I lean into it, taking in every bit of her touch. "I knew things were bad and we've talked about it before, but this . . ." She trails off and she bows her head, letting a few tears run down her cheek. I brush the tears lightly from her face and pull her against me, wrapping my arm around her shoulder.

"You don't have to say anything, you know that. Just being here with you is enough." She looks up, her gorgeous brown eyes sparkling with fresh tears, and it takes everything I have not to kiss her.

We have always just been friends, and although we've had many moments like this, we've never let anything go further. I've wanted to for so long, and not kissing her has been like a slow, painful death, but I don't want to ruin our friendship. I'd rather have her in my life as a friend than not have her at all.

She slips her bottom lip between her teeth and drops her head to my shoulder. "You promise this is enough?"

The first thing I want to blurt out is 'are you fucking kidding me?' *But I haven't watched all those romantic comedies for nothing. I know I need to play it cool. "You're my best friend, Katie. The person I trust more than anyone in this world. You're the only one on this earth that could make it better. This . . ." I pull her even closer to me and plant my lips on the top of her head. I let them linger there a bit, breathing her in before pulling away. "This is everything."*

I can see the tears welling in her eyes, and she's trying her hardest to keep them off of me. I place two fingers gently against her chin and turn her head toward mine. Her eyes still look down and her eyelids do the best they can to blink away the tears. "Katie," I say, sweet but firm. She bats her eyelids several more times before looking at me. "Why are you crying?"

She sniffs and wipes her face before answering. "God, Devin . . . I just wish . . . I wish . . . I wish I could take all your pain away." She rests her head against my shirt and wipes some of her tears on it. She doesn't know this, but I love when she does that. It feels like she's sharing a part of herself with me.

"You do take my pain away, Katie." Cupping her cheeks in my hands, my eyes roam her face, and before I realize it, my lips are on hers. To my surprise, she doesn't pull back, instead pushing her mouth tighter against mine, effectively sealing any gaps. Her lips are softer and sweeter than I could have imagined, and when my tongue traces the seam of her lips, she opens willingly. With each stroke of her tongue against mine, my heart pounds and the pain subsides just a little bit more.

I awoke to a nearly empty plane and a flight attendant poking me in my side. A Post-it note was stuck to the seat in front of me, and it read:

Tried to wake you up.
You're quite the heavy sleeper,
but don't worry, you didn't drool.
I have a connection flight I must make.
Nothing but the best to you, soldier.
Chase your heart. Find Katie.
Cheryl

The Post-it note remains clutched in my hand as I board my last flight, take a seat in the rear and buckle myself in. As the flight takes off and we gain altitude, I reread her note many times and can't help but feel disappointed that I didn't have a chance to say good-bye to my sweet but chatty seatmate. It's funny the random people you bump into and the effect they can have on you.

The violent thrashing of the plane jolts me from my thoughts and passengers start stirring in their seats. It comes and goes at first, and then a long rattle takes over that makes it feel like the plane just might break into pieces midair. Most of the passengers on the plane cry out, drowning out the pilot over the intercom, but I remain quiet. My pulse could beat its way through my veins, but I sit still, clutching each armrest tightly in my hands and watching the scenes of my life play like a movie in my head. I'm forced to realize the ironic and random nature of death. It is very likely that I could survive two deployments to a combat zone and die right here on the plane ride back home. *What a mindfuck.*

As the chaos erupts around me and the turbulence continues to make death all too real for everyone on board, I can't help but think of Katie. I can't believe how dumb I'm being, and what an insecure and jealous asshole I've been. I shouldn't have acted the way I did on the phone. It was obvious that she wanted to see me, but I sure as hell didn't make it clear how badly I wanted to see her. She was going to clear her schedule and then *I* fucked it up.

It doesn't matter though because I'll make it right, even if I have to go to Tennessee. I don't care if I have to drive all night, I *will* see Katie Devora, and I *will* tell that beautiful woman that I want her—and only her—for the rest of my life. And then I'll explain to her that every day I've been without her, I've lost a little part of myself, and I'll work my ass off to prove to her that I can be the man she deserves. No more walking away, and certainly no more hothead moments.

The turbulence eventually stops and people do their best to calm down, some muttering prayers, and I find myself taking a deep breath. Never again will I take for granted what Katie has given me and what she brings to my life. Never again will I let my pride get the best of me.

These thoughts are what get me through the hour-long flight from New York to Pittsburgh. I'm fucking ecstatic at the possibility of seeing Katie, but I'm conflicted by the death of my mother and how it will feel to put her into the ground. I need to get through the funeral and say good-bye to Josephine, and then I can focus on the reunion I've waited ten long years for.

My foot bobs rapidly as my thoughts race, and even three Bloody Marys haven't calmed me down. And then it happens . . . the loud ding followed by the flight attendant announcing our final descent. I flip open the window shade and take in the familiar sights of my old stomping grounds. *One step closer to Katie.*

Getting off the plane and walking into the airport is like getting hit by a wave of nostalgia. I haven't been in this airport since the flight that took me to basic training. And though many things have changed since then, it still feels so familiar and comforting. Before I know it, I'm heading toward baggage claim with a toothy smile that I'm sure causes a few stares. I just don't care. None of them would ever guess I was here for a funeral, and I know I should feel guilty for that, but going from a toxic war zone to a place I called home so long ago, a place without bullets, bombs, and death, is almost overwhelming. I want to strip this uniform from myself, throw on some jeans and a T-shirt, and just be normal again.

The escalator that takes us to where we pick up our baggage couldn't be longer, or any slower, and I'm anxious to the point that I'm getting annoyed. Squeezing my eyes shut, I run a hand over my face and stifle a groan. Dropping my hand, my eyes reopen, instantly landing on a familiar set of brown eyes—although they're not locked on me. My limbs tingle right before going completely numb, and when the escalator drops me off at the bottom, I nearly stumble to the ground.

Katie.

She's scanning the area to the left of me, and I know that any second she'll see me. I could call out to her, but right now I'm enjoying being able to just look at her. Her hair is longer than I remember it, and she has dark brown waves hanging messily over her right shoulder. She's *my* Katie . . . only older, more mature. Her tits are bigger, her hourglass figure clearly defined through her tight T-shirt, and her hips are fuller too. She's fucking sexy as hell, and don't get me started on those mile-long legs. Her body has definitely changed, and I can't wait to get my fucking hands on her.

My hungry gaze travels up the length of her body, and when my eyes land on hers, she's watching me, tears running down her flushed cheeks. So I do the only thing I can do . . .

Chapter 23 | *Katie*

"A Thousand Years"—Christina Perri

Pushing my way past the other passengers, I hurry up the ramp. My flight was delayed by an hour, which ultimately meant our flights landed at the same time. Normally, this wouldn't be a problem. Today, however, it is.

I haven't talked to Devin since yesterday. After he hung up, I received an e-mail with his itinerary, and I haven't heard a word since. Did I piss him off to the point where he didn't want to see me? I told him that what I had with Wyatt is over—that it was over long before he came into the picture. Shouldn't he trust me?

Running through the terminal, I find Gate 13, only there are people swarming everywhere. Weaving may way through the crowd, I get as close to the ramp as I can. Pushing up on my tiptoes, I jump around, trying to get a better look, but the crowd is too thick. And that's when I realize . . . These people are waiting to board. I glance down at my watch and then elbow my way to the information desk.

"Excuse me," I ask, tapping the counter.

The perfectly coifed woman looks up, clearly irritated with my tapping, but right now I don't have time to give a damn. "Can I help you?" she asks.

"Flight 4402 from JFK," I say, pointing out the window to a plane on the tarmac. "Did it just land? Are the passengers still on board or—?"

"They've already exited the plane, ma'am."

"Shit," I hiss, running a hand through my hair. My heart plummets inside my chest and tears prick my eyes. "Thank you." I offer her the best smile I can muster, and then I turn to look for the sign indicating Baggage Claim.

"Miss?"

I spin around and look at the woman that just inadvertently ripped my heart out. And I'm not just being melodramatic. If I missed Devin, then I have no way of getting ahold of him. I have no phone number, no address for his mom's house, and I have no idea what hotel he's planning on staying at. Essentially, I'm all alone—in Pittsburgh of all places. "Yeah?"

"The passengers probably haven't made it to Baggage Claim yet." *Yes!* A smile creeps across my face and she returns it. "If you hang a left at the bathroom right there," she says, pointing to the left, "go down the escalator, and then hang another right, you can probably beat them. It's a shortcut." She winks, and I take off.

She was right. Baggage Claim was only a hop, skip, and a jump away. The only downfall? This place is fucking packed. By the looks of it, every damn plane on the tarmac landed at the same time.

There's no way I'll find Devin in this crowd.

My eyes scan the room, and once again I'm hopping around on my toes, trying to get a good look but seeing a whole lot of nothing. What little hope I had is dwindling fast, and after a solid ten minutes of searching, I decide to call uncle. I'm exhausted, in desperate need of a shower, and my hair probably looks as though I stuck my finger in an outlet. And let's not forget my heart . . . It's pretty beat up right about now too.

Wrapping my hand around my hair, I pull it off of my neck before draping it across my shoulder. *Now what?* Spinning around, I readjust the strap of my purse and scan the room one last time before going to collect my luggage. People are bustling past me at warp speed, kids giggling and running around, men and women pushing their way through the crowd to get closer to the carousels. When I see a young woman throw herself into a man's arms, it's like a punch to the gut.

That should be me.

Tears spring to my eyes, and I take a step toward the baggage carousel when I catch a glimpse of camouflage. A wave of people walk past me, but my feet are rooted in place as I wait with bated breath to see what—or who—will be waiting for me when they pass. As though Moses himself was there, the sea of people part, leaving me with a perfect and uninterrupted view of—

"Devin." The sound of his name on my lips sounds distant and foreign. Everything around me is one big blur, streaks of color trying to break the hold my eyes have on the soldier in uniform.

There's a tingling in my chest that I've never felt before, and as I suck in a hopeful breath, waiting for him to look up, my chin starts to tremble.

He's looking at me, his gaze wandering around my body, and when his eyes finally make their way to mine, that tingling in my chest radiates outward, shooting sparks of familiarity to all parts of my body. The hair on the back of my neck stands up, my hands shake, and those tears that had been welling up in my eyes finally decide to burst free.

Devin takes a hesitant step . . . followed by another . . . and then another. Finally kicking into gear, my feet move forward, but I only get a few steps before two warm arms wrap around me, dragging me in close. A sob rips from my chest as I bury my face in his neck. Fisting my hands in the front of his jacket, I anchor myself to Devin.

"Katie." His warm breath fans the side of my neck. I can't imagine what we look like to everyone else, two people holding on to each other for dear life, both of us—well me, for sure— afraid to let go in fear of what could be lost.

Loosening my grip on the front of his jacket, I slide my hands to his back and toward his neck, holding him to me. My fingers move to tangle in his hair, only there isn't much hair, so I do the next best thing—the thing my heart is aching to do.

Cupping his face in my hands, I pull back just enough so I can look in his eyes, which are swimming with tears. Without breaking eye contact, I drag his mouth to mine and our lips crash together like waves on a shore.

My eyes drift shut, my head tilting to the side to give him better access. He takes the invitation willingly and pushes his tongue into my mouth, sliding deep, exploring and tasting.

Devin's hands are everywhere—gliding down my arms, gripping my waist, and then sliding up my back before finally settling. One hand wrapped around my neck and the other pressed firmly against my lower back, he holds me close to him. Our bodies are flush, not a lick of space between us. His heart is beating so hard that I can feel it against my chest, and his body pressed against mine is the sweetest thing I've felt in a long time. It feels like just yesterday we were doing this for the first time.

Devin pulls back and my heavy eyelids bob open. "I missed you so much," he mumbles, his lips brushing against mine. The sound of his voice causes shivers to run down my spine, and I tighten my grip on him.

"I missed you too," I say, my body relaxing against his. He groans and his lips find my cheek, my nose, my chin, my neck . . . They hit on every place they can reach before landing back on my mouth. Only this time, the kiss is sweet and gentle, completely different than the one just a minute ago.

So many things are running through my head and being said right now . . . so many emotions being conveyed. *Relief. Comfort. Happiness. Regret.*

Devin's grip loosens and I close my eyes tightly, desperate to stay in this perfect little bubble for just a few more moments—not wanting to let reality and unspoken words tarnish the here and now.

"Let's get out of here, Katie." His green eyes are swirling with so much love that it's nearly impossible to miss. "I want this more than anything, but not here, not in front of all these people."

A grin pulls at the corner of my mouth and his hand fists my shirt at the small of my back. "You can't look at me like that, Kit Kat. I'm barely hanging on by a fucking thread just being this close to you. My body feels like it's gonna explode, but I want to do this right. Just me and you."

Well shit. How the hell am I supposed to say no to *that?* It's unfair, really, that he can be so damn convincing.

"Where are you staying?"

His brows furrow and then he sighs. "I forgot to book a room. But come on, we'll find somewhere to go."

He grabs his bag off the floor, and it's funny, because I don't even remember him having a bag. Lacing his fingers with mine, he leads me toward the suitcases that are being shuffled in circles, waiting for their owners to claim them.

"By the way, I have a room at the Hilton. There's only one bed, but you're more than welcome to share it with me if you want," I say, laughing when his steps falter, nearly sending him face-first to the floor.

"I feel so much better." Devin walks out of the bathroom, a towel hung low on his hips and knotted in the front. Droplets of water are scattered across his chest, and when one slides down his abs, disappearing in the thick white cotton covering his happy trail, I bite my bottom lip.

It should be illegal for someone to look as good as he does. All straight lines and chiseled muscles. He's a hazard to women's health, really. In fact, he should have a flashing sign hanging from his head that warns—

Devin snaps, securing my attention. "Eyes up here." When I look up, he has a smile plastered to his face. *Busted!* I wait for him to say something, to make some sort of embarrassing comment about me not being able to take my eyes off of him, but he doesn't. The expression on his face shifts, his lips purse, brows dip low . . . he looks uncertain.

Devin clears his throat. "Do you want to take a shower?"

Not at all what I was expecting him to say, but okay, I'll bite. "Yes," I say with a nod. "I definitely do, but I don't think I can move." Flopping back on the bed, I close my eyes, roll to my side, and curl my body around a pillow. "I could probably sleep for days if you'd let me."

I don't hear him approach, but I can smell him. I'd know that smell anywhere. It's spicy and sweet, all rolled into one, and I would give anything to bottle it up just so I could pull it out whenever I'm not with him. A warm hand glides down the side of my face.

"I'm so sorry, Katie," he whispers, catching me completely off-guard.

My eyes fly open, my heart suddenly hammering inside of my chest. "For what?" I ask, wondering if he's going to give me the words I've been dying to hear in person for the last ten years.

He's crouched on the floor next to the bed, his face only inches away from mine, but the deep lines of tension on his face are unmistakable. "Everything," he says, his voice full of regret.

"Don't," I whisper, cupping my hand to the back of his neck. I will not let these few precious days be tainted with something that I'm already past. Yes, I still want answers, but they can wait. He opens his mouth, but I swallow his words with a kiss before pulling back. "You don't have to apologize—"

"I do."

"No." I shake my head. "Not right now." His mouth drops open, a look of astonishment gracing his beautiful face.

"Is this real?" he whispers, climbing into bed next to me. "Are you really here with me?" His voice is full of disbelief as his fingers trace along my hip and over my belly. My stomach twitches as his fingers find their way to my collarbone.

"It's real, and I am."

He smiles as though he didn't actually expect to me to answer. Those magical fingers feather across the skin of my neck before his thumb finds my bottom lip. My body is humming with sexual energy, and without thinking, I suck his thumb into my mouth, nipping playfully at the pad.

Devin's eyes widen, flashing with what I can only describe as pure desire. Releasing his thumb, I place my lips on his. "We should talk . . . shouldn't we?" he asks, sounding completely uncertain.

Reaching for the towel, I pull at the knot, feeling the soft cotton drop open. It takes every ounce of strength I have not to look down, but my hand doesn't have the same amount of self-control as my eyes. Circling my fingers around his cock, I slowly begin to work him.

Devin hisses, sucking in a sharp breath, and his eyes drift shut. I love that I can make him do that, and I wonder what other noises I can get him to make.

"Katie, if we start this, I won't be able to stop."

"I don't want you to stop." His heavy lids open and he watches me from under a hooded gaze. "I don't want to talk, and I'm tired of thinking. I just want to feel," I say, looking down. The sight of my hand on him is erotic and a surge of moisture goes straight to my core. "I want to feel you."

Finally, his hands move to my shirt, sliding under the material and slowly lifting it over my head. I sit up, just enough to let him tug it off of me. Devin flicks the clasp of my bra and the lacy material loosens around my body. In a slow and calculated move, he slips a finger under the strap and pulls it off.

"Where do you want me, Katie?"

He kisses the swell of my breast before sucking my nipple into his mouth. "Oh, God." Dropping my head back, I close my eyes, taking it all in. He releases me with a wet pop, and my eyes open to find him nose to nose with me . . . watching me. "Keep doing that," I pant, wanting his mouth back on me.

"You didn't answer me."

"Huh?"

"Answer me, Katie." The tone of his voice shouldn't turn me on, but it does, and I am in no way ashamed to admit it.

"What was the question?" Doesn't he know my brain is mush right now? I'm so turned on that it literally fucking hurts.

"Where do you want me?"

"Everywhere," I breathe. "On me, in me, wrapped around me. I want every part of you touching every part of me." My words must've been exactly what he wanted to hear because, in a matter of seconds, my panties are nowhere to be found and Devin is hovering on top of me, his thick erection cradled between my legs.

"I need to hear you say it."

"I want you, Devin." Wrapping a leg around his waist, I dip a hand between us and guide him to my entrance. "Make love to me. *Please.*"

In one fluid motion, he rocks forward, stealing every ounce of breath I have. My hands find his back and I close my eyes, memorizing the moment. The way his muscles ripple beneath my fingers, the feel of his breath against my skin, the way his hips roll with every thrust.

This isn't just sex, and it's more than making love. This is two souls reconnecting—becoming one. In this moment, we are letting go of the past and opening ourselves up to a future that's full of endless possibilities.

This is only the beginning.

Needing to be closer, I fuse our mouths together. I stroke my tongue against his, waiting for him to fight for control, but he doesn't. Surprisingly, he follows my lead. Our kiss is passionate and so different from our teenage kisses.

Breathless, I pull away. "Touch me." I don't have to ask twice, and as though he knows exactly what I need, Devin slips a hand between our sweaty bodies. His fingers find my clit and he presses down, rubbing it in tight circles. My breathing picks up, turning into a light pant, as he brings my body to the edge. Then he picks up the pace, his hips rocking into mine, faster and more demanding.

"Open your eyes," he growls, the sound nearly sending me right over the cliff. But somehow I manage to hold on, wanting nothing more than to drag this out as long as I can. "Watch us, Katie," he says, glancing down at the spot where our bodies come together. My gaze follows his and I watch for several seconds as he pumps in and out of me, the sight so damn erotic that it pushes me straight to the edge.

Digging my nails into his skin, my back arches. Rocking hard, his hips slam into me. His thumb rubs rhythmic circles on my clit, and when his body stiffens above mine, I explode into a million tiny pieces. Tossing his head back, Devin moans. The sound rumbling from his chest is hands down the sexiest noise I've ever heard come from a man.

"That was fucking amazing," he says, peppering kisses across my face.

"You're amazing," I whisper.

And I love you . . . so much.

Chapter 24 | *Katie*

"How Long Will I Love You"—Ellie Goulding

Hot. Why am I so fucking hot? And why is there an arm draped over my stomach? There's an arm draped over my—

"Shit," I hiss, flying up in bed, the sheet clenched to my naked chest. My eyes snap to the person in bed next to me, and when I find Devin's emerald eyes smiling back at me, I breathe a sigh of relief.

"You okay?" His voice is thick and husky, causing parts of me to tingle that probably shouldn't tingle at—I glance at the clock—nine o'clock in the morning.

"Yeah." Lifting the covers away from our bodies, I glance down. Yup, naked as the babies I help deliver. And *hello,* Devin is completely naked too. I drop the cover back over my body. Devin has a devilish smile plastered to his face and warmth creeps up my neck. "I, uh . . . I guess I forgot. I'm not used to waking up with a man next to me."

"We're gonna circle around and discuss the last half of that statement in a second. But really, you forgot?" Devin sits up, his movement causing the sheet to fall around his hips. I try to keep my eyes on his, I really do, but it's too damn hard. His chest is drool-worthy, and don't get me started on those abs. There are easily . . . one, two, three, four—

"Six." Devin snaps his fingers and I look up.

"Huh?"

"It's a six-pack," he says, laughing. I don't feel at all bad about getting caught ogling or counting his abs. His body is a chiseled mass of perfection. "Now let's talk about this forgetting business. If you forgot already, then I obviously didn't do a very good job." His voice softens when he brings his mouth to my neck. Running his finger along my collarbone, he slips his hand under the sheet, pushes it down, and exposes my chest.

The cool air wafts over my skin and my nipples pucker. "Maybe you should try again. Just do a better job this time . . . at, uh . . . you know . . . *oh fuck.*" I'm not sure when Devin dipped a hand between my legs, but frankly, I don't care. He pushes a finger inside of me, twisting it around before curling it upward.

"Lie back," he demands, his eyes hooded. *Well, I certainly won't make him beg.* I drop back on the bed and he rips the sheet from my body. Pushing up on an elbow, I look down. His hand is still lodged between my legs, and he's watching as his finger slides in and out of me.

Watching him work me to the brink is surprisingly erotic. It's something I'm not particularly used to, so I squeeze my eyes shut before I do or say something to embarrass myself.

"Watch me, Katie."

I don't need to watch, soldier, I can feel it and it's fan-fucking-tastic.

I peel my eyes open anyway. His eyes are on mine, intense and swirling with desire. I always did feel pretty around Devin, but right now, the way he's looking at me, I feel sexy.

"You like that, don't you?" he asks. I nod, mostly because I can't form words. My body is coiled tight and a light moan falls from my mouth. "What do you want now, Katie?"

Good God, stop talking.

"I—I don't know."

"You do know."

"Don't stop," I pant, fighting the heaviness of my eyelids. I want nothing more than to toss my head back and let myself go, but now that I've started, I can't stop watching.

"Wasn't plannin' on it. Now tell me what you want."

"Touch yourself," I blurt, feeling heat infuse my cheeks when I realize exactly what it was I just asked him to do.

"You want me to touch myself?"

I nod, watching with rapt attention as he grips himself with his free hand and slides it slowly up and down his shaft. "Does this turn you on, Katie?" he asks, picking up speed with both hands.

"Yes. *God yes.* It's . . ." My words trail off when my legs start to tremble. I won't be able to hold on much longer. Everything around me goes dark and I finally give in. Squeezing my eyes shut, I toss my head back.

Devin yanks his hand from my legs, but before I even have time to react, I'm being flipped over. My nipples push against the sheet when Devin rocks into me, and I arch backward as the sensation sends sparks of pleasure straight to my toes.

"I love being inside of you," he whispers before brushing my hair out of the way and kissing the back of my neck. "You feel so fucking good, it hurts. This is perfection. You're perfection."

His words push me over the edge, and I cry out as my orgasm slams into me with much more force than I'm used to. My toes curl, my skin igniting with intense heat as my hips rock in tandem with his. "Fuck, that's hot," he growls. Devin grips my hair, circles it around his wrist, and tugs lightly, drawing my head back. It's soft and sweet, completely contradictory to the way he's slamming into me. When his lips find my neck, he bites down lightly on the skin below my ear and I whimper. His body goes rigid above mine and his grip tightens on my hair as he pushes into me several more times.

I feel a rush of moisture and Devin groans, a string of unintelligible words falling from his mouth. There are no words to describe what he just did to me. It's never been like that . . . not even last night. My body goes limp and the feel of his weight on my back is comforting. Slowly, he pulls out of me and I'm instantly left with a feeling of emptiness—a feeling I'm suddenly not too fond of.

"Shit," Devin hisses, dropping his head to my shoulder. "I'm so sorry, Katie."

"For what?" I ask, having absolutely no idea what he could be apologizing for after what we just did.

"I wasn't thinking," he says, his voice low. "I didn't . . . We didn't use protection, last night or tonight."

Oh, that. Good thing I've got it covered. "I'm on birth control. I take it regularly and I haven't been on antibiotics, so we're good to go."

"Okay," he says, blowing out a quick breath. "Had me worried there for a second. Not that I wouldn't want to . . . you know, have babies with you and everything . . . but—"

"Just stop." I laugh, loving the way he instantly clammed up at the mere thought of me getting pregnant. *Typical man.* "We're good. It's all good." He kisses the back of my neck.

Devin slides to the left of me, wraps an arm around my back and nuzzles his face close to mine. He kisses my nose and then my mouth, and when I finally gather enough strength to open my eyes, his are closed.

Peaceful. That's the best way to describe the look on his face. He looks content and peaceful, and I have a feeling that he doesn't experience those feelings very often. His lips part, his warm breath fanning across my face. Reaching up, I run my thumb along his lip, followed by his cheekbone. I'm trying to memorize everything about him that I possibly can, because I know that soon I'll have to let him go. And after being with him again, I'm not sure how well I'll handle that.

Between his letters and the phone conversations we've had, I got the sense that he still owned a large part of my heart, but being wrapped in his arms, the familiarity of his body against mine, I realize now that was stupid. He owns *all* of it. He always has and he always will.

"I love you," I whisper, not sure if he's even awake to hear me.

"I love you more." His eyes open. They're glossy, and the way he's looking at me speaks volumes, but those words coming from his mouth pull tears from my eyes. He was gone . . . For ten long years I had to live without him, and my feelings didn't wane one bit. Sure, I was angry and pushed the love aside, but it was too strong for me to fight. All my heart needed was to be near him again to remember that it beats for him.

Wyatt never stood a chance . . . no man would've ever stood a chance. Because there is only person in this world for me, and that's Devin Ulysses Clay.

"Say it again," he says, threading his fingers into my hair.

"I love you." My lips land on his for a soft kiss. "I *love* you. I love *you. I love you.*"

His face scrunches up as though my words physically hurt him, and I pull back. But before I can ask what's wrong, he says, "I'm so sorry, Katie. For everything."

"Shhhh." I press my finger against his mouth, but he easily shakes me off.

"I need to get this out. Please, just let me get this out." I understand he has things he wants to say, but I'm just not sure I want to hear them anymore. He said he was sorry and I believe him. That should be enough, right?

But the determination I see on his face tells me this is a fight I won't win. "Okay," I whisper, cupping my hand around his neck, drawing his mouth to mine. "I want to say something first though." He nods, but his face is still drawn tight as though the words he needs to say are weighing heavily on his shoulders. "It doesn't matter what you say. In the grand scheme of things, it doesn't matter why you left. What matters is that you're here now, and when you tell me you're sorry, I know you're telling the truth because I can see it in your eyes." I kiss him once, twice, and then a third time before pulling back.

"You're perfect, you know that?"

"No, I'm not." I sigh. "But I sure do like hearing it. In fact, feel free to tell me that every single day for the rest of my life."

His eyes widen at my off-handed mention of the future, but he doesn't miss a beat. "Are you talking forever, Katie?"

"Forever isn't enough," I whisper, draping my arm over his back. The breath rushes from his lungs and I smile to myself.

"I don't deserve you." *That's bullshit.* I open my mouth to tell him that, but he pushes his finger against my mouth, the same way I did a few moments ago. "Listen. I just need you to listen, okay?"

I nod, his finger still pressed to my lips.

"Good girl." Devin lets his hand fall, but it doesn't travel far. He props himself up on an elbow, his other hand resting firmly on my hip. "You were my world growing up. I lived in a house, but I never had a home . . . You were my home, Katie." Tears spring to my eyes, and when one slides down my face, he gently wipes it away.

"I knew I wasn't good enough for you, but I was selfish so I had every intention of keeping you anyway." Devin's eyes dart to the side as though he's contemplating his next words. When they find me again, I can see the uncertainty. Whatever it is he's about to say may very well impact me more than I think. "Until I talked to your dad."

"My dad?" My brows furrow and I push up, mimicking his position. "What does my dad have to do with it?"

"Remember that last night?" I give him the patented are-you-kidding-me look and his eyes soften. "Sorry, of course you do. Anyway, I watched you walk into the house, and I was getting ready to pull away when your dad walked up."

He did? How did I not know this? "I didn't know he was even outside that night."

"Trust me," he says. "I didn't either. He scared the hell out of me."

"What did he say?" I ask. My nerves are already kicking in, adrenaline flowing in waves through my veins, because I have absolutely no idea what my dad could've had to do with Devin leaving me without a trace. Daddy knew how much Devin meant to me; he would have never done something to jeopardize what we had.

Would he?

Devin's head drops. "He didn't tell me anything I didn't already know. But the way he presented it—"

"What? What did he say?"

"He wanted the best for you, Katie. He wanted you to have a husband that could provide you with the kind of life you deserve, and he and I both knew I wasn't that guy. Wyatt was that guy for you, and your dad thought the same thing." I cringe at his words, but he continues. "I knew that if I saw you again, that if I talked to you about it, you'd tell me it was all a bunch of shit."

"Because it is all a bunch of shit."

"I know," he breathes, dragging his eyes back to mine. "Trust me, I know. It's my biggest regret in life. It's the one thing I would give anything to go back and change, but you have to understand where I was coming from. I was living a shitty life with an even shittier mother, and I was being forced to move almost a thousand miles away. There was no way I was going to be able to afford to go to college, let alone get a decent job, and I didn't want to hold you back. I wanted you to have the gorgeous house with the white picket fence and two point four kids."

"But I only wanted you."

"I know." He takes a deep breath. "I know that now. But at the time, my head wasn't in a good spot, and I knew that the only way to give you a clean break was to leave and not come back. And trust me, it was the hardest thing I've ever had to do."

Devin's chin quivers, the movement so slight I almost miss it. I have no doubt that he feels awful for leaving me the way that he did. "You broke my heart."

"I know. I broke my heart too. I thought about you every fucking second of every fucking day, and if Mom had had a phone, I probably would've called and begged for forgiveness the first chance I got. But she didn't. Hell, I couldn't even afford to call you from a payphone. Things were rough there for a while, and honestly, I'm glad you didn't have to see it. It's a good thing you weren't there, because I would've leaned on you way too much."

"I *want* you to lean on me, Dev. I want to be that person, the one you turn to when you need something—anything. I want to be your best friend and your confidant and everything else."

"You are." Sitting up, Devin pulls me into his arms. His grip on me is tight, and his chest is heaving as though he just ran a marathon. "Trust me, you are, and I never forgot that. I made a terrible mistake walking away from you, and I swear that I'll never leave you again. I know you said it before, but I need to hear you say it now. Do you forgive me, Katie?"

"Yes." With that one little word, I feel his body relax against mine. He needed to hear that much more than I realized. "I forgive you." It's easy to say because it's true, but there is still one little thing nagging at the back of my head. "I can't believe Daddy made you feel that way," I say, shaking my head in disbelief.

"Don't. Don't be mad at your dad. He only wanted what was best for his little girl, and I don't blame him. I was a hotheaded teenager, and it didn't matter how he said it, his words only meant one thing to me."

"Say it," I dare, pulling back, "and I will kick your ass."

"I love you," he says, laughing, the dimple in the side of his cheek popping out. I've missed that damn dimple. Leaning forward, I press a kiss to it.

"I love you, too." Nuzzling against his chest, Devin pulls me in close before settling us on the pillows. We lie like this for several minutes, both enjoying the quiet, but my mind can't help but wander. If he would have told me what happened with my dad a long time ago, I probably would've been pissed, because he should have known better than to think any of that. But I'm older now, and the situation he was in at the time is easier to understand as an adult than it was as a starry-eyed teenager.

Plus, as much as I hate to admit it, our time apart probably wasn't such a bad thing. Who knows what would've happened if we had tried to make it work from nearly a thousand miles away? I just wish that Wyatt wouldn't have gotten hurt in the process. And as much as I don't want to, I know the topic needs to be discussed.

"Since we're talking and opening up, is now a good time to talk about Wyatt?"

Devin rolls us over until his body is hovering over mine. "I think we've talked enough for today, don't you?" I shake my head. "Plus, we need to get to the funeral home and make sure everything is ready for tomorrow."

I've been so wrapped up in reconnecting with Devin that I totally forgot about why we're even together right now in the first place. "I'm sorry." I look down, but two warm fingers find my chin, lifting my face back up. "I've been so selfish—"

"No." That one word is spoken with an immense amount of conviction. "You haven't been selfish. You've been selfless. You took off work, rearranged your schedule, and flew all the way here just to be with me, and I can't tell you how much I love you for that. And I do want to know what happened after I left, as much as it may kill me." The last part was mumbled, and I can't help but giggle at the disgusted look on his face. "But can we wait until after the funeral?"

"Absolutely."

"I just want to get past this. And I want to enjoy having you all to myself for a little bit longer before we talk about anything else."

"That sounds like a plan. Now," I say, planting my hands firmly against his chest, "we should get up and get ready so we can go finalize plans for the funeral tomorrow and order some flowers." He doesn't budge when I push him, so I wriggle out from under his rock-hard body. I make it to the side of the bed when I feel a strong hand around my ankle, yanking me back.

"We don't have to be there for another hour."

My eyes widen. "Yes, but I have to get ready."

"I'll be quick."

I giggle when his hands attack my body, but my laughing quickly turns to a whimper when his mouth joins in on the assault.

Chapter 25 | Devin

"Body in a Box"—City and Colour

The room is filled with rows of chairs, each of them empty except the two Katie and I take up in the front row and one occupied by a great-aunt I'd never met before, who is seated two chairs down from us. Ida is nearly ninety and not a hundred percent with it, but she told us she'd promised my grandmother long ago that if anything were to ever happen to my mother, she'd take care of everything—and so here she is. But she didn't want to give the eulogy, and Lord knows I wasn't doing it. So here we are, listening to the funeral director do his best to say nice things about my mother as if he's known her for years.

It's likely he never even knew my mother beyond what my great-aunt shared with him when she planned the funeral. This is small-town Pennsylvania and most everybody knows everyone else's business, but it seems my mother became quite the recluse after I left, even more so than when I saw her last.

Katie and I stopped by Mom's house this morning to sift through a few things, and her neighbor, Shelly, stopped by. Apparently, she was Mom's only friend, although I would bet she was more of an acquaintance and was only trying to be nice. She told us that Mom quit her job at Kroger's a few years back and has been surviving off social security disability payments.

According to Shelly, it was about that same time when Mom began closing herself off, slowly becoming a hermit.

Shelly said she would check on Mom as often as she could, mostly to make sure that she had food and was keeping up on her bills, but other times to give her some social interaction. It hurt to know that this woman was the only person my mother spoke to for months at a time. She also mentioned that over the last two years or so, Mom had become paranoid and delusional, often claiming people were after her.

Shelly was sweet, cringing at her own words as if it made her sick to be the one to have to tell me all this, but I made her continue. I had to know what my mother's last days were like. She went on to tell me that oftentimes she'd find my Mom lying in a pile of empty liquor bottles, and that a few times she actually had to check to make sure she was alive. Sounds like Josephine, alright.

Now here she is, looking shiny and porcelain like a Madame Tussauds wax sculpture, the frown lines still running thick down the corners of her mouth. I try to avert my eyes, but I can't stop staring at her lying motionless in the coffin with her spindly fingers crossed together.

She looks terrible. Even after the work the mortician put in, I barely recognize her. I can't help but think that this is for the best.

Katie must recognize my internal struggle because she takes my hand in hers and pulls it on her lap, squeezing tightly.

"Are you okay?" she whispers in my ear. Without looking at her, I nod, continuing to analyze my mother's current state. I've seen too many dead bodies to count, all in various stages of decomposition, but never in my life have I seen this. I've only been to one nonmilitary funeral before—my grandmother's, and she was cremated—and the ones I've attended have never had an open casket because the bodies were in too bad of shape.

Josephine may have been a stranger to me toward the end of her life, but she was still my mother, and as distant as the good memories are, I still have some. So seeing her like this, plastic and lifeless, brings so much pain to my heart that I feel like I have to fight to catch my breath. I don't want Katie to worry, so every bit of anguish I feel in this moment is wiped clean from my face. She had to deal with this too—and not that long ago—so I'll be damned if I force her to go through it again. Nobody needs to shoulder this burden but me. I'll deal with this like I do everything else. I'll let the feelings and emotions take hold for a day, I'll process them on my own, and then I'll stuff them so deep that I can't help but forget about them . . . for a while at least.

The funeral director finishes his speech and welcomes us to say our final good-byes. My great-aunt goes up to the casket first. She touches my mother's forehead and each shoulder, delivering the Lord's Prayer before departing the room. Katie looks at me, but at first I don't move. I know I'm supposed to go up there, but my legs just aren't responding to what my brain is telling them to do. It's hard enough seeing my mom's body from this distance.

The funeral director picks up on my hesitation and moves from behind the podium. "I will leave you guys be. Please, take your time and just come get me when you're finished," he says in his most sympathetic tone before following Ida out of the room.

I rise to my feet but can't step forward just yet. My chest is burning, the lump in my throat letting me know I may just lose it if I take one step closer. I turn to look at Katie. She's standing beside me, her hand resting gently on my back. Her touch is so comforting and I don't want to ask her to leave, but I need this moment to be private.

"Baby, can I do this by myself? I just can't—"

She rests her hand on my cheek, immediately cutting me off. "I completely understand. I'll be out in the lobby if you need me." She pulls my head down to hers and kisses my lips softly. I nearly fall into her when she releases me, not wanting to stop just yet. She shoots me the sweetest smile before making her way out of the room.

My eyes move from her to my mother, and I take two baby steps forward. I don't know what exactly my problem is, but the closer I get to her, the tighter the pain in my stomach becomes. I take in a deep breath and rub a knuckle against each temple, then I move forward slowly until I'm standing beside the coffin. My eyes burn, the tell-tale sign that my emotions are taking over.

At first it's just a few tears, but the longer I stand here, the more they fall. Before I know it, the tears are running down my cheeks, many of them coating my mother's hands and the old black dress she used to wear on special occasions. It's velvet and completely swallows her frail body.

"I fucking hate that you got this reaction out of me," I say, wiping at my face. "I fucking hate crying more tears over you." The words slip out before I can even process them. I know she can't hear me, but that doesn't mean I don't have shit to get off my chest.

"You stole a huge part of my life from me. You let your own pain and anguish negatively affect me. You are the most selfish person I've ever met. So why do I still fucking love you?" The tears fall even harder now and I drop to my knees, resting my forehead against the side of the casket. I'm so fucking angry, and I can't tell whether that's because of the person she was or the mother she wasn't. Or maybe it's just because I never had a chance to say good-bye—never had a chance to mend the broken pieces.

I know it was her fault; it's not like she ever made an attempt either. But that's who she was. It doesn't mean that's who I had to be. It's too late now though, and that fact is all too clear as I bawl like a baby before my mother's withered body.

When I finally compose myself, I rise to my feet and brush the tears from my face. Taking in a long, shaky breath, I reach into my shirt and grab my dog tags, pulling them over my head.

I remove one of the tags and drape the other one with the chain back around my neck.

I place the tag between her cold hands, and the instant I touch her, the tears creep back in. Quickly, I pull my hands back and look at her closed eyes. All I need to do now is say good-bye.

"You hurt me more than anyone ever could. You made me wish every day for a different life. But that doesn't change reality. You're my blood, and no matter what happened in the past, nothing can change that. I love you, Josephine." I lean in and kiss her forehead. "Rest in peace, Mama."

We're cruising down Old Hickory Avenue in the rental car, and Katie has no idea where we're going. But I do . . . I'm just hoping they're still there. As I drive around the bend and see the massive property that once belonged to my grandparents, I'm immediately relieved to see the wild horses that my grandma loved so much. Katie catches sight of the stunning creatures at the same time I do, and the smile that lights her face is nearly my undoing.

The funeral was tough and it left my mind a cluttered mess, but Katie makes it all better.

"Oh my God!" She rolls down her window as quickly as she can. "They're so beautiful!" Closing her eyes, she takes a deep breath. The air out here is unlike anywhere in the world, and it takes me back to the days I spent with my grandmother on this property, the one place I could forget the outside world for just a while. I've missed this.

"Smells amazing, huh?" I roll down my own window and let the scent of pine and damp earth pour into the vehicle. It's freeing to be out here in the middle of nowhere, seeing, smelling, and hearing only those things that are natural to this Earth. It brings my feelings toward war and Iraq into focus, and immediately makes me yearn to get out of the military altogether. If I could—and if my men weren't still there—I'd never go back to that hellhole again.

Katie rests a hand on my lap, the biggest smile on her face. "It really does. Are we going to see them?" She's so excited that if it hadn't been part of my plan to begin with, seeing the horses would undoubtedly be added to the agenda.

"We will in just a few minutes," I say with a mischievous smile.

"What are you up to, soldier?" *God, I love it when she calls me that—and she knows it.*

"In due time, Kit Kat, in due time." I pull the rental onto a small dirt road leading to the woods beside the property.

"Are we allowed to do this?" Katie's innocence is ridiculously adorable.

"Well, I didn't ask for permission, but let's just say I was here long before any of these people were." She looks at me curiously, trying her best to figure out my meaning, before it clicks and her mouth drops open.

"Oh my God!"

"I don't know who lives here now, but I do know that"—I point to the large farmhouse off to our right that's situated in the middle of the twenty-acre land my family once owned—"my grandfather built that with his own hands. Nobody's going to tell me we can't be here."

"Yes, sir," she says with her delicate hand in a terribly performed salute. I think about the prospects of this kind of routine during sex, just as we approach a fork in the road. *I'm going to have to remember that.*

I take the path to the left, which travels further into the woods. The other road juts harshly to the right and through a gate toward the farmhouse. We are completely surrounded by trees, and I notice Katie's eyes peering out the window.

"It's so, *so* beautiful out here. I just can't even believe it. How long did your grandparents live here?" I love that even though this woman knows so much about me—probably more than anybody—she still wants to know more.

"Well, my grandpa built it after coming back from the war in '45. He and my grandmother lived here together for almost fifty-five years before he had that stroke. Then my grandma lived here for about another three years until her death."

"And she didn't leave it to any of your family? Why not you?" she asks, just as we approach the spot I've been searching for. It's a large clearing in the woods, void of anything but dried pine needles and fallen twigs. The dirt road continues down the property's northernmost fence line, and a stream runs parallel to the road on our left and deep into the woods, acting as a partial border for this spot I've come to know so well. The farmhouse is just a speck on the horizon on the other side of the fence.

I get out of the car and Katie follows, nearly tripping over herself as she stares, mesmerized by the twenty or so horses galloping across the fenced land.

"Besides my mother and I—and I guess, Great-Aunt Ida—my grandmother didn't have any family." I reach out my hand, offering Katie a seat right in the middle of the clearing, then I follow suit.

"She sure as shit wasn't giving it to my mother, and I hadn't joined the Army or anything, so I don't think she was too confident in my future at that point. She ended up donating the land, horses, and house to a nonprofit organization. I have no idea if they just sold the property, or if they're actually using it. I don't even know who owns it."

I thought about going up and asking if it was all right for us to be here, but I don't have time to fuck around—well, not with anyone besides Katie, that is.

"Did you or your grandma ever ride them?" The kindness in her eyes makes the small distance between us almost unbearable. I scoot closer to her and place an arm around the small of her back.

"Well, no. My grandmother never really believed in riding them. They've always been kind of wild and just living on the land." I throw air quotes up around "living on the land" because, in reality, they ate better than our family did most of the time. "She really just loved watching them roam free."

Katie pulls her knees toward her chest and drops her chin on them, her eyes moving in rhythm with the horses. She settles in close to me, allowing me to wrap her completely in my arms.

"I can see why. I could sit here forever." Her gaze is fixed on the horses and mine is on her. *I could too, Katie. I could too.* Although eventually we'd need to—

"Oh shit, I almost forgot," I blurt, rising to my feet. I make my way to the trunk, open it up, and grab a bottle of wine, two wine glasses, an opener, and a picnic blanket. I carry them over to Katie and set them down. "Ma'am, if I could have you please stand," I say playfully, holding out my hand so I can help her up. "I mean, seriously, what asshole would let you sit down in the dirt?" I flash her a wink and smile, and she smiles back, rising to her feet.

"Obviously, a man not as gentlemanly as yourself, good sir." She laughs and backs away a few steps. I set the blanket flat on the ground and proceed to open the wine bottle, filling each glass. I hand Katie hers and recork the bottle before sitting back down with mine.

I lift my wine glass for a toast, but I can't seem to think of anything appropriate to say. "To us?" I ask, and she scrunches her nose and shakes her head. She gives me a very dramatic thumbs-down. "No? Too simple? Okay, how about . . . To my mother, may she find herself in a better place, and to my grandmother and grandfather for having the wherewithal to see the absolute beauty of this land, and to us and the four unexpected days we get to spend together. May there be many more to follow." She smiles, her eyes welling with tears as she raises her glass, clinking it against mine.

"To Josephine, Hank and Harriet . . . and to *us*." She takes a small sip and looks at me like I'm crazy when I down the whole thing.

"Long day," I joke, setting the glass to the side and moving in front of her. I take her glass and set it down next to mine. "Katie . . ."

"Yes?"

"Isn't it funny how you can have a million different things on the tip of your tongue, waiting to be said, but when it comes time to spill it, there's nothing?" I find myself staring at the blanket and trying my best to make sense of everything going on in my head. Katie places both hands around my neck and pulls me in until I'm inches from her face. I can smell her perfume, and my eyes close as I let the scent consume me. I could sit here, just like this, forever.

"You don't have to say a word, Dev. I know."

"But I want to. I want to tell you everything. I want you to know that, regardless of the distance or time between us, I *will* make this work, and we will make up for the past ten years. We will be everything we ever dreamed of growing up." She lets out a deep sigh, and in this moment, I know she's feeling the same way I am. She needs me as badly as I need her.

We lie there for hours, completely lost in one another, talking about the past and making love like there's no tomorrow. Only Katie could do this. Only she has the ability to take this horrible day and turn it around. Watching the horses gracefully streak across the land under the fleeting summer sun, I'm completely at peace. As her head rests against my chest and my finger traces pathways across her skin, I realize I am right where I'm meant to be. If I could only hold on to this moment and never let it go. But unfortunately, the sobering realization that I only have two more days with her lingers like a bad hangover.

Chapter 26 | *Katie*

"Arms"—Christina Perri

O ur first two days together have flown by. Day one was
pretty much all travel, but remembering how the night
ended puts a fat smile on my face. Yesterday, of course, was the
funeral, and then we spent the entire afternoon watching
the wild horses. He eventually made love to me right there
on the blanket before taking me to dinner and then spending
the rest of the night worshiping my body.

And now here we are cleaning out Josephine's house. It isn't
exactly the way I planned on spending day three, especially considering Devin is leaving tomorrow, but it needed to be done.
We've been cleaning for hours, and Devin insists that whatever
we don't get through is simply going to get thrown away.

"Do you want this?" I hold up an old baseball glove I just
found shoved under a twin-size bed in the spare room, which
I assume used to be Devin's. I recognize this glove. My parents bought it for Dev in seventh grade and he loved it. His
mom couldn't afford one—either that or she didn't want to
spend the money—and he was damn proud of that black
Rawlings.

"Where did you find that?" Pushing to his knees, Devin
crawls to where I'm at and he takes the glove, brushing off
the dust.

"It was under the bed . . . *way* in the back." Reaching under the bed again, I find an old shoebox and drag it out.

Devin sighs and slips his hand in the worn leather. "I looked everywhere for this glove after we moved here, but I couldn't find it. Mom kept telling me that it would pop up, and then I guess she got sick of me asking because she finally just told me to get over it." Balling his hand into a fist, he pounds it into the glove, a wistful look passing over his face. "She said I didn't play anymore, so it didn't matter. Except it did, and I probably would have."

The look on his face tells me all I need to know—as if I didn't already—about what kind of hateful woman Josephine was. It also tells me that we need a change of subject . . . fast.

Clearing my throat, I lift the lid off the shoebox. "What do you want to do tonight? I thought maybe we could go grab some dinner."

"Dinner sounds good," he mumbles, dropping his glove to the side and reaching into the shoebox I just opened. His hand latches on to some pictures and he flips through them one by one, his smile growing bigger each time he moves to the next.

Leaning forward, I peek at the photos. "Oh my God. Give me that!" Pulling the top one out of his hand, I look down at the photo and I'm instantly taken on a trip down memory lane. "What the hell was I thinking?" *No really, what the hell was I thinking?* I know it was the '90s and all, but my bangs couldn't get higher if I tried, and was I seriously wearing layered neon socks?

"You looked hot."

"If by hot you mean I looked like a flashing neon sign that screamed '*look at me, I love New Kids On The Block*,' then yes, I looked hot."

Devin chuckles and tosses a picture at me. "Remember that?" Picking up the worn photo, I'm instantly brought to tears. It's the two of us—Devin and me—and he's sitting on one of Daddy's four wheelers. I'm sitting behind him, arms wrapped around his stomach. We're both covered in mud and laughing. We were fifteen years old, and it's a moment in time that I'll never forget.

The day this picture was taken was the day Devin told me he loved me for the first time. At the time, it was just the love of two friends, but his words meant the world to me nonetheless.

"Do you remember what happened," I ask, "right before Daddy snapped this?" My eyes drift upward and Devin is watching me, smiling.

"Of course I do. And do you remember what else we did that day?"

A grin plays at the corner of my mouth. *How could I forget?* "It's still there," I say, letting the memory wash over me.

"Were things better with your mom this morning?" I ask, tossing a rock into the creek.

Devin shrugs, his eyes trained on some unknown object off in the distance. I imagine that the fight with his mom last night must still be weighing heavily on his mind.

"We can talk about it some more if you want."

"Nah, I'm all talked out, and you've listened to enough of my bitchin'."

If he only knew how much I loved being the one he comes to. It's a good thing he doesn't, because it might scare him off. But it's true. I want to be the one he comes to when he's having a bad day and when something exciting happens. Unfortunately, the latter doesn't occur very often.

"Thank you," he whispers, glancing in my direction.

"You don't have to thank me."

"I want to." He sighs, running a hand over his face. "You're here for me when I need you, and I don't want you to think I take that lightly."

I shake my head. "I don't think that. You're my best friend, Dev, and I love you."

"I love you too, Katie." His voice is soft, and as he says the words, a crimson flush creeps up his neck. My entire body freezes, and I'm completely unable to do anything but stare at him.

"Why are you looking at me like that?"

I don't respond because I'm still in shock.

He loves me . . .

"Say something, Kit Kat."

I blink several times before I'm able to form words. "I know," I say. I love the way his eyes widen. "You know?"

"Yes," I say, chuckling. "I know you love me. I-I just didn't think you'd ever actually say it."

"Well," he says, nudging my shoulder with his. "Now I've said it."

"Now you have." I nod, looking away with a smirk.

I just wish that he loved me the way I love him.

"Want to make it permanent?" he asks. Jumping to his feet, he holds out a hand. I look at the offering for only a second before slipping my hand in his. He tugs me to my feet and I brush off my butt.

"I'm not sure I follow."

"The tree," he says, gesturing toward the old oak sitting a few feet from the bank.

"What about it?" I ask, following him when he walks toward it.

"Let's carve our names into the tree."

My lips pinch together and brows scrunch as I look at the other sets of initials carved into the bark. Both my grandparents and my parents' initials are there, and something about carving ours doesn't seem right.

"But we aren't married," I say. "You aren't even my boyfriend."

Devin laughs and pulls a pocketknife from his jeans. "It doesn't matter," he says, shaking his head. "You and me, we're forever. It doesn't matter if we're married or not. You're my best friend, Katie. You could grow up and marry some rich fucker like Wyatt and I could marry some spoiled brat like Marybeth, but it wouldn't change how I feel about you. You're always going to be a part of me, and nothing in the world is gonna change that."

His words do two things. First, they make my heart melt. Second, they make carving our initials in the bark sound much more appealing. Which is a good thing because, without giving me a chance to respond, Devin shoves the tip of his knife into the tree and carves our initials.

D.C. + K.D. = FOREVER

"Katie?" Devin nudges my leg and I look up.

"Huh?"

"You left me for a second there," he says, his brows dipped low. "Are you okay?"

I smile, but it isn't a beaming smile. It's a gentle one that says just how much I adore him. "Yeah. I'm great." And for the first time in months, I mean it. I am great, and it's thanks to this beautiful man.

"You didn't answer my question," he says, a nervous look on his face.

"Well, that's because I zoned out and didn't hear it. Repeat, please."

Devin's shoulders rise and fall on a deep breath and he rubs his hands along his jeans. "Is Wyatt's name carved on the tree?" His eyes dart away as though he can't watch me give him the answer, so I scoot closer until our knees are touching.

Screw it. Crawling into his lap, I drape my legs on either side of his hips. Devin looks up, gorgeous green eyes as wide as they can be, as my mouth descends on his.

"No." I brush my lips over his, nipping the bottom one playfully before dipping my tongue into his mouth. He opens willingly, and the kiss goes from zero to sixty in less than a second. Then a little voice in the back of my head—a really freaking annoying one—starts screaming that now is the perfect time for the conversation we still need to have.

Reluctantly, I pull back. Devin's eyes are hooded, his lids bobbing several times before his eyes seem to refocus on me.

"His name isn't on the tree because he isn't my forever." Fisting my hands in the front of his shirt, I tug him forward until we're nose to nose, our breath mingling. "You are my forever, Devin. And as much as I hated to admit it after you left, I knew that I'd never carve another man's initials into that tree."

Devin's answering smile is completely blinding, and I can't help but wonder how many times he was able to drop a set of panties just by flashing that bad boy at some unassuming woman. I cringe at the thought, and then make a mental note to ask about any ex-girlfriends.

Strong, warm hands settle on my hips. "Tell me about him . . . about what happened after I left." His face looks pained as he says the words and I know that this is the part he's dreading, so I decide right here and now to make it as painless—but truthful—as I can.

"There isn't much to tell," I say with a shrug. "You left and my heart was shattered. I was a walking zombie through my entire senior year, looking for you everywhere I went, convinced that one day you'd show up again. Every time the phone rang, I nearly jumped out of my skin, and I drove past your house so many times that I think the people who moved in thought I was stalking them."

Devin gets a chagrined look on his face, and his eyes dart to the side before finding mine again. I wrap my arms around his neck and draw circles with my fingers at the bottom of his hairline.

"Anyway, I finally realized you weren't coming back and I did the only thing I could do . . . I moved on." Devin's hands fist at my hips. I bring my lips to his cheek before peppering kisses down his neck, a reminder that I'm here and we're together. Because that's all that matters.

"I started nursing school, met Maggie, and finally started to live my life again. It wasn't until a couple of years later that Wyatt finally asked me out, and I had no reason to say no." I shrug. "He was still one of my best friends, and he knew me better than almost anyone else. He'd been completely loyal to me since kindergarten, and I hadn't dated a single person since you left."

Devin looks off to the right, and I cup his cheek in my hand and bring his eyes back to mine. "He was safe," I whisper, trying to get Devin to understand the meaning behind my words. "I knew he wouldn't hurt me, and at the time, that's what I needed. I never loved him the way I love you. You believe that, right?" I ask, dipping my head to get a better look into his eyes.

Reaching up, Devin runs a thumb along my bottom lip. I have to fight the urge to nip at it, because the weight of the moment is too strong and it's swirling with too much emotion to go there right now. His face softens and his eyes bounce around my face as though he's seeing me again for the first time.

"I believe you." His eyes close as our mouths crash together, my lips parting against his. This kiss is completely different from every one before it. Our hands are exploring and our tongues are dancing rather than dueling for power. It's as though we're saying good-bye to all of the guilt and regret, letting go of the past, once and for all.

"I love you," I say, laughing when he sucks my bottom lip into his mouth, distorting my words.

"I love you too, baby."

"Now," I say, taking a deep breath. "Want to tell me about your ex-girlfriends? There have to be a few."

Devin pulls back with a classic are-you-smokin'-crack look on his face.

"Okay," I drawl out. "I'll take that as a no." I shift to move off of his lap, because, well . . . It's not fair for me to bare it all and him not do the same. One large hand settles low on my back, holding me to him, the other wraps around my neck.

"First of all, you're not going anywhere, Miss Devora," he says, nuzzling the side of my neck. "Second, there isn't much to tell." Pushing at his chest, I separate myself from him just enough so that I can look in his eyes, which are dancing with equal parts amusement and adoration.

My legs go all gooey and I relax against him. "Tell me anyway."

"Well, we moved to Pennsylvania and I was beyond pissed. At myself, at my mom, at your dad"—he shakes his head as though he's ashamed—"and my life sorta spun out of control after that. I'm embarrassed to admit that my drinking got worse, I experimented with drugs, and somewhere in there, I made the decision to try to go to a community college. Well, that was a terrible mistake because my head wasn't in it. I was still mad, even after a couple of years, and then I got into that accident and I decided it was time to clean up my act."

"So you joined the Army. I know that. But what about girl-friends?" My heart has been pounding, waiting for him to tell me that he fell in love with the nameless woman I saw in the photo, and each second that passes drives me a little more insane. "Tell me about them."

"There was only one. She was no one. Just a girl I met in college. We got along great and she loved to party . . . It was a win-win for everyone."

"Did you love her?"

"No," he says, kissing me softly on the mouth. "I've only ever loved one girl in my life. I've only ever said those three little words to one person, and that's you. It's always been you, and it'll always be you, Katie."

"You promise?" I ask, hating how vulnerable I sound, but damn it, I'm vulnerable. He owns every single part of me, heart and soul, and if he leaves me again, I know that I won't survive the heartache.

"Katie," Devin's voice softens, his hands making their way up my body until they're wrapped around my cheeks. "I swear to you that I'm not going anywhere. I am yours, whether you want me or not. I've given you my heart, and even if you don't want it, you can't give it back because it belongs to you.

I know what I have—what *we* have. It's special. It's once in a lifetime. It's a happily-ever-after sort of love. And I may be a dumbass, but I learn from my mistakes and I don't make the same ones twice. Letting you go was one of those mistakes."

His words seep into my skin and wrap around my soul. I close my eyes, savoring the moment. "Can we go home?" I ask, hating that by "home" I mean the hotel, because right now I'd rather have him in my bed. "I just want to be with you. I want to make love to you over and over again."

"We have a lot of years to make up for, that's for sure," he says, smiling as he manages to push to his feet with me still cradled in his arms.

"Ten, to be exact." I giggle when he smacks my ass playfully. "Roughly thirty seven hundred days . . . give or take a few." Devin growls, a low rumble causing his chest to vibrate, and the sound causes shivers to run down my spine. "That's a ton of sex. Are you up for the challenge, Sergeant Clay?"

"Oh, sweet Katie. You have no idea what sort of challenges I'm up for."

"Hmmm," I purr, kissing the side of his neck as he walks through the house and out the front door. "This could get interesting."

With a speed I didn't know he was capable of, Devin opens the door of our rental, dumps me in, and then runs to his side of the car. In a matter of seconds, we're flying down the road. His hands are gripped tightly around the steering wheel, and I watch the muscles of his thighs twitch under his jeans as he shifts gears. It's fucking sexy as hell, and I suddenly can't wait for the hotel—I need to touch him now.

Turning in my seat, I reach across the gear stick. Devin gives me a curious glance. "What are you doing?"

"Nothing." I shrug, slipping my hand in his jeans. I find his erection rock solid and throbbing, and when I wrap my fingers around him, his cock jumps in my hand.

"Katie." His voice is low, raw and holds a massive amount of warning. "We're almost to the hotel, baby. Give me a couple more minutes."

"I've given you enough time, Dev." He glares at me and I can't help but smirk. He's just so damn gorgeous it isn't even fair. That strong jaw, that fucking dimple . . . those eyes. It's too much. He should be arrested for being too damn good-looking.

"Well then, you better drive fast," I say, dropping my eyes from his as I lower myself in the seat. "Because in approximately ten seconds, you'll be buried deep in my throat." He moans, his stomach muscles twitching under the weight of my lips against his belly button. "And once I start, I won't stop."

"Hold on." His voice is deep and husky, and it sounds like he's doing everything he can to keep himself together. It's a damn good thing I went without underwear this morning or they'd be soaking wet.

His legs move under me as he shifts gears, and my body jerks as we propel forward. "I am." Popping the button on his jeans, I slide the zipper down and tug his cock from the confines of his boxers. "I suggest you take your own advice, soldier." Wrapping my mouth around the head of his cock, I take him deep into my mouth, surrounding him as far as my mouth will allow.

"Son of a bitch." Devin fists his hand in my hair, and I think it's safe to say that he's not doing a good job of keeping it together now. Because when I slide my tongue along the underside of his shaft and suck hard, a string of curse words fly from his mouth.

"Katie. Fuck. I'm not gonna . . ." His words trail off as I suck even harder, pumping him over and over. His hips buck and I feel the exact moment that I've driven him to the edge. His body trembles, jerks, and then goes completely rigid. I swallow, riding out his orgasm, before releasing him with a wet pop.

I peek up at Devin while tucking him in his jeans. He looks sated and happy. He must sense me watching him, because he looks down. My head is cradled in his lap and he gives me a devilish smile.

"Your turn." The car whips to the left and he throws it into park. Before I can blink, I'm upside down, hanging off his shoulder and he's walking at a fast clip to what I assume is the hotel, considering all I can see is his ass.

His large hand slides up the back of my thigh and then disappears before smacking hard against my ass. "I hope you're ready, because I'm going to spend the entire night making you pay for that. You're going to come over and over again until you're begging me to stop."

"Will I scream your name?" I ask playfully.

"Oh, sweetheart. You have no idea what you're in for."

Right back at ya, babe!

Chapter 27 | *Katie*

"Between the Raindrops"
—Lifehouse ft. Natasha Bedingfield

A warm hand settles low on my back, and I moan when he starts kneading at my sore muscles. Devin was right; I had no idea what I was in for. That man dominated my body last night and well into the morning, and now I'm paying the price.

"Are you sore?" he asks, his fingers making their way to the exact spot that he lay claim to . . . several times.

"Mmmm . . . maybe a little."

He nods and kisses my bare shoulder. His fingers are skimming my back, and the light touch causes goose bumps to scatter across my skin.

"I love that my touch can do this to you."

"Trust me, soldier, your touch does a lot more than give me goose bumps," I mumble, my face still buried in the pillow. Devin chuckles, and I do my best to memorize the sound because I won't hear it for several more weeks.

"We should get up," he whispers.

"No. I don't want to get up." We made love until the early morning hours and then drifted off to sleep before waking up for a late breakfast. Then we made love again, fell back asleep, and now here we are. I have muscles aching that I didn't even know existed, and I'm fairly certain that I had more orgasms in the past four days than I've had in the past four years combined.

"I love seeing you like this," he says, his hands roaming my naked body.

"Like what? My makeup is a disaster, and I have messy sex hair."

"Don't talk about my woman like that." He pinches my ass playfully and I squirm next to him, rolling over in his arms.

"Hi."

"Good morning, beautiful." Dev kisses the top of my nose. "You're gorgeous, and this sated look on your face is something I could get used to."

I cuddle as close as I can get and tangle one of my legs with his. "Speaking of getting used to . . . What are we going to do when you get done? Are you going to come home, or—"

"Katie," he says, cutting me off. "You're my home. I'm coming home to *you*. Where you are, that's where I'll be."

My heart does a 360 inside my chest. If I weren't already head over heels in love with Devin, I would be after those words. "That sounds perfect."

"You're perfect," he says. "This right here, being with you again, and holding you . . . It's perfect. I don't want to leave."

Damn it. I was really trying to go as long as possible without mentioning Devin leaving, but now that it's out, I can't seem to stop the tears from blurring my vision.

"I don't want you to leave either."

Devin kisses my cheek, and then he drags my mouth to his. "We don't have much longer," he says, his lips brushing mine. "Then I'll be home, and we can start our lives together."

"That sounds good," I say, hating the way my heart is trying to jump from my chest. The mere thought of him being gone makes me want to crawl out of my skin.

Devin's mouth lands on mine and I immediately open myself up to him. We fall into a drugging kiss, a new dance we've perfected the past several days, and the thought of not doing it again tonight or tomorrow makes my stomach churn. The tears that were blurring my vision finally break free.

Devin's thumb darts out, wiping away what few tears he can catch. "Don't cry. Please don't cry."

"I can't help it." I sniff, burying my nose in his chest. "I don't want you to go. I just got you back."

Out of nowhere, my mind drifts to the what-ifs that I've been trying so hard not to think about. Panic crawls up my throat and I pull back, my eyes landing on Devin's. The words are on the tip of my tongue, but I can't get them to come out. Do I tell him that it scares me? That the thought of something happening to him makes me want to go fucking insane?

"No." Devin's voice is low and firm, the complete opposite of his eyes, which are swimming with love. "Don't go there, Katie. Please don't go there."

"Don't go where?" My voice is watery and way too shaky. I swipe away the tears running down my face and I suck in a deep breath.

"It's written all over your face, baby," he says, threading a hand through my hair. "And trust me, I get it. The unknown is scary, and there are no guarantees where war is concerned, but if there's one thing you need to know—one thing that I want you to carry with you—it's that I will fight like hell to make it back to you." Devin's eyes fill with tears. "I'm coming back to you, Katie."

I offer him a tremulous smile; it isn't much, but it's the best I can do. "Promise me," I whisper. "Promise me you will do whatever you have to do to come back to me."

Devin's eyes bounce between mine as though he can't decide exactly how to respond. I know I'm asking for a lot, but I'm desperate, and right now I need the words.

"Baby." Sitting up, Devin pulls me onto his lap. The sheet falls around my waist, leaving my body as naked and vulnerable as my heart, but Devin's eyes don't stray from mine. He cradles my neck between his warm palms, his thumbs running a soft path along my cheekbones. "I let you down once, and I promise you I won't let you down again."

"Tell me you love me," I beg, wrapping my hands around his neck, mimicking his hold on me. We're nose to nose, our breath mingling, and this moment is so incredibly perfect, I don't want it to end.

"I love you." Eyes locked on mine, Devin kisses me softly. "I want you every single day for the rest of my life." He kisses my nose, followed by each eyelid. "I want to marry you and have babies with you." His lips trail to my ear. "I want to make love to you every night and wake up to your beautiful face every morning." Wiping away more of my tears, Devin smiles at me, and it's that smile combined with these words that bring me peace. "I want to grow old with you, Katie. I want forever."

"You mean the world to me, Dev." I drop my forehead to his and slip my hands to the back of his neck. "I want all of that. What you just said . . . that's my dream."

"It's not going to be a dream for long, because when I get home we're going to start building that dream . . . together."

The urge to start building that dream now is so damn strong, and knowing that he's leaving just drives home the reality that it's going to be a damn long time until I get to be wrapped in his arms again. "Make love to me," I whisper.

Devin growls and slams his mouth to mine at the same time the alarm goes off. We didn't set it to wake us up; we set it to remind us when Devin needed to get going in time to make his flight. *I hate that fucking alarm.* Reaching around me, Devin slaps the alarm, effectively shutting it off.

"Don't go," I beg, my nerves taking over. "I need to you to make love to me one more time." Hurriedly, I pull the sheet off of us and wrap my legs around his waist. My hands roam every inch of his body, because suddenly I need one last chance to memorize everything about it so that when I'm home by myself and I'm missing him, I can pull the memories out and drown myself in them.

"Slow down, Katie." Devin wraps his hands around my wrists, then pulls them to his face and kisses them. "We have time, baby. I'm going to make love to you, and then I'm going to drive myself to the airport—"

What? Is he crazy? Hell no. "No." I shake my head, brows furrowed. Doesn't he want to spend as much time with me as he can? Doesn't he want me there right before he boards the plane? "I want to go with you."

"No," he says, gently nudging me to my back. His larger than life frame hovers above me. "I'm going to show you how much you mean to me, and then I'm going to leave you right here in this bed, sated and happy. That's the memory of you that I want when I go back to Iraq. I don't want to see you crying in the airport. I want to see you lying here in this bed, your hair fanned out on the pillow with the sexiest little smile on your lips. Because you do," he says, kissing my lips, "you get this smile on your face, and it makes me feel fucking fantastic. It makes me feel like, for once in my life, I've done something right. And I need to feel that when I leave here."

Well, son of a gun, how am I supposed to argue with that? My heart swells and I let my knees drop, allowing Devin to settle between my legs. "So this our good-bye? Right here in bed, instead of at the airport?"

"We aren't saying good-bye, Katie. *This* isn't good-bye. It's a promise . . . Remember that dream we just talked about?"

I nod, feeling him position himself at my entrance.

"This is a promise that you're going to be waiting for me when I come home . . . a promise that we're going to make those dreams come true."

"Do we need to shake on it?" I ask, finally gaining the strength to smile.

"Oh baby, we're gonna do more than shake on it."

And with those words, Devin pushes inside me.

Home.

Chapter 28 | Devin

"Tiger Lily"—Matchbook Romance

The hollow ache in the pit of my stomach is something I wouldn't wish upon my worst enemy. JFK is flooded with mobs of other passengers walking past the barstool I've claimed as my own, but I pay no attention to them. I don't see my fellow bar patrons, because in this moment, right now, I just need to forget.

I take two shots of Jameson and chase them with a shot of pickle juice. Not wanting to be seen drinking in uniform, I slide the shot glasses as far down the bar as I can. I don't like disrespecting the uniform and any other time I'd be stronger than this, but leaving Katie was unbearable. There is nothing okay about how I'm feeling right now, and there's definitely nothing okay about leaving her again. Of all the shitty things I've experienced in all the years of my life, this—this right here—takes the cake. This kind of hurt sticks with you; it fucking guts you wide open.

I wave two fingers toward the bartender and she nods in acknowledgement. She chills two more shots of Jameson and sets them before me, along with the requisite shot of pickle juice. I glance around me, making sure no one is looking, and then down all three in succession before once again sliding them down the bar. I feel like an asshole for drinking these feelings away, but the warm tingle the Jameson creates ripples through my body, just under the skin, and numbs the pain a little.

I want to call her again. I need her soft voice to help ease this ache in the center of my chest, to help me forget where I'm headed. But I have to remain strong. These feelings can't take away from me doing my job, getting back to my men, and making sure they all get back home. But I can't help but wonder how in the hell I'm going to do that when I'm leaving the best part of me back with Katie. How will I do it when a shell of a man returns to Baghdad?

Tilting my wrist, I look at my watch, which is much harder to read now than when I first walked into the bar. *Twenty minutes until takeoff.* Twenty minutes and I'm that much closer to a world completely opposite of this one. The harsh reality of it pulls the air from my lungs and sits heavily in my throat. I'm choking on the truth.

I order and down two more shots, pay my bill, and then make my way to the gate, my eyes counting the tiles on the floor as I go.

Fuck reality.

By the time I reached Germany, I had gotten drunk, sobered up, and gotten drunk again, spending more money than I'd like to admit and sleeping uncomfortably close to my flight neighbors. I blabbered to them midflight about Katie, our ten years apart, and our four beautiful days together. Somewhere over the Atlantic, several of them bought me shots, which contributed greatly to my absurd level of intoxication. Some of the women listening in bawled their eyes out, and I think at one point I did too.

As I board the plane to Kuwait, I'm no longer drunk but now have a sharp, shooting pain piercing my temples, eyes, and the base of my skull. The throbbing nearly blinds me and makes the cabin lights seem like halogen lamps burning holes through

my retinas. Several of the other uniformed personnel stagger-
ing onto the flight look the same way I do—the walking dead
lurching their way back to hell.

I want to cry so badly, but I've been fighting back the tears as
best I can. Because as much as I try and force my mind to make
that transition back to soldier, I can't fight the truth.

I need to be home, and Katie is my home.

As the lights in the cabin flicker off and the plane rumbles
forward preparing for takeoff, I think to our last phone call just
moments before boarding.

"Devin?"

*I want to speak, but I don't think I can. I'm moments away from
heading back to a war zone, and all I want is to be back beside her—to
continue the amazing journey we've restarted. The line sits silent, and
each time I try and get a word out, the throbbing in the base of my neck
takes over, the tears wanting so badly to pour from my eyes.*

*"Devin, baby, I know you're there. Say something, please . . . Did
you make it to Germany?"*

"Katie—" I croak, my voice cutting off involuntarily.

*"Oh, Devin." I can hear her voice quiver over the line and she
sniffles. I feel tears roll down my cheek and quickly wipe them away
as I conceal myself in the booth so no one can see. This terminal is full
of other military members heading back to the same place I am, and I
refuse to show weakness around them, even though weakness is the only
thing I feel right now.*

*"Yeah, um . . ." I clear my throat. "I'm a few minutes from heading
out." Swallowing hard, I close my eyes and imagine Katie being right
beside me, her arms around my lower back and mine over her shoulders. She comforts me with her words, rocking with me back and forth,
back and forth. "Baby, I miss you so fucking much." My voice cracks on
the last word, and I drop my head between my shoulders.*

*"God, I miss you too, Devin. I miss you so much." I can tell she's
crying harder now, and as much as I need her to stop, for the sake of*

my sanity, there's something terrifically heart-warming about knowing she misses me just as much as I miss her.

"Katie, baby, I just want to say that no matter what happens during the rest of my time over there, my four days with you have been the best of my life. I wouldn't change a second of our time together."

I can hear her sobbing on the other end now. "Damn it, Dev," Katie cries. "You can't talk like that, you hear me? Ever!"

I suck in a deep breath, knowing full well that I may never make it back to her. The thought fucking kills me. I hate that I have to leave her again . . . that I'm making her go through this kind of hurt. "Baby, I'm sorry, I'm just—"

"No," she says, cutting me off. Her words are much more composed than just a second ago. "I mean it, Devin. I'm hurting too much already, and I can't handle that thought."

"I'm sorry. I'm hurting too . . . so, so bad." Just then, a voice comes over the intercom announcing the boarding of our plane, and my heart sinks.

"Katie—"

"I know, baby."

"I love you so fucking much." I wish there was another word for love, because this is so much more. What I feel for this girl can't be put into words.

"I love you too, Dev, more than you'll ever know. Call me as soon as you can, okay?"

"I will, sweet girl. Bye."

"Bye, baby."

The click and dial tone hit me like a punch to the gut. I want to lie here and lick my wounds, but there's a job to be done. And even though I can't fathom the thought of getting on this fucking plane, let alone leading men in battle, I'm going to do it.

The screech of the landing gear against the pavement jars me awake. I have to sit for a moment to process where I am. Rubbing the sleep from my eyes, I look around but can't make out much of anything in the darkness of the cabin. I peek out the window and notice the tarmac lights dominating the night sky, a desert wasteland decorating its backdrop.

Baghdad.

Fuck me.

My guys welcomed me back warmly and filled me in on the uneventful past four days. I have to admit that it did lift my spirits being back with them. They are my brothers, and if I can't be with Katie, being with my guys is the next best thing.

It's been weeks since my return, and although it's been difficult, the importance of our work here and the well-being of my soldiers help to ease the pain of missing her. Thankfully, most days I'm too busy to let it dominate my head.

I call Katie every chance I get, and we've even started chatting via webcam. Lord knows I couldn't go without laying eyes on her beautiful face. While I'd rather have her with me, being able to see her makes things a lot easier.

Fighting for computer use, on the other hand, has been a pain in my ass. But I've learned to bring a book with me to help get me through the wait. Which is why I'm currently seated outside the closed communications center door reading *The Notebook,* doing my best to conceal the cover. Katie insisted I read it, and I'll admit I was a little skeptical at first, but Noah and Allie have managed to capture my attention. I've found myself imagining it's the two of us instead, and I've even laughed a few times, because when I think about the journey Katie and I have been on to get where we are, it almost feels like a love story in and of itself. Like a novel that was destined to be, set in place long before either of us were even born. She and I were made for each other, and it blows my mind that I couldn't look past my own stubborn ways to see that long before now.

The opening of the communications center door grabs my attention and I quickly close the book, hiding it in my cargo pocket while rising to my feet. Adams comes through the doorway and winks at me, motioning toward his dick.

"All yours, buddy!" He cackles and pats me hard on the back.

"Hey, man, thanks a lot for taking our shift tonight. We got you guys next time."

"No problem. I know you'd do it for me." He slaps my hand before exiting. I make my way inside, shut the door, and take a seat at the computer. The anticipation is a fucking rush. It overwhelms my senses and sends pulses throughout my body. I *love* getting to see her beautiful, smiling face staring back at me and hearing that sweet, melodic laugh.

The webcam pops up and I send a request to Katie, then wait impatiently for her to answer. It rings for longer than I would expect, and I can't help but worry that something's come up. I'd be heartbroken if that's the case. The whole reason I switched shifts with Adams was because I wanted to see Katie, and this was the only time that worked for her. I mean, my guys did want the night off and all, but it definitely helped me out.

The flicker of the screen and Katie's face popping up sends a wave of exhilaration over me. I feel like a fucking kid on Christmas morning.

"Devin!" She smiles wide and blows me a kiss. "How are you, babe?"

"Goddamn, I'm better now!" I laugh.

"How was it today?" She knows I won't tell her the whole truth. I don't want her to worry about me more than she already does, but I also don't want to lie to her.

"It wasn't too bad actually. This neighborhood has been getting out of control, and there seems to be a shitload of resentment between the Sunnis and Shiites. They just fucking hate each other . . ." My voice trails off and my eyes stray from the screen. I don't like talking about this stuff with her, not when I'm so far away and I can't be there to ease her concern. "It's been pretty quiet though. I think we're making headway. There's talk there might be an increase in soldiers out here, so that's good."

"Is it?" she says and almost immediately covers her face with her hands. "Sorry, Devin, I didn't mean that. I just want you home is all, and the news . . ." She stops herself by taking her bottom lip between her teeth. I *love* when she does that.

"No, baby, you're okay. I mean, it's not like I don't think about that stuff, you know that. I just hate seeing my guys overworked . . . getting in from mission, sleeping for a few hours, and then getting called right back out. It's wearing them out." She nods, appearing to digest my words. Katie is so patient in conversation, always attentive and waiting for people to completely finish what they have to say before she contributes. I've always been attracted to that in a woman, and I smile widely as I think about it.

"Wait"—she giggles—"what's going on in that brain of yours?"

"Just you. I love you, you know that?"

"Forever and ever?"

"Forever and ever, babe," I say, winking at her. Moments like these are when video just isn't enough. I want to pull her into my arms, wrap her in warmth, and kiss her passionately. I feel throbbing in my dick and unintentionally form a devious smile.

"*Now* what are you thinking about?" she purrs, her words thick with that playful yet sexy tone she uses when she really wants to get me worked up.

"What I think about twenty-four-seven is all. No biggie," I say, laughing and readjusting my cock.

"I saw that!" she squeals. "Does somebody want to come out and play?"

"Don't fuck with me, Kit Kat." I force the smile from my face and give her my best tough guy look, the one that brings grown men to their knees. Katie just smiles.

This girl fucking owns me.

"I'm not fucking with you," she says, her eyes hooded. "I miss you." I can see her hand slide down and out of view, and a crimson flush slowly creeps up her neck. Her eyes are burning with desire and it's sexy as hell. I fucking *want* her. "I'm all alone, and I want you inside me so bad that it actually fucking hurts." Her words send surges of pleasure through my body.

"Fuck, baby." My words are hushed as I'm overtaken by a desperate need to be inside of her. To take all of her and look into her eyes, knowing that from here on out, I will be the one and only man to have her. "Do you know how fucking bad I want you? Do you know how much you creep into my thoughts, and my dreams, and my subconscious? You're my addiction, Katie."

She moans and her arm moves, but I can't see what she's doing and it's driving me crazy. I can see through her shirt that she's not wearing a bra, and the outline of her nipples is making my cock ache. "I should be punished for taking up so much of your time," she says, her tongue darting out and running a path along her lower lip. "What will you do to me, Dev? What's my punishment?"

Son of a bitch. I didn't know she had this in her. Usually I'm the one doing the dirty talk, not her. My sweet angel has the mouth of a devil.

"Well, that all depends on how bad you've been." I shoot her a smirk, more than willing to play with her.

"Oh, I've been very, *very* bad . . ." Her words linger, and before I know it, I've pulled my dick out and into my hands. I don't stroke it immediately but rub the tip, imagining it's Katie's tongue teasing me before she takes all of me into her mouth.

"Fuck, Katie." I moan, the heat of the moment getting me all sorts of riled up. Suddenly, all thoughts of punishment fly from my head because I just want to fucking see her. My face pinches tight, and she must notice my struggle because she slips a hand to her breast and takes one of her nipples between two fingers, tugging at it lightly from the outside of her shirt.

A low growl rips from my chest. The sound seems to spur her on because she scoots her chair back to expose her other hand, which is lodged in her panties. The temperature in the room feels a hundred degrees hotter and my heart slams in my chest.

"I want to see you, baby." I motion for her to take her shirt off and wait impatiently for her to do so.

She puts one finger up and shakes it. "I don't think so, Sergeant Clay. I want to see you first. And by you, I mean Hector Sanchez." I burst out in laughter as the memory of the name overwhelms me. She asked me what I called my dick one time, and I jokingly told her Hector Sanchez. For some reason, it stuck.

She's laughing too now, but it doesn't kill the mood because that laugh is the sexiest thing I've ever heard. The curves of her neck move elegantly, causing her nipples to tease me from inside her shirt.

"Okay, I show you Hector, and then I get to see the ladies."

"Deal." She winks, removing her hand from her panties—damn!—and taking the bottom of her shirt in both hands. She holds it there, not lifting just yet, waiting for me to show the goods. I scoot the office chair back to expose my dick, and when she smiles, I begin lightly stroking. She completes the deal by pulling off the T-shirt, an old Nirvana one of mine that she stole in Pittsburgh, and tosses it to the floor. Her perfect tits sit like tear drops, her nipples perky and willing me to suck them.

"Fuck, baby. I love your body so much." I slide my other hand up my shirt and rub my tightening abs as I continue to stroke my rock-hard cock. Katie takes both nipples into her hands and pulls at them, looking seductively at me, her mouth a perfect O. Her breath is choppy.

"I want to feel you, baby. I want every part of you, and I want to take you over and over and over again."

"Mmmm, what else?" She shifts one of her hands down to her panties and slips it inside, her other hand still working her nipple.

"I want you to start slow. Tease me with your lips and tongue like you always do. Make me ache to feel you, your mouth, your pussy, everything."

"Mmm-hmm." It's all she can manage because she has her panties yanked to the side and, fuck me, she's playing with her swollen clit. Her skin is flush with pleasure, and it takes every ounce of control I have to not explode on the spot.

"Trace a pathway all over my body with your lips. Push me until I just can't take it anymore, and then take all of me into your mouth. Make me beg to be inside you." I'm fucking dying. My cock is throbbing in my hand, and I can feel my release just below the surface.

"I want you to take me," she whimpers, her hand picking up speed. "I can't take it anymore; I want you to fuck me, Dev."

"Fuck, yes, Katie. When I'm about to explode because the desire has built up so much, I'll take you by the arm and toss you to the mattress. I'll tear the clothes from your body, taking all of you in before kissing every inch of you. I want to feel your soft skin against my lips. I want to make your tight little body quiver beneath me. I'll lightly nibble from your neck to your stomach to the inside of your thigh, taking the flesh between my teeth before slowly moving to your clit. I'll lick it softly, letting you thrust your hips against me, getting it just how you like it."

"Fuck me, God, please fuck me. I need you inside me," she moans, her body writhing.

I'm caught up in the moment now, working my shaft rapidly and taking in the perfection that's playing before me. I can feel a buzz at the base of my shaft gaining momentum, preparing for climax. I move my hand faster, trying to line up my orgasm with hers.

She throws her head back and moans, her body arching up and out of the seat. The sight of her sends shudders through my body, blood rages through my veins and—

The communications door bursts open.

Navas barrels in and then stops abruptly, his jaw nearly hitting the floor. He shields his eyes with an arm at the same time my orgasm slams into me, the force of it and his interruption nearly causing me to fall from my chair.

"What the fuck?" I yell, looking at the computer as I shove my dick in my pants. Katie has somehow managed to cover herself, and she's watching the screen with a look of complete horror on her face.

"Fuck, man, I'm sorry. Shit's going down . . . I . . . fuck," Navas stammers. "I didn't know you'd be doing *that*. Sorry, man." He's trying not to laugh, but I can tell by his tone and the look in his eyes that there's something much, much bigger going on. I rise to my feet and lean in close to the computer.

"Baby, I'll call you soon, okay?"

"Uh . . . okay." She looks torn between being completely embarrassed and concerned about what's going on, but she knows now is not the time to ask.

"I love you, Kit Kat, with all my heart." Navas steps outside to give us a moment alone.

"Forever and always?" she asks.

"Forever and always."

"I love you, too," she says before the screen goes black. I log off the computer and meet Navas outside the door.

"You fucking cock! You ever heard of knocking?" I punch him hard on the arm.

"I'm sorry. I was rushing and wasn't thinking. It's just . . ." He trails off and looks to the operations center then back at me.

"What's up, dude? What's going on?"

"Just come to the ops center with me, man. Whole squad is in there. Something went down with Adams's convoy." Fear strikes me dead in the chest and the worst images flood my mind.

"What do you mean? They just set out like forty minutes ago." I follow Navas as he leads me to the operations center, where I see my guys nervously hunched over the radio.

"The other two trucks on his patrol got out to the scene and they're sending the info in now. Captain Kendricks wanted me to get all the guys ready 'cause we're probably going out."

"What do you mean *'got to the scene'*? Why weren't they together?"

"I don't know. They literally just reached out to report it. Apparently, they're still trying to figure out what happened." I have no idea what's going on or how the vehicles could've gotten separated. I turn my focus to the radio, which sits silent for a moment before relaying the message.

"Three KIA, one MIA, RPG rounds, and small arms fire. No sign of enemy combatants. Over." *Three KIA, one MIA.* The words catch me off-guard. *Please tell me I didn't just hear that.* Tavares lifts the radio headset to his ear and clicks the button.

"Names of KIA, MIA? Over."

"Akers, Fields, Dixon KIA . . . Adams MIA," the voice over the radio says, struggling to remain composed. Adams's and Dixon's faces pop into my head, and I can't help but feel terrible for everything I've ever thought or spoken about either one of them. This isn't the first time I'm hearing about the death of a fellow soldier, but it never gets any easier. It's like an out-of-body experience; you're there, but well beyond the realm of under-standing. You want to believe that if you convince yourself it isn't real, maybe it will be the truth.

The news forces me into a seat. Thomas walks quickly out of the room, and I know exactly what he's going to do. He's going to do what all of us wish we could do right now and that's cry our fucking eyes out.

Captain Kendricks grabs the headset from Tavares and pulls it to his mouth.

"Gator two Charlie, what in the hell happened out there? Over." He is furious, and rightfully so.

"Lieutenant Dixon's truck was pulling security on a bridge and we were on the other side behind cover, waiting for word from them on our next movements. The vehicles not being together was Lieutenant Dixon's call, sir. Over." Captain Kendricks squeezes the headset tightly between his hands, and it looks as if he could just about crush it into tiny bits.

"And what happened next? Over."

"We didn't immediately know where the attack was coming from, sir. We didn't have eyes on Lieutenant Dixon's truck and we were waiting on them to give us directions. Over."

"And when you finally did decide to move your ass and react to contact, what did you find? Over."

"No enemy combatants, sir. Partially destroyed Humvee, RPG and small arms fire, and the three KIA and one MIA. Over."

"Roger. You keep your asses there and don't move. Over." Captain Kendricks throws the headset to the ground and Tavares scrambles to retrieve it.

"Sergeant Clay," Captain Kendricks calls out, and I rise to my feet. "Get your men together and prepare for mission. Have Staff Sergeant Baker's squad go with you."

"Roger that, sir."

I gather my men and we make our way back to the tent without a word spoken between us. It's not like there's anything to say in this moment. There's no rhyme or reason to it. Some make it home still breathing. Others make it home in flag-draped coffins. These are the days I wish I could forget.

Chapter 29 | *Katie*

"She Is Love"—Parachute

Soda spews from Maggie's mouth, her eyes as wide as they can get, and she busts up in a full-blown belly laugh. "Oh my God! That's fucking hilarious."

"No, it's not." I shake my head, lips pursed, wondering why in the world I thought it was a good idea to tell my best friend about last night's webcam mishap. "It was horrifying. I was completely mortified."

"Who cares?" she says, waving me off as she wipes the tears from her face. "That is classic, and you're going to laugh about it for years to come."

"No, I won't," I say flatly.

She shrugs and then falls into another fit of laughter. "Fine. I will."

"I hate you."

"Don't hate me. I'm not the one that coaxed you into getting naked in front of a computer screen."

Yeah, I left out the part that I was the one doing the coaxing. She may be my BFF, but there are definitely things that are better left unsaid.

"Can we please talk about something else? This is starting to make me pissy." Plus, I've got something much bigger on my mind, and if I don't tell somebody, I'll probably burst.

"Fine," she says, taking a bite of the cinnamon roll sitting in front of her. "What do you want to talk about?"

"I think I'm pregnant." I have absolutely no control over my mouth today and the words fall out before I give them permission.

For the second time in less than five minutes, I watch Maggie spew something all over my kitchen table—only this time it isn't soda, it's her cinnamon roll. "WHAT? What do you mean *you think you're pregnant?*"

"I mean, I haven't had my period and I never miss my period . . . *ever.*"

"But you're on birth control, right?"

"Yes! That's what I don't understand. My periods have been regular since starting it years ago, so there's no other explanation."

Maggie's mouth opens and then shuts as she absorbs what I'm saying. "Okay, there could easily be another explanation."

"And what exactly would that be?"

"I don't know! I'm still thinking . . ." She rubs a hand over her head and looks down for several beats before looking up again. "Do your boobs hurt? Do you feel sick? Did you take a test? You should take a test." Her questions come out too fast, and I have to think about my answers for a second before responding.

"Yes. No. Kind of."

Maggie's brows furrow as she presumably lines up my answers to her questions. "What do you mean *kind of?* You either took a test or you didn't. It's a yes or no answer."

"I didn't pee on a stick, if that's what you're asking. But I called Dr. Bray's office and they told me to stop the birth control and come in for a blood test, which I did first thing this morning."

"Annnnd . . ." Maggie is watching me, eyes wide, waiting for an answer that's going to disappoint her.

"They're supposed to call me this afternoon." As if right on cue, my phone rings, and Maggie and I both stare at it.

"Answer it," she says, shoving it in my direction.

"What if I'm pregnant?"

"You won't know if you don't answer the damn phone." Maggie snags my cell from the table and flips it open. "Hello . . . yes, she's right here."

She hands me the phone and I slowly bring it to my ear. My heart is hammering inside my chest, and blood is rushing past my ears so fast that I'm a little worried I won't even hear her . . . in fact, I might very well pass out.

"Hello?" My voice cracks and I swallow hard.

"Hi, Katie, it's Stephanie from Dr. Bray's office. Is this a good time?"

Well, that depends on what you have to tell me. "Yes. Did you get my results back?" That was fast, I think to myself. I suck in a breath, waiting for her answer, and when I hear the words *"Congratulations, you're pregnant"* float through the line, I nearly drop the phone.

"I—I don't understand," I stammer. "How did this happen?" I shake my head, realizing how stupid that sounds. "Of course I know how it happened, but I was on birth control . . . and I know it isn't always effective but . . . *wow . . . okay . . . I'm pregnant.*"

"It's a lot to take in, and yes, these things happen. But Dr. Bray said to call her if you have any questions at all."

Okay . . . I nod to myself. I can do this . . . *we* can do this. "Wait!" I blurt. "I know this sounds stupid, and I'm a nurse and should probably know, but up until yesterday, I'd been taking the birth control. Will that affect the baby?"

"It's not a stupid question," she says before easing my mind. "You and the baby should both be fine, but Dr. Bray wants you to come back into the office for a checkup in two weeks."

My mind drifts toward Devin, and whatever else she was saying falls to the wayside. What will he think about this? Will he be excited? We just got back together . . . Will he be ready for a baby?

Am I *ready for a baby?*

"You don't have a choice." Maggie snaps the phone shut and I look up. "Don't worry," she says, "you went off into la la land, so I took the phone and wrote everything else down."

"Thank you," I whisper. Looking down, I stare at my still flat stomach and touch it gently.

There's a life growing inside there.

A tiny little life that is half Devin and half me.

Tears well up in my eyes. "I'm having a baby," I say, nearly choking on the words. "I'm going to be a mother."

Maggie's arms wrap around me. "You are going to be the best damn mother."

"You think?" I ask, turning to her with a tremulous smile.

"I know it. Congratulations, Mama. Now you just have to tell the daddy . . . and just so I'm on the right page, the daddy is Devin, right?"

"Yes!" I half shriek and half laugh as I slap her across the arm.

"Okay," she says, holding her hands up in the air. "I had to check. I mean, I figured, but you never mentioned Devin forgetting to shield the dragon."

"Shield the dragon? Where in the hell do you come up with this stuff?"

"Never mind," she says, rolling her eyes. "So, I need to know when you're telling Devin and when you're telling your mom, because this is going to be a really hard secret to keep."

"Maggie," I warn, giving her my best authoritative eye. Good to start practicing now, right? "You can't tell anyone, at least not until I give you the okay. Got it?"

"I'll do my best, but promise that you'll tell him soon, because . . . Well, you know how I get when I'm excited about something."

"I'll tell him soon, I promise. We're scheduled to webcam again in a couple of minutes anyway."

Maggie's eyes light up. "I'm totally sticking around for this."

"What? No, you're not sticking around."

"Is there any chance of some sexy times? Because if so, I'm sticking around for this. That boy of yours is fucking delicious, and I'd love to walk in and catch him naked on the screen."

"Trust me," I say, laughing, "there won't be any more on-screen sexy times for a very *long* time. Now leave," I say, chuckling as I tug her up from her chair, spin her around and guide her toward the door.

"You're no fun."

"Yes, well, I'm sure that Devin's friend who saw my lady bits disagrees with that." Spinning her around, I pull her into a hug, kiss her cheek, and then open the door and politely shove her out.

"Wait!" Maggie's arm darts out, stopping the door from closing. "What about Wyatt?"

My brows furrow. "What about Wyatt?"

"This is huge. You're *pregnant,* Katie."

"I'm aware," I say with a smile. "But what does that have to do with Wyatt?"

Maggie shrugs. "Nothing . . . But you guys didn't break up that long ago. And from what you've told me, he's been holding out hope for the two of you getting back together. I've never been a fan of his, but I hope you're planning—"

"I'll take care of it," I say, gently cutting her off. "When I went to Pennsylvania, I called and talked to him, explained where I was going and why. I made it very clear that what we had is over. But you're right, this will be touchy, and I'll talk to him about it as soon as I've had a chance to tell Dev."

"Okay." She nods, seemingly pleased with my answer before spinning on her heel. "Love you!" she hollers, walking away.

"Love you!" I yell, shutting the door.

I walk back to my room, grab my laptop, and then settle myself against the bed to wait for Devin's request. About the time I expect it to come through, my phone rings and I see the number that is now so incredibly familiar.

"Hey!" I croon, answering the phone. "I thought we were going to chat online?"

"Hey, baby," Devin says, his voice low and gravelly. It sounds as though he hasn't slept a wink since I last talked to him, and I instantly go on high alert. "I couldn't get the computer, and things have just been so . . ." He trails off, and I fight the urge to beg him to finish the sentence. Devin tries his best to shield me from a lot of what goes on over there, and as much as I appreciate it, sometimes it makes things worse because my imagination runs wild with its own scenarios.

"'Things have just been so' what?" I keep my voice soft and soothing, hoping that he'll open up. But he doesn't.

"Shit, Katie." The sound through the phone gets scratchy and I imagine he's running a hand over his face, probably completely overwhelmed. "It's just been a long-ass day, and I'm ready for this shit to be over."

"Soon. You'll be home soon, I promise." His response is a muffled grunt, so I press on. "Do you want to talk about it . . . whatever's going on? Because I'm here, you know, if you need to get some stuff off your chest."

"I know," he breathes, "and I appreciate that. But right now, I just want to forget it for a couple of minutes. Is that okay?" I open my mouth to respond, but he doesn't give me the chance. "How was your day? Anything new?"

Shit.

I want nothing more than to tell him that I'm pregnant, but now just doesn't seem like the right time. He's got enough on his mind, enough to worry about, and if I tell him about the baby, it could shift his concentration—and that's the last thing we need.

"No," I lie, cringing because I want so badly to tell him the truth. "Nothing new. I did pick up an extra shift next week for Maggie."

"That's nice, baby."

That's nice? Really, that's it?

Normally, I'd get an earful about how I should be cutting back and relaxing, since I practically ran myself into the ground. Of course, that's been months ago now, but still, he usually has more to say than *that's nice.*

"Yup, I felt like I needed to pay her back for picking up those shifts so I could come see you in Pittsburgh."

"She probably appreciates that. What did she need off for?"

Okay, well at least he's engaging some. I just hate that he sounds so distracted. "I think Sean's going to take her out of town. If I had to guess, I bet he's going to propose."

"Awesome," Devin says, his voice flat. "So, what are you up to the rest of the day?"

Other than worry about you? "Hmmm . . . Well, I have an appointment with Dr. Perry this evening, so that should be fun," I say, rolling my eyes. "And then I'm going to have dinner with Mom and Bailey."

"Sounds like you've got a full evening."

"Okay," I snap, cringing when my voice comes out harsher than I'd intended. "Enough. Tell me what's going on, and don't say 'nothing' because I'm not stupid, Dev. You're distant and distracted, and I hate hearing you like this. Let me help you, babe."

"You can't help," he growls, then quickly apologizes. "Sorry, I didn't mean to take it out on you, but you can't help. No one can help. It's just . . . this shit, all of it. I'm done, Katie."

Dropping my head back against my pillows, I take a deep breath and close my eyes. "I know." I sigh. "I can't imagine what it's like for you, but I need you to stay strong and focused"—I lay a hand on my belly, because right now those words are more true than ever—"and I need you to come home. You're almost there."

"I love you. You know that, right?"

"Of course I do, but I love you more."

"Never," he says, his voice infused with so much conviction that it causes my body to shiver. "How—" Devin's words cut off and I hear muffled voices, but I can't understand what they're saying. When he returns, his words are rushed and I'm left with yet another thing to worry about. "Hey baby, I hate to cut this short, but I gotta run."

"No worries. Will you call me later if you get a chance?"

"Absolutely."

"Bye, Dev."

"Bye, Kit-Ka—"

The line goes dead before he finishes saying good-bye. I snap my phone shut and drop it to the bed. *Well, that fucking sucked.* My mind races, going over our entire conversation again to make sure I didn't miss anything, and when I come up empty, I do the only thing I can do. Like a robot, I get dressed and go about my day, knowing full well that Devin will consume every thought until I get to talk to him again.

Soon, I remind myself, *and then I'll get to tell him about the baby—about the life growing inside of me . . . about the life we created.*

Our relationship may have had a rough go in the beginning, but the beginning doesn't really matter, and truly, neither does the ending. It's all of the substance in between that makes for a great love story—for a great relationship—and if I have any say in it, our love story is going to be *epic.*

I walk toward the mirror and slowly lift my shirt. "Hey there," I say, rubbing a hand over my stomach. "Are you ready to meet your daddy?" I ask, not caring for one second that I probably look silly talking to my belly. "It won't be long now and he'll be home safe and sound with us . . . right where he's meant to be."

Chapter 30 | *Devin*

"Set Fire to the Third Bar"—Snow Patrol

The noon sun sits heavy over this desperate Baghdad land-scape. Its rays penetrate the sixty pounds of body armor I'm wearing and sear the flesh beneath. July was bad—August is worse. The M4 rifle in my hands and twelve loaded magazines strapped to my chest aren't making things any easier, but as the team leader of these four assholes, I continue forward and keep my bitching to myself.

We were searching for our fellow soldier and we were sup-posed to push forward until we found him, but now we've received word that we have to meet back up with the rest of our platoon and head back to base. The fear of Sergeant Adams having been found dead overtakes me. We've raided hundreds of houses with no sign of him and not a damn person is talking.

Elkins and Thomas are griping behind me, but until I feel the need, I'll keep my mouth shut. My team is staggered, our backs against a long stone wall, rifles pointed in every direc-tion around us. Navas takes up the rear. His eyes are scrunched tightly watching our six o'clock, grenade launcher set and ready to fire.

The bickering continues, pissing me off, and I step in. "Elkins. Thomas. What are y'all bitchin' about now?" I don't look back but proceed along the wall, tracing its exterior to where the rest of our platoon's vehicles are located, a half-kilometer from where we are now.

"Nothing, Sergeant," Elkins answers, his voice ripe with resentment.

"Elkins, you know if you're bitchin' loud enough for me to hear, then it's not just nothing. Spit it out, kid." I scan the row of homes that runs parallel to us on the other side of a small, muddied stream. The only sounds coming from that direction—or any direction, really—are some emaciated dogs rummaging through scraps.

"It's too quiet, Sarge," Navas hollers, his voice gravelly and weathered. "These fuckin' towel heads are planning something. I can feel it."

A wave of uncertainty washes over me, unease settling deep in my gut. "It's August and hot as balls. They're probably just keeping cool inside." My words are hesitant, as if not wanting to escape my mouth at all, and I wonder briefly if my men pick up on it. *Stay calm, Clay.* I scan the rooftops intently, looking for any sort of movement or anything suspicious.

"Why are they calling us back, Sarge? Why wouldn't they just tell us if they found him or not? This is some fucking bullshit!" Elkins blurts out. I glance back in time to see Thomas smack Elkins in the arm. I shake my head and move forward, but Elkins can't seem to shut the fuck up. "I mean, how hard is it to tell us what the fuck is going on?"

I can't blame him for his frustration. I want to know why they're calling the search off too. They tell you what you need to know, and often that's not very much. I also want to know that they've found Adams alive and well, but that's not how this sort of thing works.

I look back at them again and see the worry in Thomas's eyes. He's not doing well, and I know my words must be gentle.

"Listen, we do what we are told—always. We don't question our orders, we execute them. We'll report back to base and figure out what's going on soon. I'm sure they found him and just don't need us looking anymore."

With my last word, a head pops up from a rooftop in the distance, and I immediately shift my rifle from ready at the hip to eye level. Elkins notices the same thing I do and whips his muzzle toward the activity with the enthusiasm of a twenty-year-old grunt with too much testosterone and not enough common sense. "Hold it, Elkins. It's a kid."

I pull my weapon back down and tap the top of his muzzle for him to do the same. He lowers it, and then the four of us continue along the wall. As we pass the house, I peer up toward the child—a girl, no more than five years old—who is now standing upright and curiously gawking in our direction.

So young. She doesn't have a clue why we are here, or what we are doing. At this point, she doesn't know the difference between an AK-47 and her blankie, but one day this girl will hate me just as her parents do—and as their parents did before them.

I shake the thought from my head and nod toward the girl with a smile. She giggles before taking off, her curls bobbing on top of her head.

"Let's pick it up, gentlemen, not too much further—" I'm cut off by a round screeching past our position and burrowing into the wall just a few steps ahead of me. Shards burst from the concrete in every direction as the bullet rips through the mortar. I jump back, immediately fighting to collect my thoughts. Another shot whizzes by just over our heads, forcing me to react.

"Up and over, up and over! Thomas, you lift Elkins. Navas, I got you." I drop to a knee and interlock my fingers. Navas plunges his foot onto my hands, and with one brisk push, he hurdles atop the wall. Thomas and Elkins follow suit, and then I kneel before Thomas to do the same for him.

Navas and Elkins stand behind the half wall with rifles, scanning the rooftops, searching for the culprit. Two more rounds come tearing in, hitting the wall just to the side of us. I hoist Thomas to the top so that the others can pull him over. Instead of joining them, Thomas shifts around and reaches an arm down for me. I sling my rifle behind my back and grab hold. His other hand reaches down further and he latches his fingers into my belt loop, giving me a tug. My free hand grips tightly onto the edge of the wall as he works at pulling me up. The sound of another round explodes through the air, and I instinctively duck my head. It tears through the hand I have grasping the wall, and I yank it back with a deep howl. As I do, my weight pulls me back toward the ground and Thomas along with me. He flips backward away from the wall and crumples to the earth like a ragdoll. Navas fires a few shots at no one in particular as I help Thomas to his feet. He's dazed, but quickly shakes it off. I fight the pain off as best I can, blood pouring from my hand.

"Come on, Thomas, I need to get you over." I drop to a knee to assist him, but he shakes me off.

"No, Sarge, your hand's fucked. I'll get you over first," he says defiantly. I can't argue because I know he's right. I stick a boot onto his palms and he heaves me up. I shift my weight around and lock my good hand with Thomas's just as another gunshot breaks the still air.

Thomas's eyes go wide and his hand goes limp in mine. A bullet now sits burrowed inside the wall, having made a pathway through his innards. He falls back, hitting the ground hard, and a pool of blood quickly stretches out around him. Before I can react, Elkins grabs my legs and yanks me down with them on the other side so hard that I fall to the ground. Navas locates the enemy on a rooftop in the distance and sends several of his own shots in that direction. Elkins does the same.

Adrenaline kicks in, and within seconds, the pain in my hand ceases. I scramble to my feet and use an oil drum to prop myself up onto the wall, my armpits clinging to it for support. I see Thomas reaching his hand up toward us, blood pooling in his mouth as he struggles to breathe. The return fire erupting from Elkins and Navas's rifles is muted and the wind halts, releasing grains of sand back down to the earth. Time stops. Thomas looks me square in the eye, his face void of color, and although he seems to be slipping away, his eyes are begging me for help. If they could speak, I know just what they'd say—*please, don't let me die.*

Elkins and Navas stop to reload, and three more rounds come through. One rockets past the tops of our heads. The other two rip into Thomas's dying body, successfully yanking away any remaining life.

I can't move. I can't speak. I can't think. I just stare at the new contortion the round has made of his face and I'm numb. *Completely numb.*

I don't hear my team yelling for me to get down. I remain on the wall, my head still exposed to the enemy, when something inside of me snaps. I shoot my attention back to my team—a fierce determination now blazing from my eyes. "We aren't going to fuckin' leave him here!"

"We aren't saying that, Sarge. We can come back and get him once we have some support!" Elkins hollers, his voice strained and raw. He fires three more shots toward the enemy. "No way we make it out alive going back over there, Sarge. No fucking way!"

I contemplate this for a moment as more gunfire comes crashing into our position, piercing the wall and throwing bits of rock and shrapnel into my arm and cheek. I don't feel it, but I rub my face against my arm, clearing the blood from my eyes, and look down at Thomas, then back to Elkins and Navas.

Before they can convince me otherwise, I pull myself completely up onto the wall as if I were weightless, and I sit on its edge. Navas calls for cover fire. I nod my head toward him, and with that I drop from the wall feet first.

It all happens so fast that I'm left with absolutely no time to think. A rocket-propelled grenade round heads straight for me, flames streaking behind it, and just as my feet touch the ground, the explosion takes control of my body.

The first few seconds are what I imagine hell being like. Flames race up either side of me, enveloping me in heat and blinding me of all else. The force tosses me violently into the air, and then I meet the ground so hard that all the air erupts from my lungs. I fight to breathe, struggling to put out the fire that cooks my legs—or what's left of them. The last thing I see before darkness engulfs me is a charred fusion of flesh, bone, and uniform where my legs should be.

And Katie . . . *I see Katie.*

Chapter 31 | *Katie*

"Not about Angels"—Birdy

*P*lease be okay.
   Please be okay.
   Please be okay.

Those three little words play on repeat in my head as my feet pound against the pavement. My arms pump furiously, propelling me across the parking lot. With each step my panic grows, and my heart is slamming so hard inside my chest, I'm certain it could fly right out. My lungs are burning, begging me to slow down. But I can't . . . not until I see him—not until I know that he's okay.

Thunder rumbles through the sky followed by a loud crack of lightning, and the clouds open up, bathing me in bone-chilling rain. Pushing a chunk of sopping wet hair from my face, the doors to the hospital come into view. *Almost there.* Plowing my way through a group of bodies, I sprint into the waiting room. My feet hit the tile floor, sliding out from under me, and I scramble to keep myself upright.

Everything from this point forward is a complete blur. I'm running on pure adrenaline and fear, and the need to be with Devin is consuming every single part of me. So when the blue dots that I'd been instructed to follow disappear, I look up, catching sight of a small sign hanging on the wall, and I sigh in relief.

TRAUMA ICU
PLEASE USE INTERCOM FOR ASSISTANCE
ICU VISITING HOURS
M-F 9AM–5PM
SAT & SUN 9AM–7PM

This is it.

Devin is in there. Squeezing my eyes shut, I say a silent prayer to whoever is listening. Relief that I'm going to get to see him unfurls in my chest, and for the first time in two days I feel like I can breathe.

A small black speaker is embedded in the wall next to the door and a tiny button is perched under it. Lifting my hand, my finger hovers above the unassuming button, and with a deep, optimistic breath, I push it. Several excruciating seconds later, a soft voice crackles through the speaker.

"Can I help you?"

"Um . . . yes, I'm here to see Devin Clay." Everything is quiet, minus the sound of my pulse pounding in my ears as I wait for a response.

"Ma'am, visiting hours have ended for today. If you could, please come back tomorrow any time after nine a.m."

My heart drops to my toes and I shake my head. I heard what she said, but it doesn't make sense. She isn't going to let me see him? "What?" I croak, stepping closer to the door. The familiar burn of tears builds behind my eyes, and I swallow past the lump sitting firmly in my throat. "No," I shriek, shaking my head frantically. *This isn't happening.* "You don't understand. I need to see him now. *Please,*" I plead, pushing the button again because I don't even know if she's listening—and I need her to listen. "Please let me see him."

"I'm sorry, ma'am. I apologize for any inconvenience—"

"Is this a joke?" I laugh humorlessly, maniacally. "You apologize for the inconvenience?" My body trembles as the weight of the past couple of days slams into me, and desperation quickly takes over. "You don't understand. You have to let me in there. *Please,*" I beg, banging my fist against the door. There is no response, and I pound my fist on the door again before fruitlessly jiggling the handle. Every emotion that has been building inside of me boils over. My throat constricts, making it hard to breathe. "Please let me in. There are so many things—" My words break off into a sob and I swipe at the tears that now run down my face. "I swear I won't get in the way. I'll be quick for tonight, but I *have* to see him." My words are rushed— desperate. "I can't wait until tomorrow. I have to see him now."

This isn't happening. This can't be happening. Spinning around, I thread my fingers through my hair, trying to figure out a way to get in. Oh God. What do I do? I have to get in there. What if he . . . what if I don't get . . .

No. I shake my head, refusing to let myself go there.

Turning around, I face the door. It's killing me, knowing that Devin is somewhere on the other side of this wall. I lift my hands, placing them flat against the treated wood. "*Please,*" I whisper. Something inside of me breaks and I squeeze my eyes shut, pushing another wave of tears down my face. A broken cry rips from my chest, and my shoulders heave as I fight to suck in air.

Why is this happening?
Hasn't he been through enough?
Haven't I been through enough?

Devin is finally within reach—for good—and I can't even touch him. He's in one of those cold, sterile rooms, hooked up to God knows what, and I'm not in there with him. *I should be in there.* Curling my fingers inward, I dig my nails into the palms of my hands, making a fist, and then pound furiously against the one thing separating me from him.

I have no idea how long I bang on the door, determined to get someone's attention, but no one walks by or offers to help, and eventually anger and determination overshadow my pain. Dropping my arms, I step back from the door, remembering something Devin once said to me. *"Strength comes from within. We make ourselves strong, Katie, and right now I need you to dig deep and find your strength. And when you find it, I need you to hold on to it. I don't care how many times you want to give up and let go, you hold on to that strength and you fight."*

A shiver runs through me as though he physically just whispered those words in my ear. Pushing past the sadness, exhaustion, and pain, I dig deep, finding that strength he was talking about. Straightening my back, I step up to the intercom and push the button again.

"May I help you?" It's the same woman from before. I cringe, knowing I'm not going to get anywhere but determined to at least try.

"I am not leaving." My words come out firm and strong, the complete opposite of how I'm feeling on the inside. The tears sit just behind the eyes, waiting to erupt again, waiting to pour down my trembling cheeks. "I will stand outside this door and push that annoying little button until someone lets me in there."

"Ma'am, listen—"

"No, you listen," I demand, pointing my finger at the speaker as though it's her face. "I haven't slept in forty-eight hours. I'm crabby, I'm tired, and I'm scared *to death* because the man I love is in one of those rooms fighting for his life, and you won't let me see him." Adrenaline is flowing through my body, and I run a trembling hand down the front of my shirt. The desire to see him, to feel him, surpasses any weakness in my legs. It puts the breath back in my lungs. It quells the tears that want to fall. "Devin is mine," I proclaim, fisting my hand over my heart. The truth and potency of that statement seeps through my veins, warming me from the inside out. I know that if Devin were standing here right now, he would be proud as hell. "He.

Is. Mine. And if you think for one second that I'm going to walk away now because you say visiting hours are over, well then, you've got another thing coming."

The handle on the door shifts and I step back, eyes wide, thankful that someone is giving me the time of day. The door cracks open and a short, plump, older woman steps into the hall, shutting the door quietly behind her.

"Ma'am—"

"Katie," I interject. "Please call me Katie."

"Katie, I understand that you want to see your loved one, but as I stated earlier, visiting hours are over. We have strict visiting hours for very specific reasons, and I know how frustrating it is, but you cannot stand out here acting like this. And if you don't stop, I'm going to have to call security." Without so much as a second glance, she turns away, shutting the door quietly in my face.

"Fuck," I hiss, pacing across the hall. Every ounce of strength I had managed to muster shatters. My head spins and I reach out, steadying myself against the wall. I'm completely numb—my heart, my brain, my body . . . all of it is numb. Pure and utter exhaustion takes over. Pressing my back against the wall, I slide down until my butt hits the cool tile. I bend my knees, wrap my arms around my legs, and pull them in close. "I'm here, Devin," I whisper, burying my face in my arms.

A tight band constricts around my chest, and this time when the tears fall, there is no warning. They simply fall, and I let them. My heart is telling me to get my ass up and find a way to get to him, but my head is having no part of it. The last thing I need is to get hauled out of here by security.

"Miss?"

My body jerks when a hand lands on my shoulder, but I don't look up. I can't. "I'm good," I mumble, a sob crawling up my throat because I'm anything but good. "That's a lie." I sniff, wiping my nose on the sleeve of my jacket. "I'm not good. I'm miserable. I have no idea if Devin is okay." My voice cracks when I say his name out loud. "They tell me he's alive," I cry, "but that's all I know, and all I want to do is go in there and . . . I want t-to tell him that I l-love him and that he has to s-stay strong. I need to t-tell him th-thank you for saving me and for"—I suck in a sharp breath, overwhelmed by the amount of things I need to tell him—"loving me. I don't know what I'll do if h-he doesn't make it." Blowing out a slow breath, I pinch my lips together. My chin is trembling so much that it physically hurts, and I wonder if anyone would mind if I just curled up into the fetal position right here on the floor. "I won't sur-survive without him. I know I won't." I shake my head, batting away the tears, still staring at the floor between my legs. "He has to be okay. He just has to . . ." I keep rambling because it feels good to get this all out, but I have absolutely no idea if the woman is still there or if she really did go to get security.

Lifting my head a fraction, I peek up through spiked lashes and come face-to-face with a young woman. "I don't know what to say." Flopping down next to me, she leans her head against the wall. "He sounds like one lucky man to have you."

Clearing my throat, I straighten my legs to mimic her position. I can't even imagine how horrible I look. My eyes feel puffy and swollen, and I'm sure they're about as red as can be. My make-up from two days ago is long gone and my hair is nothing short of a rat's nest, but the woman is watching me with open curiosity and unbridled compassion. And right now, that's something I could use a little bit of. "I'm the lucky one," I tell her. "He's my world and I'd do anything for him."

"And by him, you're referring to someone over there, I assume." She points her hand toward the ICU and I nod. "I see. I'm guessing that you got here after visiting hours." I nod again. "When was the last time you've seen—?"

"Devin," I answer with a watery smile. "His name is Sergeant Devin Clay, and I haven't seen him in months. Sixty-three days, eighteen hours, and"—I glance down at my watch—"thirty-three minutes."

"But who's counting?" She laughs and pushes up from the floor. I notice for the first time that she's wearing a pair of blue surgical scrubs much like the older woman from earlier. She holds out her hand and I stare at it like it's a foreign object. "Would you like to go see Devin?"

I scramble up off the floor. "You can do that?" I ask, pressing a hand to her arm.

"I can," she says, nodding. "Just as soon as the shifts change and the day shift leaves, I'll bring you back."

"How?" I breathe. "Why can you let me in, but she couldn't?" I ask, waving my hand toward the ICU. I'm a nurse; I should know this answer. But right now, my mind is focused on one thing and one thing only.

"Was the nurse you talked to older?" I nod and she smiles. "Some of the older ones are set in their ways. They don't like to bend the rules; they like to stand firmly next to them. Lucky for you, the much cooler, much younger group of nurses run the night shift, and we prefer to break the rules rather than follow them." She winks, and without thinking, I wrap my arms around her shoulders, dragging her in for a hug.

"Thank you."

"You're very welcome." Pulling away, she guides me toward a waiting room. "Have a seat in here and I'll come and get you in a bit."

"Katie!" I blurt, catching her attention after she turns to walk away. She cocks her head to the side, looking at me curiously. "My name is Katie."

A friendly smile slides across her face. "Jennifer."

"Thank you, Jennifer." I can't infuse enough gratitude into those three words, but hopefully she knows just how appreciative I am. Nodding once, she turns away.

Walking into the waiting room, I notice a young woman asleep on one of the couches. Two little girls are sitting on the floor with a box of crayons and a coloring book, and when I sit down in one of the chairs, they both look up.

"Hi." The youngest one smiles at me and I can't help but smile back.

"Hi."

"Is your fadder here too?" The question is so innocent, and if my heart wasn't already broken, it would've just now.

"No," I answer, shaking my head.

"Your mudder?"

"No." I laugh, shaking my head again. "My boyfriend." *My best friend. The love of my life. The man I want to marry. The f—*

"Ah!" The pint-sized cherub squeals, slapping a hand over her mouth. "You have a boyfwend?" she whispers. I nod with a smirk and she lowers her hand. "Daddy says no boyfwends until I'm firty."

"Well, your daddy sounds very smart. I'm almost thirty, so I think I'm good."

"Want me to pway wif you?" I cock my head to the side, trying to determine if she said 'play' or 'pray.' "My Nana says I hafta pway a wot. She says that will help bwing Daddy back. I will pway wif you, if you want."

"Stop it, Sally." The older girl slaps Sally's arm, but Sally just smiles.

"Dis is Sawah."

"Hi, Sarah." I offer a small wave at the young girl. "My name is Katie."

Sally stands up and walks around the table, not stopping until she's standing in front of me. "I wike dat name. I havva fwend named Katie."

"You do?"

Her little head bobs excitedly.

"Knock, knock." I spin around at the familiar voice and see Jennifer standing in the doorway. "Ready?"

"Yes!" Turning toward Sally, I stick out my hand, thankful that this precious little girl could momentarily distract me. Sally slips her tiny hand in mine and shakes it. "It was so nice meeting you. I'm going to say some extra-special prayers for your Daddy."

"Fank you," she says, and her smile brightens the room. But the second I move into the hallway and fall into step behind Jennifer, that brightness fades.

After she slides her badge, the door clicks and she pulls it open, I follow her into the dimly lit ICU. She asks, "Have you been updated on Sergeant Clay's status?"

"No. Actually, I don't know much at all." We pass by the nurse's station and then stop in front of room two. *He's in there.* My chest tightens and I swallow hard. "I got the call about the explosion. I was told what city and hospital he was being transported to and that his condition was labeled as critical. That's all I know."

Jennifer nods her head slowly. "Dr. Karesh has been taking care of Sergeant Clay, and he'll be in tomorrow morning around ten. If you stop by then, he'll be able to go into more detail about your boyfriend's injuries and condition."

"I'll be here."

"I figured you would be. Just remember that when we switch shifts you may have to step out." She pats my arm and I nod as I turn away. Little does she know that I'm not going anywhere, but there's no sense in starting an argument because right now I have something much more important to tend to. Gripping the knob, I crack open the door and the cacophony of sounds float through the air. How many machines is he hooked up to? Is he swollen and bruised? Will I recognize him? "Are you okay, Katie?" Jennifer asks.

Pinching my lips together, I nod jerkily and step into the room.

The sight in front of me stops me dead in my tracks. Lifting a trembling hand to my mouth, I suck in a sharp breath.

Oh my God.

A stabbing pain rips through my chest. "Devin," I breathe, rushing toward him. "Oh, God." Tears race hot down my face and I scoop his cold hand up in mine, kissing it several times before cradling it against my chest. He's always seemed larger than life, but today, tucked beneath the crisp white sheet, Devin looks so incredibly fragile. I'm reminded in the worst possible way that my hero . . . my soldier . . . is human. Squeezing my eyes shut, I send up a silent prayer.

Please, God, please let him pull through this.

Swallowing hard, I peel my eyes open and look at Devin. *My Devin.* Clear plastic tubing disappears between his lips, undoubtedly leading to his trachea, and my eyes drift toward the ventilator sitting next to his bed.

He's not breathing on his own.

Thick white gauze is wrapped around his head. Gashes and bruises mar his gorgeous face. An IV is attached to his right hand that leads to three different bags of clear fluid hanging from an IV pole at the head of his bed. He has a blood pressure cuff secured around his left arm and electrodes are visible under the neck of his gown. My eyes drift to the heart monitor. A steady beep resonates throughout the room, infusing me with hope.

His heart is still beating.

My gaze sweeps over the room, and I spot a small canvas bag tucked against the wall in the corner as though it was tossed aside and forgotten about. Without thinking, I gently rest Devin's hand on the bed and walk across the small space. Dropping to my knees, I pick up the bag and reach inside, pulling out a dark green T-shirt—at least that's what I think it is. The fabric is tattered and . . . is that blood? A shudder racks my body and I set it aside.

Glancing in the bag, a glimmer of metal catches my attention and I pull the object out. A strangled moan rips from my chest at the sight of Devin's dog tags. Gripping the chain in my hand, I reach inside one last time and pull out a picture. I choke out a watery laugh, running my thumb over the dirty photograph. Taken the last time I saw him, it's one of my favorites.

We were in the hotel room, and it was Devin's last night in Pittsburgh after his mother's funeral. Devin's gorgeous green eyes are trained on the camera. His face is split into a huge grin while I'm kissing his cheek. My chin trembles as I remember the moment. That day—that entire weekend—was pivotal for us in so many ways. *Wow. Was it really only a little over two months ago?* I feel like so much has happened since then.

Pushing from the floor, I shrug out of my wet jacket and hang it on the back of the door. Carefully, I place the photograph in my coat pocket, slip Devin's dog tags over my head, and make my way toward him.

"I feel so lost," I mumble, running my fingers over the top of his hand, wanting nothing more than for him to grab my hand, pull me in close, and tell me that everything is going to be okay. I want him to tell me that this is just a tiny bump in the road that leads to our forever.

We were so close—*so close*—to the end of his deployment and starting our lives together. What if I never again get to feel his hand wrap around my neck to drag me in for a kiss or feel the warmth of his lips against mine? What if I never get to hear him laugh again or look into his eyes as I walk down the aisle? What if I never get the chance to tell him that he's going to be a daddy?

The urge to touch him, to be close to him, to feel the warmth of his body against mine is overwhelming. My limbs grow heavy and, like a punch to the gut, everything hits me all at once. There are so many things we've yet to experience together, so many things left to say and do, and the thought of never getting the chance makes me feel as though someone is taking a machete to the center of my soul.

Lifting Devin's arm, I gently sit on the bed next to his hip and very carefully, without disturbing any of the tubes or wires, curl my body against his. Resting my head softly on his chest, I let the steady thump of his heart soothe my aching soul. I use it as a reminder that he's still here, he's still fighting and I need to fight with him—*for him.*

"Hey there, soldier." My voice cracks and a stream of tears run out of the corner of my eye, over my nose and fall from my face, only to be absorbed by the soft cotton of Devin's hospital gown. "I'm going to need you to fight, okay? I need you to pull through this, because I can't live this life without you." I sniff, nuzzling my face into him. "You know what happened to me last time. I can't go through that again. I won't survive this time, Devin, not without you. You are everything to me. You're the reason I wake up every morning. Just knowing that I'm going to get to talk to you or read your words gets me through the day. You *own* me, Dev. My heart is yours, and I gave you my soul a long time ago."

Lifting up on my elbow, I stretch my neck, peppering kisses across his jaw. "I love you *so* much. I *need* you more than I've ever needed anyone. *Please* wake up, baby," I cry. "I'm not going anywhere, I promise. As long as you're here, I'm here. As long as you're fighting, I'm fighting. I'll fight *with* you and *for* you. I'll be your rock, and I'll love you and talk to you and bring you back from the darkness, just like you brought me back." Tilting my head a bit further, I touch my lips to his, hating how dry they feel—how cold they feel.

"I want to marry you," I whisper against his mouth. "Marry me, Devin. Wake up, heal, and then marry me. Let me love you and take care of you and show you what a real family is like. And let's have babies, okay?" My voice breaks on a sob and I pull back, wiping the wetness from my face. "Lots and lots of babies. I want sweet little boys with your big green eyes and thick dark lashes. Our little girl will have your dark hair and your smile." I close my eyes, picturing it in my head. I don't know why, but I have a feeling it's a girl. "And your laugh," I whisper, the thought causing a hint of a smile to tug at my mouth. "She'll have your laugh. And she's going to love you and worship you, and I know that you're going to be the best daddy in the world."

"Katie."

The deep, gravelly voice startles me and my eyes pop open, instantly landing on the figure standing in the doorway. I blow out a slow breath at the sight of him.

Full lips drawn tight, red-rimmed eyes filling with tears, his face is packed full of emotion. I know that, right now, he needs me just as much as I need him.

"Navas." Sliding off the bed, I move toward him. He meets me halfway and I walk straight into his waiting arms. "Hi," I whisper, burying my face in his shirt. He doesn't respond, but his hold on me tightens. His broad shoulders bounce when a cry rumbles from deep in his lungs. Linking my arms around his neck, I give him what he needs . . . someone to hold on to, someone to give him hope. We stand there for a long time, but I don't let go, not until he pulls away.

"Sorry," he mumbles, taking a step back. "That probably wasn't the best way to introduce myself."

"Well, you've seen me naked . . ." I shrug and give him a what-can-you-do look. A choked laugh falls from Navas's mouth and then he shakes his head, running a hand down his face.

"Devin about fucking killed me for that. Sorry, by the way," he says, averting his eyes. A crimson flush creeps up his neck, and I get a feeling that there isn't much that'll make this man blush.

"You're forgiven." Slipping my hand in his, I lead him toward the bed. "Now, will you please fill me in on what's going on? The doctor won't be in until the morning and I'm so fucking lost." My nose burns with impending tears and I squeeze my eyes shut, listening as Navas starts to talk. I'm not sure if I take it all in, but I certainly hear the important parts.

"There was an explosion . . . damage to his legs . . . brain injury . . . needs a bilateral below-the-knee amputation . . ." I don't hear a thing after that.

Reaching out, I yank up the blanket that's covering Devin. His legs are wrapped up, but they're there. *Oh, thank God,* I think to myself. I must've heard him wrong. "What was that about an amputation?" I ask, trying to clear the cobwebs. I'm still running on pure adrenaline and probably seconds away from dropping flat on my face.

"He's going in tomorrow morning for surgery. They can't save his legs, Katie. Trust me, they've tried. But right now, Devin's only chance of survival is to have them removed." Navas's words are slow and precise, as though he knows I'm on the verge of losing it.

"I can't believe this," I say, dropping to a chair next to the bed. I look down at where Devin's legs are tucked under the covers, and then my eyes lift to Navas.

"He'll get through it," he says, conviction ringing loud in his words. "Devin is a stubborn son of a bitch, and he loves you more than life itself. Trust me, he will be okay. And we'll get each other through this so that we can strong for him, okay?" I nod feebly and Navas grips my hand in his. We watch Devin for several minutes, neither one of saying a word and one thing weighing heavily on my mind . . . one thing I'm desperate to tell someone.

"I'm pregnant!" I blurt.

Navas's eyes widen, his jaw falling slack and his gaze dropping to my stomach. "You're . . . pregnant?" he asks, looking at me.

My heart is lodged in the center of my throat and I can't seem to form words, so I simply nod. The thought of not getting to share this with Devin is too much and my emotions erupt. "I need him, Navas. I can't do this by myself . . . I don't want to do this by myself."

"Stop," he says, cupping my face in his hand. "You need to tell Devin. The first chance you get, you need to tell him. This will give him something to fight for, something to hold on to. But you can't talk like that again. It isn't good for you, and it isn't good for the baby."

I nod again, wiping the tears from my face.

"But I want you to know that you will never do this alone. Got it? Because no matter what happens, you have me, and I'm not going anywhere."

"Thank you," I whisper, choking on my words.

"Don't thank me," he says, his eyes softening. "He's my brother, and that's what brothers do."

Chapter 32 | *Devin*

"Awake and Alive"—Skillet

The faint sound of crying penetrates my head. There are muffled voices around me—a man and woman—but I can't tell what they're saying. I want to ask, but my mouth is dry. Too dry. I fight to open my eyes, but the damn things won't budge. Neither will my arms . . . or my legs.

Then another voice, this one not familiar, breaks through the air. *Where am I?* I try to scream. Nothing. *Why can't I move? Why do my legs burn?*

"He's moving!" The voice is low—muffled—but I can still make it out. It's Navas, and for a moment I wonder if I'm dreaming. I try to reach out to him, but again, nothing happens.

"Devin . . . Devin . . . Come back to us, baby." *Katie? Katie is here?* This doesn't feel like a dream. It's so very real. I try and reach out to her. Nothing. "Devin, please wake up," she cries.

A warm hand softly strokes my cheek. *I'd know that touch anywhere.* The sensations are dull, but I know it's her. I can smell her perfume. This isn't a dream. It's real. It has to be. But where am I?

"Devin, stop being a little bitch and open your eyes. Your girl misses you, dude. Why do you always have to be playin' games?" Navas heckles. A fist lightly hits my shoulder. *Son of a bitch that hurt!*

One last time I will my eyes to open, using every ounce of strength I can muster. Light breaches the miniscule crack between my eyelids, and it's so bright it feels like I'm staring into the sun. Instinctually, I lift an arm to shield my eyes and feel the back of my hand smack hard against my forehead. *Fuck, I feel that, too.*

There's commotion in the room. Navas and Katie are encouraging me, asking me to move again, to open my eyes. I try and move my arm and again feel it slap down hard, this time to my side. I give it one last go and my eyelids fly open, the sharp fluorescent rays now completely blinding me.

I snap them shut and then the light behind my lids dims. I sense that the fluorescent lights were switched off, allowing me to ease my eyes open again. This time I notice that the lamp has been turned on. "Is that better, brother?" Navas asks.

I nod my head stiffly toward Navas and Katie's distorted figures, the blur brought on by the change of brightness. Katie moves in close to me, close enough that I can make out her beautiful face, and she takes me gently into her arms, kissing every inch of my face. Each stamp of her lips leaves a tingling sensation that makes me feel like I'm glowing.

"Oh God, baby, I'm so happy you're back. I knew my soldier would pull through. I just knew it!" When she backs away, I can finally make her out completely. It looks like she hasn't slept in days and has spent the better part of that time crying, but she is still so incredibly beautiful. The sight of her causes my heart monitor to speed up. I try to smile for her, but the muscles in my face feel weak. I open and close my jaw several times to stretch it out.

"Welcome back, bro." Navas smiles widely and takes my hand in his. I meet his eyes and squeeze his hand back. I want to say, *Dude, why the fuck are you holding my hand,* but all I manage to get out is "thanks" before I break into a coughing fit.

"Don't talk," Katie says, disappearing from my sight. "They just took out your breathing tube, and they said your mouth would be dry and your throat sore. Let me grab you some ice chips." The faint sound of rustling catches my attention, but when I try to turn my head toward the noise, pain lances through my temples. *Fuck.*

Her face pops in front of mine. "Open up." I do as I'm told because Nurse Katie is fucking hot as hell. My lips part and she drops in a couple of chips, which instantly dissolve. She gives me a few more, and after I swallow a couple of times, I feel like I can actually talk.

"Where am I?" I ask, the words weakly falling from my lips, the chill of the ice chips against my throat numbing the pain.

"Walter Reed in DC, bro," Navas says.

"How long have I been here?"

"Three days. You got hit a week ago though."

Got hit? I scan my brain for what he could be talking about, but come up empty. The last thing I remember is loading up for mission to search for—

"Sergeant Adams," I blurt as soon as the thought hits my brain, "what about Sergeant Adams?" Navas looks at Katie and then to the ground, then to me again. He opens his mouth to say something but stops himself. When he shakes his head slowly from side to side, I close my eyes and let the information sink in. "What happened to me?"

"You got hit by an RPG. Got you pretty bad." I open my eyes back up, and I can see Navas's eyes have left mine again and are back on the ground. He breathes out, long and slow.

I feel the heat. I smell the burnt skin. I taste the soot.

"What happened to me?" I repeat, gritting my teeth, needing to know the true state that I'm in.

Navas looks at Katie, but she just shakes her head, covering her mouth with a trembling hand as tears well up in her eyes. My body trembles, panic gripping at my throat. "Somebody needs to tell me what the fuck is going on."

Navas looks down to my legs and my eyes follow his gaze. If it's possible, my heart fucking stops. Adrenaline, fear, confusion . . . They're all pumping rapidly through my body.

Where there should be feet, there aren't. Almost instantly, the events play through my head like a frenetic, fucked-up slide show.

The patrol . . . door-to-door raids . . . getting called back . . . taking fire . . . My vision goes black and I squeeze my eyes shut. There's something else, but I can't see it. *What is it? What else happened?*

Katie rushes to my side, climbs into bed with me, and wipes the tears from my face before wrapping me in her arms. It calms me a bit, but I need more answers.

"What are you doing back?" I ask Navas, trying to trigger the missing memory.

"I took some shrapnel from the bomb. Got me pretty good in the head. Nothing major, but they sent me here with you for some testing and to remove the shrapnel." As he says this, I notice for the first time that he's wearing a hospital gown. "Everything's good though, man. They're gonna keep me here for a few more days and then release me."

"What about Elkins and Thomas?" I ask. Navas looks confused, and then all at once his face goes pale.

"Elkins is still in Baghdad. He'll come back with the unit in a week or so. Thomas . . ." His words trail off and my heart kicks into high gear.

"What about Thomas?" I ask, feeling my voice start to turn on me, the knot in my throat getting rapidly tighter. He doesn't respond, nor does he look at me, and for some reason Katie has tightened her grip on me. She lets a few tears run down her face, which she does her best to hide from me. "Please, Navas!"

"Thomas . . ." Navas breathes out and wipes a tear from his eyes. "Thomas is dead." His eyes find mine. "He was shot, Clay.

You got hurt trying to recover his . . . his body." Navas points toward the bedside table and I slowly turn my head. A Silver Star sits beside a Purple Heart and Combat Infantryman Badge atop the nightstand. "They gave you that," he says.

His words make my blood run cold. *Nothing. They mean nothing.*

My eyes are on the awards, but my mind isn't. That horrible day finally comes into focus and I can see Thomas on the ground, helpless and reaching for me. Tears push the confines of my eyes before rolling down my flushed cheeks. A sharp pain stabs straight through my chest, and the pressure sends shockwaves through my body and up into my skull. I'm dizzy and beginning to feel lightheaded. My eyes flutter, and for a moment, I feel sick to my stomach.

"Clay, you good, man?" There's concern in Navas's voice. I feel Katie lift her head, and she does her best to wipe my face dry. My eyes drift shut and then bob heavily before opening back up.

What the fuck is wrong with me?

"Baby, are you okay?" Katie asks. Through my cloudy vision, I see a doctor approach. Katie gets off the bed, and then, in a flurry of activity, a nurse rushes in the room and starts checking my vitals. I close my eyes at the feel of her ice-cold hand against my forehead.

I listen as the doctor rattles off some orders before saying something to me. "Sergeant Clay, my name is Dr. Vincent. I'm one of the physicians that have been taking care of you. Can you tell me what you're feeling right now?"

I blink my eyes several times and watch as he slowly comes into focus. "Woozy . . . lightheaded . . . sick," I say. It's the only thing I can come up with. A chill races through my body.

The steady beep emanating throughout the room gets louder and louder. The doctor eyes the monitor and then quickly makes his way toward the door. "I'll be right back." Concern is thick in his voice, and I can tell Katie picks up on it. The tears return and she comes in close again, kissing me on my forehead and then my lips. I try and kiss back, but I can't.

Why can't I kiss her?

"Please, please, please, baby, fight for me," she cries out, nuzzling her face into my neck. *Why is she asking me to fight for her? What's going on?*

I'm so very cold, and the feeling in my limbs is coming and going. My eyes close and won't open again. I break out in a cold sweat. I can hear both Navas and Katie crying. *Navas can't cry . . . he never cries. Why the fuck is he crying?*

"Tell him, Katie, maybe it'll help. *Please* tell him," Navas begs. *Tell me what?*

There's silence for a moment and the wait is unbearable. The nurse is still flitting around the room and hands are ripping at my gown. *What the fuck is going on?*

I watch as one of the nurses nudges Katie away from the bed, but Katie nudges her way back in. "Tell me," I somehow manage to say, using every ounce of energy I have left.

The nurse pulls at Katie's arm again. "Ma'am, I need you step out of the way."

"BP is 88/50. Pulse 133," another voice calls out. *Who the fuck is that?*

"Give me a second," Katie growls before cradling my face in her hands. Her eyes are puffy and she has make-up running down her cheeks, but she's never looked so beautiful. She's my angel.

Katie brings her mouth to my ear and whispers, "You're going to be a daddy, Devin."

I repeat her words over and over in my head. *A father . . . I'm going to be a father.* I'm filled with so much joy that I feel like I'm floating.

"I'm gonna be a daddy," I say, my voice raw and scratchy. Blindly, I grab for Katie and she wraps her hand around mine.

"Yes, baby, you're—" Her words cut off when a sob rips from her throat. She kisses my cheek and then my lips, and then she's gone.

What happened? Where did she go?

I try to reach out again, but this time nothing happens. My eyes are burning and I can feel tears rolling down my cheeks. The thought of having a baby with Katie makes me want to smile, only when I try, my lips merely twitch.

Images flash behind my lids . . . *Katie and I with a beautiful little girl . . . laughing, holding hands . . . kissing boo-boos . . .*

I can see every day of the rest of my life with my perfect little family, living the life that was scripted for us by God, set in motion by *Him* long before we existed. And then darkness slowly creeps in. *Pitch black nothing.*

The unbroken buzz of a heart monitor filters through the air at the same time my body goes completely numb. My limbs become heavy before going weightless, and unless I'm dreaming, I have my legs back.

A bright white light appears out of nowhere. This light doesn't hurt my eyes, and there's something about it that makes me *want* to take it all in. I close my eyes, and when I reopen them, I see arms wide open and waiting.

CO

Katie

"Get off me!" I scream as one of the nurses applies conducting gel to Devin's chest. Someone has me wrapped in their arms, and when I struggle to break free, their grip tightens.

"Calm the fuck down, Katie," Navas growls, his mouth close to my ear. He drags me toward the door, and I do the only thing I can think of to get back to Devin. Raising my leg, I slam my foot down on the top of his as hard as I can. He grunts, his body bending forward in the process, and I use his weakness against him. When he loosens his arms, I slam my elbow into his stomach.

"Son of a bitch," he hisses, releasing his hold on me. I run straight to Devin's bed, but I can't get close because there are nurses surrounding him. One of them yells, "Get. Her. Out."

Good luck, lady.

"Devin," I cry, hoping that he can hear me. "You fight this, baby. You hear me? You're a soldier, Devin, and soldiers fight." A cold hand wraps around my arm, but I dart to the left, breaking free. "You promised me you'd come back to me, and damn it, you better pull through this because I need you!" Tears blur my vision and I push up on my toes, wanting to get a good look at him. "*We* need you!"

"Clear!"

One of the nurses steps to the side, creating an opening, and I get a glimpse of the man I love, the father of my child. His body jerks, arcing off the bed before falling limp. My blood runs cold at the sight in front of me, which instantly blurs. Tears rush down my face as a sharp pain rips through my chest. *This isn't happening.* Reaching for Devin's tags draped around my neck, I grip them tightly in my hand, needing to feel close to him— needing the comfort. My shoulders slump forward, and when I watch his body arc off the bed for a second time, my entire world shatters.

"Oh my God. *No* . . ." I whisper. Strong arms wrap around me again, and this time I don't fight it. In a matter of seconds, I'm in the hallway burying my head in Navas's chest. He's rubbing my back, whispering words of hope, and I latch on to him like he's the only thing keeping me anchored to this earth. Because, right now, he is.

"He has to be okay," I cry, gripping the front of Navas's shirt. "I-I can't lose him. This wasn't supposed to h-happen." With each word, my cries get louder, which explains why I don't hear it when someone walks up behind me.

A light tap on my back followed by a tug of my shirt grabs my attention, and I pull back from Navas. My eyes instantly land on . . . *Sally.* The little girl from the waiting room is looking at me, her piercing blue eyes swimming with tears. Sally's chin trembles as her eyes rake over my face. Lifting my hand, I wipe the tears from my face, hoping that my wails didn't somehow scare the little girl.

"You can cwy," she whispers, tears slipping down her rosy cheeks. "But don't fowget to pway." Without another word, Sally reaches out her hand as though she has something to give me. Releasing my grip on Navas's shirt, I hold out my hand and she drops something in it before spinning around and taking off toward a woman standing outside of another ICU room.

My eyes are gritty and swollen from crying, but when I look down at what the little girl gave me, a tiny spark of hope ignites deep in my soul.

A rosary.

From the mouths of babes, I think to myself. Lifting my gaze to Navas's, I hold up the beautiful white rosary. "I need to find the chapel," I whisper, my voice hoarse from crying.

He doesn't say a word, merely grips my hand in his and leads me out of the ICU. I follow behind him as he weaves down hallways, through doors, and when we eventually end up in front of the chapel, he pushes open the wood door and motions me in. The door shuts softly behind me, but I have no idea if he followed me in because right now I'm on a mission.

Sliding into a front row pew, my hands drop between my knees. The rosary hangs from my fingers as I say the most important prayer of my life to date. Except that when I give the sign of the cross and drop my head between my shoulders, it isn't the Apostles' Creed that runs through my head, it's a prayer to the first man who ever loved me . . . a man that I know would literally move heaven and earth to help me out.

I need you, Daddy . . . Devin needs you. I've prayed to you a lot over the past several months, but this time it's life or death. I'm not sure if you've got any pull up there, but if you do, right now would be the time to use it. Because I'm not ready to hand Devin over. I'm not ready to live the rest of my life without him, and I honestly don't know how I would do it. I will be a shell of a woman without him. He means everything to me, Daddy. He's my life, my heart, my soul, and I need him more than I need my next breath. Our baby needs him. He or she deserves to grow up with a daddy as great as you were, so please . . . please let him be okay. Stand beside him, give him strength, and if he tries to find his way to wherever it is that you are, push him back. Tell him it's too soon . . . tell him he has a family here waiting for him—

"Katie . . ." The soft sound of a woman's voice floats through the air, and I twirl around in my seat.

Jennifer.

My heart slams inside my chest, and my palms are growing increasingly sweaty by the second. I have no idea how Devin's nurse found me, and I don't really care. What I care about is the unreadable look on her face—the one that could potentially rip my heart out or single-handedly put it back together.

Epilogue | Katie

"You and Me"—Lifehouse

Closing my eyes, I let the warm breeze wash over me. The faint scent of flowers starting to bloom and the sound of birds chirping off in the distance tells me that spring is coming, if not technically already here.

A warm hand finds mine, and I take a deep breath before looking up. "I'm not sure I'm ready for this."

Navas doesn't say a word. He simply links our fingers, giving me the support he knows I so desperately need right now. He's been my rock through everything that's happened since Devin coded in that hospital bed. He's held me when I've needed holding, and he's talked me down from nearly every ledge I've found myself on. And trust me, there have been a lot of ledges.

He tugs my hand, leading me through rows upon rows of white tombstones. They all look alike, and if it weren't for the map in my hand, I'd certainly get lost.

Arlington National Cemetery is not my favorite place in the world. Sure, it's breathtakingly beautiful in a somber sort of way, but I hate coming here because it's a reminder of all of the lives that have been lost.

My body trembles, my legs going weak, and I quickly push those thoughts from my head. The doctor says my blood pressure is already too high, and I have to keep it down or I'll end up on bed rest. Lord knows the last thing I need right now is to end up on bed rest.

My free hand falls to my swollen belly and I rub it gently. "Are you ready to see Daddy?" I ask, loving the way my little peanut moves around at the sound of my voice. "That's what I thought."

"You really think he can hear you?" Navas asks, a curious look on his face.

"What makes you think it's a *he?*"

"It's just a feeling I've got." He shrugs and continues to lead me through rows of fallen soldiers.

"Yes, well, if you think it's a boy, it must be a girl."

"You're stubborn as hell, you know that?"

"I do." Looking up, I smile smugly. "It's one of the reasons you love me."

"Who ever said I love you?"

"What?" I scoff, stopping dead in my tracks. I'm enjoying the banter because it's keeping me distracted from the grave that's only a couple of feet away. I know it's his grave, because the flowers I left the last time I was here are still there. "Take that back," I insist. "Tell me you love me."

"Fine," he grumbles, knowing he won't win. "I love you . . . even if you are a pain in my ass."

"Who do you love?" Devin asks, wheeling his chair up to the side of me.

I look over at Navas, curious as to what bullshit answer he's going to give my fiancé. "Your woman," he says with a smirk on his face that's sure to piss off Devin if his words didn't already.

Devin glances down and a low growl rips from his throat right before he yanks my hand out of Navas's.

"Dude, get your own fucking woman. This one is taken," he says, bringing the back of my hand to his mouth before feathering kisses across my stomach. Peanut moves with the contact and Devin smiles against my dress. "I love you."

"Okay, enough of this shit," Navas barks, pushing past us. He walks straight up to Jax's tombstone, drops his hand to the top, and lowers his head. Devin and I stand back, giving him space.

"Did you have a nice visit with Jax?" I whisper.

"I did." Devin looks over his shoulder at Navas and then back at me. "Thank you for giving me some time to myself with him."

"You don't have to thank me." Bending down, I drop a kiss to Devin's soft lips. He wraps an arm around my back and drags me onto his lap. I usually resist because I don't want to hurt him, but he insists that he's fine.

That day in the hospital is hands down one of the worst days of my life. I thought Devin was gone—and for a minute there, he was. I'll never forget the way my body went numb, the way my heart felt like it was literally breaking, and then I heard my Daddy's voice. He was right there with me, telling me to be strong and reminding me to have hope. Immediately after that, I heard Devin's voice reminding me that he promised he'd never leave me—a promise that he ultimately kept.

"Plus, I think Mr. Tough Guy over there secretly liked walking my pregnant ass all the way to the bathroom."

"Trust me," Navas says as he approaches. "Mr. Tough Guy doesn't."

"Whatever." Giving Devin one last kiss, I delicately remove myself from his lap. "Now move on and give *me* some time alone with Jax."

Devin reaches out and snags my wrist in his hand. "What?"

"I said I want some time alone with Jax. Something wrong with that?"

"Uh . . ." He looks at Navas for approval—like I need any—and Navas just shrugs. "Okay. Sure. We'll be right over there."

Smiling, I rub a hand over Devin's cheek before stepping away and walking over to Jax's grave. "Hey there," I whisper, shifting to my knees. "I think I just blew my cover. Devin doesn't know we've talked before, so don't tell him, okay?"

When we come to Arlington, I always find a way to sneak out here and have a few words of my own with Jax. The first time, I merely thanked him for his service. The second time, I thanked him for saving my husband's life, and then it slowly transformed into a ritual. Today, I have something totally different to talk to him about.

"I wanted to tell you that I found out the other day—by accident—what I'm having."

Peeking over my shoulder, I make sure the boys are far enough away that they won't hear me and then I turn back. "I learned how to read ultrasounds in school. Hell, I look at them nearly every day at work. So when I had mine done, I could tell exactly what I was having. And if it's okay with you, I'd like to name him Jax. Jaxon Thomas Clay."

Running my hand along the cool granite, I picture him smiling. I never had the privilege of meeting Jax, but I've seen enough pictures to know what that smile would look like.

"I knew you wouldn't mind," I whisper. I probably look like a crazy person sitting out here having a conversation all to myself, but I could care less. I firmly believe that Jax was watching over Devin the day of the explosion and again the day Devin coded, so who's to say he's not here now? "Anyway, I wanted you to be the first to know. But I better get going. Thank you again for everything."

Jax may have been watching out for Devin, but I know that I have my own guardian angel. Tilting my head to the sky, I give a silent "thank you" to my daddy, the man who has guided me and helped me get to where I am today.

Patting the white headstone twice, I push myself off the ground, realizing for the first time just how hard it's getting to move around with this rapidly growing belly. It makes me wish that we were back at home in Tennessee—for good. I'm fully aware that right now Devin needs the best care available, and that's why we're here. But it doesn't make me miss home any less, especially with all of the exciting things that seem to be happening without me.

Sean and Maggie are engaged, although they haven't started planning their wedding, and if she knows what's good for her, she'll wait until I get home to help. Bailey is doing well in college and she finally decided on a major . . . nursing. I was beyond proud when she told me, and I know she'll make a great nurse. Mom's been doing well, and has even started taking over care of the horses. I've tried to tell her not to, but she's stubborn and won't listen. *Must be where I get it from.* I've even gotten the occasional update on Wyatt. It warms my heart to know that he's moved on, and we've even talked on the phone a couple of times. I'm grateful that he was able to forgive me, and he even said that when he had time to sit back and really reflect on things, he realized that the two of us would have never worked. I didn't push that comment any further, just took it for what it was, but I like knowing that he's still a part of my life.

A throat clears and I look up. Devin is watching me with open curiosity. He wants to know what I was doing at Jax's grave, but he's just going to have to wait. Raising his hand, he motions for me to join them. Not wanting to spend another second apart, I take a step forward . . . and another . . . and then another until I'm wrapped in the arms of my forever.

My Best Friend.
My Fiancé.
My Soldier.
My Devin.

Epilogue | *Devin*

"This Year's Love"—David Gray

The tingle transitions to a burn and I slap the end of my right nub several times in a row, dulling the nerve and quieting the pain. It's the only thing I've found that works when dealing with phantom limb pain. The sensation of still having feet, though I no longer do, is still a trip even a year after losing them. What feels like electric shocks surge from my knees down what's left of each leg, both taken about midcalf. Most below-the-knee amputees get up on their new feet in about six months or so, but infections made my wait double that.

Nothing could bring me down right now though. Not the stinging in my legs. Not even the year I waited for this day to come. *Nothing.* Today, I'm getting my new legs. Today, I feel what it's like to stand tall again. Today, I heal just a little bit more.

"Baby, does hitting it that hard really help?" Katie's sweet voice pulls my eyes from my stumps to her curious face looking back at me. I love the way her nose crinkles up when she's wondering what the hell I'm doing.

"I swear it does. It's the only thing that works. I'm finding the harder I hit it, the quicker the sensations go away." I smack my right stump a few more times and shoot a playful smile toward her. "Bad nubbie!"

She rolls her beautiful eyes, and that smile, the one that still makes my heart race, sits perfectly on her face. This journey has not been easy, but with Katie by my side, I've learned to fight harder than I ever thought possible. And now with little Jax . . . *God, how that boy has changed me.*

As if he knows his dad is thinking about him, he squeals with excitement, throwing his tiny little hands into the air. Katie pulls him tighter into her arms and sits back in her chair. She rocks him sweetly back and forth, his delicate body nestling comfortably against her chest.

He has silky, light brown hair, and each day it looks more like he got his mother's. I thank the Lord for that. Not that I don't like my hair, but you just can't beat those beautiful locks she has, which are currently held back by a hair tie and falling gracefully down one shoulder.

Just as I catch myself fawning over my beautiful wife, the door swings open and Tom, my prosthetist, comes barreling in, his arms clutching two prosthetic legs . . . *my* legs. The sight of them stirs me in my seat.

Tom sets each leg down in front of me and wipes the sweat from his forehead. He's a heavyset guy, the teddy bear type, and it's fitting because he is one of the kindest personnel I've encountered at this place. The guy genuinely cares about his patients, and it's made this painfully long wait a little easier. Excitement shines in his eyes, but it pales in comparison to the feeling that overwhelms my body right now. My ridiculous smile must be contagious, because seated just across from me is Katie smiling back so wide my heart might explode at the sight of it. Between us are two bars about waist high that run parallel to each other across most of the room. I've never used them before, but I've seen other amputees use them when they first start to walk.

"You ready for this?" Tom asks, rhetorically of course, since I've been bitching about this day to him for months.

"You bet your ass I am." I nod toward him and reach for my legs. Tom pulls them back, and the look I give him must actually scare him a little because he places them back down in front of me.

"Now, now Devin, we gotta go over some things first." I nod in acknowledgment, sitting back in my seat. I shoot him a smirk—I knew it couldn't be *that* easy—and wait for him to continue. Katie is looking intently, mentally noting everything Tom says so that she knows what to do when we are back in our little apartment.

The traumatic brain injury sometimes has its way with my short-term memory and Katie has been a godsend during my recovery, remembering medications and appointments, going over medical information with my doctors, all while pregnant with our son. And she was back at it immediately after Jax was born when I went in for my forty-sixth surgery, another irrigation and debridement—the necessary removal of dead or damaged tissue so that the remaining healthy tissue can heal. Three months ago was the forty-seventh—and final—surgery. They closed my stumps for good, which is why I now find myself seconds away from walking for the first time in a year.

"These are test sockets, that's why they're clear." He shows the legs to Katie and me before setting them down again. The sockets are plastic and nearly see-through. "We will have you up on them today in between the parallel bars to make sure you have a good fit. I'll have you tell me about any hot spots, and I'll mark them for later."

"What happens later?" I interrupt, my curiosity getting the best of me. This prosthetics stuff is fascinating, and I soak up all the information he has to give.

"Well, we have what is essentially a heavy-duty blow dryer that heats up the plastic so I can make the necessary changes." Tom looks at the two of us and waits for acknowledgement.

"So you'll heat them up today, and then I'll be walking home, right?" I push.

He looks at me, just for a moment, like I'm absolutely crazy, but I can't really understand why. I've seen enough amputees around the hospital and apartment complex. It doesn't look that hard.

Tom's face returns to normal, and he looks at Katie as if he's concerned that what he has to say next will let me down terribly. She nods for him to continue.

"Well, I will get the changes in tonight, but you won't be able to get them back until physical therapy tomorrow." He pauses, and I can tell he's biting the inside of his lip. He's my buddy and we get along great, but he's always had this odd fear of me—subtle, but odd. I smile at him and he relaxes a bit. "They'll let you take them home, but only after they feel it's safe for you to do so. After that, we'll have you keep walking on them and make whatever changes we need to. Eventually, you'll have your carbon fiber sockets, and it's nothing but up from there, my friend!"

I look to Katie and she is still smiling so sweetly that it's hard to be concerned with my own impatience. Not when she has been so patient with me through all of this. I look back to Tom and smile, and he extends each prosthetic leg out to me.

"Well, let's get this show on the road," I say, lifting both of my nubs so he can slide the prosthetic socket over my stumps, each protected by a gel liner. He rolls a gel sleeve up both legs that runs from midthigh to midsocket. Then he grabs my hands to help me get up, but I shoo him away. He looks at me as if to say I don't have an option but finally rolls his eyes and backs away from my chair, allowing me to stand on my own.

Instantly, I'm humbled. Standing isn't as easy, or comfortable, as I thought it would be. My thigh muscles ache as they flex, working harder than they have in some time. Katie looks at me concerned and nearly rises to her feet, but I put a hand up to stop her.

"Please, sweetheart . . . I've got this." She settles back in her chair with Jax, but the apprehensive look stays on her face.

I fight with everything that I have, gritting my teeth tightly together and gripping the arms of the chair before finally standing. I steady myself, wobbling a bit, before I'm able to scan the room from the perspective of a man standing six feet two inches tall for the first time in almost a year. It's like my eyes are opened to an entirely new world, foreign but exhilarating.

Tom takes me by the arm and rebuffs my attempts to push him away. He guides me as I take two slow, unsteady steps forward, stabilizing myself with a hand on each of the parallel bars. Tom backs away and waits, placing his hands on his hips. Katie rises to her feet at the other end of the parallel bars, her eyes gleaming with excitement but anxiety still present on her face.

I take two steps forward.

The nerves ache, the walls of the sockets pressing against them, but I don't feel it.

I take two more steps forward.

My wife waits, my son in her arms, and the only thing I feel is the immediate need to take them both into my own arms, to hold Katie while standing for the first time in so long.

Two more steps forward.

Tears roll down her cheek, one after the other. I want to wipe them all away. I want to kiss her, to touch her, to hold her like she's never been held. To feel whole, at peace, and so in love that nothing in this world could ever change it.

I take two more steps forward.

Katie is now standing before me, laughing because she's so happy. Jax is awake, his beautiful brown eyes curiously taking me in. I kiss Katie's wet cheek and taste the salt in her tears. I put my arm around her, gripping the small of her back, and I pull her in tight.

Letting go of the other bar, I place my hand on Jax's forehead, softly stroking his hair to one side. I kiss him lightly on his forehead. He smells of baby powder and that pink lotion Katie likes to use, and it's the best smell in the entire world.

Then I look down into Katie's chocolate eyes—after looking up at her for the past year—and all my worries and concerns evaporate. My lips meet her forehead, my other arm resting on her thigh, and out of the blue I remember something Katie said to me while I was in the hospital. She probably doesn't even know I heard her, but it was her words that pulled me through.

"I want to marry you," she says, her lips brushing mine. "Marry me, Devin. Wake up, heal, and then marry me. Let me love you and take care of you and show you what a real family is like. And let's have babies, okay?" Her voice breaks right along with my heart and I try to reach up to touch her—to comfort her—but nothing happens. "Lots and lots of babies. I want sweet little boys with your big green eyes and thick dark lashes. Our little girl will have your dark hair and your smile."

Well, I've taken care of the marriage part, and we have a sweet little boy, but I'm ready for that little girl . . . Hell, I'm ready for lots of babies.

"Hey, Katie?"

"Yeah, babe?"

"Remember when I was in the hospital and you told me you wanted lots and lots of babies?"

Katie cocks her head to the side and gives me a curious look. "You heard that?" she asks.

"I heard every word you said. Including the part about the babies . . ."

"Yeah?" she says with a cute little smirk.

"How about we head back now, put Jax down for a nap and start working on those babies?"

A choking sound comes from behind me and I glance at Tom. He looks down, but not before I notice how flushed his cheeks are. Smiling to myself, I turn my attention back to my beautiful wife. Katie's smile is blinding, and it's the most beautiful sight in the whole damn world.

"I think that sounds like a great idea."

A low growl rumbles from my throat at the thought of burying myself deep inside my wife. "Let's get me out of these things," I whisper, so only she can hear me. "What do I need these legs for when the important one is fully functional?"

Katie's eyes widen, a look of desire flashing across her face. "More than fully functional," she says, laughing.

"Damn straight it is."

"What am I going to do with you, Sergeant?" She slaps my arm playfully.

"Love me," I answer, brushing my lips across hers. "I just need you to love me."

"Sir, yes, sir," she says, and then I devour that sweet, sassy smart mouth of hers.

THE END

Acknowledgments | Kirby

A Lover's Lament holds a very special place in my heart for many reasons, but mostly because it's a story that I never thought I'd see come to fruition. Now that it has, I have a TON of people to thank for helping me get it there.

First and foremost, I have to thank my husband, Tom. The endless amount of support and encouragement you gave me while writing this novel is truly amazing. Thank you for making sure the house stayed clean, the laundry got done, and the kids were fed. Thank you for taking over nighttime duty so that I could stay up late and write. But most of all, thank you for not freaking the hell out when I showed you a picture of my cowriter. Any other man wouldn't have handled it with the grace and beauty that you have. Not only have you supported me through this, but you've supported BT as well—he just doesn't know it. You are amazing and wonderful, and I'll never know what I did to deserve you. I love you to the moon and back.

Taylor Urruela, what can I say? Thank you doesn't seem like enough, so I'm going to try really hard to find the right words. When I reached out to you last winter, I was pissed off . . . do you remember that? I read one of your short stories and I said "You can't end it like that!" That one message turned into several more and eventually led me to sharing an outline of a book—*this* book. Instantly, you latched on to this story like it was your baby too. We plotted, we spitballed, and we worked our asses off for nine long months, stretching and molding this story into something that we could be proud of. And let me tell you, I am DAMN proud of this book. It wasn't an easy journey, but believe me when I say that there isn't another writer on this earth that I would've rather taken this journey with than you. Thank you for loving this story as much as I do.

S.G. Thomas . . . oh lordy, here we go. You are still my #1 buddy reader, even though I'm fairly certain we never did finish that book! You are so much more than my editor, you are one of my best friends, my confidant, and the person I turn to when I need any sort of encouragement or advice. I've said it before and I'll say it again, you are amazing and fantastic, and I'll never be able to repay you for all that you've done for me. I love you hard, girl . . . even when you make fun of my misuse of biblical figures ;)

A big, huge thank you to my friend and proofreader, Alexis, with Indie Girl Proofs. Thank you for taking us on with such short notice. We appreciate absolutely everything you've done for us.

Whitney Barbetti, there aren't enough words in the English language to accurately describe what your friendship means to me. You spent countless hours talking with me and plotting with me over *A Lover's Lament*, and I am forever grateful that you are a part of my life. Plus, you are the greatest pillow in the entire world ;)

Lex Martin and Michelle Lynn, the two of you have been huge supporters of this collaboration from day one, and I am beyond lucky to have both of you in my corner. Thank you for the endless amount of messages and encouragement.

To my beta readers, you know who you are. Thank you for all your feedback and honesty while reading *A Lover's Lament*. We couldn't have gotten the book where it is today without you. XOXO

I've totally saved the best for last . . . To all of the readers and bloggers, THANK YOU for all the support that you've given to BT and me. Thank you for wanting this book, for begging for this book, and for all of the messages you've sent us. We are so glad to finally get it into your hands, and we truly hope that you enjoyed reading it. We are eternally grateful for all of the sharking and pimping that you've done for *A Lover's Lament*. THANK YOU for absolutely everything you've done, day in and day out, and thank you for making this book community so wonderful.

Acknowledgments | *BT Urruela*

First and foremost, thank you God for all the incredible blessings you've given me in this life. Through some of the hardest things I've ever had to deal with, things I thought would break me, you stood strong, always there to steer me in the right direction.

To my family, Pops, Britto, Brad, and Sean . . . what a ride it's been. We've all had our own challenges we've had to overcome and we haven't always been there to help each other out, but the one thing we've always had, the thing that's remained forever unchanged in my heart, is the fact that I love you guys more than I could ever put into words. I wouldn't be where I am today without you all.

To my extended family, my VETSports guys: Josh Schichtl, Rob Somers, Chris Krutzsch, Jeremy Fore, Randy Tharp, Rob Robichaux, Andrew Johnson, Bryan Belcher, Karl Dorman, Jason Wills, and whoever I may have left out that has had my back, helped support the things I believe in the most, and given everything for this organization I love so much. You guys mean the world to me.

To Michael Stokes for believing in me, for giving me a chance, and for being a true friend. I value your friendship so much. You've given me more than you could ever know.

To my book family, Randy Sewell, Eric Battershell, Golden Czemak, and the authors who had faith in me, Lexi Buchanan, Harper Sloan, Hadley Quinn, Kristen Proby, Sloan Johnson,

Heidi McLaughlin, and Jennifer Kacey. Thank you for choosing me to represent your work. I value our experiences together so much and hold you all in the highest regard.

To S.G. Thomas, our editor, for taking my confusing, often scrambled prose and making it a million times better. I have learned so much from you!

To my coauthor, KL Grayson, thank you for bringing this storyline to me, and thank you for taking a chance on a virgin author and creating this beautiful story with me. I appreciate all nine months that we spent bringing Katie and Devin together. I look forward to many more.

Finally, last but certainly not least, thank you to all my fans and supporters out there. You all are my lifeline. I couldn't be here or do any of this without the tremendous amount of support you give me. I can't tell you how much I appreciate the love and support you've given me over these past nine months. I love each and every one of you, and I fight harder for the things I believe in because of you.

Photo by Elizabeth Wiseman Photography

KL Grayson is a *USA Today* bestselling author. She is entertained daily by her extraordinary husband, who will forever inspire every good quality she writes in a man. Her entire life rests in the palms of six dirty little hands, and when the day is over and those pint-sized cherubs have been washed and tucked into bed, you can find her typing away furiously on her computer. She has a love for alpha-males, brownies, reading, tattoos, sunglasses, and happy endings . . . and not particularly in that order. KL Grayson is the coauthor of *A Lover's Lament* with BT Urruela. She is also the author of *Pretty Pink Ribbons* and *On Solid Ground*, and the coauthor of *Where We Belong* and *Live Without Regret*.

Connect with KL Grayson and visit her website at:
www.klgrayson.com

Photo by RLS Model Images Photography

BT Urruela is a *USA Today* bestselling author. He was an infantryman in the US Army for six and a half years. At the end of a yearlong tour in Baghdad, Iraq, his vehicle was hit by two roadside bombs, which took his right leg below the knee and the life of his commander. He was awarded a Purple Heart for his wounds, and also received a Combat Infantryman's Badge. He works as a director and brand ambassador for VETSports, a veteran community sports nonprofit he cofounded in 2012. He's the coauthor of the military romance novel, *A Lover's Lament*, with KL Grayson, and the author of his debut solo novel, *Into the Nothing*.

Connect with BT Urruela and visit his website at:
www.bturruela.com

CPSIA information can be obtained at www.ICGtesting.com
Printed in the USA
LVOW11s0046230916

505864LV00002B/2/P